BLACK SHADOW MOON

STOKER'S DARK SECRET BOOK ONE

A SUPERNATURAL VAMPIRE THRILLER

P.G. KASSEL

STORYTELLER WORKS

ISBN 13: 978-0-9967919-3-9

Library of Congress Control Number: 2019900860

Storyteller Works

Los Angeles, CA

Cover Design by Derek Murphy

For the family and friends who have always encouraged me in my creative endeavors. And most of all for my wife, whose love and unwavering support continuously inspires me.

"And no marvel, for Satan himself is transformed into an angel of light."

2 Corinthians 11:14

PROLOGUE

Whitby, England
1895

T he cargo hold contained a crypt-like darkness. A cold, endless blackness, so powerful the glow from the single lantern was squeezed to dimness as if a huge, unseen hand was closing around it. The sound of metal ringing against metal sent a pair of rats scurrying across a shallow pool of foul seawater.

In the middle of the hold, a seaman worked with a tangled assemblage of ropes and pulleys, straining to secure them around a large wooden box. The rigging disappeared through the framed main hatch two feet above his head. He worked skillfully, but with an anxious urgency, the lantern light catching the frost of his breath puffing in quick, short bursts.

Sweat beaded around the seaman's brow, trickling the oily dirt on his face down his cheeks. The single thought pulsing through his brain was to finish this, a job thrust on him through the bad luck of being the newest man to sign onto the schooner's crew.

With great relief, the seaman secured the final rope in place and shouted up the open hatch in his native Romanian, "They're fast. Haul away."

Not wanting to touch the thing any more than necessary, he reluctantly kept the large box from swinging as it lurched up off the floor and climbed toward the hatchway.

On deck, the light from a few scattered lanterns was of little comfort. Unusually thick fog rolled across the deck with unearthly fluidity. The ship's mate, Russian by birth, supervised as two Romanian hands strained at the ropes.

The moment the box cleared the hatchway, the seaman below scrambled from the hold. His sudden movement distracted one of the men on the ropes. The man's grip faltered and the box suddenly dipped a full two feet at one end. He hastily reapplied the proper amount of tension, but drew an angry and frightened glare from the mate on the other rope. "Hold it steady, you fool," he hissed, unable to keep the panic from his voice.

"I've got it. Just swing it over. Hurry!" the first man replied.

The brief exchange proved too much for the Russian mate, who took a quick step forward and snarled, "Shut up, both of you. Just shut up and work!" His nerves getting the better of him, he glanced up at the afterdeck where the captain, a fellow Russian, watched in silence.

The captain stood near the wheel; his hands thrust deep in the pockets of his wool great coat. He was a large man, nearing his forty-ninth birthday, once muscular, but now beginning to go soft around his broad middle. He was not as certain as his crew about the true nature of their misfortune during this last crossing, but he was as relieved as they were to be rid of this cargo.

They had sailed from Varna, on the Bulgarian Black Sea coast, down the Danube, arriving in Whitby, England only a few hours before. It was a routine voyage the captain had made countless times, but this passage had proven to be far from routine.

The hands swung the derrick's boom arm over the rail. A superstitious lot, the captain thought; most sailers were. He knew himself to be the rare exception.

Still, the captain admitted to himself he had many unanswered questions about the events of this trip. The port authorities would be certain to ask the same questions of him. They would want answers he did not have. What would he say? Would they blame him?

Two dock workers guided the box into position over a waiting freight wagon. A side panel of the wagon bore the name Carter Paterson & Co., London. The wagon was hitched to a hulking McLaren steam traction engine, its funnel streaming wisps of smoke that were soon consumed by the fog.

The dockhands manhandled the load onto a stack of similar boxes already resting in the wagon bed.

The engine driver helped pull a tarpaulin over the load and tied it down. He then climbed into the cab of his great machine. The tractor hissed and shuddered as the driver opened the throttle, and with a violent lurch, moved forward. Smoke billowed from the funnel as the tractor rumbled across the pier. Soon the machine faded away into the fog and darkness.

The captain dragged himself back toward his cabin to collect his duffel. Normally, when his ship docked in the middle of the night, he'd be content to sleep in his cabin berth until morning. But this was one night he would look forward to sleeping in the village. He had little doubt that his crew would do the same.

CHAPTER 1

Bram Stoker thought the churchyard of Saint Mary's was the most pleasant spot in all of Whitby. Research had always been a particular pleasure and on one of his visits to the village he discovered William de Percy had built the church in the twelfth century. It was still active as the local parish house of worship. Stoker watched the old groundskeeper moving among the headstones, pausing here and there to pull up the occasional weeds blemishing his yard.

Whitby rested on the sloping coast of Northern England. The charming village was built on both sides of the valley divided by the Esk River, a waterway emptying its flow into the North Sea. The village had become something of a resort in recent years, but it remained, first and foremost, a haven for fishermen.

From his bench on the path running alongside the cliff, Stoker had a panoramic view of the entire village, including a clear view of Mrs. Storm's boarding house. He and Florence had stayed there on their first trip to Whitby years before, shortly after their wedding. Mrs. Storm still provided comfortable, homey rooms and excellent meals.

Glancing back toward the church, Stoker observed that the groundskeeper had noticed him. The old fellow was heading his direction, stooped with age, but his gait strong. The groundskeeper often came over for a chat when Stoker visited the cliff, but right now he wasn't in the mood for idle conversation.

Despite the agreeable surroundings, Stoker's soul roiled with dissatisfaction. He had accomplished nothing during this trip. Finding himself with a few free days before the start of the theater season, he had journeyed to Whitby, determined to develop ideas for a new book. He found the natural peacefulness of the place ideal for his writing. There were few distractions, and the lovely backdrop often proved to be a creative stimulant. But this visit had proven to be damnably unsatisfying. He had been in the village four days and no motivating or even mildly interesting ideas had come to him.

Frustrated with his lack of progress, Stoker turned to the one thing that might make this trip worthwhile: a news clipping from The Whitby Daily dated August 23, 1895.

"MYSTERY AT SEA, ship of tragedy moored in Whitby. The Admiralty Court and local constabulary are investigating the apparent deaths of three seamen registered as crew on the Russian vessel Demeter out of Varna. According to the surviving crew, the three men simply disappeared, determined lost overboard in rough weather. Authorities are puzzled by the lack of witnesses."

The rest of the article provided a brief description of the ship, its route with ports of call and the names of the missing sailors. There was also an abridged inventory of the ship's cargo; barrels of processed grain, lamp oil, some textile bolts and several large wooden boxes. There was no record regarding the contents of the boxes.

All hands aboard described harsh weather. Considering the season, it was something of an unusual occurrence. Thick fog had enveloped the ship from the first night at sea, and a formidable storm had drenched the vessel with rain and buffeted it with wind for the last eighteen hours of its voyage.

It was no secret that Stoker possessed something of a dark side, and the sinister elements of the story fascinated him. He couldn't resist the opportunity to pursue the matter of the Russian schooner. He believed once he uncovered additional facts, the article might inspire another one of his short stories. Disappointingly, there was very little light to be shed.

The groundskeeper, now within yards of Stoker's seat, offered a congenial wave of his hand. "Good afternoon, sir." He stopped at the end of the bench, placing a hand on the back rest to steady himself.

"Good afternoon," Stoker answered, forcing his courtesy.

"You picked a fine day for taking in the air."

"It's a very nice day," Stoker agreed, hearing the hollowness in his tone.

The groundskeeper squinted at the clipping in Stoker's hand. "Ah, I see you're reading about the Demeter. Nasty business, that."

"Indeed. Do you know anything about it?" Stoker asked.

"Know anything about it?" the old man echoed. "What would I know? Only what the papers say."

Stoker nodded. "You haven't heard any talk?"

"There's always plenty of talk but it doesn't amount to much," the old fellow sniggered. "Most of the fishermen say it was just the bad weather."

"Perhaps," Stoker replied. "It's curious, though, the rest of the crew not seeing anything, not hearing anything."

"Could be nothing more than rotten luck," the groundskeeper shrugged. "You seem quite taken by it though, sir, cutting the story out, carrying it with you and all."

"I just found the report interesting. Thought there might be more of a story to tell," Stoker answered, his eyes fixed on the clipping suspended between his fingers.

"Ah, that's right, I remember. You're one of those writer fellows," the groundskeeper recalled. "Did you talk to the newspaper office about it, then?"

"I did. They claimed to know only what the local constabulary told them. So I called at the police station and all they would say is that they couldn't comment on an ongoing investigation."

"That sounds like 'em well enough," the old man observed. "Did you visit the ship?"

"It had already left port by the time I heard of the story." Stoker said. "But I did have a chat with the Admiralty Court officials."

"Did you?"

"They seemed quite irritated that I was even asking about the incident. I suspect they knew something more than they were willing to tell."

"Well, 1 don't know her schedule, but I suspect the schooner will dock back here soon enough," the groundskeeper offered. "Perhaps you'll be able to find something more then."

"I'm afraid there's no time for that now," Stoker replied. "I have to get back to London tomorrow."

"Worse the luck, then."

"And speaking of that," Stoker sighed, "I had better head back down. It's been a long day."

"A good idea," the groundskeeper agreed. "We're losing the light and you don't want to be on the stairs in the dark."

Tucking the newspaper clipping back in his pocket, Stoker stood. "Good evening, then."

The groundskeeper tipped his hat and shuffled off toward the church. Stoker turned and made his way back along the cliff side path, staring at the ruins of the old Whitby Abbey just in sight beyond the churchyard. With most of the roof gone and the broken Gothic walls worn with the passing of time, it stood forlornly against the darkening sky.

He soon reached the stairs, 199 stone steps that led up from the village to Saint Mary's churchyard. The locals referred to them as the Church Stairs, and the old groundskeeper was right. They were best navigated while there was still sunlight.

Leaving the village now was probably best, considering the visit had been fruitless. His responsibilities at the theater would consume most of his time soon enough, and only God knew when he'd be able to make any significant effort toward his writing again.

Stoker knew he had no right to complain. His job was interesting and challenging, sometimes too challenging. But he always struggled with a deep longing for something more, something greater.

CHAPTER 2

By the time Stoker reached the bottom of the Church Stairs he had worked up an appetite. He walked through the business district with its assortment of shipping offices, fish merchants, and marine supply establishments. His destination, the Boar's Tusk, lay ahead just beyond the West Pier. Stoker thought the location preferable in that it was not as boisterous as many of the pubs found closer to the commercial wharf.

Stoker didn't take long to finish his meal; an ample beef pie and a glass of dark ale. The satisfying food and the long day suddenly had him feeling tired. Setting his sights on a good night's sleep, he settled his bill straight away and left the pub.

He walked back toward Mrs. Storm's, taking a route along the jetty. The beam of the little lighthouse on the point swept across the harbor entrance, its intense brightness igniting the clouds of mist over the water in a phosphorus glow.

He heard footsteps echoing off the water long before he saw the man. Stoker watched a figure emerge from the shadows. "Why, it's Mr. Stoker," exclaimed the silhouette.

He recognized the fellow once he stepped into the dim glow of a nearby street lamp, a milliner staying at Mrs. Storm's. For the life of him, Stoker couldn't remember the man's name. "Yes. Who's that?"

"Oh, sorry. It's Moorhill, from the boarding house. Didn't mean to startle you."

"Not startled. Just didn't recognize you in the poor light," Stoker answered, adjusting the truth a bit.

Moorhill joined Stoker at the edge of the walkway. "Weather's taken to a chill again," he stated the obvious.

"Yes, it has."

"I was just on my way to the pub," Moorhill explained. "Thought I might have a glass of whisky. You know, something to warm the soul."

"I just finished supper there," Stoker replied, disguising the impatience he felt.

"Come back with me, then. I'll buy you a nightcap."

"Oh, very kind," Stoker said. "But I have to get back to London tomorrow. I'm taking the early train."

"Back to work, huh?"

"That's right. My wife is expecting me as well."

"You're with a theater, yes? I think I heard it mentioned over one of Mrs. Storm's dinners." Moorhill didn't appear to be in any hurry.

"The Lyceum. Our season opens next week."

"Sounds enjoyable. And all those actresses to work with." Moorhill was almost leering.

Stoker managed a strained smile. "Yes. Well, it's getting late, Mr. Moorhill. I don't want to keep you from your drink."

A voice came unexpectedly out of the darkness. "My pardon, sirs."

Startled, Stoker whirled around. Moorhill gave a squeak of surprise. A man stepped out of the shadows and slowly approached.

There had been no footsteps; just the gentle sound of the water against the rocks. "Dear Lord," Stoker muttered under his breath.

The man was tall and slender, dressed from head to foot in black, with a long flowing coat dropping to his mid-calf. He was clean shaven except for a long gray moustache that drooped around his thin red lips. His hair, long for current styles, was iron gray with touches of white, combed straight back, falling just past his collar.

Stoker guessed the man to be in his late forties or early fifties. His features presented the appearance of a kindly, distinguished father. Only the eyes were a contradiction. They were dark and penetrating, as if they possessed some ocular peculiarity to pry into one's soul.

"I've frightened you. Forgive me." The English was laced with a rather heavy Slavic accent, and there was a certain soothing quality to the intonation.

"You did just come out of nowhere," Stoker answered.

"Quite," Moorhill nodded.

"Again, my apology."

"No bother," Moorhill shrugged.

"I was passing nearby and couldn't help overhearing a part of your conversation," the stranger continued.

"Oh?" Stoker said.

"You mentioned returning to London in the morning. May I ask if London is your home?"

"It is."

The stranger turned casually toward Moorhill. At first, Moorhill looked back at the man with polite attentiveness, but then he appeared to grow uneasy. An expression of concern spread across his face, like a light rain pooling across a window pane. He shifted his weight from foot to foot for a few moments and then announced, "Well, I need to be getting along."

Stoker nodded, the odd behavior leaving him nothing to say.

Moorhill awkwardly turned on his heels and continued along toward the pub. Over his shoulder he called out, "Goodnight then."

Stoker watched the stranger, his eyes still locked on Moorhill. He didn't believe the man intended any mischief. If he did intend it, he must realize now that Moorhill had gotten a good look at him before his departure. The man turned back toward him.

"Mr. Stoker, is it not?" he asked.

"That's right."

"As I said, I—"

"You overheard," Stoker interrupted.

The man favored Stoker with a warm smile. It seemed somewhat perverse displayed in concurrence with the cold eyes. "I am called Tepes," he said, offering a curt bow from the waste.

Stoker gestured toward the village. "I was just on the way back to my room."

"I have only recently come to your country and my hope, my intention, is to conduct business in London." Tepes ignored Stoker's impatience. "Perhaps even make my new home there."

"A large undertaking."

Tepes nodded. "Which is why I impose myself now."

"I'm afraid you've lost me."

"It would be most helpful to me if someone like yourself could provide guidance," Tepes explained.

"Guidance?" Stoker shifted his weight, his mind still on the comfort of his room at Mrs. Storm's.

"I find myself unfamiliar with many of your customs and ways of business. Your city of London will be quite unfamiliar to me. Your knowledge would most certainly hasten my transition."

Stoker was all for helping a man when he needed it, and this man was presenting his request with no lack of charm. But the request was ill timed. His first inclination was to turn the fellow down flat, but he suspected that might delay his getting to bed. "I'm afraid you're catching me at a difficult time," Stoker said after some delay.

"Oh?" Tepes' eyes narrowed.

"Yes. There isn't much I can do for you at the moment, and as you already heard, I'm leaving the village in the morning."

The words were barely out of his mouth when Stoker found himself rethinking his resolve. It was as if his will to end this conversation was weakening.

"Perhaps you will reconsider," Tepes said, his tone soft.

No, this wouldn't do, thought Stoker. He found his determination once again. "You should look me up once you get to London," Stoker suggested. "I can be of more help to you there than here in Whitby."

Tepes' expression remained unchanged. "Perhaps that would be best."

"Indeed. Well, you can always find me at the Lyceum Theatre in Westminster. Anyone can direct you there."

"Very well."

"If you'll excuse me, I really should be on my way," Stoker said.

Tepes offered another brusque bow, his eyes fixed on Stoker.

"Goodnight, then." Fearing another delay, Stoker hurried on his way without another word.

A few seconds later, he couldn't resist glancing back over his shoulder. Tepes was nowhere to be seen.

Stoker reasoned he had handled the situation well. Pushing the odd encounter to the back of his mind, he set his sights on Mrs. Storm's boarding house and a good night's sleep.

CHAPTER 3

T he six days since his return from Whitby had been filled with preparations for opening night. After coordinating and attending countless meetings, monitoring rehearsals, and overseeing details from costuming to set carpentry, Stoker felt confident everything was at the ready.

Having completed dressing in the evening clothes he always kept in his office, Stoker made one last inspection of himself in the small mirror hanging on his office wall. At age forty-five, he was a physically powerful, large-framed man. He combed his auburn hair, once a full red in younger years, until every strand was well in place. His mustache and trimmed beard, both redder than auburn and already streaked with gray, covered his firm jaw. On more than one occasion, acquaintances had remarked on the deep, piercing quality of his eyes. Tonight, they looked rather tired.

Stoker stepped into the Lyceum's dim, lower passageway. The theater was in the process of being wired for electricity. The main floor and auditorium were already done, but the lower levels still used gas lamps. He hurried down the shadowy corridor and up the stairs leading to the main floor.

The stairway delivered Stoker backstage, to the rear of the stage itself. He offered a familiar nod to the old doorman, seated at his narrow high desk just inside the stage door, and then waded into the flurry of what society disdainfully referred to as theater people. Cast members and extras already in costume were reciting lines or heading toward the stage. The rest were hurrying toward the wardrobe rooms, dodging busy stagehands maneuvering set pieces and props.

Stoker spotted the Lyceum's stage manager, Harry Loveday, in the wings signing a purchase order for a junior clerk named Benton. Loveday, in his fifties, was a theater veteran and had been with Sir Henry since well before Stoker joined the Lyceum.

"You're right on time, as always," Loveday greeted him. "Curtain's up in twenty-five minutes."

"Anything I need attend to?"

Loveday shook his head. "Everything's been going quite well."

Stoker nodded his approval, then hurried on toward the front of the theater.

In the foyer, Stoker began greeting the celebrities and dignitaries that frequented opening night performances. The power, fame and talent carried with such ease by these select individuals always energized him.

Of all his duties as the Lyceum's general manager, he enjoyed this responsibility most of all. Stoker knew his talent and ability were just as keen as the theater's more illustrious patrons. In some cases, his abilities surpassed them, but he was never viewed as belonging to their coterie.

Stoker could keep company with Irving's friends as much as he liked, but they were just that, Irving's friends. They all viewed him as Sir Henry Irving's business manager, an employee. It didn't matter that he and Irving were close friends, as well as business associates.

Stoker felt a relentless longing to belong to this group. He was determined that one day he would walk beside them, not behind them. One day he'd be included within their circle; he'd make certain of it. He was certain that writing a successful book would prove to be his vehicle to notoriety.

The first person he spotted across the room was Bernard Shaw, looking as sour as usual. Shaw participated in an unspoken feud with Irving by writing biting reviews of Irving's productions. Irving responded by making it his habit never to read them.

Once Stoker had smoothed Shaw's feathers, he roamed about offering greetings to some of the Lyceum's more affluent patrons. He was walking past the main doors when in walked William Gilbert. The public knew him better as W.S. Gilbert, who, with Arthur Sullivan, wrote and produced the cleverest musical productions in the British theater.

While catching up with Gilbert about his latest production, a large, robust man in his early forties approached through the crowd. His movements were expansive; his broad chest appeared to strain the pearl studs of his formal wear and there was a sense of athletic power in his stride. Arthur Conan Doyle always captured attention when he entered a room.

It was a source of shame to him, but Stoker recognized he always felt a stab of jealousy whenever he encountered Doyle. Each time the man's pen touched paper it produced gold.

Doyle stopped just behind Gilbert, smoothing out his full mustache, waxed on the ends, while waiting with some impatience to be acknowledged. Noticing Stoker's gaze wander, Gilbert turned to see what his friend was looking at. "Arthur," he exclaimed with genuine warmth.

"William, how are you, and how's that scoundrel you write with doing?" Doyle asked, his voice vigorous.

"I'm doing well, considering I'm miserably unhappy with the wretched piece we're trying to finish. And I'd venture to say Arthur's feeling about the same."

"Well, I don't mean to interrupt," Doyle said. "I just wanted to thank Mr. Stoker here for his invitation."

"It's our pleasure," Stoker responded.

"You're not interrupting at all," assured Gilbert. "I so enjoyed your last installment in The Strand," Gilbert complimented his friend.

"A modest effort, but thank you," Doyle responded.

Gilbert laughed. "That from the most successful author in England."

"Oh, I don't know about that."

But it was true, thought Stoker. What must that be like, to be the most successful author in England?

CHAPTER 4

His strides were long but unhurried as he moved along the busy avenue the English referred to as The Strand. His dark, empty eyes were fixed ahead of him, but he saw everything and everyone. The tobacco shop clerk taking in a sidewalk sign before closing his shop. An open carriage passing him on his right, the middle-aged couple inside engaged in a heated discussion about some romantic indiscretion. Heading toward him through the shadows, a timid scullery maid stayed close to the buildings as she hurried home from her place of work.

He saw them all, felt them all. He sensed their hearts beating and the blood coursing through their veins. He sensed their strengths, and he keenly sensed their weaknesses.

It had been a very long time since he had been in any city and London was larger than any he had ever experienced.

The decision to enter this country from the northern village of Whitby had been wise. The village was more like home, more familiar; it helped him prepare. In good time, the large populace of London would benefit him indeed, but there was still much he must learn first.

The city crowds enabled him to move among them unnoticed. Those nearby were aware of him, but didn't really see him. Still, there was the need for caution; he was still on foreign soil in a foreign place with unfamiliar customs.

This initial journey into London was a necessity, something of a preliminary survey. He had found and secured one place to rest prior to leaving Whitby, but more would be required. This trip he'd keep as short as possible and then return to the village to see to final arrangements for his move here. He would learn quickly and assimilate. It was a point of survival, and he had been a master of survival for countless years.

He turned onto Wellington Street and in a short time was standing across the way from his destination. The light glowing from the Lyceum Theatre was brighter than any other building on the block. He learned this phenomenon was due to the new electrical light invention, and the luminance assaulted him. It streamed into the street jammed with elegant coaches and hansoms, all of them disgorging London's elite. He watched as royalty, socialites and celebrities made their way between the six Grecian columns and into the theater foyer.

Large, dramatically illustrated posters proclaimed Othello as the season's opening presentation. The entertainment was of no interest to him. He stepped off the curb and made his way across Wellington toward the theater.

CHAPTER 5

As Doyle and Gilbert exchanged pleasantries, Stoker glanced toward the far entrance in time to see his wife enter the lobby. Florence Stoker looked beautiful in a clinging formal gown of deep green silk. Accompanying Florence was her dearest friend, Lucinda Westen, also looking lovely in scarlet.

Stoker's position demanded his presence at the theater long before curtain time, so Lucinda often accompanied Florence when she attended a performance. Lucinda, widowed three years earlier, was always available and eager for any social activity. Stoker found her a preferable companion for his wife to the many men who would gladly offer their services.

Both in their mid-thirties, the women made a striking pair. Florence was green-eyed with raven hair and pearl white skin. Lucinda was blonde with a somewhat darker complexion.

Stoker was just turning his attention back to Doyle and Gilbert when an older gentleman appeared beside Lucinda. There was something nebulously familiar about the fellow. He was tall, with gray hair falling just short of his shoulders. Like the other theater patrons, he wore evening clothes.

Stoker's memory pieced together a faded image of an evening walk long the Whitby jetty. Dear God, it was the man that approached him his last night in the village. Tepes, was that his name? There was no question; it was the same man.

Lucinda appeared quite happy to see him and drew Florence into their conversation. Was Lucinda already acquainted with this fellow? That would be an implausible coincidence.

Stoker attempted to get a better view through the crowd, but it proved difficult. Florence smiled warmly at Tepes as he greeted her with a bow. After a few more moments of pleasantries, he accompanied the two women as they walked toward the nearest entrance to the auditorium.

The women disappeared through the doorway, but Tepes paused as if listening for something. He turned, and for a moment, gazed at Stoker, his eyes dark and intense. And then he was gone, swallowed up in the throng making their way into the auditorium.

Stoker suddenly became aware of Gilbert using his name.

"You know, Bram here does a good deal of writing himself, Arthur."

"Just short stories so far," added Stoker, forcing his attention back to the conversation.

"Yes, *The Waters Mou* is your latest I believe," said Doyle. "I found it admirable."

Stoker strained not to show his pride. Doyle had read one of his stories. "High praise, indeed, sir."

"Not at all." Doyle's impatience began showing again. He glanced toward the auditorium entrance and said, "Well, I'd better find my seat. Again, thank you for the invitation tonight, Mr. Stoker. And William, let's get together soon for a whiskey."

Before Gilbert could answer, an older, moneyed couple approached Doyle, blocking his path to the auditorium.

"Good evening," said the man to Doyle. "We just couldn't pass up the opportunity to meet you."

Trying her best not to gush, the man's wife blurted out, "Goodness. Mr. Sherlock Holmes, himself."

Doyle's face darkened as he glared at the hapless woman. "My name, madam, is Arthur Conan Doyle." With a final nod to Gilbert, Doyle stepped around the couple as if he'd never even seen them, and entered the auditorium.

CHAPTER 6

The moment Gilbert said his goodbyes, Stoker hurried into the auditorium. He considered avoiding Tepes, but he could not forget the image of how his wife appeared so charmed by the man. It was his responsibility to check on Florence's wellbeing and reassure himself. Stoker made his way down the aisle, still clogged with patrons slow to find their seats or pausing to greet one another.

There she was, Florence, standing at the end of a row chatting with Lord and Lady Kenniston, a wealthy older couple influential in London society. He was certain her speaking with them was not by chance; Florence was keen on her social position and made it a point to be close to those who might enhance that position. There was no sign of Lucinda or Tepes.

The Kennistons left Florence for their seats and Stoker watched her smile transform to a thin expression of cool tolerance. Now, on her own in the crowd, she appeared distant, her eyes engaging no one. He wished she could bring herself to more consistently display the warmer side of her personality that he knew so well.

"There you are," he said, catching her attention. "I thought I saw you in the lobby." He bent to kiss her.

"Ah. Careful not to muss," Florence warned, offering him her cheek. He gave her a gentle kiss.

"I thought I saw you come in with Lucinda." He surveyed the crowd.

"You did. She's gone off somewhere with her charming friend."

"Her friend? The gentlemen I saw you speaking with." Florence appeared to blush.

"They only just met, but she seems quite taken with him," Florence added.

"They met tonight, here?"

Florence nodded. "Just outside. I left her just long enough to collect our tickets from the window. When I got back, he was with her; they were already chatting away."

"Where are they now?

"I don't know," Florence responded. "But they'll be back soon. Lucinda hates to miss the curtain."

Stoker checked his watch. "Which is only a few minutes away." He looked again for Lucinda and her friend, but saw no sign of them. He couldn't delay any longer.

"I should get to my seat, then," Florence said.

"I'll see you after." Stoker took her hand in his and squeezed gently, then hurried toward the stage access door at the front of the auditorium.

Stoker caught up to Henry Irving, already made up and costumed in the wings. The actor was engaged in one of his frequent contests of the will with Walter Collinson, his competent valet of many years. Harry Loveday stood nearby, watching with quiet amusement. Despite the questionably serious bickering, Irving still kept one practiced critical eye on the stage. It was set as a street in Venice, and stagehands rushed about making final preparations for the first act.

Irving was a tall, fastidious man. His height, combined with longish hair and lean features, presented quite an imposing figure. As he came to know his friend better, Stoker realized all of it was carefully cultivated. The look, along with every move Sir Henry made, was calculated to command maximum attention. On stage, he wore his inner courage and large ego like a uniform. Offstage and out of the public eye, he was somewhat effete.

In general, Irving was not happy unless he was the eye of the storm in some minor crisis before walking on stage. Tonight's crisis involved an issue with his costume.

"Hurry. Oh, won't you hurry," Irving whined.

"Just hold still," snapped Collinson. "I can't do a thing with you twisting around like that."

Irving noticed Stoker approaching. "Bram," Irving puled. "Where have you been?"

Stoker did his best to display an appropriate amount of concern. "Is there some problem, Sir Henry?"

"Only that I should have replaced Collinson years ago," Irving replied, not meaning a word of it. "A simple bit of costume dressing seems to be beyond him."

Collinson rolled his eyes and continued to work, no doubt appreciating that Sir Henry had stopped moving about since Stoker's arrival.

"You make such a convincing Othello," Stoker complimented, taking in Irving's costume and makeup.

"I should, after all these years, shouldn't I? But how can anyone expect me to be properly prepared when I'm assaulted by last minute emergencies?"

"You'll be fine. You're always the professional," replied Stoker. "And you bloody well know it since you create the emergencies."

"And on the topic of emergencies, please tell me you've secured the proper play to open next season, something from the classics."

Stoker sighed. "We've been through and through this. We need a property with the greatest box office potential. And at this point, all we're doing is exploring the possibilities."

"But his material is so common," Irving snapped.

"It can't do any harm to talk to the man, and the next season is still many months away."

"But we must have a good play. It's the opening spot."

"More importantly, we must have a theater in which to present a play."

"You're not going to start with that financial rubbish again, are you?"

"The Lyceum does a steady business, but purchasing the lease left us low on capital. Let's just hope the press doesn't get onto it."

"We can't have that," replied Irving. "It's not their business. We need a play—"

"We need a play that'll do business," interrupted Stoker.

Irving winced. "But Sherlock Holmes?"

"His stories have outsold every author in England. It'll bring in a tidy business."

"It's true, sir," Loveday added. "I've read them all."

"I as well," added Collinson. "Quite entertaining."

Irving fixed an icy gaze on both men and then gave a sigh of surrender to Stoker. "All right, all right. We must pursue it, I suppose. But he mustn't know we need him."

"Eight o'clock, sir," Loveday reported to Irving.

The actor offered them all a final, dismissive nod and moved closer to the edge of the wings, focusing his attention on the stage. His character did not appear until scene two, but Sir Henry made it a practice to scrutinize the first scene of all his plays, regardless of if he was in it or not. He said it helped him gauge the audience.

Loveday gave the cue and the curtain went up. The stage manager shook his head in disbelief, leaning in close to Collinson. "Imagine, Sir Henry more concerned with having no play than no money," he whispered.

Collinson smiled. "Henry Irving without a role to play. Who would he be then?"

Both men noticed the look of disapproval on Stoker's face and hurried about their business.

Stoker moved to a location in the wings where he could see the audience. There was Florence, sitting in her regular seat in the third row near center stage. Lucinda was now seated next to her. He scanned the theater, row by row, and finally found him. Tepes was sitting on the aisle, several rows behind Florence and Lucinda.

It was difficult to make him out in the darkness, but one thing was obvious; the man was not looking at the stage. His eyes were fixed unwaveringly upon the two women. Or was he looking just at Florence?

CHAPTER 7

The performance perfection, and the audience enthusiastically received Irving and his leading lady, Ellen Terry. A talented performer, Ellen Terry possessed a radiant beauty and the ability to charm everyone who met her.

In the moments following the final curtain, Stoker happened to see Ellen with Sir Henry alone backstage. They were standing in the shadows, facing each other, talking in whispers.

It was long rumored that Henry Irving and Ellen Terry were lovers off the stage and on. Stoker was certain the rumors were true. However, the rumors remained only rumors. Sir Henry lived his private life with fastidious discretion.

The two actors stepped closer to each other; Stoker turned away, giving them their privacy. More distracted than he cared to admit, he walked toward the front of the theater to find his wife.

He found Florence waiting for him in the lobby. He greeted her with a gentle hug and a perfunctory kiss on the cheek. "Is Lucinda joining us?"

"Oh," Florence responded. "Her gentleman friend invited her for a late supper."

"You think it wise, Lucinda, going off with a man she's just met?"

"I suppose normally I might have objected, but I got a good sense of him," Florence said. "There's a strong character there."

"Still," Stoker began.

"I really don't believe there's anything to be concerned about, Brammie. I'm quite confident in this."

"As you say." He saw little purpose in debating the issue further. Florence was committed to her opinion of the fellow, and besides, they had to get along to the opening night festivities.

The Beefsteak Room had once served as the Lyceum's lumber room. Large and Gothic, it now bore little resemblance to what it had once been. Irving had ordered it redecorated after taking over the lease, sparing no cost. He then brought in his own chef and made it his custom to host lavish, opening night parties here.

Stoker and Florence weaved through the jolly crowd comprising the Lyceum's most important patrons and the play's cast. Stopping at the well-stocked bar, Stoker procured glasses of chilled champagne for each of them. They then made their way along the banquet table in the center of the room, considering the lavish array of fine food and drink. While preparing her plate, Florence spotted her friend Will Gilbert and wandered off to chat with him.

Irving soon found Stoker. He pointed a long thin finger toward Doyle at the far end of the room, indulging a large glass of claret while chatting with Edward, Prince of Wales. "So, you invited him to the performance and the party."

"Edward? Certainly," Bram responded, holding his smile in check.

"You know very well who I mean," Irving snapped.

"The point is to make him feel welcome, include him as a friend."

Irving continued to stare sourly at Doyle.

"Look at it as a negotiating tactic," Stoker added.

"We'll see," Irving replied.

"Sir Henry," the voice came from behind them.

Turning, Irving's smile returned. "Ah, now here's someone I invited," he said to Stoker. "Mr. Quincey," he beamed.

Following Irving's gaze, Stoker turned to see a tall man, at least six feet, approaching through the crowd, his evening clothes hanging loosely on his lanky frame. He appeared to be about thirty years of age; his weathered and darkened complexion suggested he lived a good deal of his life outdoors.

"I just wanted to thank you for havin' me here tonight," Quincey said to Irving, extending his hand. "That was a fine show."

Irving accepted the hand. "I assure you, it's my pleasure. I'd like you to meet Bram Stoker. Bram is general manager for the Lyceum and a longtime friend."

"A pleasure, Mr. Quincey," Stoker greeted, shaking the man's beefy hand, calloused by hard work. "Welcome."

"I believe I had the pleasure of meeting your wife earlier tonight," Quincey said. "Ran into her and her charmin' friend just before the play got going. Only had time to just say hello, though."

"I'll have to introduce you properly, then. You're American, I'm assuming from the accent."

"Mr. Quincey's a cowboy," Irving answered before Quincey could respond. "We met at one of Wilde's soirees last week."

"A cowboy? Really? From Texas?" Stoker asked.

"Colorado. Got a ranch there," Quincey replied. "Cattle. Built it up to about fifty-thousand acres by the time I was done."

"I don't suppose you're wearing a six-gun tonight," Irving asked, looking for signs of a holster.

"Left my Colt in the hotel room," Quincey smiled. "But I don't go hardly anywhere without this pigsticker." He reached under his coat and behind his back. With the sound of metal sliding across leather, Quincey produced a well-used Bowie knife. The weapon was beautifully crafted with a bone handle and a ten-inch blade. It looked decidedly deadly.

"May I?" Irving asked, admiring the knife.

"Have at it." Quincey handed him the weapon.

Irving hefted the knife in his hand, testing its balance. "Beautiful," he said. "First rate."

"Thanks." Quincey accepted the Bowie back from Irving and returned it to its sheath.

"So, I take it you've made your money in cattle," Stoker said.

"Silver," Quincey answered. "Well, some in cattle, I guess. But what got me here was silver."

"How's that?" Irving asked.

"Every season we gotta go up in the high country and drive our herds down for the winter. We was up in the hills doin' just that. I was up this little canyon chasing a few strays when I found it. Damn rich vein. Ran up the whole length of the canyon."

"Wonderful story," Irving said.

"That was 'bout two years ago," Quincey continued. "Ended up with more money than any man has a right to. I'd never been any place further than Santa Fe. Decided to look around some."

"Well, I'm glad you're here," Irving said. "Did you bring a guest, or are you on your own tonight?"

"I'm on my own, but don't mind sayin' I'm rather glad for it right now," Quincey answered, his eyes surveying the room. "I was kind of taken by Mrs. Stoker's friend. Is she here somewhere?"

Stoker and Irving exchanged a quick glance, amused by Morgan Quincey's forthright interest.

"You're referring to Miss Westen," Stoker said. "I'm afraid not. My wife tells me Lucy left just following the performance for a previous engagement."

"Just my luck, then."

"Well, no matter," Irving exclaimed. "Come along with me. I've got several charming women who I know will enjoy meeting you."

"Lead the way, then."

Stoker watched as Irving escorted the American across the room. The fascinated crowd closed around them.

The evening progressed and Irving was called on for a toast. He gestured for Stoker, Florence, and Ellen Terry to join him in front of the huge hearth, its fire burning briskly. The room quieted and Irving raised his glass. "Let's raise our cups to the new season. May it be overflowing with memorable performances."

"And substantial profits," added Stoker. The room filled with laughter. Stoker slipped his arm around Florence and gently pulled her closer.

CHAPTER 8

The Stokers slipped out of the party early and made their way home to Number 27 Cheyne Walk. It was a lovely street of redbrick Queen Anne and Georgian houses, tree lined and quiet, running along the north bank of the Thames at Chelsea.

Florence sat close to him on the coach's leather bench, her thigh pressed up against his, her head resting on his shoulder. He embraced this rare moment of affection.

Later, alone in their bedroom and preparing for bed, Stoker admired his wife. Her beauty could be a source of torture. Florence feared "being bloated with pregnancy." As much as he would like them to have a child, he found himself able to forgive this extreme vanity.

Watching as Florence removed her dress and stepped behind her dressing screen, Stoker directed his mind to other matters. "So, what about Lucinda and this gentleman friend of hers?"

"I don't know that much," Florence answered from behind the screen. "His name is Vlad."

"Vlad?" Stoker pulled off his shirt and hung it in the armoire. He thought that rather curious, it was not the name the man had used in Whitby.

"That's the name I heard her call him. Eastern European, I think Lucy said." Florence reappeared from behind the screen wearing a silk nightdress. "He's an aristocrat in his own country. Some kind of prince, I think."

Florence smiled as she talked about the man. The stranger's lineage made a deep impression. "What's he doing here in England?" he asked.

"I don't think it ever came up." Florence removed the pins from her hair and the dark waves fell around her shoulders. She sat down at her dressing table and began stroking the brush through her hair.

"The American seemed quite taken with her tonight, you know," Stoker said. He slipped out of his trousers, folded them, and draped them over the back of a nearby chair.

"Oh, yes. Mr. Quincey. Can you imagine? Lucy having to decide between European royalty and an American millionaire."

"Every woman's dream?"

"Oh, I don't know. I just want to see her happy. She's gone through so much, and she's been quite lonely." Florence put the brush down on the table and gazed into the mirror. "Can you imagine Lucy being courted by a prince? It's all so mysterious and romantic."

"If I try, I suppose."

Florence's voice grew soft and her eyes distant. "So charming, so commanding."

"The gentleman seemed to make quite an impression," Stoker remarked. He took his nightclothes from the armoire.

Florence suddenly turned and looked at him. "You never told me anything about your trip to Whitby. Did you enjoy yourself?"

"It was frustrating."

"How so?"

"Oh, I don't know," Stoker sighed. "I got little done."

"I'm sorry. But that happens from time to time, doesn't it?" Florence asked.

"It's always lovely there, though; that was one saving grace," Stoker muttered.

"It seems like ages since we were last in Whitby together. Remember the walks we'd take along the cliffs, the sea air? We used to have such lovely times there." She rose from the table and came to him, taking his hands in hers. His nightclothes fell to the floor.

Stoker smiled, sharing her memories. "It has been some time, hasn't it?"

"We should plan to go back soon. You could find time to get away, couldn't you, Brammie?"

He gently pulled her to him. "Remember our first holiday after we were married?" he said, his voice dropping to a whisper. Florence looked up at him and moved closer. He could feel the warmth of her body.

"That storm moved in, kept us in for two days, and two nights," he added.

She smiled. "It was freezing, and all that rain."

"That feather bed kept us warm enough."

Florence tightened her arms around him. He felt her hips pressing against him, closer than before. "I can still remember how it felt to touch you. The warmth of you, the heat of you."

He kissed her, softly at first. She responded and together they transformed the kiss into something deeper.

They pulled each other toward the bed. He was still caught off guard by her passion and proceeded tentatively, but in moments she lay beneath him, making her willingness clear.

As he moved in her, Florence pulled him down close to her. He felt her lips move across his throat, lingering there. The unusual sensation excited him.

He raised himself up, and looking down at her, took in every detail of her beauty. It was rare to see such sensuality in his wife, such lust. They were both soon overwhelmed and focused with intensity on each other. As they finished, Stoker felt a sudden ache of uncertainty whether or not his wife was making love to him.

CHAPTER 9

He gazed at the woman, Lucinda Westen, as he roamed about her bedroom. She reclined on a settee next to the window, her eyes open but unfocused, distant. The quavering shadows from the single gas lamp crawled across her face. She would remain this way as long as it suited him.

The woman, of course, accepted his offer to escort her home. She had been enthralled with him since their meeting in front of the theater. He had no true intention of supper and claimed weariness, asking if she would excuse him and allow him to see her safely home. She coaxed him for the meal, but he ended that annoyance with a slight assertion of will. The same strength of will brought him a necessary invitation into her home.

He marveled at how tractable she was, how tractable they all were. It enabled him to accomplish many things. It was the key to many doors. His strength of will served him well in life. Through the ages, it had grown immeasurably.

The Westen woman's possessions were scattered about the room, each giving him some sense of her as he gazed at them or touched them. She had told him of her husband, how he died of a sickness of the lungs some years ago. There was a portrait of them on the dresser. It was the only picture in the room; the woman had no family.

He had reasoned well in assuming Stoker's wife would attend the theater company's opening night. His senses had guided him to her as he strolled through the crowd queuing into the theater.

The moment he laid eyes on the Stoker woman, he knew he must have her. It was not lust in the mortal sense of the word; he did not experience such feelings. But in her beauty he saw a goodness and a purity that he detested. This was a peculiarity in him he had come to recognize over the ages. From time to time, he found himself attracted to prey with these qualities for the singular purpose of destroying them.

He already knew her husband's desires; he had sensed them and defined them as he watched the man interact with his wife and the wealthy patrons at the theater. Those desires were Stoker's weaknesses as well. As for the wife, she was strong willed and aloof; there would be amusement in the challenge of overcoming her defenses.

From that night in the village, listening and watching through the darkness, he knew Stoker was well suited to his needs. Learning from the man would enable him to blend into the population without notice. Yes, the fool would be very helpful in this.

He harbored no feelings in his plan for the couple. Whatever motivations or satisfactions he experienced were rooted and driven by the core of his nature. His nature was evil and evil possessed his very being. There was no pleasure in the things he did or the way he did them. There was no pain or regret in any of it.

He moved to the settee and sat down beside Lucinda Westen. Undisturbed, she held her distant gaze. His hand rested on her knee; he eased it up the length of her thigh. Her breathing deepened at the touch of his hand. He could feel the silk of her gown beneath his fingers, but nothing beyond that.

There was neither heat nor chill for him. He felt no no love, and the only hatred in him was a deep, instinctive hatred for sanctity and light. There was neither joy nor sadness. He experienced only the memories of those sensations, distant echoes of feelings and emotions that once were.

It was the stir of power that was the strongest of these echoes. He once ruled his homeland with every life subject to his mastery. His rule had been too short and his sovereignty had faded away long ago. Now his influence over the lives he encountered and often destroyed was the source of satisfaction that fed him.

He gazed impassively at the woman. She would be useful as a means to draw the Stokers closer. And in achieving that end she could satisfy one of his more immediate needs.

He reached behind her and unfastened the clasps of her gown. Her smooth, golden skin unveiled as he pulled the fabric down, the silk gathering at her waist. He touched the back of his hand to her cheek and slowly moved it downward across her throat and bare shoulders. He lowered himself to her and her flesh gave way to him.

CHAPTER 10

"So that's it then? There's nothing more to be done?" Doyle couldn't keep the sound of defeat from his voice.

"Nothing now, at least," came the reply.

Doyle sighed. Danforth Richards had been his solicitor for over ten years. He had proven himself diligent and thorough in matters both large and small. If he said there was nothing more to be done, then Doyle must accept it.

"The court is considering the buyer's offer," Richards elaborated. "It was supposed to be a bankruptcy proceeding, so it's fortunate that these fellows from Grandle stepped in."

"I suppose."

"If Grandle Ltd. can purchase Westheath Development, then there is still at least some hope for you and the other investors," Richards explained. "It may take some time, but the market will eventually recover and the properties will inevitably sell."

"That doesn't do my current situation much good," Doyle grumbled.

Richards pushed aside some papers cluttering his desk. "I know you're concerned about the expenditures for medical care."

"How could I not be? There doesn't seem to be an end to it," Doyle sighed. "Louise doesn't deserve what's happened."

"How is she doing?"

"As well as one might hope. She always puts up a brave front," Doyle replied. "But she's hardly been out of the house since the consumption began eating away at her."

He drifted into quiet thought, his vacant gaze fixing on the mahogany bookshelf built into the wall beside Richard's desk. Finally, his eyes moved back to the solicitor. "I miss her company more than I miss the money that's disappeared into that bottomless pit of doctors, treatments and household help."

"Of course," Richards nodded. "You'll give her my regards for me, won't you?"

"She'll be glad to know you asked after her." Doyle thought a moment and then added, "You think Grandle will honor the original investment agreements if and when the purchase goes through?"

"I always hope for the best. But should they not do the honorable thing, then we will deal with that problem when the time comes. In the meantime, you can always give us another Holmes story."

"I couldn't be more bored with the old fellow," Doyle scowled.

"Holmes has been very good to you."

"Yes. I'm sure I sound ungrateful."

"How are your talks with Henry Irving coming along?" Richards asked.

"If you've ever had to deal with an actor sporting a Gibraltar-sized ego, then you know damn well how it's coming along," Doyle snapped.

"I can step in and handle it if you like."

"I'd like nothing better, but you'll recall Stoker advised it would go better with me personally involved," said Doyle.

"Oh, yes. It was something about Irving feeling more comfortable dealing with another artist."

"More likely he believes he'll manage a better deal for himself if my solicitor isn't involved," Doyle replied in a sour tone. "Our discussions have just begun and I already fear the real negotiations might prove intolerable."

"If you will allow me to say so, it's important that you be patient in these dealings," Richards replied, his tone concerned. "I know you're well aware of how badly you need these proceedings with Sir Henry to go well. The Lyceum can be a prestigious and profitable showplace for your work."

Doyle absorbed Richard's words and then got to his feet. "Well, we've a meeting scheduled this morning, so the Lyceum is my next stop," he said, collecting his hat from a nearby chair. "At least Stoker is involved, and that gives me some confidence. He has a reputation for bringing a sense of reason to Sir Henry's side of things."

Richards rose from his chair and walked around the desk. "As I said, I always hope for the best."

CHAPTER 11

Florence awoke still hearing the soothing, accented voice of Lucinda's European friend. She lay in bed trying to make out the words, remaining there much longer than she intended. It was silly of her, she knew. She was married, happily married to a fine man. Still, there was something intriguing about the charming aristocrat. Well, there was nothing wrong with a little fantasy, she thought, swinging her long legs out of bed.

She saw to her toilet and dressed, and then spent some time with her Bible, as was her morning custom. By the time Florence came downstairs, Mrs. Monroe, their cook, had a simple breakfast waiting for her. A half-hour later she made a casual inspection of the house, issuing instructions to the housekeeper on a few chores she wanted to see done.

She was relaxing in the parlor with a cup of tea when she heard the front bell ring. A minute later, Tillie appeared in the parlor doorway. "Pardon me, missus, but Miss Lucinda's girl is at the door," Tillie announced.

"Yes?"

"She says she's got to speak with you. Seems a bit out of sorts."

Florence put her cup and saucer down and followed Tillie to the front door. Annie Beth stood on the front step, waiting with obvious anxiety. She had been with Lucinda forever and Florence knew her well. "Annie Beth? What is it?" Florence inquired.

"It's Miss Lucy, ma'am. I haven't been able to get her up," the girl answered.

"You haven't been able to get her up?"

"I went to wake her at 7:30, like always. Knocked on her door, but I didn't hear nothin'. I knocked again and heard her say she wanted to sleep a bit more. I could hardly make out her words through the door." Annie Beth's voice went up in pitch as she continued. "I waited an hour and tried again. She didn't say a word, so I went in."

"Very wise," Florence encouraged her.

"She was just lyin' there asleep. I shook her a bit, and she woke up, but it's like she couldn't wake up," Annie Beth explained.

"What do you mean?" Florence asked.

"I tried pulling back the curtains and she wouldn't let me. Snapped at me, she did, told me to let 'em be. I tried again; I tried to shake her awake, but she just closed her eyes. I told her I thought it best to call the doctor and that upset her. We bickered about it a bit. She wouldn't budge about the doctor, but she finally let me come for you. You'll come, won't you, ma'am? She's not herself."

Florence glanced past Annie Beth at the hansom waiting at the curb. "Tell the driver to wait another minute. I'll be right along."

Twenty minutes later they arrived at Lucinda's home on Lawrence Street, only a few blocks from Cheyne Walk. Florence dismissed the cab, and she and Annie Beth stood outside the entrance to Lucinda's bedroom. Not bothering to knock, Florence opened the door and went in. The room was dark, the curtains still drawn tight. Lucinda was lying on her back, the covers drawn up to her chin. Her face appeared drawn and troubled in the shadows.

As Florence drew next to the bed, Lucinda uttered a soft, contented moan.

"The curtains, please," Florence instructed. Annie Beth pulled them open.

Lucinda groaned in protest as the sunlight streamed across the room. She tossed uncomfortably among the covers, as if trying to throw off some unwelcome swarm of insects. Florence took Lucinda's shoulders in a gentle grip as she sat down on the edge of the bed. Her eyes opened, and she tried to shield them from the light. "No. No," Lucinda moaned. "Close them. Close them, please."

Annie Beth moved toward the window. "No," Florence stated in a firm tone. The girl stopped in her tracks. "We won't be closing the curtains, Lucy." Lucinda's eyes slowly focused on Florence and after a moment, it was clear she recognized her friend. "It's almost noon and they need to be open."

Lucinda turned her eyes away from the window. Florence noticed how pale and drawn her friend was. She felt her forehead for fever, but the skin was cold to the touch. Florence turned to Annie Beth. "Heat a cup of broth. Bring it up directly."

Annie Beth nodded and hurried from the room.

An hour later, Florence had Lucinda propped up in bed, goose down pillows supporting her comfortably. Florence had helped her take the broth and she was looking better. Some of her color had returned, though she still looked quite weary.

"I don't know what got into me," Lucinda fretted. "I still feel so tired."

"Well, you seem better now," Florence observed. "Did you eat a bad spot of meat last night, perhaps?"

Lucinda looked back at her with a blank stare. "I don't think so. I don't remember."

"You don't remember what?"

"I don't remember much about last night after the theater."

Florence smiled. "So, that's the effect your nobleman has on you?"

"Oh, Florrie, stop it." Lucinda smiled for the first time since Florence had arrived. "He is interesting, isn't he?"

"To say the least." Florence took another careful look at her friend. "Yes, I'd say you're doing better. I'm going home now, but I'll be back to check on you after dinner."

Lucinda reached out and took her hand. "Thank you for coming to my rescue. You're my angel."

Florence gave her friend's hand a gentle squeeze and then turned to Annie Beth. "Keep a close eye on her. And come get me if any need develops."

"Yes, ma'am. Thank you, ma'am," the maid replied with gratitude.

With a final, reassuring smile to her friend, Florence left to find a cab.

CHAPTER 12

I rving, a long cigar gripped loosely in his hand, was pacing outside the door of the Beefsteak Room when Stoker arrived. "I thought it best to wait for you. Doyle is already inside."

"I understand," Stoker responded with a sigh.

Irving opened the door and entered, with Stoker following behind.

A hearty fire burned in the enormous fireplace and the lamps gave the room a warm, homelike feel. Stoker watched as the game began again. Doyle and Irving's coolness toward one another vanished in a wave of professionalism.

Doyle rose from his leather wing chair in front of the fire as Irving moved across the room with a warm smile pulling at his thin features. "Ah, Mr. Doyle. Good morning."

"Sir Henry."

The two men shook hands as if they were long-lost brothers.

Doyle didn't even bother to greet him, Stoker thought, the resentment gnawing at him.

"How's your charming wife?" Irving asked. "Louise, isn't it?"

"Yes," Doyle answered with the perfect amount of appreciation in his tone. "She's well, thank you. Prefers to stay with the quiet of home when I'm in London on business. Wonderful performance last night. First rate."

"You're too gracious," Irving beamed. He always accepted compliments on his performances as sincere.

Collinson entered carrying a tray laden with pastries, fresh butter, and white bone china. He set the food on the end of the banquet table and then poured tea from a steaming pot already waiting on the massive mahogany buffet.

Doyle had piled several pastries on his plate before the last teacup was filled. "Nothing else, thank you, Walter," Irving said. Collinson left the room, closing the door behind him.

The first sign that the cordiality would fade came with Sir Henry nervously pacing past the food and picking up tidbits with his fingers instead of using a plate.

Doyle sank into his chair near the fire. "Well, Sir Henry," he sighed, setting his teacup on the small table beside the chair, "Why don't we get right to the business at hand."

The second sign, to be sure.

The professional charm between Sir Henry and Doyle transformed into a mutual wariness.

Irving appeared thoughtful as he continued to pace. "Hmm, yes. Well, actually I, I'm just unable to picture myself as this, this Sherlock Holmes fellow."

Doyle's entire body stiffened. "Oh?"

"It's just, I've built my career on Shakespeare, the classics. It's been my policy to present only the finest possible entertainment to our patrons. But a play about a policeman?"

"A policeman," Doyle responded, his temper rising. "We're discussing 'The Adventures of Sherlock Holmes,' not some news column about a south end bobby."

"Of course not." Sir Henry sounded contrite.

"If this is a way to avoid meeting my price."

"You mustn't think that, Mr. Doyle," Stoker interjected. "We're still working out the finances. It's a bit dicey since you require more than the standard royalties."

"It's been a bloody long while since I've accepted less."

"But I'm still not convinced your play is something I should undertake. Especially for a long run," Sir Henry continued.

Stoker couldn't believe Irving said it.

Doyle rose from his chair. "If that's the way you see it, I see no reason spending further time trying to change your opinion."

Stoker gestured toward Doyle. "Mr. Doyle, if you please, sit down." Doyle hesitated. "Please."

Doyle settled back into the chair with some reluctance, his suspicious eyes boring into Sir Henry. Sir Henry gazed back with a questionable innocence.

"Gentlemen. It's to all our best interests to make this work, is it not? We need this arrangement."

Doyle and Irving remained silent, tentatively eyeing each other. "Very well, then," Stoker continued. "Let me draft something informal. Some guidelines to get us on the right track, if you will. We can meet again later to look over what I've come up with."

Irving sighed. "Perhaps he's right. Perhaps the only way to move forward is for Bram to take it all in hand."

"I'll look at any reasonable agreement," Doyle said.

"As will I," Irving agreed.

"Then I'll send word as soon as I have something," Stoker confirmed.

Doyle nodded. "Good." He rose from the chair, still annoyed by Irving's "policeman" remark.

Irving dropped himself into a nearby chair as Doyle moved toward the door. Stoker got there first to open it for him. Doyle glanced back at Irving, then back at Stoker. "You highly compensate for his, his being an actor," he said.

Irving's eyebrows rose in amusement as Stoker closed the door closed behind Doyle. "Difficult man."

CHAPTER 13

Lucy was on Florence's mind throughout the day. Her friend had been through much and she was left to see to everything herself. The strain of it had just caught up with her and she was suffering from the fatigue of it all.

Early evening was a perfect time to call on Lucy. Bram wouldn't be home from the theater until late and the visit would fill her evening with something useful. After a light supper, Florence sent Tillie to the corner to fetch a cab. The girl was back with a four-wheeler several minutes later.

The moment Annie Beth opened the front door, Florence knew the situation had not improved. Annie's face was lined with worry. "I just don't know, ma'am. I just don't know. She's been half asleep all afternoon, she has. I got her to take a bit more broth at supper, but now she's napping again."

Florence handed Annie Beth her wrap. "You just see to your work and I'll go check on her." The maid nodded but stood and watched, her nerves showing, as Florence climbed the stairs.

Lucy was indeed sleeping when Florence entered the bedroom. Annie Beth had lit a single lamp and the quivering flame threw uneven shadows across the ceiling and walls. Florence sat down on the edge of the bed, and Lucy's eyes fluttered open when Florence took her hand. "Florrie," she said, still sleepy.

"Ah. There you are," Florence said, offering an encouraging smile.

"You're back," said Lucy.

"As I promised. Here, let's prop you up a bit." Florence maneuvered Lucy into a sitting position, supported by the bed pillows. "Well, aside from looking a bit groggy, you seem fine."

"I feel fine," Lucy sighed. "Just tired."

Florence made herself comfortable in a chair beside the bed. They chatted awhile about nothing in particular, recalling mutual friends, planning a day trip together, and reminiscing about trips they'd taken in the past.

An hour passed and Lucy fell asleep again. Florence was content to sit with her friend; there was still some time before Bram would be home.

"Is everything all right, ma'am?" Annie Beth asked from the doorway.

"Quite all right, yes," Florence answered. "It looks like she'll sleep well tonight. If she's still like this in the morning, I think we should call for her doctor."

Annie Beth nodded. "I'll be down in the kitchen should you need anything."

"Thank you."

Florence turned her gaze back to Lucy. The chair was comfortable and the room cozy. It was quite pleasant, really. She listened to the soft, even ticks of the hallway clock drifting through the open door, and watched the shadows slither about the room with each tiny movement of the lamp flame. The shadows began to blur, their edges seeping into the plaster of the ceiling and walls. Her eyes felt heavy and Florence gave in to their weight.

CHAPTER 14

The evening performance was a little less than two hours away when Stoker exited through the stage door on his way to find himself a light supper. He stepped out of the alley into Wellington Street, bustling with early evening carriage and pedestrian traffic.

Stoker hadn't walked fifty steps when a chill in the air overtook him. He paused to bundle his coat closer around him. Before he could continue on his way, an accented voice called his name from the shadows just behind him.

"Mr. Stoker."

Stoker pivoted around to see Lucinda Westen's mysterious nobleman standing in the night gloom a few feet away. He wore the same clothing he had in Whitby, the black coat billowing around him in the soft night breeze.

Stoker concealed the surprise he felt, and the displeasure. Where had the man come from? "Mr. Tepes, if my memory serves." Stoker was relieved to hear civility in his voice.

"Indeed. Forgive me. Once again, I have managed to startle you," Tepes smiled.

"I'm afraid so."

"You will recall our conversation in the village last week. I wondered if we might continue it, become better acquainted?" Tepes inquired.

"I'm in a bit of a hurry right now, I'm afraid," he answered.

"Yes, of course. I have detained you."

"I was just on my way for some supper before this evening's performance and don't have much time."

"I'd be honored if you would be my guest," Tepes offered. "Pleasant talk over a good meal."

Stoker felt a current of adrenaline course through his body. The hair on the back of his neck bristled like an animal in the wild, sensing a predator. He looked around him and then felt foolish. There was no danger to be seen.

At any rate, proceeding slowly in the matter before him was wise. Perhaps a meeting with the man at some point in the future would not be out of the question. Tepes watched him closely, those piercing eyes fixed upon him.

Stoker was about to decline the invitation when a feeling contrary to his decision began to overtake him. His thoughts whispered it couldn't hurt to hear the man out. After all, it was indeed possible that something propitious might come of it. Stoker surprised himself by saying, "I was heading to Christopher's Grill, just down the block."

The eyes softened and the thin lips formed an even thinner smile. "Excellent."

They chatted during the stroll to Christopher's, and by the time they were seated at a table in a corner of the dining room, Stoker had learned that Tepes did indeed have aristocracy in his blood. His family's ruling power, however, had slipped away some time ago. As the sole surviving member of his family, Tepes had developed their landholdings and had some success in acquiring additional properties.

Stoker ordered a simple roast beef with vegetables and a glass of wine. Tepes duplicated his order except for the wine, which he declined, along with the offer of any other beverage.

"So, what prompted your coming to England?" Stoker began, after the waiter left with their order.

"Necessity. The opportunities in my home country have lessened over the years."

"And where is home, if I may ask?"

"A small region now part of Romania," Tepes answered.

"Have you been in England long?

"I reached Whitby in August."

"Ah, and your passage?" Stoker continued.

"A Russian schooner."

"So, you wish to expand your holdings in England?"

"Indeed, which is why I seek your help," Tepes said.

"I'm afraid I don't have any acquaintances in land acquisition."

"I have not been clear," Tepes answered with only the slightest suggestion of a smile. "Not in matters of business, but matters related to business. I find myself unfamiliar with the customs and traditions of your country."

"That kind of thing generally comes with time," Stoker said.

"Ah, yes. But I feel some urgency. Familiarity with the ways of business here will help me in securing a more favorable position in my transactions, will it not?"

"There's no arguing with that," Stoker agreed.

"The sooner I learn about the ways of your people, your country," Tepes trailed off, searching for the correct wording.

"The proper channels," Stoker suggested.

"Yes. Then the sooner I can go about my business."

The waiter arriving with their food interrupted the conversation. Stoker was grateful for the opportunity to consider the matter. The man's story seemed reasonable enough, but he still sensed the need to proceed with caution.

As the waiter hurried away, Stoker took a sip of wine. "I'm afraid I can't be of much help," he said, returning his glass to the table. "My schedule at the Lyceum leaves me little time for anything else."

"Your answer is disappointing."

"I'm sorry. Perhaps I'll think of someone else who might be suitable."

"As you say."

Stoker attempted to ignore the awkward silence that followed by starting in on his meal. He could feel Tepes's gaze. The beef was excellent, but he found it difficult to enjoy for the disheartenment, or whatever it was, emanating from across the table.

"I should have taken your busy schedule into account," Tepes acknowledged. "Of course it is demanding of you."

Stoker looked up from his plate, relieved that his host had spoken first. "I doubt many people realize the amount of time and work it takes to manage a theater," he answered. "And then there's Sir Henry's personal affairs on top of the rest."

"It must be difficult finding time to write," Tepes intoned.

"How do you know I write?" Stoker couldn't hide his surprise. None of his work been translated or published anywhere in Eastern Europe, and it was a constant thorn in his side that none of his work had made him well known in England.

"Your stories touch on dark things."

"What have you read?"

Tepes displayed his thin smile once again. "I believe *The Chain of Destiny* is a fitting example. How did you put it? *From a cloud, misty and undefined, it became a sort of shadow with a form. This gradually, as I looked, grew darker and fuller, till at length it made me shudder. There stood before me the phantom of the Fiend.*"

"You flatter me, sir."

"It is nothing. There are elements of your stories that remind me of tales told throughout my homeland."

"You read nothing of mine there," Stoker challenged.

"I only recently discovered your writings, shortly after my arrival in your country."

Stoker took another bite of roast beef, chewing thoughtfully over the conversation. After washing down the beef with another swallow of wine, he asked, "What did you mean about the tales told in your homeland? My stories are reminiscent in some way?"

The thin smile appeared once again. "Your writings tell me you have interest in the unknown, things beyond the power of normal men. My home country is rich in legends and folk tales, many of them centuries old. The people there believe in many unusual things, many... dark things."

"For example?" Stoker asked, his interest growing.

"Witches and ghosts, curses, werewolves, the people of my country believe in these things as strongly as they believe in the rising of the sun," Tepes said.

"In this modern age?"

"There is little of the modern age in my country. Progress is slow to come there."

Stoker continued with his supper, his mind considering the possibilities.

"Perhaps you might tell me something of your next story," Tepes suggested.

Stoker shrugged. "Just now, I'm only considering some ideas. Nothing decided as yet."

No response came from Tepes.

"To be honest, I'd very much like to hear some of those stories you mentioned."

"The old tales."

"Yes, and the customs, the superstitions you mentioned."

Tepes gazed in silence across the table. The delay in his response inclined Stoker to finish the last bites of his meal.

"It would be my honor," Tepes said after several seconds.

"Wonderful. Thank you." Stoker could hardly believe his good luck, stumbling across such a wonderful source of material.

"Perhaps we might benefit one another. I tell you the stories of my country, you acquaint me with the customs of yours."

A ripple of confusion drifted across Stoker's mind. Somehow, he faced the same proposal he had rejected not five minutes before, and this time he was considering its benefits. Few Englishmen knew anything of Romania; something might come of it, some notoriety, should he write about it.

"I don't see how I can refuse after your generous offer," Stoker heard himself say.

"Then we are agreed." Tepes nodded, looking like the cat who swallowed the canary.

Stoker offered a nod and a wan smile and then noticed for the first time that his host had not touched a bite of his supper.

CHAPTER 15

After thanking him for a pleasant meal, Stoker left Tepes standing in front of Christopher's. He had felt a sense of relief once Tepes had paid the bill. Their meeting had been interesting and potentially beneficial, but he was relieved to have it end. Now there was a nagging anxiousness to put some distance between himself and the man.

Walking back up the block toward the Lyceum, he could feel Tepes' eyes on him. Glancing casually back over his shoulder confirmed the feeling. The man stood at the curb, the black coat floating around him in the evening breeze, enclosing his tall frame like dark, oversized wings.

Stoker glanced back a second time, only a moment later, and Tepes was nowhere in sight.

No longer feeling watched, Stoker slowed his pace, strolling up Wellington, his mind mulling over the topics discussed over supper. Something in the conversation was bothering him, nibbling away at the back of his brain like an annoying insect.

He felt vexed when it occurred to him that neither he nor his dinner host had exchanged addresses before parting company. How on earth was he supposed to contact the man? But nagging at his thoughts even more was the realization that he still knew little about Tepes.

It would be prudent to find out more about him. A sensible man would at least verify his background, but how? Stoker knew nothing of Eastern Europe, nor did he have any acquaintances or contacts there. Perhaps an embassy could provide information. Would anyone at any embassy answer such questions without good cause?

It occurred to him he already knew someone who very well might be helpful. He had met the gentleman at a Lyceum performance a few years ago and considered him a friend. They had met by chance in the lobby prior to the curtain; Stoker had been so fascinated by the man he had invited him to the festivities in the Beefsteak Room following the performance. Over the course of the evening, the gentleman revealed himself to be a well-traveled scholar.

Stoker altered his course, and dodging the carriage traffic across Wellington, made his way toward the telegraph office only half a block up the street.

"I'd like to send a wire, please," Stoker announced, entering the office.

"Yes, sir." The operator took up his pen and pad prepared to take down the message.

"Address it to Professor Arminius Vambery," Stoker began.

CHAPTER 16

The moon was still low in the sky. He focused his mind on a top floor window until the latch lifted.

The window swung open without resistance; he stepped through it into the darkness of a small, empty bed chamber. The door was open, leading to the dimly lighted hallway. He stood motionless only long enough for his senses to absorb his surroundings and then moved silently into the hall. The darkness of his form blended into the deep shadows.

He made his way to the stairway at the end of the corridor. The woman would be in her bed chamber off the hallway below waiting for him; he could already feel her presence. The stairs passed beneath his feet, his footsteps making no sound.

Unhurried, he moved toward the bed chamber door at the end of the passage, but his instincts soon halted his forward motion. He detected another creature; perhaps the house maid tending to her duties on the ground floor. But there was something more; there was someone else in the woman's room. He waited and listened; no sound emitted from behind the closed door, but he felt two heartbeats, each beating slowly in rest.

He continued forward and found the door to be ajar. He looked through the opening into the darkness. His blood began to sear his veins when he saw her in the chair across the room from the bed, the Stoker woman. She slept, her head tilted, resting against the side of the chair, her smooth, white throat bathed in the soft glow of moonlight filtering through the window.

Her presence was unexpected. It displeased him that the hunger welled up within him. He had come for the other woman. But now, before him, was an even more pleasing offering.

It was not yet the right time, but there she was before him. There was still much to accomplish and if he allowed himself impatience, it would amend his plans. Reason dictated it best that he retreat and return at a more propitious time. But his feet remained planted outside the door, the gnawing hunger crawling through him.

The woman in the bed, sensing his nearness, moaned softly. His long fingers spread against the wood and he pushed the door further open.

Florence felt a chill and adjusted her body in the chair, trying to find warmth. She slowly became aware of the soothing darkness and realized that she must have fallen asleep.

She willed her eyes to open and the bedroom gradually drifted into focus. The room was black, touched only by the low flame of the lamp. The shadows had grown and were crawling across every surface.

Florence sat up in the chair. Lucy was restless, her body tensing fitfully among the covers, as if tortured by some tenebrous nightmare. Soft whimpers and moans played across her lips. Florence shook off the sleep and rose from the chair. She untangled Lucy's covers and stroked her temples, hoping to calm her. The restlessness subsided, but something was still haunting her friend's sleep.

Making her way to the washstand, Florence poured some fresh water into the basin and splashed a little on her cheeks. Guided by her reflection in the mirror, she patted the towel across her face. It pleased her she didn't appear as tired as she felt.

While folding the towel and hanging it on the side of the washstand, Florence felt another presence in the room. She surveyed the mirror but saw only the shadowed room in reflection. Hearing another moan from Lucy, Florence gathered her wits and turned back toward the bed. Lucy was tossing again, battling whatever demons were tormenting her sleep.

The sudden jangle of the front door bell turned Florence swiftly around to face the source of the noise. She gasped when, for a brief, unsettling moment, she thought she saw Lucy's European prince framed in the doorway, his dark clothing indistinguishable from the darkness of the hallway behind him. And then he was gone, swallowed in an instant by the surrounding blackness.

Florence stood frozen, her eyes fixed on the empty doorway, wondering if she had really seen anything at all. The sound of muffled voices rising from the floor below restored her. Checking on Lucy once again, Florence found her to be more relaxed, her moans replaced by the quiet breaths of sleep.

Florence walked to over to the landing at the top of the stairs and was surprised to find Annie Beth speaking with the American cowboy, Morgan Quincey. He carried a mixed bouquet in one hand and his hat in the other.

The maid turned as soon as she heard Florence on the stairs. "It's Mr. Quincey, ma'am," Annie Beth explained, handing her his calling card. "Calling for Miss Lucy."

"This is such a surprise," Florence greeted the visitor.

"Not an unwelcome one, I hope, ma'am. I know it might be a bit late."

"Normally it wouldn't be at all," Florence said. "But I'm afraid Lucy hasn't been well. She isn't up to receiving guests."

"Yes, I heard of it," Quincey answered as Annie Beth relieved him of the bouquet and hurried off to put the flowers in water. "That's why I came; to pay my respects and offer help if help if needed."

"That's so kind. Right now it looks like she just needs rest, but I know she'll appreciate your courtesy."

"This must seem odd, my stopping by," the American mumbled, his shyness obvious. "I mean, I don't even really know Miss Westen."

"You've noticed Lucy's a lovely person," Florence smiled. "I understand."

"I must admit, I'm a bit taken with her."

"Perfectly understandable, and I know she'll appreciate your having stopped by."

"Well, I'll not be keeping you. Again, if I can be of some help," Quincey offered, regaining his composure.

"Thank you, sir."

Quincey offered an awkward but sincere bow and then showed himself out.

Florence felt uncomfortable and anxious once the man was gone. She was still shaken from her dream as she awoke earlier in Lucy's room, if that's what it had been.

CHAPTER 17

The week had been difficult and frustrating. Stoker had to give considerable thought to the agreement concerning Doyle's play. Keeping in mind that it had to be amenable to both Sir Henry and Doyle, and their egos, the assignment was proving to be a formidable challenge. Of course, the Lyceum's daily business did not give way just because Stoker found himself with something extra on his plate.

And on top of everything else, his mind kept returning to Tepes. He couldn't seem to get a firm grasp on what the man was about. And most distracting of all, it troubled him how the European had looked at Florence. Perhaps this was just a subtle jealousy churning somewhere deep inside him. Or was he imagining all of it?

Florence had never given him any reason to doubt her. Any flirtations had always been harmless and limited to close friends both she and Stoker knew well.

She was already in bed by the time he returned home from a long workday, propped up with pillows, and absorbed in her bible. "The scriptures," he observed. "I thought you read your bible each morning."

"Hello," she greeted him, looking up from the pages.

He leaned over, giving her a kiss on the cheek.

"I read it whenever I need comfort or strength," she replied. "I required both tonight."

"Oh, is something wrong?"

Florence didn't hesitate before answering.

"Not really. I suppose I'm just concerned about Lucy.

"Is she improving at all?" he asked.

Florence told him the latest news concerning Lucy's condition and included the visit from Morgan Quincey. He listened as he prepared for bed, but found it difficult to keep his mind on her words.

"Are you listening to me?" he heard her ask.

"I am, yes," he answered with haste. "I'm sorry. I guess I'm a bit distracted."

"Clearly. So, what is it causing you to ignore your wife?" she teased him.

"I've begun work on a new book," he said. "It's on my mind more than it should be."

"Oh, goodness. And what's this one going to be about?"

He hesitated. "I'd rather not say at this point. I need to see how it develops."

"Well, as long as it isn't the dark crack of doom of your last short story," she sighed.

"*The Invisible Giant?*" he asked, surprised. "What could you object to about that?"

"It was about an orphan girl who tries to warn everyone of a looming plague," she reminded him. "The little girl looks out the window to see a huge shadowy form approaching to consume the town. Frightening."

"I thought you liked it."

"I liked it just fine, and I love you, Bram, but you published it as a children's story."

He didn't understand her point and decided to leave it alone. Florence stretched out in their bed, and he realized he wanted to be closer to her. He slipped into bed next to her, kissing her again, this time on her lips.

His head finally resting on his pillow, Stoker took his wife's hand in his hand and stared in silence up at the ceiling. After several moments, he turned toward her and said, "I believe a child would be good for us, very good for us."

Florence squeezed his hand. "Oh, Brammie, you know how I feel about it."

"Just think of it. Think of what it would mean to us."

"I know what it would mean to me," she countered. "The horrible added weight, the labor."

"It's nothing to fear. Women have been doing it for centuries," he argued, keeping his tone gentle.

"Fear has nothing to do with it. I simply choose not to submit myself to it all."

"We should at least discuss it."

"We are discussing it."

"I mean, continue discussing it," he said.

Florence looked at him through the shadows. "If we must continue discussing it, can we do it some other time? I was just dozing off."

"Of course. I'm sorry." He gave her hand a final, gentle squeeze and then released it. She was asleep only a minute or two later. It wasn't long before, despite his restless mind, Stoker drifted into sleep himself.

CHAPTER 18

A note delivered to his desk by a young messenger late in the morning somewhat allayed Stoker's frustration. The handwritten request suggested a meeting at The Spaniards in Hampstead after the Lyceum performance that very evening. It was signed only with the initial T.

Why on earth couldn't the man schedule a meeting during acceptable business hours? Stoker wondered. He decided to suggest it.

"Wait a minute, please, and I'll have a reply for you," Stoker said to the boy as he reached for his pen.

"Can't, sir," the messenger answered.

"You can't wait?" Stoker glared at the boy.

"No sir. I mean, it's not that. There's no address for a reply."

"No address?"

"No sir. My supervisor found the message on his desk this morning with instructions and money for delivery, but there was nothing else."

"I see," Stoker sighed. "Thank you, then." He passed the boy a tuppence. It was clear Tepes had his own way of doing things.

Stoker gave the matter some thought as the messenger went on his way. Sliding a piece of stationary in front of him, he wrote a message to Florence explaining he would be working late. There was no reason he could think of he should keep the meeting from her, but an indefinable intuition suggested he should keep the matter private.

He left the Lyceum uncharacteristically early, but it was still twenty minutes before midnight when he arrived in Hampstead. He had never visited The Spaniards before, a well-known pub that had been a Hampstead mainstay since the 16th century, but he had attended the funeral of a distant relative some years earlier in the churchyard of St. John just down the road.

Now he sat across the table from Tepes, stunned to silence by what he had just heard. Their meeting had begun uneventful enough. Tepes had arrived a little more than an hour earlier, and just a few minutes late of the appointed time. He had soon directed the conversation toward his interests.

Stoker had answered the man's questions and provided examples when appropriate. Through the conversation, Stoker found it a challenge to focus, distracted by the many questions he wished to ask Tepes. After what seemed like an interminable length of time, Tepes obliged him.

Stoker began by asking a few general questions about the culture in his host's country, jotting down answers by pencil in his notebook. Out of that line of questioning evolved a discussion about prevailing superstitions. Tepes spoke of the evil eye, gypsy curses, ghosts and supernatural beasts without a hint of skepticism or derision. And then, to illustrate the deep rooted beliefs of his people, he began a story.

He referred to the protagonist in passing as a "prince" but then added that the common people believed him to be a *vlkoslak*.

"Vlkoslak? I'm unfamiliar," Stoker began.

"Wampyr," Tepes interrupted, his expression never changing.

"Vampire?" Stoker felt disappointment; he had hoped for something fresh. "I've read *Carmilla*, of course, and some of the *Varney* serials. They've been around for years."

"Perhaps you will find something different in this story," Tepes said.

"That was rude of me; I'm sorry," Stoker said. "Please go on."

And go on Tepes did, weaving a tale of a monstrous predator driven to all things by a most unnatural lust. Stoker observed the man as he spoke. Tepes' expressions varied to match the horrors he related, but the emotions portrayed in his face seemed at odds with the restrained excitement in his voice.

He painted a Gothic oil, his narrative describing a dark and brooding landscape, a rugged country with a culture imbued in long tradition, violence, and deep-seated superstition. He conveyed his story with skill and frightening detail, as if he had somehow woven himself into the fabric of an unfolding tapestry.

The story had progressed to a point where the demonic prince was about to perpetrate an unspeakable cruelty upon a mother and her infant

59

child when Tepes grew silent. Stoker leaned forward, eager to hear the rest of it.

"It grows late," Tepes murmured. "We will finish this chapter of the tale next time we meet."

"Certainly there's time to finish now," Stoker urged.

"We still have much knowledge to exchange, my friend," Tepes replied with his thin, joyless smile. "I promise; you will hear the story's end. And I have many stories."

Stoker sat in silence, his mind attempting to process all he had heard.

Tepes observed him with grim satisfaction. "Something troubles you?"

"I, no, I wouldn't say that," Stoker stumbled. "I admit there is something about it, though. Something exciting and unsettling at the same time. But that story and your telling of it, I've never heard the like of it."

Tepes raised an eyebrow, but said nothing.

"The depths of the wickedness, the evil your," Stoker hesitated, for reasons unclear to him, not feeling comfortable using the word vampire. "The evil your prince was capable of," he finished.

"So it is evil that disturbs you?" Tepes asked.

"Shouldn't it? Any decent man should be appalled by evil."

"Evil has been with man from the beginning of time," Tepes said. "It is woven into his being, it is present each day of his life, it grows and expands with its own power."

"You speak of evil as if you approve of it," Stoker challenged.

"It is not for me to approve or disapprove," Tepes shrugged. "I simply observe. Man has embraced the darkness more and more with each passing age."

He stood up, pulling his coat tight around him. "I will require a solicitor, someone well experienced in real estate transactions?" Tepes continued. "Can you refer me?"

"I don't know anyone offhand," Stoker answered. "I'll speak to our man who handles the Lyceum's business. He may work with real estate. If he doesn't, I'm sure he can recommend someone."

Tepes nodded and turned toward the entrance.

It struck Stoker what he had found unsettling about the tales he had heard this night. Feeling as if he might be about to prod a venomous snake with a stick, he blurted, "You tell those stories as if you were there."

Tepes paused. "That could not be possible, could it?" he replied without bothering to look back. In a few strides, he reached the door and was gone.

CHAPTER 19

He watched the man, Stoker, until he found a cab up the block from the inn and was driven back to London. The man's will was strong; he was not always easy to manipulate. This was unexpected, but he had little doubt the stronger will would prevail.

Now he became increasingly aware of the relentless hunger gnawing away at his insides. He had not taken nourishment for two days; the insatiable craving had grown and could no longer be ignored. Of course, he could find sustenance; refraining from doing so was a deliberate decision to avoid attracting undue attention, especially from the authorities.

In the village where he first arrived, he had lived on several farm animals to assure he remained invisible. But they served as sustenance only; their taste was unsatisfying. Now he could stand it no longer.

The little town barely breathed at this early hour of the morning. Shutters were closed and windows drawn, with no hint of light seeping through wood or glass. Inhabitants were locked within the protection of their rooms, most of them in the rest of sleep.

The scene stirred memories of his home country, of the villages that speckled the hills and farmlands at the foot of the mountain that braced his fortress. Over the ages, his people had dispelled any doubt of who or what he was. The population dwindled under his attentions, and those who lived became more cautious and clever with each passing sunset.

It had become necessary to journey farther and farther from home to find nourishment. The greater the distance traveled, the greater the risk of returning before the sun's searing light violated the soothing, early morning darkness.

He had no desire to leave his homeland, but the necessity had become obvious. It would be easier for him in the city.

He moved through the streets with increasing swiftness, his senses employed, reaching out before him like the invisible antennae of a predatory insect. For several minutes, his efforts yielded nothing, but then he felt it, the faintest measure of a tremor.

He slowed his pace, allowing his instincts to employ more fully. There it was again, a pulse that resounded deep within his being. Another came, and then another, until the pulses formed the pattern of a beating heart. It was not a body at rest; the swiftness of the pulses told him so. And then he sensed a new pattern; there were two, not one, the second beating much slower than the first.

The faint, sweet coppery scent, so arousing and familiar, began to fill his nostrils. He adjusted his course. The scent led him over a narrow lane that opened onto one of the main thoroughfares. He crossed the road and continued along a smaller lane that intersected another, wider street.

Across the juncture lay a long fence of stone and iron running along the back of the churchyard. He could see the rear of the church building on the opposite side of the yard, several hundred feet away. At the corner of the intersection stood a small house. Most of its windows were dark, but he could make out a faint glow emanating from the corner of the building.

In only a moment, he was outside the window of the house. Flickering light seeped through the closed shutters. He stepped closer, the black shadow falling from a nearby tree enveloping him, protecting him.

Through the window, he watched a woman sitting by a stone hearth. Beside her was an adolescent child, a girl, stretched out on a makeshift cot in front of the small fire. The woman bent over the sleeping girl, adjusting the blanket that covered her and then soaking up the thin beads of sweat that spotted her brow with a small, worn rag.

There was another life in the house, asleep; he could sense it. It was of little concern. Like thick oil coming to a boil over a blistering flame, the hunger inside him roiled.

Fixing his gaze on the woman he spoke to her, yet no utterance left his lips, no sound disturbed the darkness. Upon first hearing his voice, she paused, cocking her head to determine where the whispers might have come from.

He extended his will to the woman, enveloping her, taking control of her. She turned toward the window, staring, and caught sight of him. At first, alarm swept across her face, but it was soon replaced with a shallow emptiness.

She stared hollowly at him through the window as he continued the whisperings.

Your poor child is ill.

Your worry must be great.

Without proper treatment, she will surely die.

We must allow no harm to befall her.

I can help you; I can help your little girl.

Open your door to me so I might heal her.

A barely discernible tremor passed through the woman's body. She took a step toward the door but then stopped, deep rooted primal instincts holding her back.

A mother should not have to watch her child suffer.

We must allow no harm to befall her.

I bring the means to make her well.

Open your door to me so that I might bring help.

Open your door to me and see your child suffer no more.

He intensified his hold on her.

Open your door.

With a pitiful shudder, the woman turned and walked with tentative steps toward the door.

In a blur of motion, he was outside the door, waiting. He watched with anticipation as the latch turned and the door opened.

CHAPTER 20

His pen traveled swiftly across the paper. Line by line, it streamed forth ideas, recollections, descriptions and topics to be further researched. The pen filled page after page, as if driven by its own prolific power, its ink transforming thoughts into promising reality.

In spite of the hour he had stumbled into bed, sleep had been elusive. His brain raced like an overburdened engine through the night, toiling to digest the wealth of information, never allowing him to slumber.

Images of menacing, jagged peaks and treacherous narrow mountain passes occupied his thoughts. Shapeless creatures with claws and fangs, boding evil, prowled and preyed upon age-old hillside villages. His mind visualized a land of strange customs gripped by superstition and plagued by dark, incomprehensible powers.

The possibilities invigorated and excited him. Ideas gave birth to more ideas and then more still. He could see the framework of a story beginning to take place. The accented voice of Tepes telling his tale sounded in his brain. And he could hear the unique way he intoned his name. *Mr. Stoker. Mr. Stoker.*

"Mr. Stoker."

He looked up with a start. Harry Loveday stood next to the desk. Stoker hadn't even noticed him come in.

"So sorry," Loveday continued. "Didn't mean to give you a fright."

"You didn't. I was just hard at it, I guess," Stoker replied, irritated he'd been caught unaware.

"I've just brought some work orders for you to look over, and the morning paper." Loveday placed the forms and the early morning edition of the Pall Mall Gazette on the corner of the desk.

"Very good, thanks."

"Anything you need here?"

"No, no. Not at the moment. Thanks," Stoker answered.

"I'm off then." Loveday hurried out of the office.

Stoker dipped his pen in the well and went back to his notes. His lack of rest had not prevented him from rising early and making way to the Lyceum. There was plenty of theater business requiring attention, but he could think of little else other than the story of the night before, and his meeting with Tepes.

The man was odd; there was no denying it. He measured out any information he gave about himself. He thought back to their conversation at Christopher's Grill. Something still bothered him about that evening, something Tepes had said, but he couldn't put his finger on it.

"Look who I came across on the way back from my tobacco spinner," came Sir Henry's voice.

He looked up from his work to find Sir Henry and Doyle standing in his office doorway. Each smoked a cigar, undoubtedly from Sir Henry's recent acquisition. Stoker opened an accounting ledger, so its cover fell across his notes on the desk. He didn't want to risk Doyle learning about Tepes. This would be no one's story to tell but his.

Rising from his chair, he came around the desk, shaking hands with Doyle. "Mr. Doyle. How are you, sir?"

"Well, enough," came the reply. "I'll be much improved if we can make some progress in our business. I understand you have something ready."

Stoker felt himself flush. He had most of the preliminary guidelines completed, but there were still some additional points he wanted to add. He had promised Sir Henry he would see it done, but his preoccupation with all he had heard the night before had drawn his attention instead.

"Oh, yes. Yes," Stoker heard himself stutter. "It's not quite ready. I can get it to you later today if that'll be all right."

From the look on Sir Henry's face, it was not all right, but the actor said nothing.

Doyle's eyes narrowed. "I think I'd like to see what you have so far. You can tidy it up later."

"I thank that's best," Sir Henry agreed.

Where did I put them, Stoker thought, doing his best to hide his agitation. "I've got them here on my desk somewhere," he mumbled, making his way around the desk.

As he searched through the papers strewn about his desk, Doyle picked up the newspaper Loveday had delivered earlier and began leafing through it. "Tragic indeed," he muttered after several seconds of reading.

"What's that," Irving inquired.

"A murder in Hampstead."

Hearing the name of the village startled Stoker.

Doyle adjusted the paper and began reading.

"24 September. HAMPSTEAD TRAGEDY. A woman was found dead early this morning in the St. John churchyard, Hampstead. The woman, identified as Mrs. Emily Parch, was found by her husband, a local wheelwright, just after dawn.
Police told the Gazette John Parch had been asleep on the second floor of his home when he was awakened by the voice of his daughter calling for her mother from the lower floor. Mr. Parch went downstairs to discover his wife missing from the main room of the house where she had spent the night caring for their daughter suffering from a fever.
Mr. Parch searched the house and surrounding neighborhood, finally looking in the churchyard where he found his wife lying dead on the ground between a small oak tree and a family plot of headstones.
The police refused to comment on a cause of death, but confirmed Mrs. Parch had been brutally attacked, resulting in savage wounds in the neck and throat area. Police described the wounds similar to those made by a wild animal."

Stoker stood numb as Doyle finished reading, a folder of papers dangling precariously from one hand.

"Ghastly," declared Sir Henry.

"Interesting," Doyle intoned. Staring at the newsprint, his brow furrowed. "The key mystery here is the cause of death."

"The police believe it could be some kind of animal," said Sir Henry.

"Yes, but an animal with such fierceness in Hampstead? Perhaps a wild dog," Doyle answered his own question with a shrug. He dropped the

Gazette back on the desk, glancing up at Stoker as he did so. "Everything all right? You don't look well."

"Oh, no. I'm fine," Stoker answered, not fine at all. "Just thinking of the poor woman's family. Very sad." He pushed the news story to the back of his mind and turned his full attention back to his search.

"Of course," agreed Sir Henry.

In a few moments, Stoker found what he was looking for. "Here we are," he announced.

Doyle took the papers from him and began looking them over as Stoker handed a second copy to Sir Henry. "I can take this with me?"

"Your copy," Stoker nodded.

"Then I'll spend some time on it later."

"I'll review it as well," added Sir Henry.

"Just keep in mind what you've got there isn't quite finished," said Stoker.

"I'm just happy to see some sign of progress," Doyle grumbled.

"Why don't you send word once you're ready to go over the terms," suggested Stoker.

"I'll do that. Good day."

Doyle exited the office without further ceremony. Irving seemed at conflict with whether to stay or go, but after a dazed glance at Stoker, he followed after Doyle.

Stoker sank back into his chair. After staring at the newspaper for several seconds, he pulled it in front of him and read the story. He had been in Hampstead within hours of the woman's death. Both he and Tepes had been there. God knows he had seen enough death in his life, but this poor woman being murdered, and in such a manner. Tepes' stories crept to the front of his mind again.

Stoker resolved to pull himself together. His mind was full of dark, fascinating, and horrible stuff he found immensely interesting, but he had allowed himself to become too absorbed in it. That's all it was.

He took up his pen again and returned to his work. The ideas flowed again, but thoughts of the woman's death started seeping back into his mind like oil oozing its way past a valve not properly tightened.

CHAPTER 21

"Sometimes he's just an hour or two late; sometimes he doesn't come in until almost dawn," Florence sighed.

"And you've asked where he's been?" Lucy asked, taking a sip of tea.

"Several times. And I've done my best to put it as if I'm not much interested, not as if I'm trying to make him account for his whereabouts. His answer is always the same: working."

Lucy adjusted her feet on the ottoman and gazed out the window of the sitting room, her pretty face wrinkled in thought. "He tells you nothing at all?" she soon asked.

"All he'd say is that he's working on a new book," Florence continued. "He says little else, though. He won't give a single hint of what it's about."

"Well, I should imagine that writing a book takes up a good deal of time," Lucy reasoned. At a loss for any other insights, Lucy took a long, thoughtful sip from her cup.

Florence observed her friend. Lucy was having a good day. Her complexion was still pale, but her energy and spirits were higher than Florence had seen them in a month.

The first three weeks after Lucy was stricken were perplexing, and on two occasions she became so weak it appeared as if they might lose her. She had refused to see a doctor. But then her condition stabilized, although she was still quite weak and often tired.

Florence's thoughts drifted back to Bram. Five weeks had passed since

Othello opened the Lyceum's fall season, and in that time he had grown increasingly distant and preoccupied. He was normally so disciplined and reliable that the contrast was glaring.

"Oh, Florrie," Lucy said, pulling the quilt draped around her shoulders tighter. "Don't look so glum. I'm sure it's not anything at all."

"I look that bad, do I?"

"You're beautiful, as always. I'm just saying, I'm sure there's a reasonable explanation for whatever he's doing. Bram's a good man."

"But he is a man," Florence answered, her tone solemn.

"Oh, no. It couldn't be. I can't imagine him doing anything so unsavory."

"It's difficult not to think about, though," Florence continued. "At first I believed it might just be just work, but then when he started not even coming home on some nights."

"Is anything going on between you two?"

Florence shook her head, afraid that if she spoke, Lucy might see through her words to the guilt she harbored. Bram desired her in bed far more than she made herself available, and she feared he might someday do something about it.

"I just don't think Bram would do such a thing," Lucy said. "He adores you."

"If he's not doing anything wrong, I just wish he'd confide in me then. If it's just the responsibilities of work, why won't he speak to me about it? What's he afraid of?"

"Maybe it isn't fear," Lucy replied. "I'm not trying to defend him; But you shouldn't be worrying yourself to death at this point. Bram's always been a reliable sort, yes?"

Florence let Lucy's words sink in. "You're right, of course," she said, attempting to sound relieved.

"Well then," Lucy let her thought trail off.

Florence had indulged enough in self-flagellation. "Just look at me," she exclaimed. "A fine friend I am. I come to check on you and no sooner do I sit down I'm talking about all my worries."

"Oh, don't be silly," Lucy said.

"So, how have *you* been feeling? And be honest."

"Aside from being tired most of the time, I suppose I feel well enough," Lucy began. "Except for the tiredness."

"Are you getting enough sleep?" Florence asked.

"I think so," Lucy answered. "Most of the time. I think sometimes the dreams make me restless, though."

"You're having bad dreams? Why didn't you say something?"

Lucy shrugged. "Oh, I don't know. I'm not sure I'd call them *bad*."

"What are they about?"

"They're not about anything particular." Lucy's voice wavered.

"Well?"

"They're usually the same; I'm asleep in bed," Lucy began, shifting in her chair. "And then I sense there's someone else in the room, too. I open my eyes and I see the silhouette of a man."

"My goodness," Florence exclaimed, her friend's story awakening a familiar memory.

Lucy looked up at Florence. When she saw only concern and not judgment on her friend's face, she continued. "I try to see who it is, but I can't make anything out. Even as he moves closer, it's as if he is just a dark shadow. I mean darker than the darkness of the room. I try so hard to see, but can't make out any details."

"You must be terrified," said Florence.

"To be truthful, I'm frightened and thrilled at the same time. He comes closer and closer to my bed. I try to move, but I can't. It's as though he has complete power over me. It's rather exciting and terrifying all at once, I suppose."

Florence stared in silence at her friend.

"You think badly of me, having such a dream," said Lucy.

"Oh, no. No, I don't," Florence reassured her. "It's not that."

"What then?"

"It's just…"

"Just what?"

"It's just that I had a similar dream," Florence confessed. "At least, I'm almost certain it was a dream."

"What? When?"

"It was that first night I sat with you after you took ill," Florence said.

Florence grew silent and somber, seeing concern grow on her friend's face.

"What?" Lucy pressed. "What is it?"

"It's just that… I can't be certain, but I thought I might have seen your prince."

The look of shock on Lucy's face was clear. "You think it might have been *him*?" She sounded more intrigued than frightened.

"It's silly. I don't know. It was such a brief moment."

"I don't know what to say," Lucy mumbled.

Florence shrugged. "Nor do I. But I don't mind telling you, it rattled me. There was something, I don't know… something unsettling about it."

"Unsettling?" Lucy echoed. "Oh, dear."

"The moment I got home that evening I went to the scriptures," Florence said.

"Oh, Florrie."

"The Lord *is* my strength and my shield; my heart trusted in Him, and I am helped," Florence recited. "I don't mind saying I've been more diligent about my bible time ever since."

"A bit more time with the bible wouldn't hurt me," Lucy mused.

"But we went off your dream. What else happens?" Florence asked.

"He comes closer and closer until he's right next to my bed." Lucy shuddered. "He bends over me, lower and lower until I can feel his breath on my cheek. And then, nothing."

"Nothing?" Florence asked, unable to disguise her disappointment.

"I wake up. I can't remember anything after that point."

"My goodness," Florence exclaimed, blushing.

"I know," said Lucy. "I can't imagine what you must think of me."

"Don't be silly. But we don't want you having any bad dreams, and you need to make sure you're getting your rest."

"Of course." Lucy smiled.

Florence gazed at Lucy sheltered in her large, comfortable chair. She silently prayed that her friend would indeed regain her health. And then, without quite knowing why, she prayed Lucy would be protected from her dreams.

CHAPTER 22

He was now well in to the first draft of his new book and his feelings about it went beyond satisfaction. The professor had not been in the country to receive his original cable, but upon his return, provided the most generous help. Aside from the pressures of work and occasional nightmares, Stoker felt confident. He suspected the nightmares might be the result of Tepes' dark tales.

They had met on several occasions since their first conversation at The Spaniards. Their rendezvous was always at night and no meeting ever ended with another being scheduled. Either a message stating the time and location would arrive at Stoker's office at the theater, or Tepes would simply appear on the street.

One night Tepes turned up on the corner of Cheyne Walk, catching him quite off-guard. It was obvious the man desired an invitation into his home, but Stoker didn't feel comfortable with him being around Florence.

And yet, despite his discomfort, he had to battle an inclination to acquiesce. It took all the will he had to suggest a small café two blocks away. Tepes said nothing, but Stoker could feel the man's displeasure in being denied.

On this evening, they sat across the table from each other in the dining room of a small hotel off of Sackville Street. Stoker nursed a brandy while a pilsner glass of ale rested on the table in front of Tepes, yet untouched.

It was eleven thirty and the patronage in the dining room had dissipated. The meeting time was unusual for Tepes and Stoker had found it necessary to slip away from the Lyceum much earlier than normal.

"To hear you speak of it, one would think the average man has no hope at all of repelling evil," Stoker began once Tepes concluded his latest narrative.

"You disagree," Tepes said, thin lips curled in faint amusement.

"Temptation is always present, of course, but we're not animals. There's a core of good in all men, giving us the strength to resist. We have the power to do what is right," Stoker argued.

"Look at the history of the ages," Tepes countered without emotion. "The power of evil has led countless armies to glorious victory. It has conquered and ruled nations. Where perfect goodness in mortal man is impossible to realize, evil is readily attained and easily refined. It yields greater rewards and swifter satisfaction."

Stoker felt the hair on the back of his neck bristle. The man viewed the world with a dispassionate coldness that was better suited to a wild beast.

"You doubt what I've told you," Tepes stated.

Before Stoker could respond, Tepes turned his head, his eyes falling upon a young woman in her mid-twenties seated alone at a corner table. She was elegantly attired in a lavender dress. Long, chestnut hair draped over her shoulders, lending some modesty to the daring design of the gown. A wedding ring shimmered in the gaslight, bathing her left hand.

Stoker had noticed her arrive some ten or fifteen minutes earlier, and he had noticed the waiter bring the glass of sherry that sat on the table before her.

"You see the girl," Tepes stated.

"Yes, of course."

"Do you find her desirable?" he continued.

Stoker hesitated. "She's quite attractive, I suppose."

"No. Do you desire her?" Tepes pushed, his meaning becoming clear.

"Sir," Stoker recoiled, forcing his eyes away from the young woman.

"The idea is repulsive to you. You avert your eyes, but you still covet."

"Even if I did, I certainly wouldn't speak of it," Stoker said, his voice raised.

"No, of course not," Tepes mocked. "You remain silent as the girl fills your thoughts. You imagine her as yours."

"I find this distasteful, sir. Every word of it." Stoker squirmed in his chair.

A young man entered the room, pausing just inside the door. Spotting the young woman, he walked with purpose to her table. They were too far away for Stoker to hear the words he spoke, but the girl blushed when she heard them. It appeared as if they had known each other before this meeting, but not all that well. The girl turned her attention to the glass of sherry as he stood beside the table, speaking to her in soft tones.

"There, do you see? The girl has a suitor and not her husband," Tepes continued.

"You don't know that."

"She wears a wedding band. He does not. Yet he pays her careful attention."

"And your point?" Stoker asked.

"You see before you the darkness in man's soul at work," said Tepes. "The young man wants the girl for his own. That is all that matters to him."

The man slipped into the chair opposite the young woman, his smile warm and charming. The girl returned a tentative smile.

"There is the power of the darkness," Tepes droned. "It deadens any concern for the girl's husband. The potency of it even removes any true feelings the young man might have for her. He is not concerned with her well-being beyond what he requires from her in his bed. The darkness empowers his lust, not his heart."

"This is all conjecture," Stoker said.

"Is it?"

The young man leaned forward, placing his hands together in the center of the table, palms open and inviting. The girl hesitated, but then allowed her hands to intertwine with his.

"Ah, now you see the darkness extend its influence to the girl," Tepes observed. "It convinces her she deserves to be happy, deserves to be loved."

"If that fellow isn't her husband, I'd like to know where he is," Stoker growled.

"Perhaps he is away on business, or with friends at a sporting club. But it is of no consequence. The dark power convinces the girl that her husband neglects her in his absence. It persuades her that the small morsel of loneliness she feels at his being away is, in reality, a gaping hole in her heart and soul that she deserves to have filled."

The young woman was now fully engaged in conversation with the young man, demurely laughing at something he said.

"I assume you have some point you intend to make for all this?"

Tepes ignored the question. "You and he both want the same thing from the girl."

"That's not true," Stoker fumed.

"He admits it openly while you deny yourself, hiding behind the veil of righteousness. He is empowered by embracing the darkness while you are taken impotent."

"Is it your intention to insult me?" Stoker asked, anger seeping into his voice. "Because that is what you are doing."

Tepes shrugged. "Have I not spoken the truth?"

"You know nothing about those two," Stoker stammered. "And I'm certain you don't know what I want or what I'm feeling."

"I now see I chose my words in haste. Apologies, my friend. As you see, I am used to speaking plainly," Tepes said, lowering his eyes in contriteness.

"Not everyone is so easily pulled from the right path," Stoker asserted. "And good marriages, built on trust, are not shaken."

Tepes raised his eyes back to Stoker. "So you would never yield to such temptation?"

"I'm certain I would not."

"And the lovely Mrs. Stoker. Do you trust her to resist any unwelcome attention?"

The tone of the question sent a nauseating wave of jealousy washing over Stoker. He trembled at its impact. He studied Tepes, searching for the true meaning in his words. There was no expression on his face, no intent reflected in his eyes.

"I think it best that my wife be left out of our conversations," Stoker said, gathering up his notebook and rising from the table. "Especially when the topic is such as it was this evening."

"I've offended you," Tepes said, regret in his tone.

"You know you have," Stoker replied, angry. "And you know if I did allow the darkness, as you put it, to lead me to evil, then my judgment will most certainly come. Just as it will come to anyone doing evil."

"Judgment?" Tepes' eyebrows rose.

"Certainly."

"Ah, you refer to God."

"You don't believe in God?" Stoker asked, incredulous.

"I am as certain of His existence as I am of Satan's," Tepes answered. "Though I have never encountered either of them."

"Then what of the evils you've done? What judgment will you expect?"

Tepes gazed at Stoker, a hint of resentment in his eyes. "Revelation promises that at the end of time, all purveyors of evil will be cast into a lake of fire. Perhaps then I will need to consider such things."

"So you know the Scriptures?"

"I knew them once," Tepes sighed. "A very long time ago."

CHAPTER 23

25 October, 1895: 7:58PM
From: London & Provincial Telegraph Co, Ltd_Station 9
To: B Stoker, Lyceum Theatre, London
Message: Out of city for short time on matter of business. Will meet upon return. T

Stoker arrived in his office to find the telegram on his desk. He had been staring at it for a good portion of the morning, wondering what it might mean. Why would Tepes bother to send it? He had yet to reveal much about himself or his comings and goings. So why announce his departure from London?

The conversation with Tepes two nights before was vexing as well. The man's inference that he was lusting for some young woman he didn't even know was bad enough. But drawing Florence into it was going too far.

Stoker's memory transported him back to the opening night of Othello, seeing the way Florence warmed so cheerfully to Tepes in the theater lobby. He knew he was jealous; he even felt threatened, although for the life of him he could find no palpable reason for it.

And then there was that thing that had nagged at him from his first meeting with Tepes. Yet even now, he still couldn't pinpoint it.

A gentle knock on the doorframe drew Stoker from his haze. Sir Henry stood in the doorway, an opaque bottle in his hand.

"Good morning," he began, stepping into the office. "I'll just take a moment."

"Oh, whatever you need." Stoker found a welcoming smile.

Sir Henry turned the bottle over in his hands, admiring the label. "Some time ago Doyle sang the praises of this vintage port, Alambre Mar. It's from some little vineyard in the Douro region. I'll never admit to him I did it, but I ordered a case."

"That's showing quite a bit of confidence," Stoker quipped.

Sir Henry placed the bottle on the desk. "Anyway, it was just delivered. I thought you might like to try a bottle. Tell me what you think."

Sir Henry set the bottle down on the desk. Stoker retrieved it, giving it an appreciative examination. In addition to the product name and estate information, the label bore a muted color etching of three ships riding the wind over an amber sea.

"This is very good of you, thank you," Stoker said.

"You're welcome."

Stoker put the bottle back on his desk.

"On another subject," Sir Henry continued tentatively. "I've had some concerns over Doyle's ability to control extending the play's run."

The Holmes agreement. Stoker felt the tension begin to crawl up his spine.

Over the past weeks, the feelings of excitement and accomplishment he had enjoyed from his writing had been in growing conflict with the stresses emanating from his responsibilities to the theater. The efforts to bring The Adventures of Sherlock Holmes to the Lyceum stage was cursed with pitfalls.

Stoker faced increasing pressure to bring Irving and Doyle to terms. It was a laborious business and he found it a mounting challenge to stay focused on the task. He realized it was his primary responsibility, but there was always a strange pull drawing him back to his manuscript.

"From the beginning, you made your doubts about the play clear." Stoker sighed. "I would think you'd be more than happy if Mr. Doyle cut it short."

"Well, if the play is selling tickets, then we don't want to kill the goose that laid the golden egg, do we?" Sir Henry answered, pacing in front of the desk.

"It's gratifying to hear you admit the play has the potential for profit.

That's some progress, at least."

"I just think we might word the language a bit more to our advantage," Sir Henry grumbled.

"I see."

"This morning is quite busy," Sir Henry said. "But come see me this afternoon, say around four, and we'll discuss what we might do."

"All right," Stoker agreed, jotting down the appointment in his schedule.

"See you then." Sir Henry hurried from the office.

Stoker leaned back in his chair, feeling very put upon. What was wrong with him? This was his job. Why was it proving so difficult?

His eyes settled on the bottle of port, admiring the label. The three ships were very well done, each with an impressive amount of detail.

The ships. What was it about the ships? Something lingered in the back of his mind. The echo of a distant conversation returned to him.

"I reached Whitby in August."

"And your passage?"

"A Russian schooner."

The ship. Retrieving the folder containing his research and notes, Stoker began rummaging through the bundle of papers. In a few moments, he found what he was looking for. He unfolded the newspaper clipping.

MYSTERY AT SEA, ship of tragedy moored in Whitby, Stoker read. There had to be more than one Russian ship in English waters, but the schooner's presence in Whitby corresponded too closely with the date he encountered Tepes there.

Stoker read the story again from start to finish. Could it be the same ship? Was it possible Tepes had sailed on the same ship that lost three sailors under questionable circumstances? There must be a way to find out.

After staring at the clipping for several minutes, he put it aside and took up his pen and a sheet of his personal stationery.

To: Port Authority, Whitby
From: B. Stoker, Lyceum Theatre, London
Message: Please advise next scheduled arrival in your port, if any, schooner Demeter, Russian registry.

Stoker blotted the note and folded it. The telegraph office was only a short walk from the theater. Pulling his coat from the rack beside the door, he hurried on his way.

CHAPTER 24

He stood motionless in the gloom near his bed. He had been careful to place it deep in the cellars, where the risk of discovery would be unlikely.

His eyes were fixed on a narrow, dusty stream of sunlight filtering through a break in the rubble of the collapsed foundation above. The particles of dust appeared to swirl in the beam, moving slowly across the floor past the row of crumbling lancet arches that disappeared into the darkness beyond.

Preparations in the city had progressed acceptably. He had been right about the man, Stoker; he had proven useful in providing beneficial guidance and information that had been put to excellent use.

What Stoker might suspect or know at this point was of little consequence. His time of usefulness would soon be at an end. He had included an unstated invitation in his message, a mere mention of his leaving London. It would be enough, he was sure.

As for the return to Whitby, it was necessary and timely. He had acquired refuges that would be more than adequate for his needs. He was confident in his safety. Now he would attend to the last of the arrangements that would see him making the city of London his home.

As for the village, since it was unlikely he would return, there would be little reason to limit his appetites. It might even be satisfying to extend his stay somewhat.

The narrow beam of sunlight grew shorter, moving steadily across the floor toward the break in the foundation. It moved with increasing speed, the strip of dimming light creeping across the floor. Reaching the slope of the tumbled foundation, it continued upward, slithering across the broken brick and stone. It reached a hole in the rubble and moved through into the final darkness.

As the obsidian blackness closed around him, he began making his way across the dirt floor. His steps were confident and true despite the darkness. He ascended the decaying stone stairs at the opposite corner of the great cellar without pause. He climbed toward the ruined abbey above and the welcoming night beyond.

CHAPTER 25

27 October, 1895: 08:05AM
From: Port Authority, Whitby
To: B Stoker, Lyceum Theatre, London
Message: Vessel Demeter docked Whitby Harbor, East Pier, 22 October.
Further advise scheduled departure 29 October.

Not quite twenty-four hours after receiving the message, Stoker was traveling north. He told Florence he would be gone a day or two gathering research for his book. A source of information had presented itself, and he was eager to look into it. He made no mention of Tepes.

The train pulled into Whitby a few minutes before two, and after a late lunch at Mrs. Storm's, he made his way to the pier. Now he stood on the deck of the Demeter facing two crewmen who made it clear they opposed his presence and spoke little English.

"Your captain?" Stoker inquired for the second time. "I'd like to speak with your captain." He strained to understand as the seaman replied in the same imperceptible language while gesturing toward the gangway.

"No, you don't understand. You see, I just need a few minutes with your captain," Stoker insisted.

The man replied with a few terse words, one of which, without doubt, meant "no," and this time moved forward, crowding Stoker back toward the gangway. Stoker attempted to hold his ground but found himself stepping backwards before the intimidating motion of the crewman. Stoker once again insisted, "Your captain. I must speak with your captain."

"I am captain," he spoke with a heavy accent.

Stoker turned to find a bulky man with a bushy, black beard scrutinizing him with the same suspicious eyes he had already encountered in the man trying to force him off the ship.

"I am captain," the man spoke again. "What is it you want?"

Stoker felt relieved at hearing the captain's halting English. He stepped forward and extended his hand. "Ah, yes, hello. My name's Stoker. I'm hoping you can help me with a bit of information."

"What information?" the captain asked with suspicion, giving Stoker's hand a strong but brief shake.

"I read the story in the newspaper about your crossing this last August. I was wondering if I could just ask you a few questions."

The captain grew tense, almost angry as he retorted, "That is long time ago. Done."

"It's important."

"Details," the captain growled. "I tell everything to police, to writers of newspapers. They don't believe. They think me a fool. I've no more to say."

"Listen, please," Stoker said. "I've become acquainted with a man. I can't say for certain, but I think it's possible he may have had something to do with your ship."

Stoker thought he saw a hint of fear in the captain's eyes. "A man. What man?"

"I can't say, not now. But it's important you tell me what happened. Please."

The captain's eyes never wavered.

"It's rather cold out here. Could we step inside and talk?" Stoker asked.

The captain sized him up for several seconds and then gestured to Stoker to follow. They headed across the deck toward an open cabin doorway. A minute later, they sat facing each other across a small utility table in the captain's cabin.

"I know the voyage was tragic," Stoker began. "But I know little else."

"Days were good, days were fine," the captain began. "The first two nights were normal, but ship cold, very cold at night."

"So the bad weather made it colder than usual?"

"Bad weather came later. This weather was fair. The night, it was mild. But the ship is cold. On deck, below deck, cold."

"What changed on the third day?" Stoker asked.

"After sunset, much fog surrounded the ship. Hard to see. Hard to see anything on deck."

The captain looked as if he wanted to continue, but bad memories, or perhaps fear, halted him. Stoker waited for him to continue.

"I was about to sleep. I was ready to sleep when the hand on watch came down to my cabin, pound on my door. Very excited, very afraid."

"What had frightened him?"

"He says he sees man on deck, at the bow."

"Another member of the crew?"

"No. Not a familiar man. I dress quick and go topside with my man. He points and for short time I think maybe I see."

"You saw the man?"

"I think maybe I see him," the captain clarified. "But as soon as I think it, he is gone. Gone in the bad fog. So then I am not sure. We go count every man and look through ship. We carry no passengers, only cargo. All hands either in bunks or at their work."

"Can you describe this man?" Stoker asked.

"I'm not even sure I see a man. Too dark and too fast."

"And you're sure you accounted for each of your men?"

"We find nothing, no one," the captain answered. "So I go back to my bunk. Don't sleep good from worry. Next morning, word spreads. Word spreads about ghost or spirit on board."

"Your crew thought it was a ghost?"

"Sailors fast to believe in ghosts, curses, spirits. They much, much...?"

"Superstitious," Stoker said.

"Yes, they are. The crew, they want me to do something, something to protect them. They demand I do so. But what can I do? They grow more disturbed through the day. More afraid, more angry in their fear. Then rough weather begins and all grows worse. Winds and high water, and then rain. At nightfall, no man wishes to take watch. Helmsman does not wish to be at wheel. I order them. I threaten and then they do it. Palvenko at helm, and Comaneci keeping watch. But I must stay on deck with them, which I do."

"You stayed on watch all night?"

"Many hours, but then needed to rest. Need to dry some from rain. Just one hour. Then I come back. I promise them."

The captain paused again and Stoker noticed he was trembling. But this time, the man continued without urging.

"So tired then I sleep some, but not long. I am getting up again when I hear a man scream. Then running steps on deck above. I hurry topside, but nothing I can do. Nothing to do."

"What did you see?".

"I am on deck to see no man at the wheel. Palvenko, he tries to run past me, to get away. But I stop him and order him to say what has happened. He cries out that Comaneci is gone. I order him back to helm and then I look length of ship but see no one. Rain and wind are very bad, very dark."

Stoker could only imagine the terror of it all.

"I wake my boatswain. Order all hands to deck. We all look but find nothing."

"What did your man, Palvenko, say that he saw?" Stoker asked.

"Thinks he saw a man with Comaneci, but storm makes it hard. Hard to see or be sure. And then he says Comaneci just gone. He thinks dead."

"The poor fellow was probably just swept overboard with the rough weather."

"I think the same," the captain said. "But my men are still frightened. We double men at helm. We double watch. No man is alone. Then we all search. All over. Nothing anywhere but crates they themselves loaded. Just cargo, but men are afraid."

"Afraid of what?" Stoker asked. "Something in the hold?"

The captain shrugged. "I do not know, but every man hurried to leave hold."

Stoker leaned forward, eager for more information. "How long did the storm last?"

"Three nights," the captain replied. "The men believe that some evil spirit brought the storm upon us."

"And you?"

The captain shook his head. "I don't know what I think. No man slept, and everyone was still afraid. I order two men to each duty station, no one alone, but it did no good on the third night of the storm."

"What happened that night?" Stoker asked.

"I sleep almost not at all. Checking on every man. The storm is letting up, but it is still hard to see, hard to move with safety. We lose two more men that third night. Frantsev and Veselovsky. Both good men."

"How?"

"The same. Both men were forward. We hear one scream. We hear second scream, and then nothing."

"Where were you when this happened?"

"At the wheel with helmsman. We run to bow right away, but nothing. The men, they are gone."

Stoker sat in silence for some time, considering all the captain had related. His instincts told him Tepes was involved somehow with this ship, but there was little to link him to the tragic voyage. The only absolute thing about the Demeter's voyage was that three men were missing and most certainly dead. No one could say with confidence if they were lost in bad weather or by some other tragic means.

"You spoke of a man before," the captain broke the silence. "You believe him to be the same man, the man on my ship?"

Stoker shrugged. "I really don't know."

"But you come here to talk with me, to ask your questions." Suspicion had returned to the captain's tone.

"I came hoping to understand what happened," Stoker explained. "I hoped someone could describe this man, but neither you nor any of your crew ever saw more than a glimpse."

"Yes."

After a few moments the captain rose, and looking down on Stoker said, "If you *do* know this man, or *any* man who could do those things, what kind of man must you be? I must ask. What business do you have with such a man?"

Stoker stared at his clasped hands and then looked up to meet the captain's gaze. "I've begun to ask myself that same question."

CHAPTER 26

S toker left the Demeter and made his way to the port authority office just a short walk away. The administrator, after checking the logs, informed him that the Demeter was the only ship of Russian registry that had docked in port all summer. If Tepes arrived in the country aboard a Russian schooner, then it would've had to be the Demeter. But the Demeter carried no passengers, and as eccentric as Tepes might be, he was certainly no ghost.

Stoker already knew that Tepes had not taken a room at Mrs. Storm's. Lodging establishments in Whitby were few, and he spent the late afternoon visiting them all. Tepes hadn't stayed at any of them either. This confounded Stoker. Could the man have friends or acquaintances in the village?

Stoker remembered a little café, conveniently close, near the foot of the East Pier. The place did a fine job with the daily catches supplied by local fishermen and offered an interesting view of the old lighthouse. He made his way there.

He took a comfortable window table where he could watch the silhouettes of the last boats returning home and the sweeping beam from the lighthouse reflecting off the water. Between the view and an excellent grilled mackerel with gooseberry sauce, he managed to give his mind a rest from the many unanswered questions. He lingered over a rich port following the meal.

He began the walk back to Crescent Terrace just after eight o'clock. The seaward end of Church Street was still active with pedestrians, most of them seamen heading to a favorite pub or eating place, and a sprinkling of tourists. A few carts and carriages clattered along the lane. Stoker was about to cross to the opposite side of the street when he saw him.

Twenty yards ahead, on the opposite side of the street, walked Tepes. Stoker's initial reaction was one of contradiction. His senses identified the man with certainty, but at the same time he experienced a wave of doubt. Perhaps his eyes were failing him in the dim streetlight, but he would swear that Tepes looked somewhat younger than when they had last met.

Stoker remained on his side of the lane and kept moving, keeping the man in sight. In only a few moments, certainty replaced any doubt; the man was indeed Tepes. He strolled along at a casual pace, looking at something ahead on Stoker's side of the street.

Unable to make out what the European was looking at, Stoker crossed the street. Tepes' interest appeared to be a young woman. She was a working class girl, judging by her attire; perhaps a waitress at one of the pubs or restaurants in the district, or something else less reputable. There was little question she was the focus of Tepes' attention.

It occurred to Stoker that Tepes might not appreciate his presence in the village, especially if he discovered him following him. Slowing his pace, he allowed the distance to grow between them.

The young woman made an abrupt turn down an adjoining lane. Tepes altered his route and crossed the street, keeping her in view. A passing carriage blocked his view for several moments. By the time it had passed, Stoker had lost Tepes.

With a surge of anxiety that surprised him, Stoker hurried across the street, searching the gloom ahead for another glimpse of the man. He stepped into the lane the girl had taken and walked along it for several yards, but without reward. Stoker saw nothing but a few villagers making their way home. He stood his ground for a while, searching the shadows, then finally gave up.

CHAPTER 27

A few minutes before 2:00 PM, Harry Loveday strolled down the corridor toward Stoker's office. Folded under his arm was a bundle of newspapers, among them the early editions of both the Times and the Pall Mall Gazette.

Stoker was standing over his desk, frowning at an open ledger, when Loveday stepped into the office. He placed the daily newspapers on the corner of the desk, then pulled one from the top and handed it to Stoker. "The Lyceum advertisement stands out especially well in the Gazette this week," he said.

Stoker glanced at the paper. "Ah, yes. Very nice. Thank you."

Loveday hurried out of the office.

Stoker had returned to London the previous afternoon to find a note on his desk from Sir Henry stating that the actor was very cross with him for shirking his duties at the theater. The note also informed him of a 2:00 PM meeting the following afternoon with Arthur Conan Doyle. The message stated his attendance was imperative.

He had barely finished reading the note when Sir Henry gusted into his office to reinforce in person he did not appreciate Stoker's absence. Stoker did his best to explain that a time-sensitive matter had drawn him away and then capitulated to apologize. The apology appeased Sir Henry somewhat, but Stoker knew the man well enough to recognize the anger was still present.

With the meeting looming, Stoker began leafing through the Gazette. He was about to drop the paper back in the pile when the name of the village caught his eye.

Beads of perspiration gathered on Stoker's temple as he read the story. A heaviness pulled him down into his chair. This could not be dismissed as a coincidence. The theory forcing its way into his brain could not be real. None of this could be real.

CHAPTER 28

I n the Beefsteak Room, Doyle was sitting in his favorite wing chair near the fire. He was partaking of the tray of bread and cheese Collinson had placed on the table beside him. One could say a lot of things about Sir Henry Irving, but the man was dependable about the food he served.

"It's hard to believe that only three months ago we opened with Othello," Irving commented as he paced slowly around the room. "And now there's only a performance or two left of Cymbeline and this series comes to an end."

"What's hard to believe is that we've spent so much time haggling over this damn business arrangement," Doyle said, irritated.

"We've been doing what we do long enough to know what we want," Irving answered in a rare attempt to sound reasonable.

Doyle uttered a harrumph. "Well, Stoker hasn't helped matters any. What's gotten into the man, anyway?"

Irving looked stricken. "I don't know what you're talking about." He turned toward Collinson, changing the topic of conversation.

Doyle was certain Irving knew what he was talking about. Over the past months, Stoker's behavior had grown increasingly vexing. The longer they worked to complete this deal, the less reliable Stoker became. Doyle was certain that Irving was just as put out with Stoker as he was, but Irving was avoiding the subject by going on about another one of his theatrical triumphs.

Doyle would have blocked the jabber out of his mind, but it was near possible for him to do so. With few exceptions, he always heard everything; he always saw everything.

Doyle had Dr. Bell to thank for developing habits of observation that had become both a blessing and a curse. Dr. Joseph Bell was one of his professors at Edinburgh University.

Doyle recalled the first time he witnessed Dr. Bell use his highly developed powers of observation and deductive reasoning. The good doctor's assistant led a new patient into the classroom for a student case study. Dr. Bell glanced at the fellow for a moment, and then announced that the man was a left-handed cobbler. "You'll observe, gentlemen," he explained, "the worn places on the corduroy breeches where a cobbler rests his lapstone. The right-hand side, you'll note, is far more worn than the left. He uses his left hand for hammering the leather."

Doyle was skeptical at first, but he soon discovered that Dr. Bell knew nothing about these patients in advance. He was very much impressed with Bell's abilities and began practicing them himself.

Irving was now talking about one of his plays, The Corsican Brothers. Doyle checked his watch. It was after two. Where was Stoker?

"A scene in act three, I'm sure. I had over a hundred performers on stage," Doyle heard as he focused on Irving.

Collinson turned from the tea tray. "Beg your pardon, sir. Corsican Brothers employed precisely seventy-four players."

Irving looked as if he was going to argue, but then thought better of it as he stared across the room at Collinson.

Collinson shrugged. "I saw Mr. Stoker's cast sheet."

"He remembers columns of numbers after just a glance," Irving added.

"Just numbers, or do you recall words as well?" Doyle asked.

"Both, I think. Though I'm better with the numbers."

"I believe you have what's now being called a photographic memory," Doyle said.

"A photographic memory?" asked Irving.

Doyle pulled his watch from his waistcoat pocket again as he continued. "Collinson's eyes look at something—the cast sheet, for example—and his brain can record what his eyes take in as images."

Collinson appeared impressed with himself, offering a brief smug smile. Doyle snapped the lid of his watch shut and rose from his chair. "Eleven minutes past the hour. Where the devil is he?"

Before Irving could respond, a knock sounded at the door.

"Finally," Doyle grumbled.

Collinson hastened to the door and opened it. Instead of Stoker, he found Morgan Quincey, a sand-colored Stetson hat in one hand and a wrapped package in the other.

"Mr. Quincey," Irving greeted, surprised.

"The old fella at the rear door showed me where to find you. I hope I'm not interruptin'."

"Come in. We were just about to begin a meeting, but you're welcome just the same."

"If Stoker ever gets here," Doyle quipped, rising from the chair.

"Have you two met?" Irving asked as Collinson took the American's hat.

"We met at your opening night gathering," Doyle said as he shook Quincey's hand. "Nice to see you again."

"You, too."

"So, what brings you here today?" Irving asked.

"Just this," Quincey answered, handing the package to Irving. "I thought you might like it."

"Well, let's have a look?" Irving tugged at the string ties and pulled away the brown wrapping paper.

He drew a handmade leather sheath from the paper. Extending from the sheath was a beautiful stag horn handle hilt with a brass quillon. Taking hold of the handle, Irving withdrew the ten-inch Bowie knife from the sheath. The new blade glistened in the light.

"This is splendid," Irving gasped. "Thank you. This is a splendid gift."

"You seemed kind of taken with mine," Quincey said.

"I was, indeed. Thank you," said Irving.

"A pleasure."

Irving handed the new knife to Doyle. The author admired the workmanship and then returned the weapon to Irving. "It's a marvelous piece of work," Doyle said. "But we need to get back to the business at hand. What on earth's keeping Stoker?"

Collinson moved toward the door. "Shall I go find him?"

"No," Irving answered. "No. I'll go. Perhaps you wouldn't mind keeping Mr. Doyle company for a few minutes while I go see what's keeping Bram," Irving suggested to Quincey.

Irving was out of the room before Quincey or Doyle could respond.

CHAPTER 29

I rving was determined not to let anger get the better of him as he headed down the passageway toward Stoker's office. He was too eager in taking the opportunity to get away from Doyle with this errand. The man nettled him, but Doyle was right about Stoker's recent behavior.

The door to Stoker's office was ajar, and Irving pushed it open. He never knocked. After all, it was his theatre.

Bram was leaning over his desk studying an open newspaper, hastily scribbling notes on a piece of paper.

As Stoker blotted the note, Irving stepped into the office. "Bram, do you realize the time?" he asked.

Startled, Stoker closed the newspaper. Then he stumbled from behind the desk, the freshly written note clenched in his fist, and made his way to the hat rack. Irving had to move aside to make way.

"Is something the matter? Mr. Doyle and I have been waiting since well before two," Irving said, attempting to keep the impatience he felt out of his voice.

Stoker pulled his hat and overcoat from the rack, barely looking at his friend as he made his way toward the door.

Irving didn't like losing control, and the irritation he was feeling slipped into his voice. "Bram, we're both waiting for you," he snapped.

Stoker nudged past Irving, stepping into the corridor. He turned to face

Irving, but continued moving. "Sir Henry, I'm sorry. I can't just now," he stammered.

"You can't," Irving echoed, more flustered than he had been in many weeks. "But Mr. Doyle's expecting…" His sentence trailed off in astonishment as he watched Stoker turn and hurry down the corridor. "Stoker!" Irving shouted after him.

It did no good. Stoker hurried up the steps to the stage landing, then disappeared among the wing curtains.

Irving stood just outside the office doorway, trying to make sense out of his friend's behavior. As long as he had known him, Stoker had been dependable.

Irving stepped back into the office. There was nothing obvious in view that might have caused the situation. He looked to the cluttered desk and spotted the newspaper that Stoker had so hastily pushed aside. Irving stepped behind the desk and began turning the pages. A small splatter of ink, dripped from Stoker's pen, drew his attention. It was beside a brief article set near the bottom of the page. Irving quickly scanned it.

"29 October. THE WHITBY HORROR… another woman found dead. We have just received word that a woman missed two nights ago was discovered late this morning under a furze bush near Chutham Street…"

What on earth could Bram have to do with a murdered woman found in a village in Northern England Irving wondered? For a moment, he felt a small wave of unreasonable fear flow through his body. Could his friend have murdered someone?

Irving got hold of himself. He knew the answer—of course not. Stoker was a dedicated friend and employee, and a loving husband to the exquisite Florence. He had never let Irving down, and he'd never embarrassed him. Not until now, at least.

CHAPTER 30

After Irving notified Doyle of Stoker's untimely departure, the portentous author decided to confront Stoker. Irving argued to dissuade Doyle from that plan, but his efforts were futile. Doyle intended to go to Stoker's home.

The situation was so obviously awkward Irving expected Morgan Quincey to excuse himself, but the gritty American surprised him by offering to come along. "I've nothing planned this afternoon. Maybe I can lend a hand," he suggested.

Less than an hour later, Irving sat with Doyle and Quincey in a cab, making its way through mild London traffic. The coach turned onto Cheyne Walk, its wheels bumping along the roadway. The late afternoon light was soft and golden, and Irving thought the mood it evoked did not align with Doyle's disposition.

"I made it clear to Stoker. There's little value in our agreement unless we execute it immediately," Doyle said.

"Expediency is important to me as well. But chasing the man down to his home; I'd resent it if you did it to me."

"I don't much care about his resentment. An explanation's required, and I'll have our business concluded," Doyle growled.

"Stoker seems like a solid sort to me," Quincey declared. "I'm certain you'll work this out. Whatever it is."

The cab came to a stop in front of Number 27 and the three men climbed out. While Quincey remained at the curb, Doyle paid the driver, and Irving walked up the steps and rang the bell. Doyle joined him on the porch just as a maid opened the door.

"Good afternoon, Tillie," he said. "Mr. Stoker, if you please."

"Oh, hello, Sir Henry. I'm sorry, sir, but he's not at home just now," she replied.

"And when will he return?" Doyle asked, his irritation a little too obvious in his voice.

"I'm not sure, sir. He stopped in long enough to have me prepare a bag for him, then left straight away."

"He's traveling?" Irving asked.

"I'm sure I don't know, sir," Tillie answered.

Doyle nudged Irving's arm with his walking stick. "We might as well be off, then," he said. Then, tipping his hat to Tillie, "Thank you."

Tillie offered a diminutive curtsey. "Good day, gentlemen. I'll tell Mr. Stoker you called." She waited until they turned away to close the door.

Irving and Doyle began strolling up the street with Quincey trailing behind. Irving shot a sharp glance at Doyle. "I was about to inquire if Florence was at home. She'd have more information than Tillie," Irving said.

"She was home," Doyle said.

"Then why did you...?" Irving stopped suddenly, looking puzzled. "She was at home," he repeated.

"How do you know she was at home?" Quincey asked.

"I noticed someone drawing back from the second story window as I climbed the steps—the one to the left of the entrance. Although I couldn't say with certainty it was Florence Stoker, it's unlikely it was anyone else. No reputable servant would risk being caught spying on arriving guests, especially in a well-disciplined household," Doyle explained. "We already know that Stoker isn't at home. The logical conclusion is that it must be the lady of the house."

"Then why did you cut it off like that? We could have sent the maid to fetch her."

"And what if Mrs. Stoker doesn't have any helpful information, or what if she desires some from us?" Doyle asked. "Do we put ourselves in a position to lie to her, or do we alarm her without good cause?"

"Consideration to the lady," Quincey nodded. "I compliment you, sir."

Doyle's anger transformed into something else, curiosity, and Irving noticed Doyle was gazing at him with some interest. "What is it?" he asked.

"You'd think Stoker might let you know if he were going away. In case of some emergency at the theater, or some such business," Doyle commented.

"He takes a bit of time away now and then, but if he's leaving London; well, I've no idea."

"So, where would he plan to go?" Doyle asked to no one in particular.

Irving gave the matter some thought. "In his office this afternoon, he'd been looking at the Gazette. He marked an article about Whitby. You think he has interests there?"

"What was the article about?" Doyle asked.

"Something about a woman found murdered or some such rot." The fear he experienced early washed over Irving again. "You don't think he's involved in anything like that? It could ruin us."

Doyle's curiosity took on a more professional deportment.

"A rather intriguing thought. I want to see that Gazette article," Doyle said. "There are possibilities here."

It was unsettling to think that Doyle might see some kind of professional opportunity in all this. Then it occurred to him it was foolishness to spend any energy worrying about Doyle when his friend might very well be involved in a murder.

CHAPTER 31

Florence turned from the window overlooking the street, walked haltingly back to her bed, and sat down. What was her husband up to that these men would find it necessary to come here looking for him?

She leaned against the bedpost, wrapping her hands around it to cradle her head and steady herself. She wondered how their marriage could have gotten so off-kilter.

It had happened so gradually. She wanted to blame Bram and his love for his work. It kept them apart so much. But perhaps it was her fault, as well. He had always wanted a child, but she had seen what child bearing had done to her mother. She saw what it had done to so many women. Her beauty was one of her few attributes, and her greatest strength.

Now they didn't speak as often as they used to, and Bram had grown evasive about her questions pertaining to where and how he was spending his time. "Research." It was his explanation for everything. He had written several other books before and each one took his time and attention, but those endeavors had never been so fraught with secrets.

There was a transformation in Bram's mood as well. He turned quiet and introspective, as if he were always in some other place. Florence had convinced herself that it must be another woman. It had to be another woman, she thought. Bram was repaying her for what he perceived as her slight against him. Or maybe he had found a woman who wanted a child.

Florence felt like crying, but she mustn't. It would make her eyes red and the surrounding skin blotchy. She couldn't stand to see herself that way.

CHAPTER 32

He had not rested well during the train ride and had not arrived back in Whitby until after nine o'clock. Dead tired, Stoker thrust his hands deeper into his coat pockets as a defense against the cold, damp air. There was only a quarter moon, which was of little help, its muted light barely penetrating the clouds.

He had been searching for over two hours. At first, he waited in the darkness at the corner of one of Whitby's narrow lanes two blocks from the Church Stairs. Impatience soon compelled him to roam. He walked past the darkened shops and eating establishments lining the East Pier and past the taverns, still doing brisk business.

The streets, for the most part, were deserted. He passed a workingman and two seamen, all suffering from various degrees of drunkenness, but he saw no one else.

Stoker turned inland and moved down a garbage-ridden backstreet near the outskirts of the village. It was a commercial district with the buildings along the alley sheltering metal workers, coal suppliers, food processing and storage houses.

Stoker could almost feel it; Tepes was still in the village. He was determined to find him. It was clear now that Tepes had calculated everything, offering just enough information to draw him back, using the temptation of more knowledge like cheese tucked away at the end of a maze. It was disconcerting, the feeling that it was all beyond his control.

A sound brushed Stoker's ears, drifting on the chilling breeze. There was something familiar and unsettling about it. He stopped and listened, his eyes never leaving the darkness ahead of him. There it was again, a sound as subtle as the sputtering of a candlewick. He continued down the alley.

It came again, still faint but this time recognizable, a chicken squawking. It could only be a chicken squawking. Then another sound followed it, a single, dull thudding sound that lasted only a moment.

Pressing himself close to the wall, Stoker continued forward. A fire of anticipation began smoldering inside him. The answers were before him. The darkness ahead would provide what he needed. This time, he could feel it. He ran his fingers across his temples as the throbbing in his head intensified.

CHAPTER 33

H is vantage point was perfect. It was always perfect. He could make
out a dim, wavering light glowing from behind the buildings. The
clucking and squawking of chickens was unmistakable. The scent that hung
heavy in the air between the buildings was unmistakable, as well. Chickens
and blood.

He moved forward, drifting silently through the darkness that was his
protection. All his senses heightened as he drew closer, as the time drew
near.

A low, one story building bordered the far end of the yard, looking as if
it had been constructed from rotting wood. An oil lamp hanging just inside
the open doorway revealed several pens filled with chickens. The pens
extended into the building, disappearing beyond the reach of the lamplight.
A sign over the doorway in faded, green lettering read, R.W. HAGGERT,
POULTERER.

A few feet outside the doorway, a lantern resting on the seat of a small
cart burned with an inadequate light. The light was unnecessary. The dark
had long ceased to be a problem for his eyes.

Near the cart was a large wooden block, cut and leveled from a large tree
stump. The lantern light illuminated dark stains of blood splattered on the
wood. Small, drying pools of the sweet, red fluid congealed in the dirt at the
base of the stump.

The poulterer's back was to him, his frame hunched forward. He gripped a hatchet in his right hand, and a plump hen by its feet in his left. The hen clucked and screeched its protest.

His cold, emotionless eyes watched as the man, with practiced ease, stretched the chicken across the block. The hatchet sliced through the night air and in an instant, the chicken's head was removed from its body. It was a quick, efficient death. It was the best kind of death.

The man tossed the headless, bleeding carcass into the back of the cart. The hatchet dangling in his hand, he walked back to the doorway, stepped inside, and pulled another squawking hen from the closest pen.

He moved closer now, his senses and instincts sharpening. He could feel the beating of the man's heart and hear the blood coursing through his veins.

He was acutely aware of Stoker as well, thinking himself concealed in the darkness between the buildings. Stoker would benefit from a lesson learned tonight. It was important the man understand he had no power in any of this.

The time had come. He swept forward as the poulterer carried the dangling chicken back toward the block. The man must have heard the rustling of his coat and turned around. Instinctively, he raised his hatchet. It would be the last movement he made of his own volition.

CHAPTER 34

E verything was black, even after Stoker opened his eyes. His head still throbbed, though not as badly as before. A blotch of soft light crept into the darkness and he realized that his vision was still blurred. He closed his eyes tight, and then opened them again, willing himself to see. He could make out the side of the poultry yard.

Stoker became aware of a throbbing pain running up his left arm. He realized he was lying on his side with his arm folded under him. His joints stiff from the cold, Stoker rolled to his opposite side. Only inches from his face lay a dead man.

Stoker hastily struggled to his feet and backed away from the body. It was the man who had been beheading the chickens. He was sprawled on his back, his face sheet white, his half-open eyes, lifeless. The man's mouth was open wide, as if he had died gasping for breath.

His hatchet lay in the dirt beside the chopping block. It couldn't have killed him. The blade would have created obvious wounds. Stoker saw none. The only blood in sight was the chicken blood already dried in the dirt. He had no desire to draw any closer to the corpse. Fear soured his stomach.

What had happened? One moment he was moving down the alley toward the poulterer, and then just blackness. Forcing himself to overcome his fear, Stoker kneeled down beside the body and placed his hand on the man's chest. There was no heartbeat. He moved the back of his hand until it rested against the man's temple. The body still felt warmth. This had not happened long ago.

Stoker shuddered, stood up as fast as he could manage, and again retreated from the body. Why couldn't he remember? Fear overtook him with a chilling force and his body shook uncontrollably. Had he done this? Stoker examined his hands and clothing for signs of blood or any other violence. There was nothing.

Stoker surveyed the area. No one else was in sight. The only sound was an occasional clucking from the hens. He had to get away from here. He had to get back to the boarding house without being seen. Until he figured this all out, it was best that no one knew he was here. The morning would arrive soon enough and the body discovered. There was no reason to risk reporting it.

Spying his hat on the ground, Stoker retrieved it with haste. With a final, guilt-ridden look at the dead man, he hurried out of the yard.

CHAPTER 35

An aged brougham arrived at the curb in front of the Lyceum, and Bram Stoker wasted no time climbing out. Had the few flower vendors or the two bobbies lingering among the theater's mighty columns known him, they would have found it unusual to see him arriving only minutes before the final curtain of the play. They would have been outright shocked if they'd known he had missed the previous night's performance as well.

"Wait, please. I won't be long," Stoker instructed the driver as he hurried into the alley.

He stepped through the stage door, and after a wave to the old doorman, practically sprinted through the wings. Making his way along the lower passageway, Stoker reached his office and opened the door. A small flame glowed in the wall lamp, leaving the office in heavy shadows. He closed the door behind him and dropped his bag on a nearby chair. He reached up for the lamp and eased open the valve. As the flame rose, a rustling sound came from behind. He froze, an irrational chill rushing through him, and then spun around.

Florence sat on the small sofa in the room's corner, hands folded in her lap. Her eyes were fixed on him; her mouth turned down in the slightest of frowns. "Where were you, Bram?"

"Florence," Stoker breathed. "What are you doing here? I mean, you're sitting here alone in the dark."

"I was worried," she replied, her tone flat.

Stoker removed his hat and tossed it on the chair with his bag, then went across the room to kiss her. She stiffened noticeably and he thought better of it. He began to sit down next to her on the sofa, and then thought better of that, too. He rested his weight against the corner of his desk.

"Where were you?" she repeated. Her voice was cool, detached, but laced with a hint of worry.

"I had unexpected business."

"It must have been quite urgent, you disappearing without informing your family or your employer."

Stoker shifted uncomfortably. "I'm sorry. Truly. But, well, a research opportunity presented itself. There was an incident in Whitby and it was imperative that I look into it as quickly as possible."

"An incident?"

"One that could very well relate to my book, yes." He had no intention of sharing the complete truth with her. He wasn't even sure what the truth really meant anymore.

Florence's gaze stared into his eyes. "I wasn't sure what to do. I didn't know what might have happened." She waited for some kind of response but didn't get one. "You have yet to tell me what this book is about."

"It's a, I suppose it's best described as a kind of biography," he replied.

"A biography? Of who?"

A knock on the door startled both of them. "Yes," Stoker called out.

The door opened and the young clerk, Benton, leaned into the room. A cash box was tucked under his arm. "Receipts, Mr. Stoker." He saw Florence, and in an instant, felt more uncomfortable than usual. "Oh, sorry."

Stoker waved the boy into the room and then went to the safe against the wall. He dialed the combination while still trying to show Florence the proper attention. "I didn't mean to cause worry," he said to her.

"Why didn't you at least send word?"

"I meant to," he said, pulling open the safe door. "I must have just gotten too caught up in my work."

Benton put the cashbox on the edge of the desk, opened it, and removed a receipt. Stoker became more aware of Benton being in the room. He felt embarrassed as he went back to the desk and removed the money from the cashbox. Why had his wife brought their personal concerns to the theater, his place of work?

Florence shifted her approach again. "You were telling me about your book."

"You were interrogating me about my book. I have a lot to do here," he said.

He saw Florence was working hard to keep her emotions in check.

"What is it? You've changed these past months. And I seldom see you," she said.

Stoker removed the cash from the box and placed it on the desk. He began counting it. Benton looked as if he would rather be anywhere else than in this room. Stoker could feel his wife's eyes on him. His embarrassment began transforming into irritation.

The sound of muffled applause coming from the auditorium drew Stoker's attention. Benton was pointing at him.

"Uh, sir," the boy muttered.

"Now isn't the time to discuss this," he said to Florence, an edginess creeping into his voice.

"Sir, the receipt, if you please," Benton stuttered.

"All right," Stoker snapped, turning toward the boy. Benton took a step back and Stoker realized the boy hadn't been pointing at him, but was holding out the receipt to him. Stoker took the receipt from Benton, then went to his desk and retrieved his pen. He scribbled his signature and thrust the document back into the clerk's hand.

Benton picked up the empty cashbox and hurried from the office.

"Don't you see why I'm doing what I'm doing?" Stoker asked Florence as he gathered the cash from the desk and carried over to the safe. "My book, this book, it could be what we've been hoping for. This is the book that could finally make a name for me as an author."

"I know it's important to you, it's obvious," Florence responded. "But you aren't yourself."

"You know how involving writing can be. I'm just... distracted. I'm just making certain my work is the best it can be," he lied.

"But if something's wrong, won't you please tell me?" she pleaded.

"There's nothing." He placed the money in the safe, closed the door, and spun the dial.

"What keeps you away so much?" she asked.

Stoker looked at his wife. Her eyes stared coldly at him. Everything about her seemed cold. Why couldn't she just give him some time?

Florence abruptly rose from the sofa and made her way to the office door.

Stoker reached to put his hand on her arm, but she pulled away. "If you'll just wait for me to get home, we can talk then," he said.

"I asked what keeps you from me so much."

"It's just the Lyceum. You know my responsibilities here," he answered.

"And your book, you said. So, which is it?

"It's both," he almost shouted. Florence stared back at him, her face telling him nothing. "This book is important to me, but this company is my first responsibility and it's maddening. Purchasing the lease has added to it. Then there's managing the staff, the scheduling, bookkeeping, and all the rest. It takes time. My time. You know, Sir Henry depends on me for every detail of the business. You know that."

Florence glanced down at the floor, digesting the words he had given her. She pulled open the office door, holding her gaze on him. "Whatever keeps you away so much," she said, her voice shaking, "I trust it's only work."

Florence stepped through the doorway. Stoker watched as the door swung shut.

CHAPTER 36

Sir Henry had just completed one of his finest performances. At least according to Sir Henry. He felt jubilant; he felt the heated excitement of being loved and appreciated by his audience. Doyle had heard him say it several times in the last quarter hour.

Doyle feared that this was turning out to yet another wasted evening. He had planned to confront Stoker before the play got underway, but the man had failed to appear. Doyle observed Sir Henry's irritation over the situation, try as he did to behave as if all were normal.

Doyle began thinking that Irving's dressing room wasn't large enough for the both of them. He sat uncomfortably in a straight-back chair, his fur-lined greatcoat draped over the back, staring at the floor.

Sir Henry had already donned his street clothes. He leaned close to the mirror of his makeup table, wiping the last traces of pancake from his face. Collinson brushed down the costumes and hung them up on the rolling rack that would soon go to storage.

"We're capable men," Doyle volunteered. "Our differences aside, if we have to conclude our agreement without Stoker, then let's get on with it."

"But Bram manages all my business affairs. Has for years. I wouldn't know where to begin without him," Irving replied.

Collinson turned from the clothing rack. "Besides sir," he said. "You'll recall, Mr. Stoker's signature is required on all theater documents, including bank checks.

"Yes. We arranged that as a precaution several years ago," Irving explained to Doyle.

"Splendid," Doyle mumbled, not meaning it in the slightest.

A knock sounded on the door as Collinson helped Irving slip into his frock coat. The door swung open and Loveday stepped into the room. "Mr. Stoker, sir. Just arrived," he reported. "He passed so quickly he didn't even notice me."

Doyle was already out of his chair. "Where is he?"

"Heading toward his office, sir. When I left him."

Doyle grabbed his greatcoat and hat and pushed past Loveday, hurrying out of the dressing room. Irving followed him, with Collinson in tow.

"We'll have this out tonight," Doyle stated as they descended the steps into the lower level. "There've already been too many delays. The man's behavior has become intolerable."

Doyle reached the office and pushed open the door. It was empty.

Cursing under his breath, Doyle hurried back the way they came. Irving waved Collinson along and again hurried to catch up.

"I'd prefer handling this situation myself," Doyle said with a sideward glance.

"Need I remind you the man's my employee?"

"So much the better. I can speak my mind without the danger of damaging your professional relationship."

They approached the backstage area and Doyle maneuvered through the stagehands busy finishing their work for the night. He was almost through the wings and onto the stage when he spied Stoker. Doyle came to an abrupt stop and extended his arms to prevent Irving and Collinson from continuing past him. Irving collided into Doyle's backside.

"Good heavens, man," Irving began a reprimand, but Doyle brought his finger to his lips. Irving allowed himself to be herded back into the cover of the heavy draperies. Doyle again gestured for silence and pointed across the stage. Irving and Collinson leaned around him, following his gaze.

Stoker, wearing his Chesterfield overcoat and gripping a valise, stood near the stage door leading to the alley. His homburg covered his head. With him was an attractive woman Doyle estimated to be in her late twenties.

He could only make out the woman's profile. Her fair skin appeared smooth and clear. The woman's soft brown hair was done up under a stylish toque of royal blue. The toque matched her well-cut godet skirt and jacket.

Since she was not in evening dress, Doyle doubted she had been in the theater audience. A long cloak of dark blue graced her shoulders and the blush of color in the young woman's cheeks suggested she had just left the cold of outdoors to enter the theater. The couple was too far away to be heard, but Stoker was speaking to her with some intensity.

As Doyle watched, Stoker withdrew an envelope from his inside coat pocket and handed it to the woman. She tucked it into her handbag.

"So, that's it, then," Irving whispered, concern in his tone.

"That's what?" Doyle asked.

"The man's married, for heaven's sake."

"You don't know her?"

Irving shook his head, his vexation beginning to show. "I'll put a stop to this right now," he hissed, trying to step around Doyle.

Doyle took a firm hold of his arm and guided him back into the cover of the wings. "Not yet."

"Not yet? This kind of thing could cause irreparable harm. Need I repeat myself? The man is married."

"Your assumptions aren't based on fact. Right now we've more to gain by watching."

Stoker opened the stage door for the woman. She stepped out into the darkness, and he followed, closing the door behind them.

Doyle put on his coat and headed across the stage. Irving and Collinson followed on his heels.

"What are you doing? Where are you going?" asked Irving.

"This has taken a rather interesting turn," Doyle replied. "I rather fancy knowing where they're off to. I'll look you up tomorrow."

"You're going to follow them?"

"Secret trips, another woman, a possible involvement in a murder. Perhaps there's a story in it."

Irving grabbed Doyle's coat sleeve, stopping him just short of the stage door. There was no mistaking the horror lining Irving's face. "You couldn't do such a thing. The scandal; everyone would know who you were writing about. We don't know he meant them to be secret trips. I forbid you to go."

Doyle couldn't keep the amusement from his face. "You worry too much about reputation, Sir Henry. And I am going."

"You know the people who patronize us. The best of English society, the most celebrated artists in the empire, the Royal family, they all come. You mustn't write any of it," Irving begged.

"I'm offended at your implying I wouldn't be discreet in whatever I might write," Doyle replied. "I say again, you worry too much about reputation."

"And you worry too little about it. If you refuse to stay out of this, then I'm going with you."

It was Doyle's turn to be alarmed. "What? No. Why should you?"

"How else can I possibly hope to protect my interests? I'll not have your pulp stories sullying my name, nor my theater. I'm going," Irving insisted.

He rummaged through the garments on a nearby costume rack and soon found a cloak once used in Macbeth. It was a rather luminous shade of purple. He threw it over his shoulders and fastened the clasp at his throat.

Doyle sighed in surrender. "All right then. But please do as I instruct."

Doyle hurried past the doorman and pulled open the door leading to the alley before the man could rise from behind his desk. Irving followed behind him.

CHAPTER 37

S toker and the woman stood beside a brougham at the end of the alley, still engaged in conversation. Doyle thought it lucky that they were still within sight after the annoying delay caused by Irving. A fog began rolling in, and light clouds of the stuff drifted around Stoker and the woman.

Doyle and Irving peered out from behind the pile of stage flats and lumber leaning against the building. A second cab, a hansom, pulled to a stop behind the brougham. Stoker helped the woman into the hansom and spoke to the driver. The driver urged his team forward. Stoker then walked back to the four-wheeler and climbed inside.

Doyle and Irving were hurrying toward Wellington Street before Stoker's cab moved beyond the alley opening. "We'll stay with Stoker," Doyle said as he waved over a nearby hansom.

The cab pulled to a stop at the mouth of the alley, and Doyle pulled open the door. "Keep that cab in sight, but stay well back," he instructed the driver, pointing after Stoker's four-wheeler. "If we're not seen, and you stay with him, there's a sovereign in it for you." Doyle practically pushed Irving into the cab, and it lurched forward before Doyle could get the door latched shut.

"I can't bring myself to believe he's involved with that, that person. Florence is one of the loveliest creatures I've ever laid eyes on," Irving said. "You think he plans to rendezvous with this woman?"

Doyle ignored the question and leaned out the hansom window, keeping an eye on Stoker's cab. He wasn't concerned; the two-wheeled hansom was always capable of faster travel through the streets than the heavier, more cumbersome four-wheeler.

They spent the next quarter hour in silence as the cab rolled through the city streets into east central London. It wasn't long before the growing volume of music from the street caused Doyle to notice the increasing harshness of the neighborhood. The sound of drunken voices mingled with a shrill piano in need of tuning drifted into the cab.

They passed more and more pubs, or paltry eating establishments serving wine and cheap ale. The doors were always open, and the cacophonous blend of music and inebriated voices emanating from one alehouse would barely die away before being replaced by the din of the next. Men in rough clothing and women wearing too much rouge loitered on the sidewalk.

"Good Lord," Irving muttered, looking out the window. "I'm far from a schoolboy, but all those women, prostitutes?

Doyle followed Irving's gaze. If there was any doubt about the women's profession, it was put to rest as the cab rolled past an odorous, garbage-littered alley.

Looking into the alley, Doyle saw a woman half-enveloped in the darkness. Her skirts were gathered around her waist, and her legs wrapped around the hips of her customer. The man had her pushed up against the brick wall of the building, supporting her weight with his hands under her backside.

Irving turned his gaze back inside the coach. "Where on earth are we?"

"Whitechapel," Doyle answered.

Shabby rooming houses with dim gaslight seeping through their windows began replacing the pubs as the cab passed through the business district. The number of people on the street grew fewer and the night became quiet again. As their cab began rounding a corner, Doyle suddenly tapped his walking stick on the front wall of the coach. "Driver. Stop here," he called out.

Doyle opened the door and climbed out with Irving behind him. He glanced at the street signs to find that they were standing at the intersection of Bromford Road and Pincer's Alley—a dirty, narrow street, and an even narrower alley. The setting was made even more dismal in the thick gray fog.

Doyle paid the driver and surveyed the area. Only one establishment near the corner appeared to be open for business. The light glowing through its large, dirty window silhouetted lettering spelling the name of the place: Bromford Kitchen. Beneath the name, smaller lettering promised quality meals, night and day.

As the cab rolled away across Bromford Road, he took a firm hold of Irving's shoulder and guided him against the wall of the corner building. They peered around the side of the building.

The four-wheeler was already moving away at the far end of Pincer's Alley. Stoker was on the opposite side of the alley, walking away from them, his valise in hand.

Doyle waited for several seconds and then slipped out of the doorway. Irving followed close behind him.

They crossed the alley. Doyle set the pace, staying well back from their quarry, and moving into rear doorways to assure not being seen. No other living soul was within sight.

Stoker made an abrupt right turn and disappeared from view. When Doyle and Irving reached the spot, they found themselves at the entrance to a small street. The gas flame of the corner streetlamp illuminated the sign: Potter's Court.

Again, Doyle looked around the corner of the building. Certain that Stoker was unaware of their presence, he led Irving into Potter's Court. Making haste, they took cover behind a small horse cart.

Stoker appeared as not much more than a shadow in the dim light, but was still within sight. A few doors from the entrance to the street, he climbed a set of rickety stairs attached to the side of a small building.

Doyle and Irving moved forward, heading to the opposite side of the street. A slat fence fronted the property across the street from Stoker's building. Doyle soon found the gate and quietly opened it. They slipped inside, and then cautiously peered over the top of the fence.

The building Stoker entered was a shabby, two-story structure. Peeling paint hung from it in large flakes. Two windows occupied the first floor, with a door opening onto the street to the right of them. No light was visible from behind the burlap curtains. The second floor also had two windows curtained with a tattered, dark fabric overlooking the street. The entrance was at the top of the stairs.

A light suddenly burned bright from the second floor windows. Doyle and Irving watched as Stoker's shadow moved across the curtains. "He's got a flat," Irving whispered. "Not a very pleasant part of town."

"You don't know this place?" Doyle asked.

Irving shook his head. "He's never mentioned it. The woman, you think she's met him here?"

"It's clear she has not."

"No?"

"It's unlikely any well-bred woman would wait for a man in a completely darkened room, especially in this neighborhood," Doyle whispered. "We saw Stoker light a lamp upon his arrival. We also saw the woman's cab depart the Lyceum in a different direction."

"What now, then?"

Before Doyle could answer, Stoker's shadow moved back across the window and the glow of light dimmed. Stoker emerged from the flat onto the landing at the top of the stairs. He closed and locked the door, then placed the key in his pocket as he descended the stairs.

Doyle and Irving crouched behind the fence, listening to Stoker's fading footsteps. Peering over the fence, they were just in time to see Stoker disappear from view as he turned onto Pincer's Alley, heading back toward Bromford Road.

Doyle and Irving stepped back into the street. Irving headed after Stoker, but stopped when he noticed Doyle was not with him. He returned to Doyle's side and whispered, "Hurry along. We'll lose him."

Doyle didn't reply. He was gazing at Stoker's flat, studying it.

CHAPTER 38

Doyle led the way across the street to the stairs. "Where are you going?" Irving asked.

Doyle began climbing the stairs.

"Oh, no. No, no, no," Irving protested.

Doyle responded with an annoyed glance over his shoulder, but kept climbing. Looking nervously toward the corner, Irving followed him up.

Reaching the landing, they could see that the door had a small window. Tattered curtains, similar to those they could see on the front windows, obscured the view. Doyle knocked on the door.

"What are you doing?" Irving asked.

"It'd be a waste not to gather what information we can."

When his knock went unanswered, Doyle reached for the doorknob and tried turning it. The bolt rattled, but held fast. Doyle pressed his face to the window but was unsatisfied and went back down the stairs.

Doyle led Irving around to the side of the building to a small, covered porch with a low, slanting roof. He pointed above the porch roof at a single window. It was open, with a small length of wood holding the sash above the frame.

"I'll wager it opens into Stoker's rooms," Doyle commented to himself. He hurried to the side of the porch and returned with an empty wooden crate. A second trip produced another crate that he placed on top of the first. "Come along. I'll give you a lift up," he said to Irving.

"Up there? You are mad."

Doyle's tone was impatient. "I can't have you loitering about out here where you might be seen."

"It's foolishness. If I'm injured—my performances…" he trailed off, desperate to find some excuse.

"Come now," Doyle said, taunting. "How many times have I seen you on stage, leaping from a lofty set to the boards below? Now you're saying you're not up to a little climb. What would your public think?"

Irving mulled over Doyle's words. "I'm a respected performer and businessman," he replied, his resolve weakening.

"Now you can round that out with burglar."

Irving looked up at the porch roof and then fixed his eyes on Doyle's with a new resolve. "Romeo and Juliet. Romeo's ascent to the balcony—act two, scene two."

His purple cloak billowing behind him, Irving jumped up on the crates with a gesture of stage heroics that almost made Doyle laugh aloud. The boxes teetered and Irving accepted Doyle's steadying hand. Proceeding with more caution, he pulled himself up to the roof and climbed to his feet.

Doyle handed up his walking stick and then followed him up. At the window, Doyle took hold of the wooden stick and forced the sash up. "After you," he said with a tone of firm insistence.

Irving gathered up his cloak and climbed into the room. Doyle followed behind him. Once inside, he lowered the sash back onto the stick.

The room was small and sparsely furnished with a square writing table and two wooden chairs in the center or the room. Stoker's valise occupied one of the chairs. A lone oil lamp, turned down low, burned in the middle of the table. A cot and a bureau occupied the rear wall. The room lacked any cosmetic maintenance, but it was free of dirt and dust.

Doyle went to the bureau and began opening the drawers. "He left the lamp burning. He won't be gone long," he said.

Doyle watched Irving make his way over to the cot. He bent over and came up with a pair of muddy boots. "What do you make of these?" he asked Doyle in a challenging tone.

"In dire need a cleaning."

Irving appeared disappointed. "You can't tell anything by them—the color of the mud? Where he's been in London? Nothing?"

"You're joking," Doyle replied, looking at Irving as if he was insane.

Doyle was looking through the bureau when he heard Irving from the center of the room. "Hello. What's this?"

Doyle turned to see Irving moving Stoker's valise from the chair to examine a stack of papers resting on the seat beneath.

Joining Irving at the table, Doyle looked at the papers in the actor's hand. Stoker's bold, neat handwriting covered each sheet. A page heading on the top page read "Jonathan Harker's Journal." As Irving read, his eyes widened. "Dear God," he exclaimed.

"What is it?"

"A journal. Here, listen." Irving moved the papers down next to the lamp and began reading.

"There, indeed, was a woman with disheveled hair. When she saw my face at the window she threw herself forward, and shouted in a voice laden with menace: "Monster, give me my child!" I heard the voice of the Count calling in his harsh, metallic whisper. His call seemed to be answered from far and wide by the howling of wolves."

Doyle reached around Irving and adjusted the papers so he could see them more easily. He took up the reading.

"Before many minutes had passed a pack of them poured through the wide entrance into the courtyard. There was no cry from the woman, and the howling of the wolves was short. I could not pity her, for I knew what had become of her child, and she was better dead."

"Fascinating," Doyle mumbled, taking the papers from Irving and leafing through them.

"Disgusting. How could any man stand by while such a thing occurs?" Irving asked.

"Stoker's handwriting, is it not?" Doyle asked.

"It is. But it's this man's, this Harker fellow's journal. And who is this Count, and what became of this poor woman's child?"

Doyle looked more intently at some of the following pages. "Hmmm, a vampire," he said.

"A vampire. Oh, poppycock," Irving exclaimed.

"The child succumbed to a very powerful vampire."

"You surely don't believe in such nonsense?"

"No, though I've seen many strange phenomena since I began my studies in spiritualism. There's much we don't know," Doyle answered. He took an even closer look at the pages. "This is a manuscript."

"A manuscript?"

"The journal form is quite effective—an eyewitness telling of the tale— quite powerful. Almost as if someone had been on hand," Doyle said, giving it deep thought.

"Harker. The Lyceum's scenic designer is a fellow named Harker," Irving said. "Joseph Harker."

At that moment, the sound of footsteps echoing off the street reached the room. Doyle rushed over to the front window.

Stoker appeared through the shadows, only a building away from the flat. He carried a small bundle wrapped in heavy paper and a bottle of ale.

Hurrying back to the table, Doyle returned the manuscript to the chair and replaced the valise. "He's back."

After hastily making certain that everything was as they found it, Doyle hurried back to the window.

Stoker was just reaching the bottom of the stairs. He would be at the door in seconds.

Doyle and Irving moved to the side window. Irving almost knocked over the empty chair, but caught it before it clattered to the floor.

Doyle took hold of the supporting stick and held the sash up as Irving scrambled over the sill. Irving did the same for Doyle. The author replaced the length of wood under the window sash as Irving lowered himself over the edge of the roof.

The sound of a key turning in the lock reached Doyle as he dropped to his knees and eased himself off the roof.

"I'll never be able to set foot on the stage again," Irving muttered as they rushed down the alley.

CHAPTER 39

S toker entered the flat feeling tired and troubled. He wasn't all that hungry, but he hoped the food he purchased at Bromford Kitchen might fuel him with enough energy to think through just what had happened to him in Whitby.

As he bolted the door, an odd feeling overtook him. It was vague and unexplainable, but the room did not feel the same to him.

He moved to the window and looked out onto Potter's Court. A movement of shadow at the corner of the street drew his notice. Two dark shapes in the roadbed rapidly diminished and disappeared.

Turning from the window, Stoker surveyed the room again. Everything looked as it should. Nothing was out of place. His uneasiness upon entering the flat had probably been because of the troubles he was struggling with, nothing more.

Seating himself at the table, he opened his bottle of ale and unwrapped the sandwich. He gazed blankly at it for more than a minute before taking a tentative bite. Considering the turmoil, he felt it was an accomplishment that he could eat at all.

He could see the face of the poulterer, his lifeless eyes glassy and blank, his skin pale white, the mouth gaping open. The image occupied his dreams, along with impressions of Tepes following the young woman down the darkened street and the fearful eyes of the sea captain.

What did it all mean? What had he done? Had he involved himself with some kind of criminal, or worse still, a madman? His very reputation was at stake, not to mention the Lyceum's reputation. He felt a strong need to tell someone, perhaps Doyle or Irving. But the fear he felt was even stronger; the fear that he might put his friends in danger.

Stoker pushed the unfinished half of the sandwich aside. Perhaps if he could undertake some writing tonight, it would help clarify his concerns. Absorbing work would provide some distraction and perhaps some relief.

He gathered his notes and set to work.

CHAPTER 40

S toker didn't know how long he had been working. He wasn't even certain what time it was, but he knew it must be early in the morning. The light burning in the master bedroom window surprised him as he neared his house on Cheyne Walk.

Stoker unlocked the door and stepped inside. He hung his homburg on the rack in the foyer's corner and trudged up the stairs.

Florence was lounging on the small chaise in the far corner of the room, reading the latest issue of the Strand. A lamp burned on the table beside the couch. A half empty glass of sherry rested beside the lamp.

She wore a long, crème-colored silk robe over her nightclothes. Involved in her magazine, she did not notice him at first, and when she finally did, she appeared somewhat startled.

"Oh, Brammie," she said as he stepped into the room. "I didn't hear you come in."

Stoker went to her, leaning over to give her a kiss on her full, sensuous lips. She avoided his approach, offering him her cheek instead. He accepted it, but felt a disappointment that smoldered deep within him.

"Didn't mean to scare you," he said.

"You didn't. I just didn't hear you, that's all."

As he began undressing for bed, Stoker thought he heard a voice, a barely discernable whisper. Only weeks ago, he would be looking around the room to locate who might be speaking, but now he didn't bother. He knew the whisper was in his head. It was telling him that his wife had no right to avoid his kiss.

"More theater problems?" Florence asked.

"What's that?"

"You seem preoccupied. I wondered if there were more problems at the theater," Florence clarified.

"There are always problems at the theater, but no. I'm just tired, I think."

"Considering the time you spend at work, I see no reason to bring any of it home with you," Florence lamented.

"The books, the scheduling, keeping Sir Henry out of difficulties. I have responsibilities," Stoker answered.

"To your family, as well, I imagine."

Stoker ignored the remark, hanging his shirt in the armoire. "I was surprised to find you up at this hour," he said, placing his boots beside the bed.

Florence sipped the last of the sherry. "I was having trouble sleeping." She rose from the chaise and walked to her dressing table.

He watched as Florence let the robe drop from her shoulders. The lamp-light beyond revealed the outline of her body underneath the delicate night-dress. She removed the pins holding up her hair and it fell down around her shoulders.

He stood there, gazing at her as she stroked the brush through her hair. "A bit more rest is what you need. Sleep can perform minor miracles, if that's all it is," she said.

The whisper rose from the back of his mind, like some unimaginable sea creature moving from the murky depths toward the surface. The soft, metallic voice declared that she was his wife, and he could kiss her whenever he wanted. He closed his eyes and squeezed his head between his hands, trying to shut out the sound.

"Tired or not, you won't forget the Beacons charity dinner," Florence said. "The fourteenth."

"The fourteenth. Yes, of course." He watched the rise and fall of her shoulders as she raised the brush, then pulled it down through her hair. She gathered the hair, revealing the smooth skin at the back of her neck. Stoker felt a stirring deep inside him. He took an involuntary step toward her.

"Really, Bram. This dinner is most important to me. You've missed most of our other social events this season."

Florence rose from the dressing table. The nightdress clung to her hips and thighs as she moved. She turned down the gas lamps.

Stoker moved toward her, reaching her as she arrived at the side of the bed. He stood behind Florence, taking in the length of her body with hungry eyes. Reaching up, he began softly stroking her shoulders. She tensed. Then with a single movement she patted his hand, descended to the bed and slid under the covers.

"I'm rather tired, too," she said, stretching to a comfortable position.

The whisper continued as Stoker looked down at her. It reminded him again that she was his. It urged him to reach out for the warmth and softness of her body.

He could make out the contour of her hips beneath the comforter. Stoker leaned down and began kissing Florence's neck and shoulders. With the covers around her and his weight holding the covers in place, she had no way of retreat.

"Please, no. Not tonight," she said, her voice gentle.

Stoker paused, but did not draw away, his breathing growing heavier. The warmth of her skin against his lips combined with the scent of her was intoxicating.

"Try to understand," she continued, trying to maintain her calm. "It's difficult for me to, well, be with you—that way, when I hardly see you any other time."

The whisper insisted it didn't matter what she wanted.

"You look exquisite," he said.

"Perhaps with a bit more time. If we could just spend a little more time together."

He brushed his lips against hers. Florence turned away again and then placed an affectionate but cool kiss on his cheek. She rolled onto her side, turning her back to him.

"Goodnight, darling," she said, a stiffness in her voice.

Stoker felt the frustration churning up inside him.

The whisper told him again of the heat, the comfort, the satisfying power that he would find in the depths of her. He pulled her back toward him. Florence gasped with surprise.

Stoker held Florence's head in his hands, then pushed his lips against hers. She squirmed, but he held fast. He glimpsed the panic in her eyes.

He threw the bed covers aside and took hold of her wrists, pinning her arms back against the pillow. Florence attempted to roll away from him, but his full weight pushed her back into the bed.

"Stop. Stop it," she gasped as he moved his lips to her throat.

Stoker released Florence's wrists, but his full weight was on her. The whisper murmured something about how he should enjoy this power, how he should revel in the control. He pushed the hair away from her eyes and began stroking her brow. Then his hands moved down across her breasts, and then lower still.

He pulled at her nightdress, and she began struggling with renewed resolve. He got it high enough up her legs to lodge one of his knees between hers. Watching her panic turn into a full-fledged fright excited him.

A sudden shift of his position and he was on top of her, prying her legs open. He traced the inside of her thigh with his hand. Tears began welling up in her eyes. She twisted under him.

Stoker grunted, exerting more effort to hold her down under him. It was time to take her now. The voice told him so. He shifted most of his weight to his knees and then reached for his trouser buttons.

The move put himself off balance. Florence rapidly pulled her right leg up, bending her knee, and then twisted violently to the side. He gasped as her knee slammed into his chest, forcing the breath from his lungs.

Taken by surprise, he rocked backwards and moved both hands to his bruised chest. With a cry of rage, Florence rolled out from under him.

She scrambled for the far side of the bed, but he lunged after her. Catching her by the shoulder, he spun her around, ripping the nightdress free from her shoulders. The sound of the shredding fabric pierced Stoker's head with the intensity of a shrill factory whistle.

"Stop it," Florence shouted, angry tears reddening her beautiful eyes. She scrambled off the far side of the bed, gathering the nightdress up to cover her breasts. "What gives you the right?"

Stoker couldn't move. Frustration flowed across his face, then shock. By the time he dragged himself around to sit on the edge of the bed, shame sculpted his features.

Florence moved around the end of the bed, staying as far from him as possible. "What gives you the right?" she shouted again as she bent down to retrieve her robe, never taking her tear-swollen eyes off him.

Stoker's chest heaved as he tried to comprehend what he had done. Florence began making her way toward the door. She paused in the doorway and again hissed, "What on earth's happened to you?"

Tears began creeping down his cheeks. He buried his head in his hands. "I don't know," he sobbed as she hurried from the room.

The whisper had grown silent.

CHAPTER 41

Henry Irving left his rooms at 15A Grafton Street in Green Park for the Lyceum about ten o'clock in the morning. Arriving at the theater, he avoided Bram's office, and searched out Joseph Harker in the scenery workshop. Their conversation had been brief, and Irving found himself back at Grafton Street well before noon.

He spent the rest of the morning reading a new script proposed for the Lyceum's next season. Promptly at twelve thirty, Doyle rang the bell.

Doyle seated himself in a comfortable leather wing chair in the parlor and Irving, hands clasped behind his back, advised him of his morning's visit to the theater.

"Harker told me he has no relative to his knowledge named Jonathan. He's never even heard of a Jonathan Harker," Irving explained.

"And he had nothing else to add?" Doyle asked, munching on one of Collinson's excellent raspberry tarts.

"Said he was happy for the extra work we've been giving him. His family needs the money."

Doyle seemed to contemplate the last bite of tart he held in his fingers. "It appears our little adventure last night has just raised more questions."

"I've never undertaken a more humiliating course of action in my entire career," Irving stated. "Climbing through an alley window like a common thief."

Doyle's eyes glinted with amusement. "You did insist on coming along."

"You mentioned more questions," Irving said, ready to change the subject.

"We found no signs of a woman in Stoker's flat, yet we saw him with a woman at the stage door."

"So we must ask ourselves if Bram's lack of attention is because of the woman, or to some other distraction."

"You're getting better at this."

"I certainly hope not," retorted Irving. "I still wonder about that horrible manuscript, or whatever it is."

"It's a manuscript. But why is it so upsetting to him, if that's the reason he's been behaving so vexingly," Doyle added.

"So, what now?"

"Hmmm. It appears a different approach may be called for."

"A different approach," Irving repeated.

Doyle popped the morsel of tart into his mouth. "Yes, perhaps a more investigative—"

A loud pounding on the door interrupted Doyle. Collinson hurried into the room, as much appalled at the rudeness of the intense banging as Irving and Doyle.

Collinson hurried to the door, turned the knob, and pulled it open. Bram Stoker, glowering with anger, pushed past Collinson into the room.

Caught completely off-guard, Irving stepped forward to greet Stoker. "Bram," he began, but Stoker stopped him.

"Where did you hear the name of Jonathan Harker?" Stoker challenged, struggling to control his anger.

Doyle rose from his chair, but remained silent.

"I beg your pardon," Irving responded, stalling for time.

"You both heard my question. Where did you hear the name of Jonathan Harker?"

Irving gathered himself. "This is a most inappropriate way to enter these rooms," he said, his voice indignant.

Stoker glared at Irving, his fists clenched. "Joseph was quite impressed that Sir Henry himself paid him a visit this morning," he said. "Did you have even the slightest intention of being truthful with me?"

Irving thought a moment before responding. "We're only concerned about the harm… the harm that can come from, well, a scandal."

Stoker appeared confused for a moment, but then his angry glare returned. "Listen, both of you. I'm simply working on a book. A new book, a challenging book. That's all." And then pointing at Doyle, "You shouldn't mind that, should you? Nothing I've ever written has ever taken away from your stories."

"I wish you all the best success, of course," Doyle assured him.

"Do you?" Stoker responded.

Doyle was about to respond when Irving stepped in again. "What about this young woman we saw you speaking with last evening?" He asked.

"The man says he's writing a book," Doyle said.

"Please keep in mind the Lyceum's reputation with which I am strongly identified," Irving continued, ignoring Doyle's comment.

Stoker took a threatening step forward, exercising little control over his anger. Irving took a step backwards, glancing at Doyle, who remained silent in front of his chair. "Leave her out of it," Stoker snapped. "Stay out of it."

Irving called upon the full strength of his personality. His eyebrows almost met as he locked a debilitating stare on Stoker. "Considering you're still in my employ, I find myself unable to stay out of it," Irving said with an even forcefulness.

Stoker had no immediate response.

"A difficult thing to say, after so many years of friendship," Irving continued. "But in this transaction with Mr. Doyle, I've found your behavior to be damnably embarrassing."

"I've always been most efficient in handling your business affairs," Stoker said, a defensiveness in his tone.

"But timing is critical, and I need your full attention now."

Stoker glanced helplessly at Collinson who remained standing at the edge of the foyer, and then down to his feet. "I, I've been distracted," he muttered, a hint of defiance in his tone.

"By this woman?" Irving asked.

Stoker's head jerked up, his anger flaring again. "No," he spit. "I don't know how you found out, but your respect for my property and my privacy is severely in question. Now, mind your own business, and leave me to mine."

Stoker spun around, bolted past Collinson, and was out the door in the span of a moment. The slam of the door behind him made them all flinch.

Irving stared at the door and then looked over at Doyle. "Well, you didn't have much to contribute to that conversation," he observed.

"I saw little point," Doyle replied. "It's obvious our friend won't be open to further questions, of any sort." Doyle retrieved his walking stick from its place beside the chair.

"But what now? We have no other course of action left," Irving said.

"Not altogether true." Doyle walked across the room and took his hat from Collinson, who had already taken it from the rack. "I mentioned a course earlier, and now I'm convinced of it. I've put it off, but now I see little choice."

Irving hurried across the room. "No, wait. I'm going with you," he said.

"No need. I just have some errands to attend to," Doyle answered, stepping toward the door. Collinson opened the door for him.

Irving's eyes narrowed. "I want to know what you're up to."

Doyle offered a smile of reassurance. "I just want to look into something. I'll let you know should it lead anywhere."

Irving looked doubtful.

"I won't go near Stoker or the Lyceum. I swear," Doyle promised.

"All right," Irving responded. "Then I suggest you stop back for me once you've finished your errands. That is, if you want your play to appear on my stage."

Doyle sighed. "I'll call for you around four."

"Then I have ample time to acquire body armor from the theater before you return," Irving quipped.

"Why Sir Henry, you just might have a sense of humor after all," Doyle smiled. With that, he took his exit.

Irving shook his head. *"What have I gotten myself into?"* he wondered.

CHAPTER 42

S toker sat at a small desk in the Reading Room at the British Museum.
He often ran into Lyceum regulars here, such as Bernard Shaw and
Oscar Wilde. Today he wanted to avoid seeing anyone; still upset with Sir
Henry, he knew he could not keep his mind on simple pleasantries.

Sir Henry had been more than an employer for many years and Stoker
felt anger at his friend for betraying him. He didn't know how Irving and
Doyle had come by the information they had, but there was no question it
came to them through a gross violation of his privacy.

The anger was distracting enough, but his mind also raced with the
details of his research and where it all appeared to be leading.

Stoker looked down at the book open before him on the desk. It was a
small, cheaply bound volume—a travel book titled "The Land Beyond The
Forest," authored by Emily Gerard. Stoker was familiar with the book; he
had looked through it on two previous occasions. He turned to a chapter in
the middle of the book and began to read.

"More decidedly evil is the nosferatu, or vampire, in which every
Roumanian peasant believes as firmly as he does in heaven or hell.
Even a flawless pedigree will not insure anyone against the intrusion
of a vampire into their family vault, since every person killed by a
nosferatu becomes likewise a vampire after death, and will continue
to suck the blood of other innocent persons till the spirit has been

exorcised by opening the grave of the suspected person, and either driving a stake through the corpse, or else firing a pistol—shot into the coffin. In very obstinate cases of vampirism, it is recommended to cut off the head and replace it in the coffin with the mouth filled with garlic, or extract the heart and burn it, strewing its ashes over the grave."

Stoker leaned back in the chair; his eyes still fixed on the open book. It was nonsense; all of it was nonsense, of course. The text made it clear that these were the beliefs of peasants, uneducated and unsophisticated peasants. He closed his eyes and pulled his hands down across his face, trying to massage some of the tiredness away.

Stoker reached for the Whitby Daily and opened the paper on top of Gerard's book. The small headline read:

"WHITBY MYSTERY... public concern for missing woman."

Much of the information Tepes provided was subject to interpretation. He was full of the dramatic, too, and Stoker suspected he took a wicked delight in confusing him. He was a master of answering a question with a question and was doubly skilled at providing half-answers.

More disturbing was the fear Stoker had begun to experience in their meetings. It crept up on him, barely discernible at first. From the beginning he had sensed that there was more to the man than his engaging charm and aristocratic air. There was coldness there, a ruthlessness that was difficult to define, and it chilled him. It chilled him because he felt helpless in its presence. It chilled him because he began believing the man was a lunatic.

A dull ache began throbbing in his head, and he again massaged his temples. Afraid or not, he had to get answers to all of this; he had to discern the truth. If Tepes were still in Whitby, then the truth was in Whitby. He would return to the village, and this time he would not allow himself to be manipulated or confused. This time, he would push and keep pushing until he knew the truth.

CHAPTER 43

Doyle and Irving walked along Gordon Street beside University College. "Ah, I believe this is what we're looking for," Doyle remarked as they turned on to Endsleigh Place.

"Really, Doyle," Irving grumbled. "If I'm to be towed about London on a damp afternoon, the least you might do is tell me why in blazes we're here."

"You did insist on coming along," Doyle said. He noticed Irving didn't appreciate the reminder, so continued. "The envelope the young woman gave to Stoker."

"Yes?"

"It had rather distinctive qualities. The paper weave and unusual beige hue is peculiar to the Morley & Bowling Paper Company in Leeds; the principal supplier of stationery to the British Museum."

Irving was quite impressed and unable to disguise it. "I see the power of deduction isn't limited to your stories," he said. "Extraordinary."

"Not in this case," Doyle replied. "I'm on the museum's honorary board. Been receiving their correspondence for years. I was at the museum this afternoon, asking a few discreet questions about Stoker's young lady friend."

"If you've known so long where to find this young woman, why didn't we just come here in the first place?

"As long as we could deal directly with Stoker, I saw no reason to embarrass or compromise the young lady," Doyle answered.

"And just where is she?"

"She resides here, unless I'm very much mistaken," Doyle answered, leading Irving up to the front door of a pleasant home. He reached out and twisted the bell knob. A muffled chime sounded through the door.

After several moments, the door opened, revealing a man in his mid-fifties. He had a strong nose and a prominent forehead made more noticeable by a receding hairline. His full beard was short and neatly trimmed. He was rather short, the top of his head just clearing Doyle's shoulder. He wore a well used green silk lounging jacket, black trousers, and worn slippers.

From the man's initial reaction, Doyle was certain he recognized them. "Professor Vambery?" Doyle inquired.

The man squinted. "Yes, Vambery. Professor Arminius Vambery," he replied.

Doyle extended his hand and Vambery accepted it. "My name is Doyle. Arthur Conan Doyle. And this is Sir Henry Irving," Doyle said. "Can we intrude on you for a few minutes?"

Vambery finished shaking Irving's hand. He stepped back from the door and waved them in. "Yes, of course. Do come in."

They stepped into a small foyer, and Vambery closed the door behind them. To the left of the foyer was a study, and it was into this room Vambery led them.

The study was cluttered with books. Every shelf and every available flat surface, including the floor, held books. Artifacts from all over the world were exhibited as well; all mementos and objects of study from the professor's extensive journeys.

"Please gentlemen," Vambery said, waving them over to rugged, comfortable chairs. He sat down on a cluttered sofa in front of his desk and leaned back in the cushions.

"You said 'professor', at the door," Irving remarked to Vambery as he sank into the chair.

"Professor of Oriental Languages, University of Budapest," Doyle responded. "I've read two or three of your monographs, sir."

"Ah, and I've read some of your fictions. Very... amusing," the professor said. He turned toward Irving. "This must be more than a coincidence. I was planning on coming 'round to see you, Sir Henry."

The statement surprised Sir Henry. "Me? Why?"

"Our friend, Stoker."

"And how do you know Bram Stoker?" Doyle asked.

Vambery put his feet up on the sofa and stretched out. "I first met him at the Royal Lyceum some time ago. Almost five years now, I think. *Ravenswood*, I believe, was the play. Fine performance; very convincing, very fine," Vambery said, nodding at Irving.

Irving nodded back with a practiced humility.

"Bram invited me to dine with him in your Beefsteak Room after the performance. We'd become quite absorbed in talk of my travels," Vambery continued.

"Your travels? Why's that?" Irving inquired.

"I'm one of the great adventurers of our time, sir," Vambery said, puffing up like a strutting rooster. "One of the brilliant researchers. I was telling him about the superstitions of Eastern Europe."

"Eastern Europe," Doyle muttered to himself.

"Bram and I share a deep interest in the supernatural. He's fascinated by the history, the legends," Vambery explained.

Doyle leaned forward. "What in particular?"

"At the time, our conversation was quite general. But just over two months ago he wired me, asking if I'd look into the background of some fellow he'd met."

"Why would he ask you for such a thing?" Irving asked.

"The fellow is from somewhere in Eastern Europe," Vambery answered. "Stoker is aware of my background and familiarity with the area. He thought, correctly, that I'd be able to turn something up."

"And did you?" Doyle asked.

"Not so far," Vambery sighed. "I was out of the country when Stoker's telegram arrived. Since I was traveling in rather remote regions, it wasn't possible to have the message forwarded. I only recently started looking into the matter. Haven't turned anything up as yet, but I'll continue my research."

"You mentioned you were planning to come see me," Sir Henry said.

"Ah, yes. I sent word to Stoker once I was back home. He wanted to come 'round to see me."

"And this time he wanted to discuss something specific," Doyle stated. "What was it?"

"The vampire tales," Vambery answered with the slightest hint of embarrassment. "Yes. He pursued it quite seriously."

"Children's stories," Irving snorted.

"The roots of such stories run deep, Sir Henry. I gave him what information I had, but he did a great deal of work on his own. Told me he's outlining a book on the subject. I thought it a splendid idea. Nothing worthwhile has been done on it up to this point."

"You encouraged the project?" Irving asked.

"I even gave Bram the loan of a little flat I keep for investment purposes in Whitechapel, in Potter's Court. A place he could work without distraction."

Irving snorted again. "Yes, I've seen…" Irving let his sentence trail off as a young woman entered the room. There was no doubt. It was the same young woman he had seen with Stoker at the stage door of the Lyceum.

CHAPTER 44

The men rose to their feet. The young woman seemed surprised by Doyle and Irving's presence. "Oh, sorry, father. I thought I might've heard the bell, but I didn't know you had visitors," she said to Vambery. Then, nodding to Doyle and Irving, she added, "Gentlemen."

The woman wore a simple home gown of a soft green. Doyle observed she was much more attractive viewed this closely, than from across the stage at the theater.

Vambery stepped over to her, affectionately placing a hand on her forearm. "Ah, Clarise," he addressed her. "Allow me to introduce Sir Henry Irving, Arthur Conan Doyle." He beamed with pride. "Gentlemen, my daughter, Clarise."

Doyle and Irving managed a simultaneous "good evening."

"Yes, of course," Clarise responded. "I know of you both. Good evening, gentlemen."

"It was Miss Vambery's name I secured earlier today," Doyle explained to Irving.

Professor Vambery returned to the sofa, and his daughter sat down beside him. Doyle and Irving waited until Clarise was seated, then sat back down in their chairs.

"Not only is Clarise a delightful daughter, she also serves as my secretary. She's been a great help with carrying books, notes, a variety of things between Stoker and myself in the past weeks," the professor said.

"That would explain our seeing you at the stage door," Irving said with obvious relief.

"Yes. Mr. Stoker told me what you thought. I'm really quite mortified by it, Sir Henry," Clarise replied with a mischievous glint in her eye.

Doyle was certain that seeing Sir Henry squirm with discomfort, and the red flush in his cheeks made the entire visit worth the time. "You still haven't explained why you want to speak with Sir Henry," he said.

"Yes, of course. I'm concerned for Bram, concerned for his safety," Vambery replied.

"His safety? Why?" Irving asked.

"In one of our early meetings, Bram showed me a newspaper clipping, a report about the schooner Demeter arrived in Whitby from Varna.

"Varna?" Doyle echoed.

"On the Bulgarian Black Sea coast. The Demeter sailed from points down the Danube from Transylvania. Clarise, dear. The Demeter clipping, please."

Clarise rose from her chair, rummaged through a bundle of papers on her father's desk, and soon produced a scrap of newspaper. She handed the clipping to Doyle.

Doyle noted that the clipping came from the Whitby Daily. "Ship of tragedy moored in Whitby. Three seamen dead," he read aloud.

"Good God," exclaimed Irving as Doyle passed him the clipping.

"Bram began to suspect there was a man on board during the voyage, not a member of the crew," Vambery explained. "The same man he asked me to look in to."

"But the ship carried no passengers," Doyle observed.

"It didn't," Vambery confirmed.

"Bram was greatly disturbed by it when he told us," added Clarise.

"A stowaway?" Doyle pondered aloud.

"We believe Bram still has some connection to this, this stowaway, if that's what he is," said Clarise.

The professor leaned forward, concern lining his features. "He's cited this acquaintance of his as a key research source. He's shared some of his notes with me. Such stories; not even I've been able to unearth such information."

"And the details, quite chilling," Clarise said, with a shudder.

"His writings of the vampire existence. It's a violent way of spending eternity, you know. And Bram's work contains tremendous detail. I fear it may be more than imagination," the professor said.

Doyle was incredulous. "You're not saying—?"

Vambery interrupted him, holding up a hand.

"Last night Bram passed along some more notes to Clarise." Vambery leaned over to retrieve a newspaper clipping from the side table of the sofa. "Found this tucked among his papers."

"We only get the Times here. We weren't aware until we saw it," Clarise explained as her father handed the clipping to Doyle.

Again Doyle read aloud. "THE WHITBY HORROR. Another woman found dead."

"Yes. We saw this one," said Irving.

"Just one of those stories is an incident, but together they can't be ignored," Doyle added.

"You're aware he's been back to Whitby more than once in recent weeks," said Vambery. "I don't like it. I believe he risks much, perhaps even his life for this research of his."

"Oh, really," Irving sputtered. "You're not saying there's such a thing as vampires? Please."

Vambery leveled his gaze at Irving, his pompousness subdued. "In this day of modern science, Sir Henry, I hesitate to make such a claim. But you've seen Stoker. He's not himself. Something indeed happened aboard that ship and people have been murdered in Whitby."

"My concern, our concern, is that he's looking into these murders. Perhaps even trying to solve them for the sake of getting a good story," said Clarise.

The room was silent for several seconds. Irving was at a total loss for words, and Doyle was deep in thought. Doyle suddenly rose from his chair.

"We thank you, professor," he said. "It's time we went directly to the source."

CHAPTER 45

"He's been gone several hours now," Florence told them. "There's nothing wrong, is there?"

Doyle and Irving stood in the foyer at Number 27 Cheyne Walk, their hats in their hands. They had made their way to Stoker's home immediately after leaving Vambery's. Florence had opened the door herself, and Doyle thought he noticed some disappointment on her face when she recognized them.

Doyle did his best to give Florence a reassuring smile. "Oh, not really, no. But it's rather important. Do you know where we might find him?"

"He didn't say."

"Really." Doyle sounded disappointed.

"He just rushed in. Took a bag Tillie had made ready for him the other day, and left. He said he'd return as soon as he could." Florence couldn't keep the hurt and concern from her face. "He's made several unplanned trips north in recent days. It's possible he's gone back to Whitby."

It surprised Doyle to feel his heart tighten with a subtle, throbbing pain. Something in the woman touched him. Perhaps he recognized the anguish and suffering he had seen in the eyes of his own wife. He stepped forward, reaching for Florence's hand. "Are you all right?" he asked, his tone gentle.

Florence slowly gave him her hand. "Oh, yes. Yes, I'm fine," she answered. "It's just Bram's been so, so unlike himself. His work, it must be his work, isn't it?"

She received no answer. Withdrawing her hand from Doyle's, she looked down at the floor. "And these unexpected trips and the like. I suppose it can put a strain on the best of marriages."

Irving shuffled uncomfortably. "Yes. Well, then, it's best we say good evening," he said.

As abrupt as the suggestion was, Doyle had to agree it was unlikely that Florence could provide more information. He nodded his agreement. "Sorry to have disturbed you," he said.

"Not at all," Florence said, looking up and willing a smile to her beautiful face. "Good night."

As they walked down the steps and turned onto the sidewalk, Irving shot Doyle an accusing glance. "I can tell what you're thinking."

"I'm thinking we see if Stoker is back at the Potters Court flat," Doyle answered.

"And if he isn't, you'll want to go to Whitby," Irving said.

"Well, you have me there."

"I say no. You will not go to Whitby."

"And why not?"

"Because if you go, then I'll have to go. And I can't go. I'd have to have my understudy take on the last few performances of the season."

"Then I'd suggest you give your understudy notice," Doyle quipped.

"I can't miss the last performances."

"I've urged you from the start to let me handle this," Doyle answered.

"And let you stir up a scandal? You saw it yourself. Florence seemed quite disturbed."

"Yes. There can be little doubt she reached the same conclusion you first did. That is, before our meeting the charming and chaste Miss Vambery." Doyle took a moment to collect his thoughts, and then continued. "We'll go to Potters Court straight away. If Stoker isn't there, we'll take one of the morning trains to Whitby."

Irving drew a deep breath. "God in heaven, help us."

CHAPER 46

Stoker had paid the thirty-four shillings for a first-class compartment. He needed time to be alone, time to rest and to think. The trip, as always, took almost seven hours. It still amazed him that a modern locomotive could pull half- dozen carriages and still travel at fifty miles an hour. His train arrived in Whitby just before nine thirty at night.

Now, partially dressed, he stood wearily in his room at Mrs. Storm's Boarding House on Crescent Terrace. The only light in the room came from a moon somewhat obscured by thick, rolling clouds. He always asked for this same room. It was at the front of the house, overlooking the street, and afforded a view he found absorbing.

He leaned on the windowsill and looked out across the river at East Cliff. It rose as a dark mass above the village. The 199 steps appeared as a single, dull-white strip rising from the village to the churchyard. Stoker could just make out St. Mary's Church through the darkness. The moon-light reflected off the rows of gravestones. They radiated an unearthly glow through the mist. The imposing ruins of Whitby Abbey were barely visible beyond the gravestones.

Stoker shivered as he turned away from the window. He knew he must have a plan. He must be sure of every argument. But he feared how his decision would be accepted. He fell onto his bed, careless in pulling the covers over himself.

Sleep finally came to him, but it was an uneasy sleep. The image of

Tepes appeared as he tossed in the bed, tangling himself in the sheets. Stoker could hear his voice. Then he saw Florence, her beautiful face contorted in anger and fear, as he pinned her to the bed. What he did to her never should have happened. Why did it happen? This had to stop. It all had to stop.

Stoker rolled over, pulling the bed sheets tight around him. The constriction awakened him and he felt himself breathing too rapidly. Untangling himself, he lay on his side staring at the moonlight floating through the half-open window.

At first, Stoker couldn't be certain he was seeing it in the darkness. Then it gradually became more visible. An unhurried ribbon of mist swirled into the room; its end split into tendrils like long, white fingers pointing at Stoker, gesturing to him.

He felt a presence in the fog, and the familiar feeling of disquiet surfaced from deep within him. The drifting fingers curled back, beckoning him. Something was pulling at him, calling for him.

Stoker willed himself out of bed and made unsteady steps to the window. He looked out onto the street. At first, he saw nothing but the mist. Then, two buildings away, Stoker made out the faint outline of a man exiting an alley. The moonlight reflected off the figure as it moved away from him, hidden in the shadows.

Stoker turned away from the window, pushing his back against the wall beside the frame. He felt his heart beating in his chest; he felt the air straining through his lungs. Stoker fought to calm himself, to think clearly. He must keep his head clear.

The man wanted Stoker to follow. Of course, that's what he wanted. There was no reason to put it off. He made haste, gathered his clothes and dressed.

Stoker encountered no one else in the house as he made his way down the stairs to the front door. Why would he? It must be close to two o'clock in the morning.

Once he was in the street, the fog appeared thicker, and the gloom deeper. He glanced up. It was not quite a full moon-perhaps the next night it would reach fullness.

Stoker made his way across Crescent Terrace to the opposite side of the street, finding himself in the same shadows that had obscured his view of the man he followed. He pulled his coat tighter around him and began trudging up the street.

He walked with hurried, long strides, his intention to overtake the figure. His eyes strained to see through the darkness and the eddying clouds of mist.

Several minutes passed, then the silhouette of a man appeared. It was as if the figure was a part of the mist; more of an apparition than a flesh-and-blood man. And as Stoker drew closer to it, it materialized into a solid form. The silhouette hesitated, as if to acknowledge Stoker's presence, then continued forward. Stoker remained several yards behind it, no matter how he adjusted his pace.

The figure in the fog led Stoker through the empty village lanes, heading toward the coast. They continued along the jetty past the West Pier. Stoker lost sight of the shadow, but the disappearance did not disturb him. He knew where he was going. He could already see the beam from the light-house sweeping across the bay between the East and West piers.

Stoker turned toward the point and the small, stone block lighthouse faded into view. The building had no residence; it was a utility structure. The keeper appeared to ignite the lamp at sundown, and then reappeared in the morning to shut it down. Stoker followed the little path to the base of the tower, stopping a few yards short of the structure.

The rotating lamp caused the shadows around the building to move, with patches of mist, wood and stone transforming from light to dark every few seconds. Muted grating sounds of the gear mechanism drifted down from the top of the tower, accompanied by the softer throbbing whir of the recently installed electric motor housed inside the building.

A silhouette of the man moved in the shadows next to the tower, the small waves of the bay breaking behind him. The light moved over him in unpredictable, angled shafts, but left him predominately in darkness.

A soft, metallic voice crawled from the blackness.

"Good evening, my friend."

CHAPTER 46

"What has brought you to this village?" Tepes' voice came from the darkness.

"I thought it would be good for us to talk," Stoker answered.

"And you have come all the way here to find me."

Stoker heard something disturbing in the tone, as if Tepes already knew his intentions. "I, I've been looking over my notes," he continued in a nervous tone. "There's a great deal of material."

"Yes."

"I mean more than enough. I wanted to thank you for all your help."

"Thank me?" Tepes feigned confusion.

"Yes," Stoker answered, wondering if Tepes could detect the tremor in his voice. "I have more than enough material, so I'm here to thank you and end our collaboration."

"You've come all this way only to say this?" Tepes' voice contained a barely discernable measure of disdain.

"I thought it was the least I could do."

Stoker drew a deep breath. "I'll be returning to London tomorrow. It's time I settled in and finished my book.

"I must admit, I still have so many questions about your country, about London," Tepes continued.

Stoker took a few hesitant steps backwards. "No," he responded. "I've no more time for it."

"Why do you say this?" Tepes inquired. The moving shafts of light revealing his thin smile.

"My work has suffered. I have responsibilities. I've explained that before," Stoker answered. "My employer is quite put out with me right now, and with good reason. And my wife has seen precious little of me these past months. I'm afraid she has the wrong idea about all this."

Tepes' smile grew thinner. "That's the cost. The price one pays."

Stoker remained silent, his mind struggling, trying to stay ahead in the conversation. He knew what the statement meant, of where Tepes was leading, but he didn't want to reply. It was more prudent to wait for Tepes to explain himself. Stoker didn't have long to wait.

"Immortality has its price," Tepes said in his harsh whisper.

"Immortality?"

Tepes nodded. "Isn't that what you really want?"

Tepes had stirred Stoker's repressed fear with a single word. "I don't know what you mean," he said, amazed the words came out unhampered.

"Oh, but you do. Tell me again, how many works have you already written?"

Stoker considered the question a few moments before answering. "Two books and a collection of short stories."

"And who knows them?" The smile was gone.

"I'm an excellent writer," Stoker replied, too quickly, hearing the defensiveness in his voice.

"You want recognition. You wish to be remembered alongside the Victor Hugos of the world. Dickens, or perhaps Byron."

Stoker took a clumsy, involuntary step toward Tepes, recognizing the truth in his claim. "I suppose I do," he said, his voice weak.

"Work that lives forever. This might be your last opportunity."

Stoker sensed himself weakening, giving in, and the feeling disgusted him. He had spent so many years at the Lyceum in the presence of greatness. He regularly interacted with men whose pens flowed with magic ink, creating works of art eternal in their substance. The public recognized and admired them for their accomplishments. The world acknowledged them as special, and their contributions as important.

Stoker considered several of these men his friends, but he often grappled with envy. Stoker was ashamed to admit this, but the shame did not overcome his longing to walk among them, to have his work admired as being among the best.

Tepes took another step out of the shadows. The twisted shafts of light drifting over him revealed a cruel gash where the smile had once been. "For work that lives forever, one needs something unforgettable—an unforgettable book. And haven't I been of help to you? Did I not promise that, through me, you would reveal natures of evil the world has never known?"

Stoker found himself inexplicably drawn toward the possibilities. He had suspected the nature of the man from the beginning, but had not wanted to admit it to himself. Now, there could be no more denying what he was dealing with. It was terrifying, but Stoker had to know more. How could he live with himself if he let such a unique opportunity slip away?

A smile of some warmth appeared from nowhere, and Tepes began walking inland. "Come," he said to Stoker, ushering him along with him. "I've an ancient story I know you'll find useful. Then you must tell me more about London, and about your family."

The wandering beams of light from the tower lamp reached out for the two men as they walked back toward the village. The uneven shafts passed over them for a moment, illuminating small portions of their figures, then lost them to the darkness.

CHAPTER 47

Arthur Conan Doyle sat alone in the first class compartment gazing out the carriage window. The further north the train traveled, the more rural the scenery became.

He had just enough time to explain to Louise where he was going and the reason for the trip. She was always so understanding. A thorn of guilt pricked him. He knew he shouldn't spend so much time away from home.

Doyle knew Stoker wasn't having an affair, at least not with Clarise Vambery. The young woman's word, and that of her father, was beyond reproach.

His interest and ongoing research in psychic phenomena had exposed him to many unexplainable situations over the years, and a small part of him entertained some hope that a vampire could be at the root of the problem here. But he didn't actually believe it and he wondered if Vambery did.

The newspaper clippings had mentioned crewmen missing from a storm-battered schooner, and a missing woman. Stoker may have clipped out the articles, but that didn't mean he was collaborating with a murderer. And crewmen were sometimes swept into the sea and lost; it was one risk of the job. Doyle did not intend to jump to conclusions.

The compartment door slid open and Sir Henry Irving slipped inside with an impatient sigh, closing the door behind him. "Each time I'm forced to use one, I can't help wondering if it's possible to construct a railroad carriage water closet any smaller. There's barely room to breathe."

Much to Doyle's great surprise, Irving had arranged for his understudy to take over his role in the last two performances of Cymbeline.

Finding the flat at Potters Court abandoned, Doyle insisted they take the five-fifteen morning train from King's Cross. Irving had objected to the early hour and to almost everything else from the moment they boarded the train. Doyle supposed it was Irving's way of dealing with giving up his glory of the season's closing performances.

The actor slumped down in the seat opposite Doyle and picked up a copy of Horne's Guide To Whitby, a paperbound volume that he had purchased at the Shelby station while changing trains. He leafed through the book for a few moments and then tossed it aside. "Oh, to be home in the comfort of my rooms now," Irving puled.

When Doyle didn't engage, he continued on a different tack. "I daresay your Holmes fellow wouldn't have to do all this running about."

Doyle realized he had grown increasingly sensitive whenever Irving mentioned his fictional creation. Something about the condescending tone irritated Doyle beyond reason. Forcing himself to remain silent, he glared at the actor.

Missing the meaning behind Doyle's silence, Irving continued. "It's obvious you lack any of the actual skills that make the series so vital. How do you manage it? Do you consult with someone at the Yard?"

It surprised Doyle at how quickly his smoldering impatience burst into a full conflagration. "Consult with someone—how dare you," Doyle sputtered, rising to his feet.

Irving watched, his mouth hanging open, as Doyle pulled open the compartment door.

Halfway through the doorway, Doyle paused, glaring at Irving. "Stoker's lack of attentiveness has brought our mutual business to a complete halt. Less ambitious men might sit by, but I rather enjoy the thrill of the chase. And I'm not acting."

Doyle stepped into the passageway and banged the door shut.

CHAPTER 48

"I wonder what got into him," Irving asked himself, while the slamming of the door echoed through the compartment. Picking up the Horne's travel book, he spent the rest of the trip absently thumbing through the pages.

The train pulled into Whitby twenty minutes short of one o'clock in the afternoon. Irving had not seen Doyle since he had stormed out of the first class compartment forty minutes earlier.

After giving the matter some thought, Irving concluded Doyle had good reason to be impatient with him. He had been rattling on about anything and everything, and complaining like one of those overindulged actors for whom he had so little patience. Further reflection led him to a conclusion why he had been behaving so; he and Bram were longtime friends, and his friend's state of mind concerned him.

Friendship was the main reason he originally hired Bram Stoker. Bram's love of the theater was a second reason. Irving had only a vague awareness that his friend had an aptitude for business. Over the years, he came to realize how truly lucky he had been. He'd hired a young man for the wrong reasons and ended up with a general manager who was remarkably skilled at the job.

Irving had no real interest in business and he was grateful for Bram's efforts; efforts that undoubtedly had saved him from professional and financial disaster.

As the train lurched to a stop, Doyle slid open the compartment door. He retrieved his bag and walking stick from the overhead rack. He then waited for Irving to gather his belongings. His bag in one hand, the Horne's Guide To Whitby in the other, Irving followed Doyle off the train.

The station was small by London standards. A sign on the building identified it as West Cliff Station — Whitby. Irving spotted a porter and motioned the man over. "Porter. Can you tell us where we might find decent rooms?" he inquired.

"Mrs. Storm's about the best in the village, sir," the man responded. "Just follow the road 'bout one mile up to the end of West Cliff. Look for Number 4 Crescent Terrace. Or you can hire a cart, if you please, in front of the station."

"Number 4 Crescent Terrace," Doyle repeated. "Thank you."

The porter tipped his cap and hurried off to the train.

Doyle and Irving made their way to the street and had no difficulty finding a cart. Settling onto the wooden benches behind the driver, Doyle gave the man their destination.

As the cart rumbled up the street, Irving opened the travel book. "I believe I saw something about a Mrs. Storm's," he said. Turning a few pages rewarded his memory. "Ah, yes. Here we are, an advertisement." Irving began reading. "Mrs. Storm. Four Crescent Terrace, West Cliff, Whitby. Furnished Apartments. Uninterrupted Sea Views, Close to the Saloon, Tennis Courts, Golf Links, and the Beach. The House is certified as possessing perfect Sanitary Arrangements."

Irving snapped the book shut. "Well, that's a relief," he said, a sardonic lilt to his voice.

In a few brief minutes, the cart stopped in front of a two-story house. Four dormer windows jutted out from the roof. A decorative iron balustrade ran the length of the building on a shallow balcony.

Mrs. Storm proved to be a plump, pleasant woman in her late forties. She assured her new guests that since their visit was taking place in the off-season, she had individual rooms available for each of them.

Their landlady led them upstairs, showing them to their rooms. She then urged them to join some of her other guests in the dining room. She always provided a late lunch to accommodate guests arriving on the afternoon train.

Lunch was a pleasant affair with cold slices of mutton, fresh bread, and an apple and beetroot salad garnished with capers. Cups of perfectly acceptable tea complemented the meal.

Doyle and Irving enjoyed the lunch with three other guests, a married couple on holiday, and a representative for the local jet mining company. Most of the other guests had already dined or had eaten elsewhere.

Doyle washed down the last of his mutton with a sip of tea and placed his folded napkin on the table. "I suggest we look around while we have an opportunity," he said. "Can't hurt to become familiar with the place."

"If you insist. It'll help with the digestion," Irving replied, pushing away from the table.

They exchanged courtesies with their dining companions and returned to their rooms to retrieve coats and hats. They met in the hall at the top of the stairs and descended to the foyer together.

Irving was reaching for the front door when it unexpectedly pushed open. He stepped back to avoid being struck. A man hurried into the foyer, almost colliding with Irving and Doyle. The man came to an abrupt stop and they found themselves face-to-face with a very surprised Bram Stoker.

CHAPTER 49

S toker's surprise turned to shock, then to anger. He glared at Doyle and Irving as if they were the most hideous creatures he had ever laid eyes on.

"Good afternoon," Doyle greeted him.

Stoker endeavored through his anger to respond. "What are you doing here? How did you—?"

Irving interrupted his friend. "I assure you we have the best of intentions."

"Your intentions be damned," Stoker lashed back. "You must leave here. Today."

Doyle stepped toward Stoker, leaning his weight on his walking stick. "We came all the way up here to speak with you. Offer help if it's needed."

"It's not needed," Stoker snapped, his voice growing louder.

The guests still in the dining room began noticing the intensity of the conversation. Mrs. Storm entered the dining room from the kitchen. Sensing the tension, she stopped and stared as well. His lips forming a silent curse, Stoker turned on his heels and walked out to the street. Doyle and Irving followed close behind.

Reaching the sidewalk, Stoker turned. His mouth formed words, but Doyle spoke first. "We understand you're gathering research material for your book. Perhaps there's something we can do to help?"

"There's no help needed. And who told you I was gathering research here?" Stoker asked.

"We've worked together for years, Bram. I've never seen you so troubled," Irving said.

"We have worked together for years," Stoker responded without waiting for Irving to finish. "Does that make every part of my life open to you? Aren't I entitled to privacy?"

"Certainly," Doyle answered. "We only wish to—"

Stoker cut him off as well. "I'm writing a book. All right? How I go about it is my own business. Who I associate with is my own affair. Can't you stay out of it?"

Irving's troubled features softened as he looked at his friend. "Well, at least you acknowledge the years we've worked together, worked as friends," he said. "I thought we'd developed some trust along the way."

Stoker allowed the statement to sink in before answering. "Then in the name of that friendship, for the sake of trust, take the evening train back to London. Please. Let me do what I must do."

"But what is that?" Irving persisted.

"No, no," Doyle said to Irving. "Mr. Stoker's point is well made." Turning to Stoker, he added, "We haven't respected your privacy. You're quite right about that and you have my apology, sir." Doyle continued addressing Irving. "I detest a lengthy trip for such little result, but we must agree to his request… for friendship's sake."

"What are you talking about?" Irving asked.

"I'll rest much easier if you go. Take the evening train, please," Stoker pleaded.

"We'll return to London," Doyle assured Stoker. "But it must be tomorrow morning." Stoker stiffened noticeably and began to object, but Doyle held up a warning hand and continued. "No, please. Sir Henry and I have been on a train all day. We've only been here just over an hour. We're exhausted."

"You'll nap on the train home," Stoker suggested.

"Really, Stoker. I know you understand," Doyle insisted. "We'll rest here tonight, then take the ten thirty back to London in the morning. It'll give us time to gather our things as well."

Doyle was resolute. They watched as Stoker again struggled to find the right words. "You're better gone tonight, but it's obvious I've no power to make you leave," he responded. "But please make certain you're on the ten thirty. It's on your honor."

Doyle nodded. Stoker climbed the steps of Number Four, opened the door and went back inside. The door slammed closed behind him.

CHAPTER 50

"Such unpleasantness," Irving sighed.

Doyle continued staring at the door, as if Stoker were still standing in front of it. "He was quite keen on disposing of us before tonight. I wonder why?" After considering the question for a few moments, Doyle waved Irving along. "I suggest we familiarize ourselves with the village."

They spent the remainder of the afternoon exploring. Eventually, they found themselves at the foot of the Church Stairs. Doyle suggested they climb the 199 steps for a closer look at St. Mary's Church, and to explore the abbey ruins. With one glance at the steep climb, Irving vetoed the idea. Doyle shrugged and continued on toward the pier.

The coarse, aged pubs, and variety of marine-related businesses fascinated Doyle, as did the fishermen, sailors and dockworkers they encountered. He drank in each site and each human character with great intensity.

Ambling along East Pier, Doyle was disappointed to discover that the schooner Demeter was not in port. With that being determined, he decided it was best to get back to Mrs. Storm's before nightfall.

Once there, Doyle inquired of Mrs. Storm if Mr. Stoker was currently in the house. She assured him that Mr. Stoker had returned not long after exchanging words with Doyle and Irving earlier in the afternoon, and had been in his room ever since. Satisfied, Doyle suggested to Irving that they get a little rest before dinner. They parted company and went to their rooms.

Mrs. Storm was prompt with dinner, serving it at seven o'clock. Stoker did not glance up from his plate and ate in a sullen silence. None of the guests could engage him beyond a single word answer to their questions.

Stoker's mood didn't appear to bother the other guests, but Doyle noticed it bothered Irving. His attempts to speak with his friend went unacknowledged. Each time he tried and failed, it seemed to wound him, and he soon fell into silence himself.

The meal mercifully ended. Doyle and Irving followed Stoker up the stairs and watched him enter his room without as much as a sideward glance.

Doyle looked up and down the hallway and then turned to Irving. "I think it's important to monitor our friend tonight," he said. "There's no back stairway, and your room is right across from his. Do you think you can stay alert? If you hear his door, make sure you see what he does, where he goes."

"Of course I can stay alert," Irving assured him. "Where will you be?"

"I'll post myself downstairs in the sitting room. There's a clear view of the foyer and I'll see anyone who comes in or goes out."

Irving opened the door to his room. "I hope he's satisfied to stay in. I'm far too tired for any nonsense."

"Quite so. Good night, and do stay alert."

Doyle watched Irving enter his room and then descended to the sitting room.

Doyle found a comfortable, overstuffed chair and a pleasant fire crackling in the grate. His chair provided him with an ample view of the foyer and front door. He also had an adequate view of the street through the large front window. Stoker's room was located right above the sitting room. It would be difficult, if not impossible, for Stoker to make a move this night without Doyle knowing it.

Doyle settled back in his chair and lit a pipe. It could very well turn into a long night.

CHAPTER 51

S lipping out of Mrs. Storm's boarding house undetected had taken little ingenuity. Stoker suspected that Doyle and Irving would be watching him. Their well being concerned him and he didn't want them stumbling into something dangerous.

Upon entering his room after dinner, Stoker had donned his hat and coat. Opening the casement window, he squeezed out onto the narrow balcony, climbed over the iron railing and then lowered himself down until he was hanging by his hands with his feet only a little more than a yard from the street. Dropping to the bricks, he was well away from Number 4 Crescent Terrace in a few minutes.

Now, at almost twelve thirty in the morning, he was seated in front of a hospitable fire at the Boar's Tusk Inn.

Stoker looked across the table at Tepes. His long coat hung on a stand next to the hearth. A small portion of white silk shirt and formal wing collar was visible above a black waistcoat, the only hint of brightness on the man. His tailored black jacket covered the waistcoat.

A tankard of untouched dark ale sat on the table in front of Tepes. He ran his fingers up the side of the tankard and around the handle, but never lifted it.

"You have been quite helpful," Tepes said, gazing down at his ale. "It is all interesting to me, so very useful."

Stoker shook his head. "Useful. I don't see how."

"Any small scrap of knowledge is a source of comfort."

Tepes looked up from his tankard. The firelight flickered off his eyes and then seemed to be absorbed in them as if it never existed.

Once again, the vague, nagging feeling that it would be best to end this collaboration revisited Stoker. "I'm pleased that I could be of some help," he said. "And it's good you have all you need because the demands of my job are increasing. It's probably the best timing for me to thank you for your stories and be on my way."

"Be on your way?"

"I think it best," Stoker pressed. "Besides, I've taken enough of your time."

"I do not yet have all I need." Tepes stared, frowning. "You will know when I do."

Stoker wanted to press forward with his argument, but couldn't will himself to speak.

A thin, wintry smile formed on Tepes' lips, and then widened, giving an illusion of warmth.

"But you have been doing all the work and now it is my turn. I promised you another story, yes?"

Stoker dearly wanted to hear the story. Feeling the sense of anticipation disgusted and confounded him. He dreaded the man; he knew he would do well never to see him again, yet hungered for the tale he offered to tell. Stoker withdrew his notepad and pencil from his inside coat pocket.

"This is a Carpathian tale, a very old story. It has been told among the mountain peasants for hundreds of years," Tepes explained.

"I'm all attention," Stoker assured him.

Tepes slowly turned his gaze toward the fire. He studied the embers as if searching for the details of his story among them. "There once was an army officer," he began with tempered enthusiasm. "A dashing army officer, some might have said."

Stoker thought he heard the slightest trace of disdain in Tepes' voice.

"The officer was known to have two loves. The first was the land. He hungered to own more and more land. He was always looking for ways to increase his holdings and was shrewd in bargaining. His second love was a village maiden, a gentle beauty adored and sought after by all the young men in the region. The maiden, however, chose to give her heart only to the officer.

162

One evening the officer was making love to his maiden in the forest. The moon was pale and full, and a wealthy landowner came upon them."

Tepes' voice softened, causing Stoker to glance up at him. He was staring into the fire again.

"The maiden's beauty consumed this landowner, and he desired her for his own. Now, there was a rumor in the village that the landowner was a wicked man." Tepes' fingers roamed over the tankard.

"At the very least, a nosferatu, a vampire," he said with a humorless chuckle. "Many believed him to be in the direct employ of the devil. The jealous peasants felt that wealth as great as his could not have been accumulated through honest toil, but only by supernatural means."

"I assume you're saying that the rumors about the landowner were just that, rumors," Stoker said.

The edges of Tepes' mouth curved up slightly in a faint, satisfied smile, and without answering, continued.

"Their passions spent, the happy couple made their way out of the forest. The landowner, taking care not to be seen, followed them as the young officer returned the maiden to her parents' cottage. After the officer bid her good night and was making way toward his own lodgings, the landowner approached him.

'You have something I desire, and I have something you desire,' he told the officer. 'Come along with me.'

"The young officer was wary of the landowner's approach, for he was not unaware of the rumors. But the landowner was charming and seemed quite sincere. So, the officer accompanied him.

The landowner led the officer to a knoll overlooking the outskirts of the village. From this place, they could see across an expanse of lush forest and rich meadowland.

'You see these lands?' asked the landowner.

The young officer acknowledged he did.

'From the trees to the edge of the meadow, the land is yours, in fair exchange,' promised the landowner.

'In exchange for what?' asked the baffled officer.

When the young officer learned it was his maiden the landowner wanted, he stepped back, repulsed. But after a few moments, the officer regained his control. It is excellent land, he thought to himself. Perhaps I can turn this proposition to my advantage.

The officer apologized for his rudeness and explained that the young maiden was not his to give. She still rightfully belonged to her parents.

The landowner reminded the young fellow that he was not accustomed to being denied.

The officer feigned helplessness, stating he was certain the maiden's devotion to him was so complete, she would reject the landowner should he approach her directly. He suggested that perhaps the landowner would be interested in putting this truth to a wager. The landowner was indeed interested.

'Approach my love tomorrow evening and make your wishes known to her,' the young officer proposed. 'If she accepts you, I lose both her love and the land. Should she turn you away, your land is mine.'

'She will know nothing of this wager,' the landowner instructed. 'She will not be given warning.'

The young officer agreed to the condition, adding that the wager would mean little if his maiden was not free to make her own choice. With the bargain struck, the landowner melted into the shadows of the forest.

Returning to his room, the young officer was at first delighted with his cleverness. But as the night wore on, the officer slept less fitfully. After all, his gentle maiden was a great treasure. And then there were the rumors about the landowner. Should he take them seriously? By sunrise, he knew what must be done.

The young officer called upon the maiden first thing in the morning. Conveniently forgetting the terms of his wager, he warned her against accepting the overtures of the suitor who would call on her that very night. He warned her it could be a question of life or death.

The loving girl assured him that no other man could displace him. And he promised the maiden that he would conceal himself in her room that night to insure no harm would come to her.

That night, at the appointed time, the officer returned to the girl and hid in her room. They waited.

The hour grew later, and the night longer as the village clock counted the hours. But when the night was at its darkest, the landowner suddenly appeared in the room, although neither door nor window was given open to him.

The maiden made the landowner as welcome as she could at that late hour. He made his affection and intentions known to her, and as planned, she insisted that her love was forever pledged to the young officer.

Of course, the landowner was not satisfied with her answer, and being a reasonable man, he asked again. But the girl showed resolve and assured her caller that her answer to his proposal was final.

Taking insult at her request for his departure, the landowner's features contorted in a silent rage. His probing eyes swept across the room. It was only a moment before he located the young officer in his place of concealment.

The landowner crossed the room with great swiftness and pulled the young man from his hiding place with unstoppable strength. The landowner's mouth pulled back in a loathsome grimace, revealing teeth as sharp as needles.

'Our bargain is broken, and our wager finished,' he said to the officer, struggling like a helpless insect in his grip. 'And those who do not honor an agreement must expect to pay the price.' With that, he threw the officer across the room. The man struck the wall with such force as to render him half-conscious.

The maiden, overcome with terror, attempted to flee, but the landowner caught her well before the door. He drew her to him, and consumed with rage and lust, took her before the pained, helpless eyes of her lover.

The landowner finished with the girl and looked down at her body lying limp across the bed. The officer, near death from the violence done to him, watched as his attacker turned from the bed, and was horrified to see landowner's lips smeared with the maiden's blood.

Helpless to act, the young officer watched his love's life ebb away as the winner of the wager took his leave, the blood of revenge still dripping from his lips."

A feeling of foreboding floated up from the depths of Stoker's gut. He looked up from his notepad to find Tepes staring at him, a grim, satisfied smile on his lips.

"Some of the old stories have a moral, as does this one," Tepes said.

"I'm not sure what you mean," Stoker replied, his voice shaking.

Tepes rose from the table and retrieved his coat from the stand, never once taking his eyes off Stoker. He threw the coat over his shoulders.

"There is a kind of man who wields true power," Tepes whispered. "He has a power grown over centuries. He has a purpose that commoners cannot understand. Such a man will not be obstructed. He shall not be denied in the fulfillment of his needs."

Tepes moved around the table to stand over Stoker.

"Look at the unfortunate man in my story, the officer," he continued. "He made a poor decision. He made a pitiful attempt to betray a man whose power was beyond his ability to understand. And someone dear to him suffered for it."

Tepes leaned toward Stoker. "You're a wiser man than that fool in my little story. You would never risk harm to someone dear to you."

Tepes turned and strolled unhurriedly across the room toward the door. He did not turn back, but Stoker heard him clearly, the tone harsh and cold. "We will meet again tomorrow night."

CHAPTER 52

Doyle and Irving were both up early. Despite keeping a vigil from his chair until well after two o'clock in the morning, Doyle appeared even more robust than usual.

As they headed downstairs, Doyle explained he had seen no sign of Stoker the entire evening. Irving reported that he, also, had observed nothing suspicious.

Mrs. Storm served a delightful breakfast of egg croquettes, tea, and sautéed kidneys. Doyle and Irving lingered over two additional cups of tea, and some pleasant conversation with the other boarders, but Stoker didn't appear in the dining room. After an hour or so, Doyle suggested they retire to their rooms.

"We'll need a bit of time to pack," Irving said as they reached the upstairs hallway.

"There'll be plenty of time," Doyle answered. "I'll knock on your door in about twenty minutes. We'll take another look around the village. Perhaps we'll come across our friend."

Twenty minutes later, Doyle knocked on Irving's door. Wearing over-coats against the chill, they made their way back down the stairs and out the front door.

Doyle and Irving had not walked far when Stoker came rushing out of Number 4 Crescent Terrace. The door slamming in its frame drew their attention, and they turned toward the sound.

"Good morning, sir," greeted Doyle as Stoker approached them, almost at a run. "We were rather hoping to see you at breakfast."

"Where are your things?" Stoker asked.

"Our things?" Doyle replied.

"Your baggage for the train."

"Ah, well, we saw no reason to carry it around the village with us," said Doyle.

"Carry it around the village? You're supposed to be taking this morning's train."

"And we are, of course," Irving said.

"But we wanted to see a bit more of the shore while we were here," Doyle added, drawing his watch from his waistcoat pocket and flipping open the lid. "There's enough time."

"I'm aware of the time. You've not much more than an hour."

"Then we'd better hurry along." Doyle smiled, continuing along down the street. Irving hesitated and then followed him.

"You gave me your word," Stoker called out. "You assured me you'd leave this morning."

Doyle answered with a friendly wave without even glancing back in Stoker's direction.

When they were well down the street, Irving looked back toward Number 4 Crescent Terrace. "He's still standing there, watching. I wonder what all that's about," he said, turning back toward Doyle.

"Indeed."

"That's all you have to say?"

Doyle shrugged. "What else is there to say?"

"It would appear that Florence's wifely instincts have out-done the art of detection," Irving responded.

"Repartee, Sir Henry? Your actor's training, no doubt."

"Well, at least it has nothing to do with Clarise Vambery," Irving mused.

"Several of the villagers I spoke with are familiar with Stoker, but none of them have ever seen him here with a woman. And except for Clarise Vambery, we've never seen Stoker with a woman other than his wife."

"Ah, just so," Irving acknowledged.

"Of greater concern, the unsolved murders in the area have most of the villagers I spoke with frightened. Assuming it's not just common gossip, the locals say that there've been more murders than reported in the papers."

"More?" Irving's eyebrows arched.

"The authorities found two or three bodies they kept out of the news. And there've been some disappearances. Most of the people I chatted with believe those people were murdered as well. Nothing proven, but considering the circumstances, it's a reasonable conclusion."

"How do you mean?" Irving asked.

"No one, especially the local constabulary, has any idea who is committing these murders, or why. There are no witnesses, no murder weapon. The only commonality is that all the victims were murdered at night. Most murders occur at night, so it's useless information."

"How were they murdered?"

Doyle shrugged. "I'm not sure anybody knows, and if they do know, they won't say."

"What do the police say?" Irving asked.

"Very little. The constable I spoke with seemed almost embarrassed by the question. He just mumbled something about it being ghastly."

"Do you, do you think Stoker might have something to do with all this?"

"All we know for certain about Stoker is that he's not himself. And that's an understatement."

Irving brooded over Doyle's observations for a few moments. "Well, you saw how he was. You know he won't let up until we leave for London."

"We'll see what we can do to put that off as long as we can," Doyle responded.

"To what end?"

"Stoker's insistence on our leaving this morning makes it clear he doesn't want us present. And I believe at least some answers we seek can only be found here tonight."

"Then what do you propose?" Irving asked.

"We do our best to avoid him for the remainder of the day. The longer we stay, the more we stand to learn."

CHAPTER 53

D oyle and Irving spent little of their morning in Whitby. Doyle
thought it prudent to find another location for sightseeing, if for no
other reason than to avoid being pestered by Stoker.

They strolled down to the West Cliff train station and made an inquiry
of the stationmaster. He suggested they investigate Robin Hood's Bay, a little
fishing village five or six miles south of Whitby. Hiring a cart in front of the
station, they soon found themselves heading south on the main coastal road.

Robin Hood's Bay was like a picture postcard. Red pantiles decorated
the roofs of stone cottages. A labyrinth of cobbled streets connected the
cottages and several shops, pubs, and inns. Most of the buildings appeared
to be built into the cliffs. It seemed as if the entire village was clinging
precariously to the limestone walls.

They explored the twisting village streets for an hour before wandering
into the village square. Doyle spotted a shop that brightened him. The
lettered sign above the doorway attracted him as the proverbial mouse to
cheese: A. W. Drewett, Fancy Bread & Biscuit Maker, & Confectioner.

They sat next to a window overlooking the bay. The only other patrons
in the shop were an elderly gentleman attired in walking clothes and
enjoying a slice of orange cake, and a pair of middle-aged women
exchanging the latest gossip over tea.

Irving took a sip of his tea and arched an eyebrow as the shopkeeper delivered a large butterscotch scone to Doyle. Doyle thanked the man and enthusiastically attacked the scone.

"How many is that now?" Irving inquired.

"No reason to go hungry just because there's some waiting to be done," Doyle answered with his mouth full. He reached for his teacup.

"I can't help wondering if we should be waiting."

"It's half-past two," Doyle said, glancing at the wall clock above the pastry counter. "I think we can make our way back after tea."

"That's not what I meant. Bram is furious about our being here. Perhaps it's best to just let him be," suggested Irving.

"You aren't interested in tracking down a vampire?" Doyle asked.

"You're serious," Irving said, shocked.

Doyle shrugged. "Once you eliminate the impossible, whatever remains, no matter how improbable, must be the truth."

"You're saying—"

"I'm saying we still don't know what we're dealing with," Doyle interrupted.

They passed the next couple of minutes in silence, drinking their tea and looking at the ocean through the window. Irving broke the silence, turning his attention back to Doyle. "I can't remember the last time I saw you in London with your wife," he said.

Doyle did not turn his gaze from the window, nor did he answer.

"Mr. Doyle?"

"It has been some time," came the quiet reply.

"I trust all is well between you two."

Doyle fixed his eyes on Irving. He appeared haggard, but his voice remained even when he spoke. "Since you're being so courteous as to inquire after my wife, Sir Henry, allow me to respond in kind. How is the lovely Mrs. Terry? I can't recall the last time I saw you two about London together."

Irving was stunned at Doyle's angular response. He stared down at his teacup, at a loss for words.

Several moments passed. "Louise has been quite ill," Doyle said.

Irving leaned forward a bit. "I had no idea. I assure you, when I asked, I didn't know."

"No, of course not," Doyle said, only a trace of sadness forcing its way into his voice. "Louise hasn't been very keen on her condition becoming common knowledge."

"May I ask what it...?" Irving cut himself off, fearing that he might further offend Doyle.

"Consumption."

"I am sorry."

"She seems to lose a bit more strength every day." Doyle added.

"I didn't mean to bring up any unpleasantness. I was only trying to pass the time in idle conversation," Irving said.

"Of course. I don't know what came over me to answer you as I did. I do apologize." Doyle paused for a moment, then continued. "I didn't intend to malign Mrs. Terry's reputation, or your own."

Irving nodded. "It's difficult at times, isn't it?" he said. "Being a public figure while trying to keep some kind of a private life. Trying to love someone without the entire country having a say in it."

Doyle nodded. "Indeed."

"Is there anything I can do? For Louise, or you?" Irving asked.

Doyle could not hide his look of surprise. Irving noticed and smiled. "I may be a self-absorbed actor, Mr. Doyle, but I'm still capable of helping my friends," Irving said.

"Yes," Doyle answered. "I'd say you've already proven that."

It was late afternoon by the time Doyle and Irving returned to Whitby and dropped off the cart at the station. Only a few minutes later, they were walking up Crescent Terrace with Mrs. Storm's in sight. Stoker stood on the front steps, waiting for them. Beside him were their traveling bags.

"I spent a good deal of time looking for you today," Stoker said, his voice strained.

"And here we are," Doyle answered. "Good afternoon."

"Those are our bags," Irving pointed, annoyed. "What do you think you're doing?"

"I took the liberty of telling Mrs. Storm of your urgent need to return to London on the afternoon train," Stoker responded. "I explained how you were otherwise engaged, and it would be a great help if she could pack for you."

"Very thoughtful of you," Doyle said.

Stoker came down off the steps. "Now, if you would be so kind as to fetch your bags, I'll go along with you to the station."

"That's about enough," Irving began.

Dole held up a hand and Irving stopped. "No," Doyle said. "The morning gave me some time to think, and if he is so keen on our leaving, then perhaps we should go."

"What?" Irving was incredulous. "You might have mentioned this earlier and we'd already be on our way back to the city."

"I'd prefer to stay, of course," Doyle continued. "But Mr. Stoker has made it clear he has no use for us here, and it's obvious our presence is distressing to him. I don't know about you, but I've no desire to stay where I'm not wanted."

Irving, confounded, just kept staring at Doyle.

"Let's hurry along, then," Stoker said.

"But there's our bill to settle," objected Irving.

"I've taken care of it," Stoker snapped. "You came all this way on my account. It's the least I can do to compensate for your effort and wasted time."

"Then I suppose it's settled," Doyle nodded to Irving.

With a frustrated sigh, Irving grabbed both bags and passed Doyle his.

"It's for the best, I assure you," Stoker told them, forcing the first smile they'd seen from him in ages.

They walked to the train station in silence, the air around them thick with tension.

CHAPTER 54

The sun was low in the sky when they arrived at the West Cliff station. The train was already at the platform and there were still ten minutes before its scheduled to return to London. Heavy clouds that had lingered on the ocean horizon the afternoon through now rolled steadily toward land.

Doyle, his demeanor calm, waited on the platform with Stoker while Irving went inside the building to purchase their tickets. Neither of them attempted to make conversation.

The train was boarding by the time Irving returned to the platform holding two first class tickets. The final whistle sounded as Stoker ushered them into their carriage.

"Please believe me. This is best for everyone," Stoker assured them.

With a loud hiss of escaping steam, the train began steaming out of the station. Doyle's last glimpse of Stoker was through the still open doorway of the moving train. He soon disappeared from view as the train picked up speed.

Irving was already seated in their compartment by the time Doyle slid the door closed and sank into the opposite seat.

"Do you mind telling me what all *that* was about?" Irving asked. "You were the one who was so keen on finding out what he's up to tonight."

"I still am," Doyle responded.

"You've an interesting way of showing it. You didn't even put up a fight back there."

"If we insisted on staying, he'd be more cautious."

Irving leaned forward with interest. "You think he might not follow through with whatever is happening tonight if he knew we were there?"

Doyle nodded.

"But if he thinks we've gone, then he might very well carry on with less caution," Irving reasoned.

"The question is, how do we get back to the village by nightfall?" Doyle wondered.

Irving leaned back and his seat, giving the question some thought.

The compartment door slid open and the train ticket inspector stepped into the compartment.

"Excuse me," Doyle greeted, as Irving handed the inspector their tickets.

"Yes, sir," the official replied.

"Can I arrange to stop this train?" Doyle asked.

The ticket inspector made little attempt to hide his amusement. "Well sir, as soon as we get to Selby station, I'll arrange to stop her for you."

"And if I told you it was quite literally a question of life and death?"

"Sir, I'd say the chairman of this line might be dying, but I still can't stop this train 'till we get to Selby to change locomotives for the main line."

The ticket inspector returned the punched tickets and hurried from the compartment.

"We should jump," Irving said.

"Excuse me?"

"We'll need to jump."

"*You* want us to jump from the train," Doyle repeated, amazed.

"You don't like the idea?

"I think it's an excellent idea. I'm just surprised it came from you."

"I don't see why," Sir Henry was indignant.

"Sir Henry, you have become much less predictable since we began this adventure," Doyle chuckled.

Irving slid over to the window, taking a hard look at the terrain outside of the carriage, and then rose from his seat. "The sooner the better, I would think."

"Agreed."

Doyle rose from his seat, opened the compartment door, and stepped out into the passageway.

"What about our bags?" Irving questioned.

"They'll hold them at the station for us."

With a last longing look toward his bag, Irving followed Doyle out of the compartment. A few moments later, they were standing on the platform at the rear of the carriage, watching the landscape rush by.

Doyle gripped the handrails and lowered himself onto the bottom carriage step. "We'll look for the best spot. Preferably a slope down from the tracks."

Doyle scanned the approaching countryside for a safe place to jump. The light was fading enough that it was a precarious business at best.

He felt the train's speed slow slightly. "There," Doyle cried, pointing to a spot ahead of them.

The train reached a slight grade and the locomotive had slowed to climb it. Coming up beside the roadbed was a grass-covered slope with a gentle slant down from the tracks.

Doyle could make out one or two good-sized boulders, and several smaller stones spotting the knoll, but it was by far the best place they had seen so far. "This will do," he informed Irving.

Irving nodded and readied himself as the train approached the slope.

Judging the timing the best he could, Doyle targeted what appeared to be an unobstructed area. "Now," he cued Irving.

Doyle leaped from the carriage steps. Irving followed, launching himself from the train behind the author.

Doyle hit the ground hard and tumbled down the slope, which turned out to be steeper than it had appeared. A boulder at the bottom of the slope halted his forward progress. He twisted around to protect his head, but his side slammed into the rock, and he felt the air rush from his lungs.

Irving somersaulted past Doyle and landed on his back further down the hill. His left leg came down hard on a small outcrop of rock. He pulled himself into a sitting position. A patch of blood stained his trouser leg.

Irving pulled up the fabric and looked. Even from ten feet away, Doyle could see that it wasn't bad. The rock had cut the actor, and he was bleeding a little, but the wound was slight.

Both men sat where they had landed, grateful for the time to rest and catch their breath. The train was already out of sight, but they rested and listened until the sound of it faded into the distance.

Doyle gingerly felt his side where it impacted with the boulder. He winced; there was nothing broken, but he knew there would be a nasty bruise.

"Are you all right?" Irving asked.

"Just bruised a bit. You?"

"The same, though I don't think I'd want to try that again any time soon."

Doyle smiled his agreement and pulled himself to his feet. "We need to get moving. We must've traveled at least three miles from Whitby."

"Just what we need, more exercise," Irving said, climbing to his feet.

"The road runs parallel to the tracks. It should be just through those trees," Doyle pointed.

They made their way through the trees. The foliage was not thick and it took only five minutes to reach the road. Doyle and Irving followed it back toward Whitby. The shadows lengthened across the road, and darkness soon enveloped them as the sun disappeared from the sky.

CHAPTER 55

After leaving West Cliff station, Stoker walked aimlessly through Whitby's gaslit streets. It was dinnertime, and driven more by habit than hunger, he made his way to a small restaurant he frequented in the village.

He sat alone at his table, staring vacantly at a mostly untouched plate of roast grouse and peas with mint. His mind ran through the events of the past weeks. His repeated attempts to end his association with Vlad Tepes had failed, and for the life of him, Stoker could not determine why. Despite all the confusion, his instincts cut through the haze enough to tell him again that it was more and more dangerous to let things remain as they were.

An old story his mother had told him as a child began surfacing in his mind, surfacing from the murky waters of the past. It was during a cholera epidemic that raged across Ireland in 1832. His mother had been in her mid-twenties and living with her parents in the town of Sligo.

The disease had struck down an unfortunate traveler on the road a few miles outside the town. Several representatives from the town, exercising great caution, approached the man as he lay too weak to walk, or even crawl, at the side of the track.

The poor man must have at first viewed the townspeople as coming to his aid. But the doctors had ordered that any person who died of the affliction be buried within an hour of their demise.

The townspeople made haste in digging a pit, and using long poles pushed the feverish man, still very much alive, into it. And then they shoveled the dirt over him, covering him up, alive.

Stoker had vivid images of that roadside scene when his mother first told him the tale, and the images remained. He wondered what it must have been like for that man, still alive but too weak to move. Looking up at his last glimpse of the sky. Lying in his grave as shovelful by shovelful, the soil covered him. The dirt and dust filling his nose and mouth as an eternal blackness pressed in around him.

Stoker picked at his food, wondering why such dark thoughts filled his head. His mind had been full of too many such reflections since he had met Tepes. What was it about the man that made it so?

The restaurant was filling up. Stoker paid his bill and walked back toward Crescent Terrace. He still had a little time and wanted to rest in his room before facing Tepes.

A few blocks from the boarding house, Stoker turned onto a pleasant, shop-lined street. Ahead of him, at the mouth of an alley, a crowd had gathered. The gas flame from a nearby streetlight projected their movements in twisted shadows across the cobbles and up the building walls.

He heard their excited murmurs and whispers as he drew closer. Stoker saw a constable, just inside the alley, doing a reasonable job at keeping the cluster of people out. Reaching the outskirts of the assembly, Stoker caught the attention of an elderly man. "What is it?" Stoker asked.

"Another killing," the old man answered, unable to conceal that odd excitement humans experience upon witnessing violence against one of their own.

"Murder?" Stoker asked, weakness in his voice.

The man nodded. "Katherine Fraley, it is, poor thing."

Stoker pushed into the crowd and wedged his way through to the front. He could now see that a second constable was also on the scene, about twenty feet into the alley, kneeling near the left wall. Stoker trembled when he saw the body beside the constable.

The late Katherine Fraley was in her mid-twenties, sprawled on her side, her head facing the alley opening. Her right arm was folded under her body. Her left arm hung limp across her chest. She was clothed in a simple brown woolen skirt and a white blouse ripped away at the neckline. Blood stained the white fabric and the area around the girl's throat. A nasty wound was apparent at the base of her throat, obviously the source of the blood. The wound looked bad enough to suggest that the bleeding should have been more extensive.

Stoker took another uneven step toward the body. The first constable stopped him. "Sorry, sir, but you understand."

Stoker could only stare at the lifeless body. He should have made the authorities aware of his theory. They would have thought him insane, but he should have at least tried. Then no one could say he'd remained silent. Was he responsible for this? Was it possible that he was an accessory to this crime?

The constable noticed Stoker's rapt attention on the body. "Do you know her, sir?" he inquired.

"No."

The elderly man who had provided the victim's name weaved his way through to the front of the crowd, coming to a stop next to Stoker. "When did it happen?" he asked the constable with almost gleeful interest.

"We think she's been there most of the night 'an all through today. Worked at her father's tailor shop."

"I know that already," came the old man's irritable reply.

"Stayed behind after closing to finish the stitching on a pair of trousers. Then didn't come home last night." The constable paused, noticing Stoker's eyes still fixed on the body. "If you're given ill by it, sir, perhaps you should turn away," he suggested, attempting to be helpful.

Stoker forced his eyes away from the dead girl and looked into the face of the constable. "Yes. Yes, of course." Did he see suspicion in the constable's eyes?

The constable continued. "We never found her. A crewman from one of the cargo schooners did. Cutting through here on the way to his flop after drinking all afternoon. Almost scared him sober, it did."

A middle-aged woman made her way through the throng, an old woolen blanket draped over her arm. "'Ere ye' go, then," she said, handing the blanket to the constable. "Give the poor girl 'er privacy."

Stoker turned away as the two constables took hold of the blanket corners, spread it open and covered up Katherine Fraley's body. The queasy illness began to pass, but not quickly enough. He had to pull himself together. Resisting the urge to break into a full run, Stoker continued on his way back to Mrs. Storm's.

CHAPTER 56

S toker entered his room at Number 4 Crescent Terrace as if chased by an army of demons. He closed the door and pushed his back against it, surveying the shadows for any potential threat. Reaching through the darkness, Stoker turned up the gas lamp. The flickering flame provided some sense of comfort, but not near enough.

He walked unsteadily across the room to the window, dropping his hat on the end of the bed. He peered around the frame.

The dark form of East Cliff reached up into the night. He could make out the Church Stairs climbing from the village, winding up the cliff to the churchyard above. Ominous storm clouds drifted over the churchyard. Their movements made the gravestones appear and disappear in the dim moonlight, as if the hood of a lantern aimed at the stones slowly opened, and then shut.

The abbey ruins were barely visible in the darkness beyond St. Mary's. The Gothic arches appeared to rise from a sea of torpid, swirling mist.

That is where he would be tonight, Stoker thought. "It can't be," Stoker whispered, surprised by the sound of his own voice.

Stoker removed his travel bag from a chair in the room's corner and placed it on the bed closer to the lamp. Rummaging through it, he removed a simple silver cross suspended on an inexpensive chain.

The knock at the door made him jump. Pocketing the cross and laboring to move in silence, Stoker approached the door. He stood in front of it, staring at the doorknob. The knock repeated, causing him to start yet again.

"Bram," the familiar voice called from the other side of the door.

Oh, God, no, he thought. Stoker pulled open the door. Florence stood before him wearing comfortable travel clothing covered by a short wool cloak. Her face was stony and tired with worry.

"Florence."

Florence pushed past him into the room. She stood beside the bed, her eyes scanning the room, taking in every detail.

"Florence," Stoker said again. "What are you doing here?" He could not hide the fear and concern he felt, nor could he ignore the fresh resurgence of guilt welling up inside him.

Ignoring her husband, Florence continued to look over the room, uncertainty growing in her eyes. She hurried to the closet and pulled open the door. She stared inside, slowly running her hand across Stoker's clothing hanging there.

Florence closed the closet door, her beautiful face flooded with confusion. She removed the cloak, dropped it on the end of the bed, and then sat down beside it. "You're alone," she said, mild surprise in her tone.

Stoker tilted his head, confused for a moment.

"I'm no longer certain what I expected to find here," she continued.

Stoker suddenly realized what she meant. He realized what she had been thinking, and what had driven her to follow him all the way to this place. "Oh, no. No. How could you think such things?"

"I suppose I thought, I don't know."

"No. It never occurred to me."

"There's no other woman?"

She still needed assurance.

"There never has been." His chest ached. How could he have caused her this kind of pain?

"I've misjudged you badly," Florence said, her relief obvious.

"You must go."

"What?"

"I'm so sorry. I'm truly sorry if I've caused you to think, if I've caused you to worry about such things, but you must go. You must go at once."

Florence rose from the bed and circled her arms around him, pulling him close, resting her head on his chest.

"What's wrong, Bram?" she asked. "What's all this about?"

"You must trust me a while longer. You must return to London right away," he insisted.

"There are no more trains tonight. It's posted at the station."

Stoker gently pushed away from her and began pacing the room. "Dear God in heaven, what should I do?" he prayed silently. The fear he felt for himself paled against the fear he felt for his wife. Perhaps that was a good thing. He needed his wits about him tonight.

"Please, tell me what's wrong," Florence pleaded. "Let me help."

"Let me think," he snapped at her, not meaning to.

She was right, of course, about no more trains tonight. If he couldn't get her out of the village, then there was no place that was safe for her.

Reaching into his pocket, he fingered the cross on its chain.

"There's no time, and I must go out," he said.

"Go out? Now?"

He slipped into his overcoat and picked up his hat from the bed. "Just a short while. I was just leaving when you arrived."

"Then I'll go with you," Florence volunteered.

"No," Stoker answered, unable to conceal the panic he felt at her suggestion. "You mustn't. But I won't be long."

"You're frightening me."

"I'm sorry. But you'll be fine. Everything'll be fine if you just do as I ask." His voice lacked conviction.

Florence moved to intercept him as Stoker made his way toward the door. "Bram, please."

Stoker withdrew the room key from his pocket and pushed it into her hand. "Here. Lock the door behind me. Don't open it for anyone but me. And close that window. Latch it, as well."

Before she could object again, he was out the door and it was closed between them. His voice came through from the hallway.

"Lock it now."

CHAPTER 57

Florence locked the door, then sat down on the edge of the bed to think. She had convinced herself that another woman was the only explanation for his unusual behavior. It was a tremendous relief to discover that she had been wrong. But if it wasn't an affair, what was causing him to be so preoccupied? What had prompted his moodiness and the many trips to this village?

Florence relished the relief she felt, but was keenly aware of the fear Bram could not conceal. She wanted to hemp him if he was in danger. He shouldn't have to face whatever the problem was alone.

The danger must be real; Bram wanted her locked away in this room. Glancing up, Florence noticed the window was still open.

She got up from the bed and hurried across the room. She began pulling the window closed when she thought she heard a voice. It was more of a whisper. She turned to look about the room and was relieved to find that she was still alone. Then she heard the whisper again, and this time there was no imagining it.

Follow me.

Was it Bram's voice? Florence turned back to the window and peered into the darkness. She spotted a slight movement in the distance.

Come to me. I need your help.

Florence couldn't help but look around the room again.

Come.

It sounded rather like Bram, but she couldn't be completely sure.

A beam of moonlight broke through the clouds, bathing the cliff side in a gray light. Florence looked again. There it was, higher up the cliff this time.

A man climbed the steps. Her instincts and something in his movements told Florence it was her husband. She was sure of it. The clouds moved again, extinguishing the light. Bram disappeared in the darkness.

Follow me. Follow me now. I need your help.

A feeling sidled through her. She could not stay any longer in this room. She must go.

Come.

Her husband was calling for her and he needed her help.

Florence retrieved her cloak and the key from the bed. She unlocked the door and stepped into the hallway. Hastily closing the door behind her, she hurried away, leaving the key in the lock.

CHAPTER 58

D oyle and Irving hurried down the hallway and stopped in front of Stoker's door. Doyle knocked hard against the wood. "Stoker," he called out. "Stoker."

Irving stepped forward and knocked. When there was still no response, Doyle twisted the doorknob. The door swung open.

"Blast it all," Doyle cursed in frustration, surveying the empty room.

"Marvelous," Irving added. "We jump from a train and march all the way back to see him, and now he's not here."

Doyle paced around the room, turning over the possibilities in his mind. "If one were meeting with a vampire," His voice trailed off.

"Or someone pretending to be a vampire," Irving interjected.

"Where would one go?"

Doyle peered out the window. He could just make out the outline of St. Mary's Church, framed by heavy clouds.

"The churchyard!"

Doyle and Irving ran from the room, neither of them looking forward to climbing 199 steps.

CHAPTER 59

S toker was only a few stone steps from the top of the cliff. Ugly dark clouds formed a ceiling above the precipice. Thunder cracked somewhere among the condensed vapor. The steps could be treacherous without a lantern and he had to make the climb by the moonlight seeping through the infrequent gaps in the clouds.

Reaching the top of the Church Stairs, Stoker stopped to rest. To his left was St. Mary's Church. The gravestones in the churchyard glowed unearthly in the reflected moonlight. Mist swirled in an ever-widening whirlpool among the markers.

At least one murder had occurred in the churchyard. He did not believe that its proximity to the abandoned abbey was a coincidence. His breathing gradually returned to normal. He stepped off the path and headed away from the church.

Stoker made his way through the grass and weeds that were knee high and damp from the weather. Traversing this uneven ground in the dark was troublesome business, but the moonlight continued to filter through the moving clouds, enabling him to better choose his footing.

It only took a few minutes to reach the grounds of Whitby Abbey. Thunder threatened again in the distance. Stoker stopped at a low, stone wall that extended into the property to form a large, empty rectangle. The area may once have been a residence hall. But now, most of the wall had fallen away from the passing years and the harsh elements of Northern England. At its highest point, the wall reached only about six feet.

The far end of the residence wing connected to the tower building. Twin two-story walls, formed of Gothic arches, were mostly intact, but the roof had disintegrated ages before. The two-story section of the building jutted out beyond the residence area, forming an inverted 'L'. A square-walled, three-story tower rose above the lower portion of the building.

The main sanctuary was by far the largest building of the abbey. It extended perpendicular from the tower building. Its walls, too, were constructed of Gothic arches. Three-quarters of the sanctuary's roof was gone. The small portion that remained was riddled with large, jagged gaps and supported by rotting beams.

Stoker spied a half-moon shaped gap in the wall of the residence building where stones had been dislodged from their mortar. Using the gap as a natural gate, he stepped over the wall into the ruins. He felt the temperature drop. The air was cold, but an even greater chill cut through him as he stepped onto the abbey property. Pulling his greatcoat tighter, Stoker peered into the darkness.

The moon broke through the clouds again, bathing the abbey in a murky light. Shadows extended from the building's pillars, dark tendrils that reached out to Stoker. The mist hung close to the ground, drifting in and out of the arches and appeared to be growing thicker. He looked harder. His eyes were not playing tricks on him. The fog was gathering into large, churning clouds. It was almost as if the storm clouds above had descended into the abbey and were now pouring through the arches.

Stoker drew on what little courage he could find and walked toward the tower. He stepped through an archway, using his hands to steady him in the darkness. He waited a few moments until his eyes adjusted to the blackness and then continued through to the main sanctuary. It was even colder now. He flinched as several explosions of thunder followed one upon the other.

Stoker looked up and saw the moon framed by heavy clouds. When he looked down again, he saw Vlad Tepes walking toward him through the mist, his black coat billowing around him. Stoker blinked, trying to be certain of what he was seeing. It was difficult to tell if Tepes was approaching through the mist, or being formed out of it.

The man's face was cold and expressionless. He moved with an unearthly grace. Stoker felt almost numb with fear. And now he was certain of only one thing; he should never have come here.

Tepes stopped in front of Stoker and the mist thinned out around him.

The expressionless mask transformed into a warm smile, but the dark eyes maintained their usual coldness and distance.

"Good evening, my friend," Tepes greeted.

Stoker stared back at Tepes, trying to build up his nerve. "Who, who are you?" he finally managed.

"An interesting question after all this time."

"Who are you? Who are you really?"

Tepes looked up through the open roof at the moon, then at the Gothic walls surrounding them. "What brought you here tonight?" he asked, the cold eyes fixing on Stoker again.

"I wanted, I needed to speak with you."

Tepes' smile thinned. "I meant, why did you come here tonight?"

"I had a feeling. I thought I might find you here."

"I see."

"Who are you?" Stoker's tone was insistent.

"As I've told you, only a prince who has left his home for a foreign land."

Smoldering anger overtook Stoker's fear. "I didn't want to know the whole truth. I convinced myself it was all harmless."

"You are unhappy." Tepes said it with some sarcasm. "My stories of my homeland, they've not been beneficial to you?"

Stoker fought to keep himself on track. He would not. He could not allow this man to manipulate him. "The attacks. The killings. You're responsible?" It was the most difficult question Stoker could ask. And he was fearful of the answer.

Tepes stepped toward Stoker. Even though there was nothing threatening in the movement, Stoker took a step back.

"Strange occurrences kill people every day... and night," Tepes replied, his smile thinning even more, his eyes void of any feeling or life.

CHAPTER 60

F lorence reached the top of the Church Stairs, her breathing strained. It was frightfully dark, and she had stumbled on the steps several times on her way up. But her eyes had grown accustomed to the night, and she was driven by the desire to help her husband.

She looked at St. Mary's church. It was close enough, and the area between the steps and the church building was open enough to offer an unobstructed view. There was no light or movement visible in or around the church. There was no sign of Bram. She surveyed the area and turned toward the walls of the abbey. It was the only other building in sight.

Florence pulled her cloak tight around her and walked toward the abbey. A few minutes later, after tripping over a low stump once, and then again when her boot heel sank into the soft ground, Florence reached the abbey. Discovering the low gap in the residence building wall, she entered and walked further into the ruins with caution.

Florence had just reached the tower building when she thought she heard voices. She stopped and listened. A man's voice. It wasn't Bram, but was hauntingly familiar.

Choosing her steps with care, Florence continued on toward the archways leading into the main sanctuary. Bending low, she made her way to the outer sanctuary wall. She straightened up and looked around the pillar that concealed her.

Bram was standing forty feet away, inside the sanctuary, his back to her.

Florence watched him take an uneasy step backwards as he listened to a tall, older man. It appeared as if her husband feared this man. And then she recognized him through the darkness.

He was dressed almost completely in black. Florence remembered him as a kindly, older gentleman, but now he looked ten years younger than when she had first met him. And there was something else about him, a coldness that filled her with dread.

"I won't be coming back again," she heard Bram say.

"Our business is unfinished," replied Tepes.

"I want nothing more to do with you," Stoker said, taking another step back from Tepes.

The slight hint of kindness on Tepes' face melted away. "The timing of your decision is poor. I fostered our relationship because you are useful to me."

"So, we've traded information. That'll be the end of it."

"It is time for me to complete my transition to London. I wish to experience it, the crowds. So many people out at night." Tepes smiled the most unpleasant smile. "I've already made certain arrangements, but I'll require your help for a while longer."

Florence watched Bram shake his head, shivering at the cold and with fear. A peal of thunder rolled through the ruins and Florence chose that moment to rush into the sanctuary.

"Bram," Florence called to him.

Her husband spun around in surprise. "Florence," he groaned, clearly horrified at her presence. He looked back at Tepes. Tepes did not appear surprised at all.

"Ah, the lovely Mrs. Stoker," Tepes acknowledged her, taking a step forward. "How fortunate to see you again."

Bram rushed to position himself between Florence and Tepes.

"What's this about, Bram?" she asked.

"Please, come closer," Tepes smiled at Florence. "Allow me to greet you properly."

Florence sensed something in Tepes, a tangible feeling that terrified her. She couldn't believe that she hadn't felt it those months ago in London.

"Bram, come back with me now. This is an evil man. I know you sense it, too," Florence said, her tone urgent.

"So very foolish," Tepes whispered, the charm replaced with menace.

"She's right. I'll have no more of it," Bram insisted.

Florence moved forward and took her husband by the arm. "Let's go. Let's go right now."

Tepes leaped forward. In a single, violent motion, he shoved Bram to the ground and took hold of her. The blow sent her husband tumbling across the ground. Florence was stunned at how swift and fluid the movement had been.

Florence screamed, but the scream was strangled as Tepes wrapped his fingers around her throat and, with a single arm, lifted her off the ground. She could see the fear in Bram's eyes as he scrambled to his feet and charged at Tepes. With his free arm, Tepes sent him sprawling again.

The pain from Tepes' grip was excruciating and Florence struggled to draw air into her lungs. Her vision darkened.

CHAPTER 61

D
oyle and Irving were making their way across the abbey grounds near the tower building when they heard Florence scream. Breaking into a full run, they raced into the ruins, heading for the main sanctuary. Entering the open, cavernous room, neither man was prepared for the scene that met their eyes.

A man in dark clothing was holding Florence in the air by her throat with a single arm, and she was choking. Stoker was a few yards away, climbing to his knees.

Before Doyle and Irving could take action, Stoker dug a hand into his trouser pocket, then leaped to his feet and ran like a madman at the older man. Stoker thrust his hand into the man's face. The man released Florence and delivered a rough blow to Stoker, knocking him to the ground.

Florence dropped unconscious to the ground beside Stoker. The older man backed away a few steps, holding an arm up as if to protect himself.

Doyle and Irving ran to Stoker and Florence. Doyle kneeled down to help as Irving took a defensive position between his friends and the man who had attacked them.

The mist in the abbey appeared to be thickening and gathering around the darkly clad man. The man lowered his arm, pointing it at Stoker. His eyes flashed with rage. "You think yourself so wise, so very clever," he snarled. The harsh, metallic sound of his voice reverberated off the ancient stone walls.

Doyle watched as Stoker stared in disbelief at his own clenched hand. He opened his fingers, revealing a small silver cross.

Stoker looked up at him, and Doyle stared at the cross with the same shock and incredulity that he saw on Stoker's face. Stoker struggled to his knees, kneeling beside his wife with the cross dangling from his hand in clear view.

Doyle looked back at the stranger, his face drawn taut in a quiet fury. His eyes bored into Doyle and Irving, then focused again on Stoker.

"You betray me even further," he growled. "You'd have found me to be a better friend than to have me against you."

"I cannot be a part of these crimes. Not any longer," Stoker answered, almost in tears.

"London is not all that far away. Once I am there, I'll find someone who can assist me in my tasks. Perhaps…" The man let his voice fade away as his eyes turned down to envelop Florence.

Stoker's face contorted with rage and terror as he turned to face the man. He rose unsteadily to his feet.

The man in black was already backing into the mist.

"Noooo," Stoker screamed, bolting forward.

Doyle and Irving rushed forward as Stoker leaped into the air, reaching for the stranger. The man jumped back with an animal-like quickness, disappearing into the fog. Stoker came into contact with nothing but vapor and slammed into the ground. Doyle and Irving almost tripped over their friend, stumbling to the ground beside him.

The three men got back on their feet. Stoker rushed back to Florence, kneeling beside her and looking in every direction. Doyle and Irving did the same from their position a few yards away.

A fluttering sound suddenly cut through the mist, similar to that of a bird's flapping wings.

Doyle looked up into the fog as something swooped out of the mist, wings beating wildly. It happened so quickly, and the night was so dark, none of them could make out what it was. Doyle and Irving ducked, swatting the air with their arms to keep whatever it was away from them. The creature circled their heads, then shot up through the open roof, disappearing into the night.

A gentle but bone-chilling breeze sprung up and the mist began to clear. "What in bloody hell was that?" Irving cried out.

"I couldn't make it out," Doyle replied.

Doyle returned to Stoker and Florence while Irving kept a keen watch. "Did you see where he got off to?" Irving called out.

"No, but keep a good watch," Doyle answered.

"Should we go after him?" Irving asked. "He can't have gotten far."

"Mrs. Stoker is our first concern," Doyle replied as he knelt down beside her. As Stoker worriedly looked on, Doyle drew on his early medical training. He checked Florence's pulse, and then gently probed her neck and shoulders for injuries.

"What if he's still here? He could come at us again," Irving said. Neither Doyle nor Stoker replied. "The place is so large. It's likely he's still here. We have to—"

"He's gone," Stoker interrupted. Then more evenly, "I assure you, he left us."

Doyle helped Stoker move Florence into a more comfortable position. "She's got some nasty bruising around her throat, but there's no permanent harm," Doyle assured Stoker.

Stoker nodded, but kept his eyes on his wife.

Irving joined them, his eyes still roaming around the sanctuary. "Well, there's no sign of him, thank God. Good heavens, what was all that about?"

"We're fine," Stoker moaned. "We're fine, now."

"Who was that?" Irving asked. "And what's his quarrel with you?"

"He must be mad, whoever he is," Doyle posed.

Florence moaned, beginning to regain consciousness. Another clap of thunder seemed to crack open the clouds and a heavy rain began falling.

"Please, help me get her down to the village," Stoker implored. "Please."

CHAPTER 62

Doyle stepped away from the bed and joined Irving near the door of Florence's room. "She'll be fine with a good night's rest," he announced. "Although I suspect the memory of it will take longer to heal."

The three men had helped Florence down the Church Stairs in the pouring rain and through the village streets to Number 4 Crescent Terrace. The exhaustion showed on them all, and they were chilled and soaked to the bone by the time they reached the boardinghouse.

Florence lay in bed under the covers, Stoker sitting beside her on the bed. They all had changed into dry clothes. Doyle had returned to check on Florence's condition one more time before letting her get to sleep. Irving had stopped in to show his concern just as Doyle was finishing up.

From the warmth and comfort of the room, the sound of the rain hitting the roof and splashing against the windowpanes was almost comforting. The thunder was infrequent, now, and some distance away.

"I'm sorry," Stoker said to his wife.

She gripped his hand tightly. "What is all this about?" she asked him, her voice thin and tired.

"I will tell you everything. But after you've gotten some rest."

"The blighter's insane," Doyle stated for at least the fifth time that evening.

"That's obvious," Irving agreed.

"We'll inform the police straight away, Mrs. Stoker. You have our assurance," Doyle said, reaching for the door.

"No," Stoker cried, jumping up from the bedside.

Doyle paused, looking back at Stoker. "Why on earth not?"

"No. Not the police, please."

"Think of what you're saying, man. You saw what he did. The man's dangerous. You want him taking hold of some other innocent woman in the village?" Doyle argued.

"Please, out of consideration for my family," Stoker pleaded, looking down at Florence.

Florence was watching her husband closely, just as confused by his position as the rest of them. There was more to this matter than any of them had imagined.

"A scandal now would certainly hurt the Lyceum. It's not only my livelihood, but Stoker's as well," Irving observed. "And then there are the negotiations for the rights to your play."

"I'm not totally convinced, but your point isn't lost," Doyle answered. He took a few moments to consider the situation. "You needn't worry about any bad publicity, not from me," he added. "But my condition is that we receive a full explanation of this madness. Tonight."

"Of course. I owe you all at least that. Especially after what you've risked because of my foolishness," Stoker agreed. "But I'd like to speak with you gentlemen, in your rooms, if you don't mind." He bent over Florence and kissed her forehead. "I won't be long. Please, rest."

Florence nodded. She was halfway to a deep sleep before the three of them had even left the room.

CHAPTER 63

Once in the hallway, they agreed to continue their discussion in Doyle's room. They were no sooner inside with the door closed behind them when Stoker said, "Florence and I must return to London at once."

"We all must, but would you mind telling us what it was we saw tonight?" Doyle asked.

"You saw him looking at her like that. I must get her away from here."

"What was it we saw up there?" Irving asked.

Stoker slumped, exhausted, into a wooden chair. Doyle and Irving sat down on the bed facing him.

"I'm not certain myself," Stoker replied. "I thought I knew once, but not now. Our meeting, I thought it was a blessing. Now what have I become? An accomplice to murder? I don't even know."

"Murder," Irving repeated.

"I haven't hard proof, but you saw him. You saw what he did," Stoker moaned.

"What's his name?" Doyle inquired.

"Tepes. On one occasion, he referred to himself as *Voivode*.

"Voivode?" Doyle repeated.

"Romanian for, well, some kind of ruler or warlord. He's referred to himself as a prince on more than one occasion. It's possible he truly has some kind of aristocratic heritage, but so far I've found no records documenting it."

"I still don't see how all of this started," Irving said.

Stoker buried his head in his hands, rubbing his temples for a moment, and then straightened up again. "I was just interested in starting a new book," he began. "I'd written nothing in some time and that frustrated me. So I took a few days to spend here."

"In Whitby?" Irving asked.

"Florence and I came across the place on our way to Scotland several years ago," Stoker explained. "I've vacationed here many times since. If I'm writing, I'll often spend a weekend. There are few distractions; I get a good deal done."

"But how did you meet this Tepes fellow?" Doyle asked.

Stoker explained how Tepes had first approached him walking along the jetty those few months ago. He continued with all the events that came to mind leading up to their first exchange of information at The Spaniards.

"I still didn't know what I wanted to write about," Stoker revealed. "But then he told me a story involving a vampire preying on a village at the foot of the Carpathians. Well, several years ago I met Professor Arminius Vambery at the Lyceum."

"We had occasion to meet Professor Vambery as well," Doyle admitted.

"That explains a great deal," Stoker remarked. He paused to collect his thoughts and then continued. "Vambery and I dined together after the performance, and somewhere in the course of our conversation he mentioned a few of the superstitions he'd encountered during his travels. The stories concerning vampires from the Moldavia, Transylvania, and Wallachia districts particularly intrigued me. A short time later, I was spending an evening in the library, just leafing through a few books. I came across two or three fictions about vampires. They were older works and really quite dreadful. Very melodramatic and not based on any factual information."

"Factual information. About vampires?" Irving chuckled.

"What I meant was that none of them seemed to draw from the original superstitions, the authentic folktales, like those I heard from Vambery," Stoker clarified.

"Alright," Irving acknowledged.

"Years passed without me thinking about the topic," Stoker continued. "But when Tepes first spoke of the creatures, it fueled my interest again."

A passionate spark replaced the tiredness in Stoker's eyes. His voice took on a fervent energy as he continued. "I was certain I could write a better book than those others. Perhaps even a brilliant book. None of my other work, none of my other stories have made a mark. I was certain that this topic, if handled properly, could be remarkable."

"I've found all your writing to be quite good," Irving said. "A bit dark, perhaps, but entertaining."

"I'd have to agree," Doyle added.

"Even so, hardly a soul knows I've written anything at all."

"How can you say that?" Irving asked.

"All I want is recognition of my own. Recognition for my work."

"Dear Lord, man," Irving asserted. "Everyone in England knows you're the backbone of the Lyceum. The place would be boarded up in a fortnight without you."

"Yes, and that's it exactly," Stoker scoffed, resentment again returning to his tone. "Sir Henry Irving and Stoker. Stoker and the Lyceum. Sir Henry's man. That's what I'm known for."

"That's not true. Not to me," Irving insisted.

"Do you know what it's like?" Stoker asked. "Do you know what it's like to work among the Bernard Shaws of the world, the heads of state, the performers celebrated everywhere they go, royalty that calls us by our given names? Can you imagine how I feel when they look at me but all they see is you or the Lyceum?"

Irving was preparing to respond, but Stoker continued. "And you," he gestured at Doyle. "At least before you began working on producing your play at the Lyceum, Sherlock Holmes remained at a tolerable distance. Now I have to stare into his face every day. I don't begrudge you your success, but I can't help envying it. For once, I wanted to accomplish something that would set *me* apart. Something that would bring genuine success."

The outburst plunged the room into an uncomfortable silence.

No one spoke for several moments. Irving stared at Stoker in disbelief.

Doyle waited and watched until the scowl on Stoker's face softened.

"So, you saw this new book as an important opportunity?" Doyle prodded.

Stoker nodded, his eyes fixed on the floor.

"For as much as it might matter, I've written plenty of things that've flopped. It's happened to every author I know."

Stoker nodded again, but remained silent.

"I'd like to get back to Tepes, if you don't mind," Doyle continued. "You were, what, collaborating?"

"Yes, in a way," Stoker replied, his face darkening at the memory. "He was visiting England with the idea of moving here as a permanent resident. Tepes knew things; he had stories you can't even imagine. His perspective, the way he viewed everything, and the things he'd seen. Extraordinary. He told me he could help make my book something different, something exceptional. And as it happens, he wasn't boasting about that." Stoker paused, beginning to feel rather ill.

"Are you all right?" Irving inquired.

"I don't know. There's something insidious about him. When I realized he might be connected to murder, I kept it to myself. I think I knew, somehow, that I shouldn't be involved, but I couldn't bring myself to stop. And I was afraid to tell anyone should my telling cause them danger. I wanted to keep it from you as well, Mr. Doyle."

"Me? Why on earth would my knowing concern you?"

"Because you've authored stories from actual crimes before. If you, if you wrote a book about all this, it would be your work the public would want to read, not mine."

"My dear fellow," Doyle replied. "I fall short more often than I care to admit, but I've never stolen a story from anyone."

"I don't understand what made me stay silent for so long," Stoker said. "There's something hypnotic about him. It wasn't just his stories; there was something about *him*. He seemed like such a blessing in the beginning; a great stroke of luck to help me get what I've always wanted. Now what's happened? All I've accomplished is to help a murderous madman."

"And no marvel, for Satan himself is transformed into an angel of light," Irving quoted.

"Second Corinthians, chapter eleven, verse fourteen," Doyle said.

Irving's surprise was obvious.

"Being an atheist doesn't mean I haven't read the book," Doyle quipped. He then turned his attention back to Stoker. "What about your book? Is your research in a secure place?"

"Oh, what does it matter?" Stoker replied, anguished. "I didn't want anyone else involved in all this, but I must do something. I can't risk him ever getting near Florence again." Stoker rose from the chair, his eyes desperate. "Can I count on your help?"

"Of course," Doyle assured him. "But there's nothing to be done tonight. And there'll be no more trains until tomorrow, so we might as well try to put all of this aside until then."

"You can count on us. We'll see it through with you," Irving added.

Stoker nodded as he made his way to the door and pulled it open. He glanced back at them, the pain and exhaustion plain on his face.

CHAPTER 64

D oyle was so exhausted that he didn't rise until mid-morning. It turned out to be of no consequence when he discovered that Irving and the Stokers had overslept as well.

Mrs. Storm had been good enough to prepare a simple breakfast for them, even though they had missed the scheduled breakfast hour. Doyle appreciated that Mrs. Storm recognized Florence was in a fragile state and pampered her with attention.

Now Doyle, Stoker, and Florence stood on the platform at West Cliff Station, preparing to board the early afternoon train to London. Irving was inside the station purchasing their tickets.

The good night's sleep and a pleasant breakfast had especially benefited Florence. She seemed much more herself, although a bit more quiet than usual.

Doyle watched her, standing next to Stoker, her arm linked through his. She was a most remarkable woman, strong, and understanding of her husband's character. Doyle was certain Louise would like Florence very much if they ever met.

Irving returned with the tickets. "Here we are," he said with cheer, glad to be returning home. "We'll all be safe at home in a few hours."

"I'd like to think so," Stoker remarked.

"Why wouldn't we," Doyle asked. "Tepes may have intentions of traveling to London, but he has no way of locating any of us."

Stoker's face darkened at the remark. Doyle felt uneasy at the reaction and began to ask Stoker to elaborate regarding his concerns, but the boarding call sounded for their train. Along with the other passengers gathered on the platform, they began moving toward their carriage.

☧

While the Stokers and their companions entered their compartment, two porters pushed a large cart across the platform toward the baggage carriage at the rear of the train. Resting on the cart were two large crates. The crates were uniform in size, about seven feet in length, not quite a yard in height, and not quite a yard wide. Stenciled onto the side of each crate in flat, red paint was the name of the shipping concern: CARTER, PATERSON & CO., LONDON.

Doyle waited until they had settled in their first class compartment and the train left the station before he voiced his question to Stoker. "Is there reason to believe we won't be safe in London?"

"Aside from the fact that he may be in the city, you should be safe enough," Stoker replied.

"But not you?" Doyle pressed.

Stoker averted his eyes, embarrassed or uncomfortable at the question.

"How could he possibly find your home?" Irving asked.

Stoker hesitated before answering. "My own foolishness, again. He always maintained an aloofness, but our talks did often take on a rather friendly air."

"Friendly," Doyle repeated.

"I know, I know," Stoker sighed. "He asked a myriad of questions. Customs, traditions, prices. He wanted to know which areas were suitable for buying property. I suppose that's when I told him where I lived, why I liked the area and such."

"Oh, dear God," Florence cried.

"I never mentioned our house number, but he knows we're in Chelsea Walk."

"Anything else you told him that might help us?" Doyle asked.

"Not much, really. I gave him the name of a solicitor, which I regret now, along with everything else."

Florence took her husband's hand. "I wish we could just stop talking about him."

"We must find him and stop him if we're ever to have any peace," Doyle stated.

"Stop him?" Stoker was incredulous.

"He's just a man," Doyle insisted. "Insane, but just a man."

"I hope that's the case," Stoker said.

"Of course it is," Irving insisted.

"At any rate, I think Florence should get away from London until this is settled," he said.

"That's wise," Irving agreed. He looked at Doyle. "Why not your place?"

"Undershaw? Certainly."

"Oh, but I wasn't thinking," Irving said. "What about Louise? Her condition?"

"I think it's the perfect answer. There's plenty of household help and I think company might do Louise some good." Addressing Florence, Doyle added, "She'd love to have you."

"What condition are you referring to, Mr. Doyle?" Florence asked with concern.

He explained the details of his wife's illness while Florence listened. Once he had finished, she reached over and took his hand.

"Considering how ill she is, how could I possibly impose?" Florence asked.

"Look here, I'll check with Louise first, and if I detect the slightest reluctance, we'll look for another solution," Doyle promised. "But I think having some company will do her some good."

"I don't know..." Florence hesitated. "Perhaps it is the best thing. That man is the last person ever I want to see again."

"Then it's settled," Stoker said. "And I'm going to find him," he added with resolve.

"*We* are going to find him," Doyle corrected.

CHAPTER 65

While the train changed locomotives in York, Doyle and Irving took a walk to stretch their legs. Left alone with Florence, Stoker told her the entire story regarding Tepes. He left out nothing, including his fears about possibly being a facilitator of murder.

Florence clung to her husband. "I still don't understand all this," she said.

"I know. There's much to explain. And I owe you far more than just an explanation."

"What do you mean?"

Stoker pulled her close to him. "The way I turned from you. The way I treated you. I still don't fully understand it myself. My pride, my selfishness, I let him use it all. I let him use it to turn me from everything that's important."

Florence rested her head on his shoulder. He placed a tender kiss on her forehead. After a few moments, she looked up at him.

"Bram, do you still want a child with me?" Florence asked.

Surprised, he looked at her with wide open eyes. "I always have."

"I think we should, then."

"What?" He couldn't seem to grasp what she was saying.

"It's what I want, too, now. I don't know what I was thinking before, all those years. I'm ashamed."

"But what's brought this on? Why now?" he asked.

"I've never been so terrified, last night, thinking I might lose you."

"But you didn't."

She looked up at her husband. "But if anything had happened, what would be left? I mean, what would be left of you, of us? Do you understand?"

"I think so."

"And I've had so much time to think; all this time I thought you might be leaving me," Florence continued.

"I never thought of leaving you," he reassured her.

"Perhaps not, but I just kept thinking of the things we've done together. There weren't enough of them, not for me. But having a child, what more important a thing could we do together? What could be more lasting?"

"Nothing I can think of," he answered.

They held on to each other in silence for some time. And then a lengthy kiss lasted until the train began moving again.

It was eight o'clock in the evening when the train pulled into King's Cross Station. Their cab stopped at the curb in front of Number 27 Cheyne Walk less than an hour later. Stoker retrieved his and Florence's bags from the driver. Insisting on seeing the Stokers inside, Doyle instructed the driver to wait.

"Tillie," Stoker called out, once they were in the foyer.

The young maid appeared from the rear of the house and carried the Stokers' bags upstairs. Florence thanked Doyle and Irving for their help and then followed the maid.

Stoker waited until Florence had climbed the stairs and was out of earshot. "We must act quickly."

"I agree," Irving said.

"As do I, of course," Doyle added. "But there's nothing more we can do tonight. I suggest we all get a good night's rest, and then go about this fresh tomorrow."

"Florence cannot remain here," Stoker insisted.

"I'll wire home in the morning and make arrangements for her stay at Undershaw," Doyle promised.

"You'll not be leaving her tonight. She'll be safe with you here," Irving pointed out to Stoker. Then, to Doyle, "Meet us at the Lyceum. Say, around eleven," Irving said.

"Eleven?" Stoker protested. "We're wasting valuable time."

"We've been away from the theater for days. There's business to conduct, and you do still have a job," Irving reprimanded.

Stoker did not look happy, but shrugged his agreement.

"We'll begin tracking your man tomorrow," Doyle assured him. "You said earlier you referred Tepes to a solicitor. Who would that be?" Doyle removed a pencil and notepad from his inside coat pocket.

"Billington," Stoker replied. "A Mr. Morris Billington."

"Address?"

"All I can recall is the name."

"He's not your man?"

Stoker shook his head. "Our solicitor specializes in contracts and copyright work. He referred me to Mr. Billington as a man with a more general practice."

"All right then, I'll see what I can find on him in the morning and we'll have something to start with by the time we meet," Doyle said.

Stoker nodded. "Whatever we do, we're best doing it during daylight."

CHAPTER 66

I t was shortly after ten o'clock when they found the body. Doyle knelt over Tillie, holding a lantern. Stoker, doing his best to hide how upset he was, stood beside him. Sir Henry remained with Florence, offering her what support he could, at the foot of the porch steps several feet away.

"I called out for her," Florence sobbed. "She's always so prompt, but this time she didn't come."

"How long ago was this?" Doyle inquired.

"Shortly after we arrived from the station. Not even a half-hour. When I couldn't find her, I came to you."

The dead girl was stretched out at the rear corner of the house. The neckline of her dress was ripped away and a small, but swollen and discolored wound marred her throat. It was as if some animal had fiercely torn away the flesh. And every inch of visible skin was disturbingly pale.

"Perplexing," Doyle muttered.

"What's that?" Stoker asked.

"There's no blood. She's lost a good deal of it, but there's no pooling anywhere. The wound on her neck is the only sign of violence I can see. It's enough for substantial blood loss, but there's no blood on or around her body."

"Are you ready to consider what I've been trying to tell you?" Stoker asked.

Ignoring the question, Doyle studied the corpse, trying to make sense of what he was seeing.

A deep sob from Florence drew Doyle's attention. "I'm very sorry," Doyle said as he stood up, observing she was shaken.

Florence began crying. Doyle ushered the Stokers back to the house, guiding them inside with Irving following along. They settled in the sitting room, with Bram sitting next to Florence on the sofa, holding her close.

There had been a rough agreement that involving the police could be counterproductive and even dangerous. But Tillie's brutal murder went far in changing opinions. Florence, especially, felt they had a responsibility to their employee to handle the situation properly. Tillie had been like family all these years. Bram, surprisingly, supported her position.

"We may be in agreement the police are going to be involved," Irving said. "But we still have to determine what exactly to tell them."

"They won't believe the truth," Stoker insisted.

"They'll see for themselves that a man free of his right mind did this killing," Doyle retorted. "Stay as close to the truth as possible. Mrs. Stoker went looking for her maid. We joined the search and found the body. None of us witnessed the killing firsthand, so don't know who might have killed the poor girl."

"There's no way to anticipate all the questions the police might ask," Stoker cautioned.

"No, but I'll have considered most of the reasonable questions by the time I return," Doyle answered.

"You're leaving? Where?" Irving asked.

"They're in no condition to go for the police right now," Doyle said, nodding toward the Stokers. "I'll fetch them. And I suggest you return home, or to the theater. Anywhere but here."

"I'll go with you. None of us should be out alone right now," Irving said.

"Your celebrity is certain to draw a good deal of unwanted attention, being connected to something like this."

"We've moved well beyond the point of being concerned with our own bad publicity," Irving sighed. "There's much more at stake here and we best look out for each other."

Doyle nodded and then turned to Stoker. "We won't be long. I'll do most of the talking once we're back with the police. Just try to follow wherever I go with it all."

Stoker nodded his understanding.

With a last sympathetic nod to Florence, Doyle gestured to Irving and the two men left on their errand.

CHAPTER 67

Within twenty minutes, six uniformed bobbies arrived at the Stoker home. Stoker directed them to the rear yard where they began looking over the crime scene. A few minutes later, Stoker answered the front bell and showed a middle-aged, serious man with an impressive moustache into the sitting room.

"Good heavens, Lestern. You pulled this one?" Doyle greeted the man.

"I did. You know something about it?"

"What could I possibly know?" Doyle gestured toward the Stokers. "Mr. and Mrs. Bram Stoker. This is their home. And you must recognize Sir Henry Irving."

The police officer greeted everyone in turn.

"This is Inspector Gregory Lestern. Many years with Scotland Yard," Doyle concluded the introductions.

"I'm very sorry we're meeting under such sad circumstances," Lestern addressed himself to Florence. "My condolences."

She managed a sad, grateful smile.

"I'll need to see the body," the Inspector said to Doyle. "And then I'm sure I'll have some questions for you."

"Of course," Doyle answered. "This way."

Doyle showed the Inspector from the room and returned a few minutes later, a bobby following behind him. The bobby stood in the doorway as

Doyle took a seat. Ten minutes later, Lestern returned and began his questioning.

Stoker explained the events leading to the discovery of the body, telling the truth, but omitting he was certain about the identity of the killer. Florence sat in silence while her husband related the facts, staring at her hands folded in her lap.

"How are you involved, Mr. Doyle?" Lestern asked, turning his attention to Doyle.

"I wouldn't say I am," Doyle responded. "Sir Henry and I are in negotiations on a business venture."

"You may know Mr. Stoker handles business matters for me and the Lyceum Theatre," Sir Henry offered. "We were all meeting here tonight to discuss details of our arrangement."

"The tragedy took place while we were here. That's all there is to it," Doyle said.

"A coincidence, then?"

"Nothing more."

"You touched nothing on or around the body?" Lestern asked Doyle.

"Of course not," Doyle answered, sounding just offended enough.

Inspector Lestern remained quiet for some time, studying each of them closely. "And you, Mrs. Stoker, do you have anything to add?"

Florence looked up at him through tear-glazed eyes. "It's as they've said, Inspector."

Lestern turned his gaze back to Doyle. "We've known each other for some time, you and I."

"We have, indeed."

"I've seen you at several murder scenes over the years. You normally have a good deal more to offer than you're saying here."

"I'm finding it quite vexing myself that I can't help more." Doyle felt himself growing flushed as he spoke.

"Very well," Lestern sighed in frustration. "You'll be available, of course, as we proceed with the investigation. I'm sure we'll have more questions."

"Of course," Stoker responded.

"We're at your disposal," Doyle added. "And one other thing, if you will, Inspector?"

"What's that?"

"Sir Henry and I would be grateful if you can refrain from mentioning our names should you find yourself talking to the press. We're both fairly well known and it would be unseemly to bring any more upset to this family through additional publicity."

"I'll do what I can." Inspector Lestern eyed them all with a thoughtful gaze for several seconds. "My men will attend to the body," he said, striding from the room.

Irving waited until the Inspector was gone and then looked at Doyle with some amusement. "Really?"

"What?" Doyle asked.

"Lestern?"

"What of him?"

Irving was incredulous. "Lestern, Lestrade? He's your Inspector Lestrade."

"I thought you never read my books," Doyle returned with a dry tone.

"I don't believe I ever said I hadn't read one," Irving answered, chagrined.

Doyle had little desire to discuss a character in one of his stories. He still felt the frustration of not being able to tell Lestern all he suspected, all the facts he'd begun to fear.

With no clues to find, the police remained at the house for less than an hour. Doyle made certain that Stoker kept Florence distracted as two bobbies carried Tillie's body away on a cart.

Now, with the house to themselves, the discussion turned to how they had handled the police. "That was damn frustrating," Doyle began. "My apologies," he added for Florence, aware of his language. "A much as I'd have liked to tell Lestern everything we know, I've still got no reasonable explanation for it all."

"No explanation they'd believe, anyway," Stoker agreed.

"We're certain as to the identity of the murderer and still don't know enough to help the police, let alone ourselves," Doyle continued. Not to mention how it would look, the creator of the famous Sherlock Holmes at a loss for answers in an official police investigation, he thought to himself.

"I'd say our greatest risk is in the police finding out that we've withheld information," Irving said.

"Telling the police the whole truth in this matter might prove disastrous," Stoker fretted.

"You're holding onto that supernatural nonsense?" Irving groaned. "What he did is sick and brutal, but he's a madman and nothing more."

"That's your explanation for it?" Stoker challenged. "We'd better make it our business to find him before the police do. They won't know what they're dealing with, and I don't want to see any more killings."

"Enough," Florence ordered, rising from her seat. "I can't stand any more of it. Not tonight."

The men, surprised at her sudden outburst, stood silent, staring at her.

"I cannot stay in this house tonight. I will not," she exclaimed.

"Of course not," Stoker assured her.

"A hotel for a night or two isn't a bad idea," Doyle agreed.

"I'll see to it straight away," Stoker said.

"Then I'll put some things together for us," Florence said. "And once we've settled in, we need to send word to Tillie's sister. She's her only family." Without another word, Florence hurried from the room.

CHAPTER 68

The police learned very little from Tillie's corpse and released the body late in the day following her murder. Her funeral took place at twelve thirty the next afternoon in the graveyard behind a little church in Clerkenwell, the church she and her sister had attended since they were children. Society considered it unseemly for an employer to attend any event connected with the personal life of a servant, but the Stokers never even considered this social distinction.

Stoker chose to remain with Florence throughout the morning. The night before, Doyle explained he had business to attend to and would not be available until the late morning. Irving, too, expressed the need to attend to some personal matters before going to the theater. So, there was nothing to be done about their manhunt until later in the day and his wife needed him more.

Standing close to Florence, Bram found his mind drifting away from the words of the minister, an older man with many funerals behind him. He gazed at Tillie's sister, a few years older than her deceased sibling, weeping at the side of the grave. The thought that he had brought this tragedy to her family troubled him deeply. There was little he could do to put it right, but he would do everything in his power to make certain no one else suffered. Stoker found himself drawn back to the words coming from the minister.

The old man was reading, his well-worn bible open in his hands. "Behold, I show you a mystery; We shall not all sleep, but we shall all be changed. In a moment, in the twinkling of an eye, at the last trump: for the trumpet shall sound, and the dead shall be raised incorruptible, and we shall be changed. For this corruptible must put on incorruption, and this mortal must put on immortality. So when this corruptible shall have put on incorruption, and this mortal shall have put on immortality, then shall be brought to pass the saying that is written, Death is swallowed up in victory. O death, where is thy sting? O grave, where is thy victory? The sting of death is sin; and the strength of sin is the law. But thanks be to God, which giveth us the victory through our Lord Jesus Christ."

The ground crew lowered the coffin into the freshly dug grave. The service was well attended and Stoker thought it likely that most of the congregation had turned out. They were all working class folk, stoic and quiet as they grieved the loss of a friend.

The mourners began filing past Tillie's sister as the first shovelful of dirt fell on the coffin lid. They offered their condolences and prayers before returning to their jobs where they'd work longer shifts to make up for taking time off.

Stoker ushered Florence through the assemblage. He felt his soul being pulled in two different directions. He was impatient to return to the Lyceum, to get back to the hunt with Doyle and Irving, but his affection for Tillie and the guilt he felt over her death dictated that he do exactly what he was doing at the moment.

Florence, in an impressive act of will, held back tears as she expressed her own grief to Tillie's sister. The woman was grateful for the words and even more so when Stoker assured their help should she need anything.

With everything said that could be said, Bram and Florence walked from the graveyard.

That morning at their hotel, Florence had expressed her readiness to return home. He would see her safely back to Cheyne Walk and then proceed on to the Lyceum to meet Doyle and Irving.

CHAPTER 69

T he morning did not begin well for Arthur Conan Doyle. He had spent the night at the little flat he maintained for short stays in London on Berkley Street, just off of Piccadilly. Being more tired than he realized, he had overslept.

He was preparing to leave the flat when the front bell rang. Doyle found a young messenger at the door with an envelope addressed to him. It was from the manager of a bank he used, requesting that he come round at his earliest convenience to discuss a matter of great importance.

Doyle rushed through a mediocre breakfast at the nearest cookshop he could find and then stopped at a telegraph office to send a wire to Louise regarding Florence's visit. He instructed her to reply to the Lyceum where he planned to be sometime later that morning.

The bank problem was nothing more than a need to exchange funds between two accounts in order to pay some of Louise's medical bills. By the time an appropriate strategy had been determined, wires sent and paperwork signed, it was almost lunchtime.

Doyle was late, not arriving at the Lyceum until after two o'clock. He had no sooner stepped through the door than he spied Stoker hurrying toward him. "Where on earth have you been?" Stoker blurted. Then, seeing Doyle's austere reaction to the greeting, "I'm sorry, Mr. Doyle. It's just been very difficult... the waiting."

"Of course," Doyle replied. He described the difficulties of the morning, but his explanation did little to calm Stoker.

There was a fair amount of activity backstage. Harry Loveday was engaged in a somewhat heated conversation with a thin, odd looking man. The odd little fellow was holding an open blueprint, and there was a good deal of pointing and gesturing originating from Loveday's side of the discussion.

"Are you preparing another production?" Doyle asked Stoker.

"Not us. A producing company we've leased the facility to. They opened last night."

Irving was waiting in the Beefsteak room, leafing through a manuscript in one of the leather wing chairs near the hearth. As they walked in, he rose and came forward, picking up a telegram from the banquet table.

"Thank heaven you've gotten here," Irving said. He handed Doyle the telegram. "This arrived for you."

Doyle placed his hat on the corner of the table and then opened the telegram.

"I'm just about at my limit with him," Irving said, glaring at Stoker.

"I am sorry," Doyle apologized. "I've already explained my morning to Stoker.

"Not that it should have mattered. I had enough to catch up on here, and Bram's only been back from the funeral a short time."

Doyle skimmed the telegram. "Well, we still don't have an answer from Louise."

"The wire didn't come from Undershaw?" Stoker couldn't hide his disappointment.

"No, it is, but from our butler. Apparently, her doctor took Louise to a sanitarium near Chippenham this morning to try a new treatment. They're expected back this evening."

"Can't we send a wire to the sanitarium?" Stoker asked.

"Considering the hour they're likely already traveling," Doyle answered. "It's certain they'd be traveling by the time the wire reached Chippenham."

"We must think of something else," Stoker insisted.

"I didn't know Louise would be gone today."

"Of course not."

"It's only one more night," Irving observed.

Stoker shook his head. "I won't rest easy until I know Florence is out of the city."

"Well, as Sir Henry said, it's only another night. I'm happy to stay in Chelsea with you, if that's a help," Doyle offered.

"Yes, thank you. Since there doesn't seem to be much else to do," Stoker conceded.

Collinson entered carrying a tray laden with an antique silver tea service and a plate of lemon biscuits. "Gentlemen."

Doyle acknowledged Collinson with a polite smile and then turned back to Stoker and Irving. "I'm certain we'll hear from Louise this evening. In the meantime, there's much to discuss."

Collinson put the tray down on the end of the banquet table.

"I thought we could all use a bit of refreshment," Irving explained.

"Lovely silver," Doyle said, looking closer at the tea service.

"From America," Irving explained. "I found it on one of our tours there. Colonial. Cost me a pretty penny."

"Forty-nine dollars and eighty-two cents American. Plus two dollars for the packing," Collinson reported.

Irving's eyebrows arched.

Collinson shrugged. "I saw the bill of lading when I uncrated it." When Irving's eyebrows failed to return to their normal position, Collinson retreated. "Gentlemen." He closed the door behind him.

"Remarkable," Doyle commented as he sat down at the table. "That memory of his."

Following Doyle's lead, Irving and Stoker took seats. Irving poured tea for Doyle and himself; Stoker declined with a brusque wave of his hand.

"I did manage to accomplish one thing this morning," Doyle reported, pulling a piece of notepaper from his pocket. "Morris Billington's address acquired from Kelly's Post Office Directory. He keeps offices in Sackville Street."

"That's excellent," Stoker responded. "And I went around to see Professor Vambery before I came here. I gave him what latest information I have on Tepes."

"What can Vambery do?" Irving asked.

"Perhaps a bit of research will tell us more about what we're dealing with. He'll contact me if he finds something."

"Who knows how long that might take?" Irving sighed.

"Yes, but we need to call on Billington in the meantime, anyway," Stoker stated, clenching his fists. "We'll see him at once."

"What can we hope to get from this Mr. Billington?" Irving asked.

Doyle thought a moment before answering. "If Tepes followed Stoker's recommendation and secured the man's services, then there'll be documentation of some sort. But Billington won't want to give us much, I would think. He won't want to violate the confidentiality of a client."

"And if we get some scrap of information that leads us to the man?" Irving inquired.

"Then I think we should notify the police. We keep watch on him until they arrive."

Stoker shook his head, exasperated. "No. No, we cannot bring in the police."

"I don't understand your reluctance about the police," Doyle argued.

"I've told you. They won't know what they're dealing with."

Irving scoffed. "You don't believe that Scotland Yard can handle a madman?"

"If that's all he is."

Doyle leaned toward Stoker. "We've already had this conversation. Do you seriously believe that this man is anything more than a violent maniac?"

Stoker stared at Doyle, the tension coiled within him like an overwound spring. "After all, we've seen, can you say with all certainty that a maniac is all he is?"

The two men glared in silence at each other for several moments. Finally, Irving broke the stalemate. "All right, all right. We've been around and around about this. And it's obvious we'll not settle it now. I propose we move forward and find the man, then let the circumstances dictate our decision."

"Well, as long as we make some forward progress, I say it's an acceptable suggestion," Doyle commented.

"Yes," Stoker added. "Anything to get us out of this room. The sooner the better."

Doyle nodded, leaning back in his chair. "Then the first order of business is to call on our Mr. Billington. We collect whatever information we can from him. We return to Chelsea to assure Mrs. Stoker's safety. When we receive Louise's wire, we'll be well positioned to make arrangements for Florence's travel to Hindhead. And then we can pursue whatever information we have from Billington first thing in the morning."

"Excellent," Irving agreed. "Florence will be safely away by the time we take any action against our man."

Stoker practically leaped from his chair. "Then let's be off. We've wasted enough time."

CHAPTER 70

A twenty minute cab ride brought Stoker, Doyle and Irving to Sackville Street. The street constituted a respectable business area just west of Piccadilly Circus. A simple brass plaque mounted beside the building entrance displayed the name of Morris Billington, Solicitor. The building entrance opened into a small foyer where a stairwell led to the upper floors.

They climbed the stairs and found themselves in a spacious hallway. They found Morris Billington's office at the very end of the hallway.

Stoker reached to open the door, but the knob would not turn. "Locked," he muttered, tapping his fist against the wood. Receiving no answer from within, he knocked again, harder. Still, there was no response.

"The chap must be out," Irving observed.

"Hello," Stoker called out, expressing his growing frustration by knocking harder than before. "Mr. Billington."

The door of the office belonging to an adjacent bookkeeping firm opened and a bespectacled man in his late twenties poked his head out into the hall. He took his time looking them over as Stoker hammered his fist against the door. "Can I help you, gentlemen?" he asked.

"Ah, I'm sorry," Doyle responded. "We've obviously disturbed you."

"Not at all. I heard the knocking and heard Mr. Billington's name."

"It's important we see him," Stoker said.

"He's not in, I'm afraid. That's why I came out," the man explained. "He asked me to tell anyone who might stop by that he's in Bedford for the day on behalf of a client."

"That's just wonderful," Stoker fumed.

"He's traveling back early morning and said he'd do his best to be in the office by ten or ten thirty."

"Do you know where we can find him in Bedford?" Stoker asked.

"I'm afraid I don't."

"We'll return tomorrow, then," Irving smiled. "Thank you."

The man nodded. "Not at all," he replied, withdrawing back into the office and closing the door.

Stoker appeared tired and frustrated as they made their way back toward the stairs. "What else can go wrong?" he asked.

"Perhaps it's best none of us ask that question at this point," Irving responded.

"There's no use dwelling on it. We can only do what we can do," Doyle said, checking his watch. "And all that's left for us at this hour is to return to Chelsea."

Doyle led them down the stairs and out onto the street. He couldn't help but note the position of the sun. Another night would be upon them soon enough.

Arriving in Chelsea in a four-wheeler, they found Florence waiting for them in the doorway of Number 27, a coat draped over her arm. Next to her, Stetson in hand, stood Morgan Quincey. "Hold the cab," Florence called out.

Stoker could see she was anxious and upset.

"Thank God you're back," she blurted out.

"What's wrong? You're all right?" Stoker asked.

"I'm afraid I've upset your wife," Quincey said.

"I'm such a fool," she continued. "If anything's happened to her."

"To who?" Stoker asked.

"Lucy." she lamented.

"What's happened, Florrie?" Stoker probed.

"Mr. Quincey's just come from Lucy's. Something's wrong," Florence lamented.

"What's happened, Mr. Quincey?" Stoker asked.

"I've kept hoping to see Miss Westen again ever since I met her at the theater on that opening night, but with her illness and all haven't managed it," Quincey explained. "Last week I finally sent word to her home, asking if I might call. She agreed to a visit. It was set for this afternoon. I guess I'm not too patient."

"She didn't answer," Florence said.

"When I saw nobody was home, I came over here," Quincey continued. "Thought Mrs. Stoker might know what'd happened, the ladies being friends and all."

"Bram, he knows Lucy. Tepes knows Lucy and he's been to her home."

"Who's Tepes?" the American asked.

"Dear God," Stoker said.

Florence's concern infected them all.

"You said no one was home?" Doyle asked Quincey.

"I rang the bell, knocked on the door. More than's considered polite, I'm sure."

"We need to go there now," Doyle insisted.

"We'll see to it," Stoker assured Florence, starting for the cab with Doyle and Irving close behind him.

"I'm going, too," Florence insisted, pushing past her husband. Her tone was so determined that the men offered no argument.

"Count me in," Quincey volunteered.

CHAPTER 71

They spent the cab ride filling in Morgan Quincey on the circumstances leading up to his arrival at the Stoker home. He remained quiet for the most part. His only comment was that he thought he'd seen and heard everything, but guessed now he hadn't.

Lucinda Westen's Lawrence Street home was quiet when they arrived. Their repeated ringing of the bell and knocking went unanswered. They made their way around to the back.

Arriving at the service door, Stoker broke the small window beside the door without hesitation. Reaching through the window, he unlatched the door, and they entered.

Stoker knew that something was wrong the moment they stepped into the kitchen. Quincey sensed it, too, pulling his knife from under his coat, holding it at the ready. A faint, coppery smell of blood hung in the air and the stillness, the unnatural quiet of the place was unsettling.

"Lucy," Florence called out. "Lucy. It's Florrie and Bram, and Mr. Quincey." A void of silence swallowed her voice.

His wife looked up at him, apprehension filling her eyes. Stoker took her hand, offering reassurance he didn't feel himself. He led them through the kitchen doorway and down the hallway toward the front of the house.

He saw the body before the rest of them and instantly turned, trying to block Florence's view. Despite his effort, she saw it, began to scream, but stifled it by burying her face in his chest. Doyle, Irving, and Quincey stepped past them into the foyer.

"God in heaven," Irving muttered.

Annie Beth lay on her back, her head lodged up against the wall beside the door at a grotesque angle. Her eyes, empty of life, stared up at the ceiling. Her face was drawn in an expression of terror and pain. A pool of partially dried blood had soaked into her clothing and stained the floor beneath her body. A smeared trail of blood led from the corpse straight to the bottom of the stairs where a patch of the girl's bloody hair and scalp appeared to be growing from the splintered second step.

Florence wept as Stoker held her close. "I'm so sorry," he said.

While Quincey checked the adjoining rooms, Doyle stepped closer to the body. Looking up at the top of the stairway, he said, "This happened sometime last night."

"You're saying he did murder at Bram's home and then came here?" Irving asked, disbelief strong in his tone.

"Or he was here first and then moved on to your place," Doyle's voice trailed off as he looked from the stairwell to Annie Beth's body. "He threw her down the stairs with such force that when she struck the bottom, the momentum slid her across the floor to the wall."

"She was thrown?" Stoker tried to grasp the concept.

"It looks like her head didn't even touch the steps until here," Doyle said, pointing to the second step.

Quincey returned to the foyer. "Nothin' else down here I can see."

"We need to find Lucinda," Stoker said, his voice trembling. "Stay here," he instructed Florence.

Florence nodded, looking frail.

"Sir Henry, if you wouldn't mind staying with her?" Stoker asked.

Irving stepped over to Florence and placed a long, protective arm across her shoulder. "My privilege."

Stoker could hear his wife's whimpers as he, Doyle and Quincey climbed the stairs to the second floor. At first he had considered the American's presence an intrusion. But now he felt a certain comfort knowing that the man and his Bowie knife were bringing up the rear. They made their way along the upper hallway to Lucinda's bedroom door. Stoker hesitated a moment, then pushed the door open, and they stepped inside.

Lucinda, her body half-naked, was stretched on her back across the width of the bed. Her shoulders and head hung over the edge of the mattress, her long hair flowing to the floor. Her eyes were half-open, as if she were tired and having difficulty staying awake. An ugly wound, similar to the one on Tillie's body, blemished the beauty of her throat.

"God have mercy," Quincey murmured.

"We should've thought of this sooner," Stoker lamented.

"It's no one's fault," Doyle responded.

With focused urgency, Doyle approached the body, inspecting it closely. "There's no blood. Just like your girl."

"What have I done?" Stoker asked, panic surfacing in his voice. "We shouldn't stay here."

"Another moment," Doyle answered. Bending lower over the body, he asked himself, "What's this?" He touched his index finger to the corner of the dead woman's mouth and it came away with tiny flakes of dried blood. Using both hands, Doyle parted the cold lips.

"What are you doing?" Quincey asked, his nerves showing.

"There's blood in her mouth," said Doyle.

"A result of her injuries?" Quincey asked.

"I've no idea. It's all very odd." Doyle stepped back from the body.

Glancing anxiously at the bedroom door, as if Scotland yard might burst in on them at any moment, Quincey removed a handkerchief from an inside pocket and handed it to Doyle, who wiped the blood from his hands.

"I brought it on us all. First Tillie and now this. He's sending a message. He warned me not to trifle with him. We have to leave now."

Doyle gestured to Quincey to follow, took hold of Stoker's arm and ushered him back into the hallway. "As I understand it, Miss Westen met him before any of you."

"What does that matter now? Florence will never look at me the same again," Stoker groaned.

"Honestly, Stoker, I don't see how any of us will look at each other in the same way after all this," Doyle snapped. "Placing blame or taking blame is just a waste of energy at this point. We need to keep our heads. Mr. Quincey, I'm assuming we can count on your discretion."

Quincey nodded. "Anything you need, just tell me. Any man who'll do something like this doesn't deserve livin'."

Doyle hurried them toward the stairwell. "All right, then. Let's go back downstairs and decide how to handle this."

CHAPTER 72

It seemed prudent to handle the loss of Lucinda Westen just as responsibly as they had with Tillie's murder, through proper channels. It was the right thing to do for their friend. The police would easily see the link to the Stokers, but there was little sense in trying to hide it. It was also decided that, if possible, it was best to keep Doyle and Irving out of it this time.

After getting their stories straight, Doyle and Irving left Lawrence Street with the plan that the Stokers would meet them at a neighborhood pub three blocks away. Morgan Quincey left to find a cab that would return him to his hotel. There was no direct connection between him and Lucinda Westen, and Doyle saw no reason for him to submit himself to the scrutiny of the police.

Bram and Florence, clenching each other's hand, went in search of a constable and found one patrolling only a half-block away. It wasn't long before Lucinda Westen's home was swarming with police, once again directed by Inspector Lestern. He questioned them at the bottom of the front steps as several neighbors looked on.

For the most part, Florence remained silent while Bram provided the Inspector with their story. Just as he had in explaining Tillie's demise, he held mainly to the truth. His wife had scheduled to call on Miss Westen that afternoon. Arriving for the visit, Florence could get no one to answer the door. Her friend was always reliable and Florence became alarmed.

Returning home just ahead of her husband, Florence enlisted him to join her in a visit to Lawrence Street to check on their friend's welfare. Drawing no answer at their persistent ringing of the front doorbell, Bram broke in.

"Do either of you know anyone who might wish to harm Miss Westen?" Inspector Lestern asked.

It was the inevitable question and Stoker was ready for it. "We know she'd become involved with a foreign gentleman she met on opening night at the Lyceum. I saw them once together there."

"Name?"

"I'm not sure I ever heard Miss Westen give it," Stoker answered.

"Can you tell me what he looked like?"

"Rather tall, slender, an older man. Perhaps in his fifties."

"You didn't meet him at the theater?" Lestern probed.

"I only saw them from across the room."

Lestern remained silent for several seconds, absorbing the answers and never taking his eyes off of the Stokers.

"Your house girl and a dear friend murdered on the same night," Lestern cited with an insinuating tone. "Extraordinarily unusual, wouldn't you say?"

"Too horrible is more like it," Florence responded, tears beginning to well up in her eyes again.

"Are you accusing us of having something to do with this, inspector?" Stoker challenged.

Lestern looked apologetic. "You're a gentleman, sir, and considering your social and professional status, you'd never be seriously suspected for something like this."

"I was beginning to wonder," Stoker responded. "Are you saying the same person did these crimes?"

"I'm not saying anything. But two of the bodies bear similar wounds." Lestern shrugged.

"So, they were killed in the same manner?"

Lestern uttered a frustrated sigh. "We aren't sure what killed them as yet. The medical examiner says he's seen nothing like it before."

Florence, her emotional strength fading, issued a sob. "Do you have to go on about it so?"

"I am sorry, ma'am. It's my job but I don't mean to upset," the Inspector responded.

"If there's nothing more, Inspector, perhaps I can take her home now?" Stoker said.

Lestern hesitated, again staring unblinkingly at them for several seconds. "I suppose that's best for now," he answered. "Again, I'm very sorry Mrs. Stoker. Both of you." With a tip of his hat, the Inspector made his way back inside the murder house.

CHAPTER 73

After rendezvousing with Doyle and Irving, Stoker filled them both in on his encounter with the police as they all headed back to Cheyne Walk. Florence was weeping when they first arrived at the pub, but she soon regained composure as they made their way home.

Doyle had always shared the opinion that Florence Stoker was cold, but he believed now that the coolness was nothing more than a superficial, protective layer. He saw a warm and caring woman concerned for her husband, and grieving the loss of a dear close friend.

The moment they stepped foot in Number 27, Florence slumped into the nearest chair.

"Florence?" Stoker asked with concern.

"I'm just tired," she answered. "But there's so much to do, the arrangements for Lucy's funeral. She had no other family."

"Let's get you upstairs for some rest."

Florence objected, but he stopped her. "You'll feel much more capable once you've slept awhile."

Florence nodded her surrender and Stoker helped her up the stairs. Upon his return, he sought out the cook and issued instructions for dinner, advising her that Doyle and Irving would join them.

Doyle and Irving then followed Stoker into the sitting room where they sat and rested.

"She's exhausted," Stoker said, gesturing toward the upper floor. "And frightened."

"Who here isn't?" Irving asked.

From that point on, the conversation was sparse until the cook announced dinner well over an hour later.

Stoker excused himself and ascended the stairs. A few minutes later, he returned with Florence. Color had returned to her cheeks; the rest had apparently done her some good.

The cook prepared an excellent beefsteak pudding, serving it with a celery and chestnut salad. Dessert was a caramel custard that Doyle was so taken with, he requested and received, a second portion.

The entire meal was quiet and somewhat surreal, considering the events of the past two days. When someone spoke, they refrained from speaking about the heartbreaking events earlier in the afternoon. Even Stoker limited his conversation to Lyceum business and to asking Florence for details about the society events she was involved with.

As they left the dining room, Stoker turned to Doyle. "Would you consider staying here tonight? It would save some time in the morning."

"That would be a great help to me. The sooner I can get to bed, the better," Doyle answered. And then turning to Florence, "If it's not an inconvenience."

"Oh, no, Mr. Doyle. Honestly, I'll feel a good deal safer having both you and Bram here," Florence responded, her voice cracking with tension. "I'll just go see to your room."

She hurried up the stairs, shoulders bent low in her sadness. The men returned to the sitting room and sank into chairs, exhausted.

"It should be clear to you both now what he's capable of," Stoker said.

"After what I saw today, I'm not eager to get to the man before the police do," Irving remarked.

"I don't understand why we haven't heard from your wife," Stoker addressed Doyle.

"I suspect the doctor thought it wise to keep her in Chippenham a bit longer. I'll send another wire in the morning."

Stoker shifted uncomfortably in his chair, his fists clenched in his lap.

"This will all turn out well. We'll all see to it," said Doyle.

"Yes. I'm sorry. This horrid day, the waiting, it's just all so infuriating," Stoker responded. "If anything happens to Florence it'll be my fault."

Doyle leaned forward. "We'll certain make sure nothing happens."

"It was bad enough with those people in Whitby found dead," Stoker continued. "But now Lucy and her girl, and Tillie. Tillie, in our own home."

Doyle could see that Stoker was torturing himself. It must be like a nightmare that was becoming tangibly real for him, he thought.

Doyle observed Stoker staring at his clenched fists. Now that Florence was out of the room, the anxiety and tension began surfacing. To his credit, the man had forced it back for the comfort of his wife, but now it was boiling up again. Doyle understood and sympathized, but it was as if the man was about to explode.

Irving took a sip of sherry and stretched his long legs out from the chair. "So, tomorrow's going to be difficult. Billington won't be available to us until late morning."

"And at some point there'll be Miss Westen to attend to," Doyle posed. "Once the police release the body, there'll be the funeral, I mean."

"There must be something else to do," Stoker fretted. "I'll go mad tomorrow."

That was Doyle's concern. He was not looking forward to being in Stoker's company for the greater part of tomorrow, considering the man's current state. "We'll all have plenty to do," he responded. "Your wife is going to need you to see to the funeral arrangements."

"That should fill your morning," Irving said.

"I have some business in the morning, and Sir Henry, you have responsibilities that require your attention at the Lyceum."

"Indeed."

"We're all in need of some rest, but I wager you'll sleep better if we discuss the details of what's to be done tomorrow before we get it," Doyle said to Stoker.

Stoker nodded.

"Then let's get to it."

CHAPTER 74

Doyle and Irving were waiting in the hallway outside of Morris Billington's office by the time the solicitor arrived shortly before eleven in the morning.

Billington was in his early forties, a man of medium height and rather rotund in build. His blonde hair was beginning the transition to silver, with the most prominent patches evident on his muttonchop whiskers.

The solicitor recognized Sir Henry Irving and was rather excited by a visit from the well-known actor. When he discovered his other visitor was Arthur Conan Doyle, his excitement doubled.

Billington's suite comprised a roomy reception area and his personal office. Besides a sofa for guests, the outer office was heavy with bookshelves lined with the countless volumes mandatory to any office of law.

Billington opened the door to his private office to drop his satchel inside the door, and Doyle could see that there were even more filled bookshelves housed inside.

When he told the solicitor the purpose of their visit, his excitement dampened. Billington went on the defensive so quickly he forgot to even invite his guests to sit down.

"I'm sorry," Billington told them. "I shouldn't even confirm that the gentlemen you mentioned is one of my clients, but you're already certain enough of that."

"Mr. Billington," Irving began.

Billington held up his hands. "Sir Henry, you must understand. I have a responsibility to assure the confidence of every client I serve."

"Sir, it's important we locate this man as soon as possible," Doyle said. "At this point, you're the only hope we have."

Billington gazed down at his boots for several moments, then looked back at Doyle. "May I assume you're working for the police, sir?"

"I am not."

"Perhaps the purpose of your visit relates to another Holmes tale?"

"No. No on both counts," Doyle sighed with impatience. "But the matter is of even greater importance."

"Can you tell me what it is?" Billington asked.

"I'm afraid that we also need to maintain a certain confidentiality."

Billington again held up his hands in a helpless gesture. "Mr. Doyle, Sir Henry, you must understand. If only this were some sort of official inquiry. In that case, I might be able—"

A loud sigh from Henry Irving interrupted him. Irving slumped into the nearest chair, burying his head in his hands. "That's it, then," he moaned. "We're through."

Doyle stared at Irving with confusion.

"My dear sir," Billington stammered.

"We'll never find him, and mother'll soon be gone," Irving groaned. He began weeping, his head still cradled in his hands.

Doyle looked at his friend in horrified astonishment. Good God. Was he actually crying?

"Gone?" Billington inquired with concern. "Excuse me?"

Irving looked up at Doyle, his eyes wet with tears. "We might as well tell him. I mean, there's nothing left."

The man was crying. He was crying. Doyle was still too confused to be certain of his response. "As you say."

Irving sniffled an explanation through his tears. "My mother. She's afflicted with a growth, I'm afraid, in her brain."

The information moved Billington. "Oh, my good man. I'm so sorry."

"Our physicians in London have done all they know how. Now they've referred us to the only two surgeons in the world who can help. One's in America and could never reach mother in time. The other is the man we seek, and he's in London now."

"A physician?" Billington fretted. "He never indicated he was a physician."

Irving withdrew a silk handkerchief from his coat pocket, wiped his eyes, and noisily blew his nose. "That's why we're having such difficulty. He's traveling under this assumed name. God only knows why."

"His schedule is so hectic. I just assumed he wanted to be left alone on his holiday," Doyle offered.

Irving gestured toward Doyle. "That's why I went to Mr. Doyle, here. His abilities at detection, you know. I thought he'd be able to help, but so far we've accomplished little. Oh, I can't possibly tell mother."

Billington stared agape at Irving as he issued a fresh volley of tears. Doyle winced. But then he observed a slight change in Billington's deportment. His embarrassment transformed into hope when he saw Billington pace across the office. Doyle could hardly believe it. Was the solicitor's resolve weakening?

"You say this man's a physician? A surgeon?" Billington asked.

Irving could only bob his head, sobbing.

Billington turned to Doyle for further confirmation.

"Indeed, yes," Doyle answered, too fast.

"Give me a moment, gentlemen," Billington said. He walked into his office and returned in less than a minute holding a folder. Turning his back to them, he placed the folder on the corner of the clerk's desk. He opened it and began shuffling through the contents.

A few moments later, Billington turned to face them. "It occurred to me that there might be a way I can help you without directly providing the information myself."

"Oh, sir," Sir Henry wailed. "If you only can."

"Considering it's you, Sir Henry, and Mr. Doyle, of course," Billington continued.

"We'd be most grateful for any help," Doyle assured him.

"You understand I could never provide you with an exact location for my client. The truth of it is that I don't know myself where he is. I can, however, tell you I arranged transport for this man through Carter Paterson & Company."

"Carter Paterson & Company," Doyle repeated as he withdrew his notepad from his coat pocket and scribbled the name.

"They're in Goswell Road," Billington added. "And I'll very much appreciate your confidence as to where you got that information."

"When you say 'transport,' can you be more specific?" Doyle asked.

"No, I cannot," Billington responded in a sharp tone.

Irving leaped to his feet, now crying tears of joy. "Oh, thank you!" Irving cried. "Hope once more. Thank you, sir, with all my heart."

Doyle winced again. The men shook hands, and then Doyle and Irving stepped into the hallway. Billington stopped them. "Sir Henry."

"Yes?"

"Please know that our prayers will be with your mother."

The tears glistened in Irving's eyes. "Thank you, sir. You've done us a great service."

The office door closed and Doyle and Irving were alone in the hallway. The spring bolt had barely slid into place when Irving stopped crying. He wiped the moisture from his eyes and cheeks, and then returned the hand-kerchief to his pocket, his normal composure restored.

"Your mother?" Doyle inquired.

"Passed away some twenty years ago. Rest her soul."

Doyle couldn't help chuckling.

Irving shrugged. "On to Goswell Road, Mr. Doyle?"

"Indeed. And I would appreciate it if you address me as *Arthur*."

"Goswell Road, then Arthur."

CHAPTER 75

The mid-afternoon November sun cast long shadows across the churchyard of Saint Luke's in Chelsea. Some forty of Lucinda West-en's friends and acquaintances gathered around the small crypt where the body of her husband was already entombed.

Florence had cried herself to sleep the night before. Lying next to her in the dark, listening to her soft, anguished sobs in the hours before she surrendered to sleep, Stoker never imagined that such a sound could make him feel so much pain.

Earlier in the morning, a stoic silence had replaced the tears. Florence had risen early and set upon preparing for the funeral. Stoker provided whatever support he could and made it his business to remain close to her.

Now, holding her husband's arm, she stood beside the coffin containing the body of her dearest friend. Stoker glanced through the sea of mourning faces until he found Doyle and Irving standing next to Professor Vambery and Clarise. The Professor wore a dark, wool suit that was at least five years out of fashion. Clarise looked lovely, even dressed in black.

Mr. Quincey was also in attendance to pay his respects. He had not known Lucy well, but was taking her loss personally. His eyes also shared the glint of anger they all felt over their friend's murder.

Doyle and Irving had arrived just as the service was beginning. Stoker was impatient to hear what had transpired with the solicitor Billington, but knew it would have to wait.

The church rector prayed a blessing over the body and concluded the service. Stoker, Irving, Quincey, and three other men then carried the coffin into the crypt, placing it next to her husband's. They filed back out of the crypt and the church groundskeepers stepped forward to close and seal the door.

As the metal door swung shut with a dull clang, Stoker watched Florence fight back more tears, her mouth pursed by the effort. He moved back to her side where she took his arm for support.

As the mourners dispersed, moving away through the headstones, Stoker and Florence gathered with Doyle, Irving, Quincey and the Vamberys. After introducing the American to the professor and his daughter, they walked together toward the cemetery gates. "Was Billington able to help?" Stoker asked, unable to restrain himself.

"We have a good deal to tell you," Doyle reported.

Stoker felt Florence shudder against him.

"I really don't think Mrs. Stoker is up to any of that just now," observed Clarise.

"Ah, yes. Of course," said Doyle.

"My mind isn't where it should be," Stoker admitted. "I am sorry, my dear."

"I understand," Florence said, managing the slightest smile.

"Our task will still be with us tomorrow," Irving said. "Let's plan on gathering in the morning, in the Beefsteak room."

"Tomorrow then," Doyle proclaimed. "I suggest eleven."

With everyone in agreement and sharing a growing sense of purpose, the band of comrades made their way from the churchyard.

CHAPTER 76

The last golden-red rays of the sun had disappeared from the hazy Chelsea horizon two hours earlier. A groundskeeper for Saint Luke's Church relaxed on the wooden bench outside the tiny, two-room cottage at the back of the churchyard provided by his employer.

He sat in the dark because a lantern might reveal the large tankard of ale in his hand. It was his second of the evening. A doctor he had seen for a minor leg injury, noting his ample belly, strongly recommended he cut back on his drinking. Besides, the rector wasn't too keen on one of his employees enjoying the hops in such generous quantities.

The groundskeeper took a good swallow from the tankard and gazed with contentment across the churchyard. The gas lamps lining the street outlined the silhouettes of the gravestones. A low mist was beginning to creep through the yard, glowing dimly in the lamplight.

He enjoyed these evenings and didn't even mind the chill. The ale warmed him, and he used the time to plan his work for the following day. His ale was near gone and he was thinking about moving back inside the cottage when a slight movement caught his eye.

The mist had become denser, swirling around the headstones in flowing currents. The groundskeeper had to squint to make sure, but it slowly became visible; a figure of a man stood well across the yard near one of the crypts. A body had been interned there earlier in the day. He was on hand to seal the crypt along with young Richard.

He relaxed on the bench again. The man was just paying respects to the deceased. It was an odd time to visit a graveyard, but he would give him a few minutes and then run him off if need be.

He took a few slow sips at the tankard; he didn't want to run out just yet. Dulled by the ale, his mind wandered as he gazed into the gloom. The sound of metal scraping against stone drew him back to attention.

Leaving the tankard on the bench, he stood and peered into the darkness. The man beside the crypt had moved from his original position, but he was still there among the gravestones. A muffled moan drifted across the graveyard, and then something else was moving within the heavy mist. A dull, metallic reverberation followed soon after; the sound of a crypt doors slamming shut.

The groundskeeper felt a chill that penetrated down to his soul. He rubbed his eyes, trying to clear them of whatever impairment his drinking had planted there. He stared through the gloom, determined to see more clearly through the fog. And then he saw the man, barely discernable in his dark clothing.

The mist gathered close to the man, churning and growing denser until the figure of a woman seemed to be formed out of it. She appeared not much more than a silhouette, the murky light giving her cream-colored gown a dull cast.

Without a sound, the two figures turned and drifted through the shroud of fog. The groundskeeper registered a strong feeling of relief that they were moving away from him. But then the man paused and turned in his direction. Even in the gloom, the groundskeeper could make out the malevolent pair of eyes staring at him.

Leaving his tankard on the bench, he frantically hurried inside his little cottage and locked the door. He huddled down next to the small fire crackling in the hearth, hoping the flames would quell the numbing chill.

CHAPTER 77

"You're certain you're up to it?" Stoker asked.

"I'm not certain I'm up to anything," Florence replied, gathering her wrap from the chair in the foyer. "But you won't keep me out of this. I was kept me in the dark long enough and worried myself sick because of it."

She had not named *him* as keeping her in the dark, and Stoker was grateful for her diplomacy. "I understand," he acknowledged. "I just don't want anything to happen to you."

"We're going to face this thing together and I want to know everything that's going on. That monster murdered my friend."

"All right, but you still agree that staying at the Doyle home is the safest course for you. Once we hear from his Louise, you're off to the country," Stoker insisted.

Florence sighed in surrender. "Yes, all right. But until then, I'm going to be at your side."

Stoker looked at his wife and knew she was determined. "Let's get going, then. Our meeting begins at eleven and we've barely the time to make it."

He opened the front door for her and they both stepped through. It wasn't until he had closed the door behind him that Stoker noticed the uniformed constable standing on the sidewalk at the bottom of the steps. He was young, still in his twenties.

"Mr. Stoker. Mrs. Stoker," the young man greeted them.

"Yes," Stoker confirmed.

"Inspector Lestern's compliments, sir. He would appreciate it if you'd come along with me to the yard," the bobby explained.

"Well, we have a meeting of some importance just now," Stoker responded. "Perhaps sometime tomorrow."

The bobby straightened up a bit. "I'm sorry, sir. The inspector is quite insistent. He'll see you now."

Stoker glanced at Florence. He knew her well enough to sense her concern, but she wasn't showing any of it to the constable.

"You'll leave our colleagues waiting for us with no notice," Stoker argued, allowing the irritation he felt to enter his tone.

"I'm sure they'll understand," the bobby answered.

"Are we charged with something?" Stoker asked.

"No sir, but the inspector is waiting. Now, if you'll follow me up to the corner, we'll get ourselves a cab."

"And where are we going, exactly?" Stoker pressed.

"The old headquarters at Whitehall Place, sir."

Stoker reasoned that arguing further would only create greater problems. "Let's get on with it, then," he surrendered.

Arm in arm, the Stokers followed the constable up the lane.

Some forty minutes later they arrived at Metropolitan Police Headquarters. The young bobby escorted the Stokers through the public entrance off of Great Scotland Yard, the street running along the rear of the building. After two busy hallways and a flight of stairs, they found themselves in a cluttered, windowless office, where their escort asked them to wait.

Stoker's frustration at the disruption of his day's agenda had increased with each passing minute. Now Florence watched as he paced the small office like a tormented dog, looking for the opportunity to sink his teeth into an abusive master. After being kept waiting for twenty minutes, Inspector Lestern stepped into the office.

"Thank you for coming," Lestern said.

"It didn't seem like we were given any choice," Stoker said.

"Oh, we always have a choice, don't we?" Lestern countered, his tone pleasant enough, but his expression remaining serious and focused.

"You've disrupted a very busy day for us," Stoker said. "I can't imagine why we're here, so I'd appreciate it if you'd get on with it."

Lestern settled into a nearby chair. "Well then, let's have a seat and get at it." The inspector gestured toward the remaining chair next to Florence.

Stoker hesitated and then sat down, realizing that his indignation had no effect on Lestern.

"I've called you in because we need help," Lestern continued.

"How can we help?" Florence asked.

"Yes, we've told you all we can," Stoker added.

"There've been very few leads in this case," Lestern explained. "You two are the most obvious connection, and I can't ignore that. Lucinda Westen was your close friend and Tillie Grover your housemaid."

"Are you accusing us of murdering our own housemaid and Miss Westen?" Stoker asked.

"Nobody's accused anyone of anything," Lestern answered. "You must know there've been other murders in the city in the past several weeks."

"Why would we be aware of such things?" Stoker asked.

"If you read the papers you should know," Lestern responded, a sharp edge to his voice. "The victims all died the same way and with the same wounds. And the medical examiner hasn't been able to explain or identify those wounds."

"Perhaps you should be searching for a vampire," Florence blurted out.

Stoker turned to stare at his wife with stunned disapproval.

Lestern, too, stared at Florence, a look of shock and confusion shaping his face. And then he broke into a hearty laugh. "Yes, of course we should. Vampire indeed," he guffawed.

The inspector's amusement turned to disapproval in a blink. "Really, Mrs. Stoker, as much as I appreciate such a humorous observation, don't you think it's in poor taste? Especially considering your long relationship with two of the victims."

"You're quite right, of course," Florence answered. "I don't know what I could have been thinking."

"Now, if we can get back to the business at hand, I want to go over the facts with you again," Lestern said.

Lestern asked them the same questions he asked the night of the murders, watching them closely as they answered and scribbling notes on a tablet.

After twenty or thirty minutes of covering the same material, he would excuse himself, leaving them to wait alone for his return. He would be gone another twenty minutes and then revisit the little office.

This routine continued for over two hours with Stoker checking his watch through all of it, growing more frustrated with each passing second.

Returning to the Stokers after one of his absences, Lestern left the office door open. "I think we've gone over everything we can here," he announced.

"It's unclear to me why you couldn't realize that two hours ago," Stoker groused.

"Yes, well, you're both free to go."

Lestern followed the Stokers into the hallway. They hadn't walked very far when they spotted Doyle and Irving moving away from them at the far end of the corridor.

"Sir Henry. Mr. Doyle," Stoker called out.

The two men looked back and reversed their direction, meeting the Stokers and Lestern in the middle of the hall.

"You, too?" Doyle growled as he approached.

"I'm afraid so," Stoker answered.

"And you, attempting to use my own interview techniques against me," Doyle accused, pointing an angry finger at Lestern.

"I wouldn't want you to think we hadn't learned something from you," Lestern responded.

"Well, you see what's come of it. A monumental waste of everyone's time," Doyle proclaimed.

"Let's just be on our way," Irving urged, just as annoyed as everyone else.

"Yes," Stoker agreed.

Without another word, the group hastened to the stairwell. They could feel the inspector watching them with each step.

Once back on Great Scotland Yard street they rallied. It was soon determined that no one had veered from their original accounts to Inspector Lestern. Lestern might be suspicious of the circumstances, but he'd learned nothing new from them.

"The day is almost gone and I can only imagine what our associates must be thinking," Stoker began.

"This morning when the inspector's messenger boy demanded my presence, I instructed Loveday to send word to the Vamberys and Mr. Quincey before they dragged from the theater," Sir Henry explained. "I suggested we delay our meeting for two hours, so they've only been waiting a short time."

"Then we best hurry," Stoker urged.

Doyle stepped into the street to hail an approaching cab.

CHAPTER 78

As Irving projected, the Vamberys and Morgan Quincey were waiting for them in the Beefsteak Room. Tension filled the room. A copy of the Pall Mall Gazette, one of several papers Collinson had placed on the banquet table for Sir Henry's convenience, contributed to the tension.

Professor Vambery slid the Gazette copy across the table. Stoker picked it up, reading it for the second time.

BOY FOUND DEAD IN REGENT'S PARK.

"Lord, protect us," Florence said, almost under her breath.

"Women and boys. He sure plays it safe, doesn't he?" Quincey observed with disdain.

"Don't be fooled," Stoker countered. "He's not afraid of any man, and he's deadly dangerous." Growing more agitated, he pushed back from the table and stood.

"I sent another wire home first thing this morning," Doyle interjected, holding up a rumpled telegram. "Your stage manager handed me this just as we walked in the door. Louise writes that Mrs. Stoker will be more than welcome at Undershaw as long as she wishes to stay."

"Thank God," Stoker exclaimed.

"I don't really want to go now," Florence said.

"Perhaps Mrs. Stoker would allow me to escort her to, what is it, Undershaw?" Quincey asked. "I'll see she's not bothered in any way."

"I'd be grateful," Stoker answered. "Mr. Doyle, would you write instructions for Mr. Quincey?"

Collinson fetched paper and pen from a nearby cabinet and placed them in front of Doyle.

"I suppose there's little doubt your man was involved with this Regent's Park affair," Irving said.

"No doubt at all," Stoker responded. "Don't misunderstand me; it's a tragic thing, but the boy's murder and the murder in Hampstead Heath have saved us a good deal of trouble from the police. Lestern must be going mad that he can't find a logical connection between those crimes, Tillie, Lucy and Annie Beth."

Doyle finished jotting down the directions, blotted the paper and handed it to Quincey. "I've noted the train and the stops. You shouldn't have any trouble."

"We'll be fine," Quincey assured him, rising from the table.

Stoker helped Florence from her chair. "Mr. Quincey will make sure you get there."

"I'd rather stay with you right now," Florence said, a quiet anguish in her voice.

"This is the safest way. I'll do nothing but worry if you stay."

Florence could see there would be no arguing with her husband and summoned the strength for a pleasant smile as she joined the American at the door. "Mr. Quincey, if you please. I have some packing to do at home."

"Yes, ma'am," Quincey answered as he escorted her from the room.

"That'll have her out of London before nightfall," Stoker sighed with relief. "How did you two do?"

"Bloody irritating work yesterday morning, but we've got something," Irving said.

"Carter Patterson, the shippers, delivered five large boxes to four different addresses around London," Doyle explained. "The first some two months ago, about the same time Stoker says he met Tepes. The last of them only yesterday morning." Doyle pulled a slip of paper from his inside coat pocket and consulted it. "To 197 Chicksand Street."

"Yesterday," Stoker repeated, considering the information.

"Chicksand Street. Drab neighborhood," Collinson commented, glancing over Doyle's shoulder.

"What could this man need with so many boxes?" Irving asked.

Stoker exchanged a long glance with Professor Vambery. "Earth boxes," Stoker said.

Irving's brow knitted in puzzlement. "Earth? Dirt?"

"That would explain his scattering them all over the city," Stoker said to Vambery.

"Affords him some protection," Vambery agreed.

"Just a moment," Irving said. "You're saying these boxes contain nothing but dirt?"

"The vampire must return to rest during the day on his own soil," Vambery explained.

Doyle sighed. "Well, this fellow must *believe* he's a vampire if he gone to such lengths."

"Once you eliminate the impossible, whatever remains, no matter how improbable, must be the truth," Irving interjected with a sly nod to Doyle.

"Quite so," Doyle muttered.

"You mentioned you had some information, as well," Stoker addressed Vambery.

"A bit of research uncovered some information linked to the name. It took longer than it should have because we weren't looking back far enough?"

"What do you mean?" Irving asked.

"The records we searched were too recent. Once some of these more recent developments came to light, it occurred to me that starting back further might be helpful. I have access to private collections that our friend Stoker here does not, and it would seem they paid off," Vambery said.

"Tell us, please," said Stoker.

"I started with the name, Tepes," Vambery began. "It comes from tzepa, which means spike. And I found it used as a direct reference to one Vlad Tepes."

"Spike? But what an odd name," Irving commented.

"It was a name his countrymen attached to him after his death. Apparently, he was rather fond of impaling his enemies on tall stakes."

"God in heaven," Irving grimaced.

Vambery continued. "It's a horrible way to die, very slow. Tepes used it as a warning to anyone who might oppose him, and it appeared to be very effective. The man was considered a great warrior in his own time. I found one manuscript asserting after one battle he impaled 20,000 of the enemy. Turks, in that instance."

"In his own time? When did this take place?" Doyle asked, confused.

"I believe the date of the battle was recorded as 1456. Vlad Tepes died in 1476."

"1476," Irving repeated, incredulous.

"Tepes was drawn to other cruelties," Vambery continued. "When his mistress told him she was pregnant, he ordered her cut open to prove it. He invited all the beggars in one village under his rule to a large feast held in a barn. Once they were inside, he had the doors fastened shut and then set fire to the place. He reasoned he was eliminating an inferior breed and preventing the possibility of plague. Oh, and there was one reference to him forcing mothers to eat their babies."

Clarise shuddered. "I think I've heard enough. Thank you, father."

"I am sorry, my dear."

"Well, there's no doubt the man was bloodthirsty," Irving observed. "But spike? You mentioned he got the name after he died."

"We have his given name, too," Vambery stated.

"Yes?" Doyle asked.

"Dracula, Prince Vlad the Third, Voivode of Wallachia."

CHAPTER 79

"Some translated the name as 'Son of the Devil'. But *Dracul* can also translate to 'dragon.' Tepes's father was a member of the Order Draconis," Vambery explained.

"Order of the Dragon," Doyle mused.

"And what about *voivode*?" Irving asked.

"Ruler or warlord. He ruled no less than three separate times during his natural lifetime," Vambery answered.

"So we're searching for someone who's been dead over four-hundred years," Doyle sighed.

"It doesn't matter what you believe at this moment. We must destroy those boxes before Tepes can move them again," Stoker insisted.

"Destroy them?" asked Doyle.

"The earth boxes."

"If these are, indeed, earth boxes—if his sleeping places are found out and eliminated — he has no place to rest. He'll have no place to hide," Vambery explained. "The legends make it clear. He'll be prey to the cleansing rays of the sun."

"I'm wondering if we shouldn't tell the police all we know," Doyle suggested.

"We've been over and over that," Stoker almost shouted.

"It's just that this all seems to be getting out of hand. I'm not certain we're up to it all," Doyle argued. "And as hard as it is for me to admit, I don't have one reasonable theory. Nothing makes sense. For instance, the blood in the mouth of Miss Westen."

Vambery leaned forward. "There was blood in her mouth?"

"No blood anywhere else, not even much on the throat wounds, but blood on her lips and in her mouth."

Vambery ran a hand through his white mane, his eyes troubled.

"What is it, father?" Clarise asked.

"The legends," he answered.

"What of them?" Stoker asked.

"The legends tell us that the vampire can drain a victim to their death or turn them."

"Turn them?" Irving asked.

"Transform them into one of their own, a vampire," the Professor continued.

"Oh, father," Clarise murmured, dismayed.

"But what's the foolishness of some legend have to do with this?" Doyle asked.

"The vampire takes the victim to the point of death. Then makes them drink of his blood before killing them," Vambery explained, disturbed by the thought.

Stoker looked horrified.

Doyle sighed. "And you're certain you don't want the help of the police?"

"Florence already suggested to Lestern he should be looking for a vampire," Stoker said.

"What?" Irving exclaimed.

"He laughed in her face, thought she was joking. And then he just moved on. He didn't consider it for even a moment."

"I can imagine," Doyle mumbled.

Stoker pulled his coat and hat from the rack. "I'll do this myself if I have to." He held out his hand. "The addresses, please."

"Stoker, please," Irving pleaded.

"No matter what you believe he is or isn't, you've already agreed we must stop him. I don't know about the rest of you, but I'm going. Alone if I have to."

Stoker slid the address list into his coat. Doyle gazed at the floor for a few moments and then pulled a Webley revolver from his coat pocket. "In for a penny, in for a pound, I suppose," he said, checking the revolver's chambers.

"I suppose," Irving sighed, eyeing the Webley warily.

Professor Vambery rose from the sofa, his face dead serious. "Take caution with you, gentlemen. Remember, you fight with the power of God on your side."

"The power of God?" Doyle asked.

"You must know God is light and truth. The thing you battle loathes this light. For him, it carries only death, for true evil can survive only in darkness. This creature exists, and has existed these many years, by distorting and twisting the truth. He manipulates and misleads. He exerts his powerful influence to destroy lives, and he has done it all while staying concealed in the shadows."

"If you don't mind, I'd rather rely on the strength of this," Doyle said, gesturing with the revolver before slipping it back into his pocket.

"I understand, Mr. Doyle," Vambery replied. "But I assure you the power of God will prove the mightier weapon. The legends supply a variety of methods with which to dispatch these creatures. Let me review them with you before you go."

"All right, but we've got to hurry," Stoker urged. "I don't want to be doing this after sunset."

CHAPTER 80

There was a great deal about the proposed trip that Florence found stressful. Foremost, she did not want to leave Bram to face the monster that was hunting them both. She had never seen him so frightened. There was little she could do to help, but she was terribly anxious having to be away from him now.

Morgan Quincey was wonderful about it. Upon their arrival at Cheyne Walk, he made it clear that they had to leave Chelsea as soon as possible, and did whatever she asked to help. He had a four-wheeler waiting and helped the driver with the luggage to assure that everything moved along. Mr. Quincey was efficient and implacable, but he was gentle and patient as well.

The weather was turning bleak, but at least no rain interfered with their ride to King's Cross. The one thought that cheered Florence was that this entire mess had clarified her feelings for her husband. More to the point, it had enabled her to see that his feelings for her were still strong.

Florence always found King's Cross Station to be busy no matter what time of day she visited it. Passengers bustled across the platform in every direction, all of them seeming to be in a great hurry.

Florence watched as Mr. Quincey supervised a porter loading the bags onto a pushcart. She found some comfort in that he was accompanying her to Hindhead. She didn't relish the thought of being alone right now.

P.G. KASSEL

Mr. Quincey bought first class tickets and they made their way across the busy station platform to their carriage. They climbed aboard, located their compartment, and made themselves comfortable inside. It wouldn't be long now, and they'd be on their way.

CHAPTER 81

The sky had grown overcast, and the clouds were threatening rain by the time Doyle, Stoker and Irving reached 220 Jamaica Lane in Bermondsey, the first address on the Carter Paterson & Company list. The Bermondsey address was the furthest south from central London, a commercial and shipping district known for its tanneries, glue factories and wool warehouses. They agreed that the most efficient approach would be to begin in Bermondsey and then work their way back into the city.

Doyle drove their four-wheeler while Irving and Stoker rode inside. The driver of the first cab they attempted to hire had driven off the moment he saw the ax that Stoker carried and the crowbar in Doyle's hand. The second cabby didn't bolt, but when they weren't forthcoming with straightforward answers to his questions about the tools, he insisted on them paying double-fare.

Stoker was about to agree to the arrangement, but Doyle stopped him and dismissed the cabby. He decided that hiring their own coach was a superior idea.

It did not take long to find a livery and strike an acceptable agreement. Doyle appointed himself the driver. Now he climbed down from his seat and placed the ground tie in front of the horses. He tied the lead to the iron ring set in the weight and then joined Irving and Stoker at the side of the coach.

The neighborhood was working class and had grown out from the edge of the warehouse district. More likely, Doyle thought, the warehouses had consumed a portion of the older neighborhood. The afternoon foot traffic was moderate and an occasional wagon rolled past. No one paid any attention to the three men.

The housing was a holdover from Elizabethan England—four and five story, peaked roof affairs with each floor jutting out beyond the one below it. Built close together, heavy wooden beams spanned between the buildings, across the narrow mews, to support the high, grimy walls.

At the end of Jamaica Lane, the high houses gave way to a few freestanding structures. The residents probably viewed them as mansions for the well heeled. Number 220 was one of these. It was once white, judging from the paint flakes peeling from its walls. The structure was small and dilapidated, fitting perfectly into the neighborhood that was uniformly shabby and rundown.

Doyle tucked the crowbar under his arm and consulted the address list a final time. "220. Yes."

Doyle and Irving followed Stoker around to the side of the house where a footpath led to the rear of the structure. Listening for any signs of life from inside, they walked around to the back of the property.

The house was quiet. Three worn and splintered steps reached up to the backdoor. A narrow, filthy window was mounted on either side of the door. Stoker used the ax handle to break the pane of glass nearest the doorknob.

Irving flinched at the sound of the glass breaking, and looked somewhat nervous, but made no comment. "You seem to have grown used to this business of burglary," Doyle said to him as Stoker reached through the broken window and unlatched the door.

Irving favored Doyle with a brief, sideward glance. "You've compelled me to grow used to a good many unsavory things since meeting you, Arthur," he replied.

Doyle allowed himself a chuckle as Stoker pushed open the door. They entered with caution and found themselves standing in a small pantry that opened into a kitchen. None of them made a move or a sound for several seconds. The silence that greeted their ears made them relatively certain they were the only living creatures in the house. Still, they were not willing to let down their guard.

Stoker stepped into the kitchen. Doyle and Irving followed close behind him. The room was almost dark, with the only illumination coming from the gray afternoon light seeping through the dingy windows. It was was completely empty. The one thing the kitchen had in abundance was dust. It covered every exposed surface. Most of the cupboard doors hung open, some dangling on a single hinge.

Moving through the house, they found the other rooms in a similar state. Dirty windows, empty floor space, dirt, dust and too little light epitomized this dreary dwelling. Making their way down the central hallway of the house, they all noticed it at the same time.

CHAPTER 82

The sound of an explosion reached their compartment, shaking the train carriage. A woman's scream immediately followed the short, loud bang.

Outside the train, people began shouting. Through the carriage windows, Florence could see several people on the platform running toward the front of the train.

"I'll go see what all the fuss is about," Quincey told her, rising from his seat.

"I'll go with you," Florence insisted.

"Yes, ma'am."

Florence and Quincey stepped into the passageway and made their way to the end of the carriage, along with several other curious passengers. Once on the station platform, they could see a large gathering of people at the front of the train, near the locomotive. The air beyond the crowd was full of smoke and steam. A loud hissing sound hung in the air, along with the sound of excited voices.

Quincey led Florence through the crowd. It took some maneuvering and some pushing, but they soon found themselves near the front of the assembly, close enough to see what had happened.

The first thing that Florence noticed was a porter helping the locomotive's stoker to his feet. Behind the porter and the stoker, the engineer and another railroad employee were examining the locomotive's boiler, which appeared to be the source of the smoke and steam. Two other railroad employees were doing their best to keep the crowd back.

The stoker was in pain; Florence could hear his moans over the noise of the crowd. As he turned, it became obvious why. The left side of the unfortunate man's face was bright red and beginning to blister. The left side of his clothing appeared wet. Another railroad employee joined the porter and together they helped the stoker away from the train.

Florence and Quincey moved to another location in the crowd. From her new vantage point, she could see the source of the explosion. A large pipe, about four inches in diameter, snaked out from under the locomotive and ran along the base of its long boiler. A jagged hole was visible at a point on the pipe near the front of the boiler. Steam hissed angrily from the opening, its pressure forcing out large droplets of water. The pipe looked as if it had been peeled back and shredded.

This was all unfortunate. It would most certainly cause a delay, Florence thought. If Bram knew of this, he would be worried to the point of distraction. Worried about her, about her safety.

Quincey tugged gently at Florence's hand and guided her through the crowd back toward their carriage.

CHAPTER 83

S everal footprints were visible in the thick layer of dust on the floor. A larger, heavier object had also disturbed the dust. The footprints pointed in both directions, forming a trail leading to the front of the house. The dusty path of prints and scuffs stopped in front of a closed door in the center of the hallway.

"They carried it in from the front of the house," Doyle observed in a whisper.

Stoker approached the door and placed his hand on the doorknob. He hesitated, working up his nerve. He tightened his grip and turned the knob. The sound of rusty metal scraping against rusty metal issued a muffled screech in the hallway as the bolt drew back. He pushed the door open. The hinges squeaked as the door swung back to reveal little but blackness.

They all stared into the darkness for several seconds. When their eyes adjusted to the blackness, they made out some kind of covering placed over the only window in the little room. Irving walked across the floor and reached for the fabric covering the window. He tugged and pulled. There was a sudden ripping sound and the cloth tore free from the top of the window. A tiny ray of light drifted into the room through the dirty glass pane.

The light revealed that the fabric was a heavy, hunter green velvet drapery. Apart from a little dust, it appeared new. It had been nailed to the window frame. Irving renewed his grip on the velvet and pulled again. It tore away from the window, allowing more light into the room.

They could now see the box. Doyle withdrew the Webley from his coat pocket.

Constructed of low-grade lumber, a tongue-in-groove design held the planks solidly together. The lid was nailed shut. Stenciled onto its side in red lettering was CARTER PATERSON & CO., LONDON.

"What now?" Irving asked.

Stoker answered by raising his ax over the box.

"Wait," Doyle stopped him. "I want to know what it is we're dealing with." He pocketed the revolver and wedged the crowbar beneath the box's lid.

Stoker watched with impatience as Doyle methodically worked his way around the box, using the crowbar to pry up the long nails holding the lid in place. The nails squeaked as they pulled away from the wood, the sound cutting through the still air. It only took a few minutes and Doyle was at the last nail. He pulled it out and the leverage from his pull dislodged the heavy lid.

Stoker handed the ax to Irving and moved around to the opposite end of the box from Doyle. Doyle passed the crowbar to Irving and then nodded his readiness to Stoker. The two men took hold of the lid and pushed it aside.

A sudden rumble of thunder sent a long vibration through the house. They jerked away from the box. After a few moments, their breathing returned to normal and they resumed their positions. They pushed hard against the lid. It slid off the side of the box and thudded against the floor, the weight of it forcing a flurry of dust into the air.

Almost filling the space inside was another box with the dimensions of a standard coffin. Like the outer crate, the box was a simple design constructed from common wood. The lid was hinged, but no locks or other fasteners were evident.

Stoker stepped forward and lifted the lid. A sour odor spilled into the room; a smell of mold and decay. The inner box was empty except for a thick layer of dark soil packed along its floor. The dirt was somewhat damp.

Doyle and Irving stared at the dirt. "I was rather hoping we'd find a wardrobe, or table linens or the like," Irving said in a quiet tone.

Doyle nodded, looking back into the box.

"It's dirt," Irving continued. "Just as Stoker and Vambery predicted."

Doyle stepped over to Irving and retrieved the crowbar. Returning to the end of the box, he took the end of the crowbar and thrust it into the dirt at the end of the box, pushing it aside and turning it over. He moved to the middle of the box and repeated the process. It was just dirt, nothing but moldy soil.

Stoker took the ax from Irving and fixed his eyes on Doyle. Doyle shrugged in surrender. "We said we'd be with you in this, so do what we came to do."

Doyle and Irving stepped back from the box as Stoker raised the ax over his head. He swung it down fiercely. The wood cracked and splintered as the first plank broke loose. He destroyed the outer crate first and then went to work on the box inside. Stoker channeled all of his fear and all of his anger into the ax. He brought it down again and again. Splinters flew into the air and dirt poured onto the floor.

In a few minutes, both the crate and what it contained were a pile of broken kindling. Using the ax head, Stoker spread the dirt across the floor.

"Now for the others," Stoker said.

They searched the rest of the house. Finding nothing, they left the way they came and returned to their coach.

After consulting the list, Doyle snapped the reins. The weather had turned even bleaker and another peal of thunder sounded in the distance as they rolled away from the ruined hiding place.

CHAPTER 84

The next street number on the list was near an industrial area a few blocks from the Thames. They found the Grange Street address in another dingy, uncared-for neighborhood that appeared to be home to dockworkers and seamen who worked nearby. It was another single level house, smaller than the first one they had visited, but in an equal state of disrepair.

There were no windows near the door at the rear of the house, so Stoker used the ax to shatter the lock.

The back door opened into a kitchen that contained an old stove and some broken sticks of furniture. This time, they were rewarded with footprints on the dusty floor. They had tracked into the kitchen from the front of the house and ended in front of a closed door. Doyle pulled open the door. A wooden stairway led down into the black pit of a cellar.

"Did anyone think to bring a lantern?" Irving asked. The others shook their heads.

Doyle began opening the cupboard doors and drawers around the kitchen. Stoker and Irving joined in the search and soon produced a handful of candles, matted with dust, from a cupboard. He gave a candle to Doyle and Stoker, kept one for himself, and placed the rest back where he found them.

Doyle found a box of matches in his coat pocket. Rain began beating against the roof as Doyle lit each of the candles. There were two or three more crashes of thunder, then just the steady pelting of the rain.

Doyle gave the crowbar to Irving and again removed the Webley from his pocket. With great caution, led the way down the stairs into the darkness. The candles cast a pitifully inadequate light, but their flame was better than nothing.

It was a small cellar, built solely to house the old coal furnace that faced the stairs. The rusted furnace looked like it had not enjoyed the heat of a fire in many years.

Another Carter Paterson & Company crate rested on the floor in the middle of the cellar. This time, Irving ripped the nails loose from the lid. Moving it aside, they found the same simple coffin. Within that, they found the same fetid earth. Stoker took his ax to the boxes and within a few minutes splintered them to pieces with the soil scattered across the cellar floor.

They climbed the cellar stairs and searched the rest of the house. Finding nothing else of concern, they left through the damaged back door. They hurried along the side of the house through the steadily falling rain. Their clothes were dripping wet by the time they reached their four-wheeler.

The third address was on the outskirts of Whitechapel near Mile End Road. This time it was not a house, but a basement level flat. The front entrance to the place was not on a principal street, but accessed through an alley.

Finding the address number, they descended ten steps to a tiny patio area and the front door. Trash littered the area, now soggy from the rain that had blown down from the street level.

Irving surveyed the steps and the small patio. "If there's another box here, one has to wonder how they got it into the place," he said.

"Probably lowered it over the side with ropes so they wouldn't have to make a turn into the doorway. Of course, they'd have had to push it through the door almost on end," Doyle surmised.

The front door had a small window set in its upper half. The only other window they could see was set in the bricks to the right of the doorway. It was only about a foot square and covered with iron bars.

Stoker used his ax handle to break the window in the door, reached in and tripped the latch. They hurried in out of the rain.

The flat was dim and carried the faint smell of rotting garbage. Irving produced one of the candles he had brought with him from the last house. Doyle struck a match and put it to the candle.

Two rickety wooden chairs and a lopsided wooden table occupied the room. A closed door opposite the entrance was the only other door. Doyle opened it and Irving moved into the open doorway with the candle. The large proved hard to see in the shadows, but there it sat against the wall at the back of the room.

Stoker swung the ax and within minutes, the now familiar ritual was complete. They left the room with shattered wood and moldy dirt spread across the floor.

The rain had lessened by the time they climbed the steps to the alley. Stoker's eyes looked to the horizon. "The sun will be down soon," Stoker observed. "And we've still got two more boxes to find."

Shivering from their wet clothing, they hurried along to the street and were soon back in their coach. Doyle climbed inside with Irving and Stoker to get out of the rain for a few minutes. The four-wheeler was dry but did little against the chill they all felt.

"The last address. What is it?" Stoker asked Doyle.

Doyle reached into his pocket, withdrew the folded notepaper and spread it open. He frowned, looking hard at the list. "Bloody hell," he cursed.

"What?" Irving asked, but he could already see the black smudges of ink on Doyle's fingertips.

Doyle turned the paper toward them. The rain had soaked through his coat and through the list as well, smudging the ink. The list was unreadable. "Can you make any of it out?" Doyle asked them, but already knowing the answer.

Irving shook his head. "I think it's an 'n' and a 'd'. But that's all."

"We must have that address," Stoker shouted.

"Blast this weather, anyway," Irving muttered.

Stoker was growing agitated again. "What do we do?" he asked.

"We've nothing here," Doyle answered, crumpling the list.

"And the transport house will be closed at this hour, or closing soon at the very least," Irving added.

"We'd never get there in time," Doyle agreed.

"There's no time anyway," Stoker complained. "It's almost dark. We must have those addresses."

Doyle stared at the crumpled list in his hand. Something was stirring in his recent memory. What was it?

"Collinson," Doyle almost shouted the name.

"What?" Stoker asked.

"Collinson," Doyle repeated. "He looked over my shoulder when I first brought out the list. Back at the Lyceum when we were discussing what we should do."

"That memory of his. If Collinson saw the list, there's a good chance he'll still remember the addresses."

Doyle adjusted his position to look out the cab window. "There must be a telegraph office nearby," he said.

"That's no good," Stoker argued. "We could end up waiting half the night for a reply."

"Perhaps we could find a telephone," Doyle suggested. "I didn't see one at the Carter Paterson office, but—"

Stoker shook his head, interrupting Doyle. "We haven't put one in the theater yet."

"I'm not sure I trust the things anyway," Irving said. "It'll be faster to just return to the theater."

Doyle nodded and climbed from the coach. Moments later, he was whipping the horses back toward the Lyceum.

CHAPTER 85

I t had been almost a half hour since the night had overtaken the house on Grange Street. The soft wind blowing in from the river made the cold air even more uninviting. The wind had also blown at least a few of the clouds away from the full moon. Somewhere, two cats wailed at each other, readying for a fight.

The house was darker than the night surrounding it. The only sound penetrating from outside came from the sporadic dripping of rainwater off the eaves. Pitch blackness filled the cellar. A small puddle of water had formed in the corner where the cellar had flooded.

The squeaking hinges of the cellar door being pulled open broke the silence. The stairs groaned and strained as he descended into the cellar.

His boots stepped down onto the packed dirt of the cellar floor. His eyes surveyed the damage. The broken and splintered wood, the soil of his homeland defiled and scattered, and now mixed in with the dirt of this floor. He stepped over to the edge of his ruined property. There was no question who had done this thing.

A low, angry, animal-like growl formed in his throat. It expanded into a full-throated scream of rage. The sound echoed around the cellar as he grabbed hold of a jagged corner that remained of his box and hurled it across the room. The wood frame struck the brick wall with tremendous force and disintegrated.

His long, black coat flowing around him, Tepes whirled around before the last scrap of wood hit the ground. He ascended the cellar stairs with a plan gestating in his mind. They would all pay for this impudent attack. He would see them all dead before the sun came up.

CHAPTER 86

S toker, with Doyle, and Irving close on his heels, charged through the stage door. The Lyceum was bustling with activity because of the producing company that was leasing the facility. Stoker spotted Benton keeping a careful watch on the visiting company's personnel. This was not a Henry Irving production, so the role of the Lyceum staff was looking after the interests of the landlord.

"Collinson. Where's Collinson?" Stoker asked.

"I believe I just saw him on his way to your office," Benton answered.

Stoker, Sir Henry, and Doyle ran to the office.

Collinson was placing a small stack of receipts on Stoker's desk when they all entered.

"Ah, Mr. Stoker," Collinson began. "I was just leaving Sir Henry's personal receipts for last month and the—"

Stoker interrupted him. "You were here this afternoon when Mr. Doyle arrived with a list of addresses."

"Yes, of course."

"Do you remember the numbers?" Stoker continued.

"We only need the last one on the list," Irving interjected.

"Oh, of course," Collinson said. "I got a fine look at them. Just let me think." They waited impatiently as Collinson mentally ran down the list to visualize the last address. "Ah, yes. Chicksand Street. 197 Chicksand Street."

"Remarkable," Doyle mumbled, scribbling down the address on his pad.

"That's it, then," Stoker stated. "We'll need a lantern before we leave this time."

He turned to leave the office and almost collided with Florence, who suddenly appeared in the doorway. Behind her was Morgan Quincey, looking rather timid, and behind him, Harry Loveday. Stoker glanced at the American.

"There was an accident," Quincey volunteered.

"What's happened?" Stoker asked Florence, alarmed.

"As Mr. Quincey said, there was an accident at the station. Only with the train. We're both fine." She stepped into the office and sat down in a chair near the door.

"A boiler exploded on our locomotive," Quincey explained.

"You're all right," he repeated.

"Just tired. I knew you wouldn't want me going home, so I thought coming here was best."

"It was," her husband responded. "But we must get you on the next train."

"But that's just it. That's why we came back here," Florence sighed. "The accident blocked the line. They sent for a switching engine, but no one has any idea how long it'll take to clear the track."

"It would appear that London is reluctant to let you go," Irving remarked.

"We left the luggage by the stage door," Florence said.

"It'll be fine there," Irving assured her.

Florence looked more closely at her husband, and then at Doyle and Irving. "What's happened to you?" she asked.

Stoker ignored the question, rubbing his hand across his eyes. "What can we possibly do now?" he asked.

Doyle shrugged. "All that's required is a safe place for tonight where she won't be alone."

"Mrs. Stoker'd be welcome at my house," Loveday offered. "We don't have the space you're used to, but we'll make you comfortable."

Stoker could see that his wife was even less enthusiastic about this suggestion than she was about her trip to Hindhead, but she read the concern in his eyes.

She nodded to Loveday. "You're very kind. That would be lovely."

"I'll take her along myself and introduce her to the Missus," Loveday offered.

"Could I go, as well, if Mrs. Stoker doesn't mind?" Quincey asked. "I like to finish what I start."

"Call a cab for them," Stoker ordered Collinson. The valet hurried from the office.

Stoker looked as apologetic as he did anxious. "We have to go out again, right away," he said to Florence.

Doyle and Irving moved toward the office door.

Stoker reached into his coat pocket and withdrew the small cross and chain he had grasped in his hand that night at Whitby Abbey. He knelt down next to Florence and pushed the cross into her hand.

"Take this," he insisted. "And don't part with it."

Doyle couldn't help rolling his eyes.

"But Bram," Florence began.

Stoker didn't give her time to finish. He kissed her forehead and then straightened up, turning to Harry Loveday.

"Stay with her now and don't let her out of your sight the rest of the night."

"Certainly."

Stoker started for the door, but Loveday stopped him. "Uh, Bram."

Stoker paused.

"It'd help to know what it is we're protecting Mrs. Stoker from."

Stoker exchanged an embarrassed, uneasy glance with Doyle and Irving.

Irving answered first. "The truth of it, Harry, is that we're not certain what we're dealing with."

"True enough," Doyle added. "This is just a necessary precaution. The man we're concerned with appears to be a lunatic."

Loveday appeared properly concerned, but not at all alarmed or frightened. "Am I putting my wife in any danger with this?"

"I won't deceive you. It could be dangerous," Stoker admitted. "He has no way of knowing where you live, but there's nothing to say he couldn't find you if he made it his business. Leave instructions that none of the staff provide anyone that information," Stoker answered.

"Right," Collinson began. "Well, for the sake of Mrs. Stoker, I think it's a risk worth taking."

"And you'll have Mr. Quincey standing by you," Irving added.

"That you will," the American confirmed.

"Just make sure that nobody approaches unless you know them. Keep as much distance as you can between Florence and any man you don't know," Stoker advised him.

"I understand."

Stoker gave Florence the most reassuring smile he could muster and then headed for the door. "Let's get that lantern," he said to Doyle and Irving as he pushed past them through the doorway. They were gone.

Florence gazed down at the little cross and turned it over in her hand. She slid back the tiny clasp, separated the chain and then fastened it around her neck. She took a last look at the cross and then tucked it inside the bodice of her dress.

"The fog's gotten thick tonight," Loveday observed, glancing up at the transom window set high in the office wall.

Florence and Quincey looked up at the small window. It was there for ventilation and positioned about a foot above the alley that ran along the side of the building. An unnaturally thick mist swirled against the pane of glass.

CHAPTER 87

T he four-wheeler drove through Whitechapel on Commercial Street. The rain had stopped, but the clouds still hung heavy and gray in the moonlit sky. A right turn on Old Montague and a left on Brick brought them to 197 Chicksand Street.

Of all the houses they had visited, the Chicksand Street address was the largest. At least it was large for the class of neighborhoods they had found themselves in during their hunt.

The house was a pale yellow, the paleness further exaggerated by aged, peeling paint. A narrow porch ran along the front of the house, with two dark windows set in the wall, one on either side of the front door. A narrow chimney of crumbling brick poked out of the dilapidated roof at a slight angle.

The neighboring houses were all built close together and several of them displayed soft gaslight in their windows. Still, most of the light on the street came from the full moon.

"I don't like this. Not after dark," Stoker muttered.

"Let's have a look," Doyle said, walking up the three wide steps to the front porch. Irving and Stoker followed him.

Doyle tried the front door and found it locked. They peered through the windows but could see nothing in the blackness. Doyle tried opening one window and Stoker the other.

"It's just occurred to me you two are cut from the same cloth," Irving quipped.

Stoker and Doyle descended the steps with Irving behind them. Stoker pointed with his ax handle to the path leading alongside the house.

Overgrown weeds and shrubbery covered the path. When they reached the rear of the house, Irving held up the lantern while Doyle struck a match and lit the wick.

A small porch jutted out from the rear of the house. Three steps led up to a narrow door with a window set into its upper half. Stoker tried the door. Finding it locked, he broke the window with the ax handle. A few moments later, the door was open and they were inside.

The house was deathly silent. The flickering light from the lantern revealed another dusty kitchen. If there had ever been cupboard doors, they were gone now. Empty shelves lined one of the inside walls. Cobwebs hung from the ceiling corners and covered the wall shelves. Dust and rat droppings speckled the wood plank floor and countertops. Several empty food tins, along with some other litter, were scattered around the room.

A swath in the thick dust ran across the kitchen from the door where they entered. Something heavy had been dragged across the floor. The trail led through the only other door in the kitchen, opening into a narrow hallway. Looking closely, they could make out a few footprints.

Doyle took the lantern from Irving, and leading the way, followed the path in the dust. The hallway ran past a small bedroom with one bare window. The door was ajar. Doyle paused and peered inside. Aside from a deteriorated mattress and an assortment of trash on the dirty floor, it was empty.

The trail in the dust led to the next door on the opposite side of the hall. The door was closed. Doyle handed the lantern back to Irving and raised the Webley. He turned the latch with his free hand and pushed it open.

The room was pitch black when they entered, but the glow from the lantern revealed a small table, worn and scarred with age, and a rickety chair resting against the wall.

A small fireplace was the source of the tilted chimney they had seen from the street. A few loose bricks had fallen away from the mantle and lay in a random heap on the floor. Chunks of charred wood and piles of ash lay in the hearth.

Torn, faded wallpaper of a flowered print adorned the walls. Heavy curtains of a somber maroon were nailed over the only window.

Irving went to the window and looked at the curtains, running his hand along the fabric. "These are new," he announced.

"This is the last address on the list," Stoker said. "I was certain we'd find the remaining two boxes here."

"We need to look through the rest of the house," Doyle said.

A search of the house turned up little of interest. The last door in the hallway opened into a large storage closet. It was completely empty.

The front room of the house was just as dusty, bleak and empty as the rest. Cobwebs hung everywhere. There was no indication anyone had been in the room for years.

"They must be here," Stoker stated.

"Those boxes are too large to miss. If he was ever here, he's not here now," Irving observed.

"The lantern, please, Sir Henry," Doyle requested.

Irving handed it to him. Doyle circled the room, looking at every wall and every foot of the floor. "I was certain they'd be here myself," Doyle said. "It doesn't add up."

Stoker and Irving followed Doyle back to the hallway. Doyle opened the closet and stepped inside, moving the lantern to every corner, pushing against the walls and tapping them with the crowbar. The examination revealed nothing.

They went back to the sitting room, and Doyle followed the same procedure. Holding the lantern close to the fireplace, he peered at the bricks. He pushed on a few with the heel of his hand, but their mortar held them firmly in place. Doyle even looked behind the curtains.

"The place is empty," Stoker fumed.

Doyle led them back to the bedroom. There was very little to explore there. The kitchen yielded nothing, as well. He stood near the center of the kitchen, slowly turning in place, his eyes searching.

"The boxes may not be here, but this place has some purpose for him," Doyle said.

Stoker shrugged, full of frustration. "If he returns to any of his other places, it won't do him any good. Not with the boxes broken to splinters."

"I agree," Doyle responded. This place just might be his last option… and ours. He walked back into the hallway.

"Where are you going?" Irving called after him.

Irving and Stoker followed and found Doyle in the bedroom.

"What're you doing?" Irving asked.

"Finding a place to wait."

CHAPTER 88

H e watched the middle-aged cab driver from his perch atop the three-story building overlooking Wellington Street. The man from the Lyceum had caught the driver's attention with a wave from the corner cabstand just up from the theater.

The cabbie twisted around to check traffic, straining against his sizable paunch. He ran the back of his hand across his unkempt beard and then reined his team diagonally across the road. A few moments later, he pulled his four-wheeler up beside the Lyceum.

He observed the driver exchange a few words with the Lyceum man who pointed down the alley.

So, there would be a passenger waiting at the stage door. Good, he thought, the alley would be more convenient to his purpose.

The cab moved forward again and turned into the alley, disappearing from view. He gazed down for another moment, and then with a swift, graceful movement launched himself from the building into the night.

His feet touched the stones of the alley as the cab pulled to a stop a few feet from the theater's stage door. The driver shivered in the sudden fog and pulled the collar up on his well-worn ulster. He tied his reins and climbed down from his bench.

The driver had only taken two steps toward the door when his team of horses, sensing his presence, snorted and skittered backwards against the harness. Their master spoke to the beasts as he stroked their noses and patted their heads. They calmed under his attention.

The driver first caught sight of him as he turned back toward the stage door. The fool looked surprised at first and then befuddled.

"You my fare?" the driver asked, apprehension obvious in his voice.

There was no reason to answer.

"Did you send a man for a cab, sir?" the driver tried again.

Tepes smiled a pleasureless smile. "No," he answered in a whisper as hard as iron. "But it is good fortune that you've come."

A knock sounded at the stage door. The doorman got up and walked around his desk. He opened the door to find a rather tall, slender cab driver standing in the alley, his four-wheeler waiting behind him in the fog. The driver was wearing an ulster that looked a bit small and had seen better days. The wide collar was turned up.

"Cab," the driver said.

"I'll go fetch 'em for you," the doorman answered.

"Should I wait out here?" the driver asked. He spoke with a bit of an accent.

The doorman glanced at the mist drifting through the alley. "Step inside if ya' like. Get out of the chill for a couple of minutes."

He nodded and stepped inside as the doorman hurried off to the opposite side of the stage. He waited by the door, his eyes taking in his surroundings.

The stage wing draperies hung about thirty feet away. Several men in working clothes were going about their duties, moving in and out of the wings. None of them paid attention to him.

In the corner to his left was a storage area for scenery flats and prop furniture. There was a desk and chairs, a small double bed with an end table and bureau, and several other smaller items. Probably for use in the current production, he thought.

To the right, beyond the doorman's desk, there was a large panel mounted on the wall. Copper wires strung across white ceramic knobs covered it. The thing must have something to do with the electricity for the building.

Stoker's woman was walking toward him between the drapery rows at the rear of the stage. Close behind her were the two men he had seen in the office, the one called Loveday, and the man with the broad-brimmed hat. He turned away from the woman and hunched down into the ulster, pulling up the collar even more. It would not do for the wife to recognize him, not until he wished her to.

"The lady's luggage is right there," Loveday said, pointing to the bags beside the doorman's desk.

He turned his back to them and gathered up the bags. "If you'd just wait a moment while I take care of these," he said to Loveday in a low voice.

He walked into the alley and hoisted the bags into the coach. Stoker's woman was stepping through the door as he finished. The men followed a few feet behind her. Keeping his back to her and his head low, he pulled open the coach door. He offered his hand and helped her aboard.

While she still faced away from him, he slammed his hand hard into her back, shoving her violently against the opposite door of the coach. She struck her head and crumpled to the floor half-conscious. He threw the coach door shut and whirled around.

The man with the hat had paused to close the stage door behind them and was reaching for the handle.

Tepes jumped forward, grabbing Loveday by the throat with his left hand. His strangled scream drew the second man's attention. He spun around and ran forward to help. Tepes' right hand intercepted him, locking around his throat as well.

He never stopped moving. Holding them each by the throat, he lifted their feet off the ground and hurried back into the theatre. He slammed the two bodies together and then hurled them like rag dolls toward the storage area.

Loveday landed on the bed stored there first, slamming into the headboard. The other man landed on top of him. The mattress sprung back under the weight and bounced him to the side of the bed. He came to rest with the upper half of his body slumped off the mattress, his head almost touching on the floor where his big hat now rested.

Tepes was moving back through the stage door before either of them stopped moving.

He slipped out of the ulster and leaped up to the cab's driver seat. He snatched up the reins, then grabbed the whip from its mount and snapped it over the team. The four-wheeler lurched away down the alley.

CHAPTER 89

The silence within 197 Chicksand Street was almost maddening. The place was little more than a tomb of dust and darkness.

There was some evidence of life. A spider scurried across its web in the kitchen. In the sitting room, a rat poked its head out from a small hole in the wall beside the hearth. Its nose twitched, surveying the room for signs of danger. Smelling nothing of a threat, the rat ran across the room, through the doorway and into the hall.

In the bedroom, the only illumination came from the few beams of moonlight the dirt-caked windowpanes allowed to pass through. None of them needed much light at this point. With the hours spent waiting, their eyes had become accustomed to the dark.

Doyle adjusted his position to ease his stiff joints. When one of them changed their position, it triggered the other two to do the same. It had been going on all night.

"How long must we keep this up?" Irving whispered.

Doyle kept his eyes on the doorway as he answered. "I told you it could be some time, Sir Henry."

Stoker held his finger up to his lips, gesturing for silence. The men listened. Several seconds passed, but they heard nothing.

Then they all heard it, drifting through the emptiness of the house, the faintest squeaking sound.

CHAPTER 90

Tepes had walked up the path beside the Chicksand Street house, not making a single sound. Toward the rear of the place, he had stopped beside an outcropping of thick shrubbery. He moved the shrubbery aside, uncovering the double cellar doors set into the side of the house at a shallow angle. A heavy padlock held the doors secure. He produced a key from his pocket and removed the lock. The hinges squeaked as he pulled the doors open. Standing at the top of the steps, Tepes turned and pulled the doors closed behind him as he backed down the stairs.

His eyes surveyed the blackness. Resting in the cellar's corner, the earth box was still intact. The fools had not discovered it.

It was an outrage, an injustice that he forced to live in this manner. A boyar, a man of power, forced to hide in hovels.

The world had changed and changed for the worse. Gone were the days when the peasants remained silent about him, their lips sewn shut by fear. Over the years, they had learned that light and truth provided them with at least some strength, some power. It began gradually, but they began speaking about what they knew, and in their words were stories laced with cautions and warnings.

London would be different with its teeming populace; sheep with pride that would not allow them to even consider the truth. Stoker had been an unexpected mistake. Tepes had misjudged him, never expecting that the fool's will could be so strong

Tepes' eyes moved across the cellar to the second staircase leading into the house. He moved toward it.

The faint scent of food drew the rat from the sitting room into the kitchen. It scurried from food tin to food tin, sniffing the aroma of nourishment, even though the last remaining morsels had been carried away long ago.

The rat froze at the first sound of the muffled footsteps. It sensed the vibration in the floor before it saw or smelled anything. The rat jerked around to face the center of the room and then held still again.

A section of the floor, three feet square, shuddered slightly and little geysers of dust spurted into the still air. The rat bolted across the kitchen as the floor rose on hidden hinges. The rodent only glimpsed a tall, dark shadow rising out of the floor before it ran into the hallway.

CHAPTER 91

The old house became thick with tension, filling the thick in the blackness. Doyle, Irving and Stoker dared not move.

Stoker moved across the room and flattened himself against the doorway wall, the ax gripped in his hand. Doyle shifted the crowbar to his left hand, removed the Webley from his pocket and took up a position on the opposite side of the door. Irving positioned himself beside Doyle.

The sound of creaking hinges traveled down the hallway, and then a dull thud. Doyle, Irving and Stoker tensed as they heard the approaching footsteps. Each breath they took sounded like a gale wind blowing through their ears. The men fixed their eyes on the open doorway.

The footsteps drew closer. Doyle looked at Stoker. The man appeared as if he was about to leap into the hallway. Doyle risked raising his hand, signaling Stoker to wait.

The footsteps were almost directly outside the bedroom door. They seemed to slow. The three men held as still as statues, barely daring to breathe. A shadow filled the doorway for a moment and then moved on.

Doyle waited a few moments and then, with great caution, shifted his position. He leaned forward and peered around the open bedroom door. The angle of sight was fortuitous, allowing Doyle to see into the sitting room without risking moving into the hallway.

Tepes stood just inside the sitting room doorway, his eyes searching the room. Turning, his gaze fixed on something out of view. He took a step in the box's direction and then seemed to think better of it. He turned back and proceeded to a corner of the room near the hearth.

Just above eye level was a large strip of faded wallpaper hanging limply off the wall. Tepes reached up and peeled back the section of paper. Feeling behind the wallpaper, he withdrew a large, thin envelope and carried it to the table.

Tepes hunched over the table, his back to the door. He opened the envelope and removed several documents and some paper money.

Doyle motioned to Irving and Stoker to follow him. Moving slowly, they made their way into the hallway. Doyle kept waiting for the floor to creak under their weight, but miraculously it did not. It was not until they stepped into the sitting room that the floor groaned under them.

Tepes whirled around, his eyes fired with hate. He did not appear surprised to see them.

Doyle leveled the Webley at Tepes and took a step further into the room. "Stand where you are," he commanded.

CHAPTER 92

With an animal-like snarl, Tepes leaped across the room, smashing into the three men. The revolver and crowbar went flying from Doyle's hands as stumbled backwards. His back struck the wall and he felt the breath forced from his lungs. He fell hard to the floor.

Stoker regained his balance. He raised the ax over his head and charged. The ax hissed through the air. Tepes darted under it with the speed of a striking snake and grabbed Stoker's wrist, then twisted it. Stoker yelled in pain as the ax flew across the room, clattering into the fireplace.

Irving rushed forward to help Stoker, throwing his weight against Tepes. The three of them staggered across the room and crashed into the table. The rotted legs gave out under the weight and the table collapsed, spilling the money and papers across the floor.

Tepes stayed on his feet and effortlessly shook Irving loose. With a sweep of his arm, he sent the actor rolling across the floor. Stoker took advantage of Tepes' momentary distraction, twisting away from him.

Never releasing Stoker's wrist, Tepes brought his free hand up to grip him by the throat. Stoker gasped for breath as Tepes lifted him up off the floor.

Doyle and Irving scrambled to their feet and rushed at Tepes, trying desperately to pull the lunatic's hands off Stoker. Tepes struck out with one arm, beating them away. Doyle tripped over the tabletop, now lying on the floor, and fell backwards.

Stoker's feet were still off the ground as Tepes, his lips pulled back in an ugly sneer, pinned him against the wall. Irving rushed forward again. Before Tepes could throw him off, Irving thrust his hand into the man's face. Tepes hurled Stoker into the corner of the room and leaped away from Irving.

Doyle pulled himself to his feet while Stoker struggled to work his way into a sitting position, his back against the wall. Both of them stared in amazement at Irving. Irving shrugged and held up a cross that was cradled in the palm of his hand.

Stoker pulled himself to his feet while Irving gripped the cross in his hand, his arm extended toward Tepes in a defensive stance.

Tepes' face contorted with rage, the corners of his mouth curled down in an angry snarl. He kept his eyes fixed on Irving, his gaze fixed on the actor's face and not the cross held in his hand.

He began moving along the edge of the room, keeping his back to the wall. His eyes swept across the three men. When he spoke, he did not raise his voice, but for the fury in his tone, he may as well been shouting. "You'll not inconvenience me again."

Tepes' lips formed an ugly, sneering smile. Then, before any of them could make a move, he leaped through the doorway into the hallway.

Stoker and Irving rushed after him. Doyle retrieved his revolver from the floor and followed them.

By the time they were in the hallway, Tepes had already reached the room facing the street at the front of the old house. He was moving fast, his long coat trailing out behind him.

Tepes went into a crouch without slowing and sprang into the air. His body struck the window. Glass and wood sprayed into the air as he flew through the damaged frame and landed on the porch outside.

"Dear God," Irving exclaimed.

Avoiding the jagged fragments of glass still lodged in the frame, the three men followed him through the window. But they had lost ground. Tepes ran toward a four-wheeler parked at the curb in front of the house. The horses weren't hobbled, but oddly, the animals hadn't wandered away.

Odder still, a rope was looped through the luggage rail on the roof of the coach. One end was tied around the driver's handgrip; the other end disappeared through the passenger window into the coach. Florence, framed in the coach window, dangled from the end of the rope knotted around her wrists, her head slumped down against her chest.

Doyle, Irving and Stoker raced across the porch and down the steps as Tepes reached the coach.

"Florence," Stoker wailed as he sprinted into the street.

With a single jump, Tepes was in the driver's seat with the reins in his hands. He yelled something they couldn't understand at the team and the coach sped away.

Doyle and Irving raced ahead. Stoker followed them, forcing his legs to move. "He's murdered Florence," he cried.

"She's not dead," Doyle called back. "Or he wouldn't have bothered tying her."

They reached their four-wheeler. Irving and Stoker jumped into the coach. Doyle untied the horses, climbed up to the driver seat and snapped the reins.

The four-wheeler careened around the corner. Doyle gave the team plenty of rein and they picked up speed. At the far end of the block, Tepes' coach was just disappearing from view as it turned onto Brick Street. Irving and Stoker leaned out the windows on either side of the coach, trying to keep Tepes in view.

"For God's sake, don't lose them," Stoker screamed.

Doyle snapped the reins and yelled the horses on. By the time the four-wheeler reached Brick Street, he had the team running near a full gallop. The coach's four wheels skidded sideways across the wet road as Doyle steered the horses through the turn. He breathed an audible sigh of relief when the four-wheeler regained its forward momentum in time to just miss a signpost.

CHAPTER 93

Tepes was just in sight, reining his horses dangerously around a slower-moving freight wagon. If they were going to keep up, Doyle would have to do the same thing. It was fortunate that it was the middle of the night; the streets were practically empty.

Doyle came up fast behind the freight wagon. The clatter of the horses' hooves on the bricks and that rattling of the coach and wagon created a din. The driver shook an angry fist at him as he pulled the four-wheeler along-side and passed him.

No sooner had they cleared the freight wagon than Tepes turned left and disappeared. Doyle yelled another encouragement at the horses. Reaching the street, they hurtled through the turn on two wheels.

Irving and Stoker saw the turn coming and realized they were moving too fast for it. Stoker jumped to the left side of the four-wheeler next to Irving and held on. Throwing his weight against the turn made the differ-ence between tipping over and landing back on all four wheels. Again, they rounded the corner just in time to see Tepes' coach disappearing around another corner a block ahead.

The turn put Tepes on Commercial Street, a wide thoroughfare that during daylight hours would be heavy with traffic. Doyle followed, driving expertly, weaving around an occasional delivery cart or open wagon. "He's heading to the West End," Doyle shouted.

"You must stay with him," Stoker called back.

"Where on earth could he be going?" Irving wondered aloud.

Doyle kept the kidnapper in sight, but couldn't seem to close the gap between them. By the time they turned onto Euston Road, Doyle's horses were tiring.

Almost two blocks ahead of his pursuers, Tepes almost tipped his coach, careening around a sharp corner onto Park Square East, a minor road leading into Outer Circle at Regent's Park.

"The park," shouted Stoker. "He's going into Regent's Park."

Doyle made the turn onto Park Square East and followed it to Outer Circle. He guided the horses up Outer Circle along the east side of the park. Ahead of them they could see Tepes' coach. It stood motionless in the center of the lane. Doyle reined in behind the coach and jumped down from his perch. Stoker and Irving were already climbing out of the four-wheeler and running toward the other coach.

"Florence," Stoker called out. "Florence."

There was no sign of Tepes. The horses stood snorting and panting. Stoker pulled open the passenger door. The coach was empty.

CHAPTER 94

"There," Doyle cried out, pointing to a footpath leading through the trees.

They ran toward the path. The only logical place to start.

Shadows closed around them as they sprinted along the path. The only light came from an occasional gas street lamp. A fog had rolled in, making navigation on the dirt path even more difficult. They had not run very far when Stoker suddenly stopped and peered through the darkness.

"There," he said, pointing. "He's left the path."

To the right of the path was a small stand of trees. On the far side of the trees, they could see the glow of a street lamp set next to another footpath. Silhouetted in the lamp's glow, Tepes carried Florence through the trees, moving away from them at a fast pace.

Stoker broke from the path, leading Doyle and Irving through the trees at a run. Low branches and shrubbery grabbed at their clothing. More than once, they stumbled over tree roots or rocks, almost blind in the growing fog and dim light.

Breaking through the trees, they faced a large expanse of lawn. The fog rolled low over the lawn and churned around the trunks of the trees. Several yards ahead of them lay another path. Beyond the path, they could see the walls of the Zoological Gardens.

They spotted Tepes at the same time. A grove of trees had blocked him from view for a moment, but he still carried Florence in his arms and he was hastening toward the south wall of the Zoological Gardens.

"Why is he letting us keep him in sight?" Stoker wondered aloud as he began running again.

"He's carrying your wife, for God's sake," Irving wheezed. "How fast can he possibly go?"

Just as they ran across the path intersecting the park, Tepes disappeared into the shadows. Stoker strained to see through the blackness. "Where are they? Do you see them?" he asked.

"There," Irving pointed.

Tepes stood at the base of the ten-foot wall. The heavy mist swirled around him, seeming to tug at his long, black coat. He lifted Florence over his shoulder and began climbing the wall.

The sight stopped the three men dead in their tracks. Tepes ascended effortlessly, zigzagging up the wall resembling a large black lizard.

They watched, astonished, as Tepes reached the top of the wall and disappeared, head first, over the crest.

They ran full out to the spot where Tepes had begun his climb. The brick and mortar was flush; there were no handholds.

"I don't see how he did it," Irving said.

Stoker backed up from the wall, looking up at its peak. "Wait here. I'll be back," he said, rushing back in the direction they had come. He soon disappeared among the trees and fog.

A few minutes later, Doyle and Irving heard horses snorting and neighing. They turned to see Stoker driving their four-wheeler across the lawn.

They moved out of the way as Stoker drove the horses in close to the wall. He pulled the reins tight when the four-wheeler was parallel to and only a foot from the wall. He handed the ground tie down to Doyle, who placed it in front of the team and secured the lead.

Stoker extended his hand to Irving and helped the actor up to the top of the coach. Doyle followed behind Irving. Standing on the four-wheeler's roof, they could easily see over the wall. The clouds drifted clear of the full moon, allowing a sliver of its soft light to reach the park.

The Zoological Gardens spread out before them, shrouded in shadows and mist. They were looking down on an area of small ponds that stretched out to their left. To their right were four more ponds laid out in a half-circle. A path ran through the inside of the half-circle, creating a viewing area for another, larger pond.

There was a sign mounted on the railing around the large pond, indicating some kind of exhibit lived in the water. Beyond the ponds, a maze of cages, pens and low buildings extended into the darkness, all connected by a network of walkways.

There was no sign of Tepes or Florence. Somewhere off in the distance a big cat, a lion or leopard, issued a low, threatening growl. The high-pitched screech of a tropical bird followed the growl. One or two other birds joined in. Then, as quickly as it started, the screeching stopped, the last of it echoing eerily across the park.

Stoker led the way, swinging his leg up and over the top of the wall. Hanging from his hands, he lowered himself down to arm's length and then dropped the remaining six feet to the wet grass. Doyle followed, using the same technique, and then Irving.

They stood still for a few moments, listening, their eyes searching the darkness. The mist had grown thicker, drifting through the trees and congealing at the foot of the buildings.

"Why is it the darkness of the shadows always seems directly proportionate to how damn scared one is?" Irving asked.

"Black shadow moon," Stoker replied in a whisper.

"What?" Doyle wanted to know.

"Superstition," Stoker explained. "A full moon lights a man's way at night, but shadows on such a night are uncommonly dark, to better conceal the evil things that hide there. Black shadow moon, the Romanian peasants call it."

"Lovely," Irving sighed.

The three men walked around the pond and headed into the zoo.

CHAPTER 95

The odd shadows cast by the cages and other animal enclosures made the darkness of the place even more eerie. The shadows shifted and moved as the clouds drifted past the full moon.

Stoker led the way. The other two followed him along the path that wrapped around the larger pond. A sign indicated that sea lions resided there. There was no sign of the beasts in the calm, murky water.

Off to the left, a common roof provided shelter to a row of pens. A peacock's mournful scream came from somewhere on the opposite side of the pens. The unexpected sound made them all jump.

Stoker chose a route heading to the center of the zoo. They entered the wide thoroughfare that stretched almost to the opposite end of the property. Several smaller walkways intersected it along the way.

They approached the lion house, moving slowly but steadily. Four huge restless cats paced in their cage. One lion roared. The sound was blood curdling and the three men veered to the side of the walkway farthest from the cage.

The bars of the lion cage obstructed his view of the three men. Tepes shifted his position to keep them in sight. He was too far away to hear them, and their backs were to him.

The outcome with Stoker's woman had been disappointing; he had been robbed of the time to fully enjoy her. Perhaps it was for the best. He would lead them all to death with a single stroke. They would watch each other die. They would hear each other's screams. And then she would be his completely.

A wolf barked, and the bark became a howl. Tepes' lips pulled back in a cruel smile. He turned and walked into the darkness.

CHAPTER 96

"This is all quite unsettling," Irving complained, his head turning this way and that like a nervous rabbit.

Stoker's eyes never stopped scanning the darkness. He had not expressed his opinion aloud, but he considered every shadow, every alcove of darkness, a potential source of violence.

"I agree," Doyle added. "Too many places to hide. And it's too bloody dark."

Punctuating the remark, a monkey chattered somewhere in the distance.

"I'm not as concerned with where Tepes might hide as much as I am about finding Florence," Stoker said.

"The issues are the same," Irving commented.

"I don't think so," said Stoker.

Doyle glanced at Stoker, then reached into his coat pocket and removed the Webley.

Another howl penetrated the darkness. Stoker strained to hear, trying to determine the direction the howls came from as they continued forward.

The three men approached the northeast corner of the gardens. Ahead on the left they saw the camel house, and to the left of that, the clock tower. Just beyond the clock tower was an open area with a bandstand.

Stoker suddenly broke into a run. At first, Doyle and Irving were confused. Then they saw it. Something or someone was lying on the upper steps of the bandstand. Doyle and Irving ran after Stoker.

"Florence," Stoker cried out. "Oh, dear God. Florence."

She was lying at an angle with her head angled toward the bottom of the steps and her legs up on the platform. Stoker stared down at her, numb with fear.

Within seconds, Doyle and Irving were at his side. Florence's dress was ripped open at the collar, exposing her throat and shoulders. The little cross Stoker had given her hung in clear view against her unscathed skin. The men exchanged relieved glances. Even Doyle appeared to accept the significance of the cross, considering the situation as he pocketed the revolver.

"Thank God," Irving said.

They moved Florence into a sitting position on the platform. Doyle knelt down on the steps and began examining her, checking her pulse and checking for any obvious wounds. He found none. Her breathing was deep, and she muttered unintelligible phrases or groaned, as if she were having a bad dream.

Stoker cradled her head against his shoulder, his arms supporting her. He fought back tears of relief. It wouldn't do to have Sir Henry and Doyle see him cry, not now. He ran his coat sleeve across his eyes.

Somewhere in the darkness, a wolf howled. Then a second joined in. The sound was haunting, disturbing.

"She's all right, I think," Doyle reported.

"Yes, yes. Thank God." Stoker was relieved, but his eyes probed the darkness from whence they'd come. "Wolves," he said.

"Let's get her up," Doyle said. He gently slapped her cheeks. "Come along. Come along, now," he urged her.

More wolves had joined in the distant clamor. Stoker stared into the darkness as Florence's eyes fluttered open.

CHAPTER 97

The mist had grown heavy around the wolves' den. It swirled through the metal mesh fence and crawled along the base of the rocky hill. The wolves paced, fevered with instincts that had been dormant for a very long time. They barked and howled; a few of them snapped at each other.

Tepes emerged from the mist beside the den. The wolves fell quiet as he ducked under the guardrail. He stood watching them for a few moments and then moved closer to a metal door set in the side and to the rear of the pen. A large padlock secured the door.

Tepes walked around the back of the enclosure. He found the area littered with cleaning equipment and a variety of maintenance tools. His eyes cut through the blackness and found a two-foot length of old pipe lying in the soil at the base of the pen. He picked up the pipe and walked back around to the metal door.

The wolves watched him in silence, their heads hung low, as Tepes inserted the pipe through the padlock's shackle. He pushed forward on the pipe; the shackle snapped and the lock fell into the dirt. Tepes dropped the pipe and pulled open the door. The wolves never took their eyes off him.

The fog thickened and eddied around Tepes. He stood deathly still, watching the wolves, his eyes glowing in the darkness like burning coals. They were moving in the den again, alert and hungry, ready to hunt.

Tepes drew his arm across his chest, his palm extended toward the wolves. Once again, the animals quieted. He extended his arm in a sweeping motion. One by one, snapping and snarling, the wolves hurried out the door.

As the pack passed through the portal, a large female wolf emerged from the foliage near the cage and stood beside Tepes. The vapors of her breath lingered in the chilly night air for several moments before fading into the darkness.

The wolves congregated outside the den, circling Tepes and the she-wolf for a few moments, and then ran off into the night. Tepes gestured toward the pack as they ran away and the large female set out after them.

CHAPTER 98

F lorence was disoriented and frightened when she first regained
consciousness. Doyle and Irving waited while Stoker assured her she
was in good hands. Aside from being terrified, she appeared to be in good
health.

"I thought I was murdered," Florence sobbed.

"You're safe now," Stoker assured her, not convinced himself.

"Where is he?" she asked.

"We don't know."

"Our first obligation is to get Mrs. Stoker to safety. We can worry about
our madman later," Doyle said.

"Yes," Stoker agreed.

"We're close to the main entrance. I suggest we head there," Doyle said.

"Perhaps we can find an easier way out than the one in. Although we're
certain to encounter a locked gate," Irving said.

A wolf howl floated through the night. Stoker's head snapped around in
the sound's direction. "We must hurry," he said.

The night filled with howls, their cries echoing among the buildings and
through the cages. The baying began stirring the other animals. Monkey
screams, bird screeches, cat roars and other unidentifiable noises under-
scored the howling.

"They're hunting," said Doyle.

"This way," Stoker said, feeling a sudden sense of urgency. He put his arm around Florence and helped her to keep up with the men. Doyle and Irving flanked the couple, watchful for any danger.

As they hurried along, Florence regained more of her senses. She ran her tongue over her gums and teeth and then touched her fingers to the tongue. Drawing them back, she discovered her fingers were stained with blood. Had she bitten her tongue or lip?

They passed the clock tower and the polar bears' pit. Terrace Walk, leading north to the main entrance, was ahead of them. The animal cries grew louder and more frantic.

"I don't think I can take another minute of that blasted din," Irving grumbled.

As they approached Terrace Walk, the howling of the wolves subsided. The other animals calmed down as well. The change brought Stoker no comfort.

They reached the intersection and made a hurried right turn onto Terrace Walk. Ahead of them they could see the main gate illuminated in gaslight diffused by the fog. It wasn't more than forty yards away.

"It's locked," Irving sighed.

"At least there'll be footholds," Doyle said.

No sooner had the words left Doyle's mouth than three wolves emerged from a side path and fanned out between them and the gate. Everyone froze.

The animals stood their ground. They held their heads low, three pairs of dull yellow eyes fixed unwaveringly on the humans.

"Dear God," Stoker said. "He trapped us."

Two more wolves appeared, approaching from the opposite side of the walkway. A third group trotted out from among the trees in a small land-scaped area across from the pelican house.

Doyle slipped his hand into his coat pocket and withdrew the revolver. The wolves lowered their heads and growled menacingly.

"Back away from them. One step at a time," Doyle instructed in a whisper.

They made it two or three steps before the wolves stepped forward. When they froze again, the wolves stopped their advance. Several began snarling, their black lips drawn back, baring long, sharp fangs.

A wolf from the group closest to the humans lunged forward. As the beast leaped into the air, Doyle took quick aim with the revolver and squeezed the trigger. His Webley jumped in his hand, the explosion splitting the night air.

The wolf yelped, twisted in mid-air, then dropped to the ground on its side and lay still.

The rest of the pack stopped their advance. A few of them backed up a few steps. Two of the animals approached their fallen comrade. Before they could reach him, the wolf twitched and straightened itself, raising its head.

They all watched with astonishment and horror as the beast slowly rose to its feet. With unnatural strength, the wolf faced them, saliva dripping from its open jaws. They could see a dark matting of blood in the fur where the bullet had entered its chest.

Irving and the Stokers had already begun retreating when the wolf attacked again. Doyle mustered his nerve, allowing the beast to get close before he fired two more shots. The animal slammed into the ground with another chilling yelp. This time, it stayed there. Doyle turned and ran as if the demons of hell were chasing him.

The rest of the wolves leaped forward, some of them pausing to sniff at their dead comrade.

"This way," Stoker shouted, leaving the walkway and cutting across a planted, grassy area. He led them toward the closest building.

"I have just three cartridges in the chamber, then I have to reload," Doyle called out as they ran.

Stoker's instincts urged him to look behind them. The pack was gaining, and one wolf was only a few yards away.

Doyle stopped, brought the Webley up as he turned and fired.

The explosion spooked the wolves again and they slowed their pursuit, scattering. The bullet drilled into the animal's side. It tumbled over with a high-pitched yelp.

As Doyle started running again, the wolves behind the injured animal tripped over the body. They stopped long enough to snap at their comrade. In a fevered rage, one of them buried his teeth into the fallen wolf's neck and shook the beast.

The injured wolf opened its eyes, shook off its attacker, and rose to its feet. The pack regrouped and resumed their pursuit. Stoker risked another look behind him and saw that the animals were closing fast.

The Stokers and Irving reached the aviary building. Stoker grabbed the doorknob and twisted. The bolt slid back and he pulled open the door.

Doyle caught up to his friends. He turned back, took careful aim with the Webley and fired at the closest wolf. The animal went down. He chose the next closest target and pulled the trigger again. The shot missed. Doyle knew it was his last cartridge, but in a reflex spurred by fear, he pulled the trigger again. The pistol clicked empty.

"Doyle," Irving shouted.

Doyle whirled around and bolted through the door Irving held open for him. Irving slammed the door shut. Several large, lupine bodies slammed into it. Irving rotated the thin metal slat into the latch to hold the door shut.

The aviary was a long, narrow building divided down the center by a brick walkway. Floor-to-ceiling cages on either side of the walkway housed hundreds of exotic birds.

The human intruders awakened the birds. Outside, the predators threw their bodies against the door. The aviary erupted in a cacophony of squawks, screeches, and flapping wings. Added to the barking and snarling of the wolves, the noise was almost unbearable.

Stoker was already pulling Florence toward the door at the opposite end of the building. Irving was close behind them. The wolves began jumping at the metal screen, growling threateningly. The door hinges strained and the heavy bodies bent the screen.

Doyle snapped open the revolver and dumped the empty cartridges onto the bricks. He reached into his coat pocket, withdrew a handful of shells and began reloading as he backed away from the door. Doyle couldn't keep his hands from shaking as he inserted the shells into the chambers. Snapping the cylinder closed, he speeded up his retreat, keeping his eyes on the door.

The wolves were relentless, lunging against the door and the screen. The hinges rattled. Then two of the animals struck the screen at the same moment and a corner of the mesh broke loose. Another square hit and the entire side came free.

"Hurry, Mr. Doyle," Stoker shouted.

Doyle turned and ran to catch up with his friends. Looking past Doyle, Stoker watched as a wolf began squirming through the opening in the screen. The beast snarled, baring its fangs, saliva streaming from its jaws.

The Stokers and Irving reached the opposite door. Doyle was still about twenty feet behind them when the wolves smashed through the screen. The panicked birds fluttered around their cages, screaming as the pack leaped through the opening one at a time, howling and barking.

CHAPTER 99

S toker got the door open and ushered Florence and Irving outside. Fortunately, none of the wolves had bothered running around the outside of the aviary. They had all followed the scent and rushed inside.

Doyle leveled the Webley and squeezed off one shot after the other. The narrow passageway pressed the wolves together, so almost every shot hit the target. Some of the beasts went down and stayed down, but the bullets only temporarily disabled others.

Doyle emptied the chambers, turned and rushed through the door. Stoker slammed it closed and slid the bolt home. They ran from the aviary, listening to the wolves hurling their bodies against the door, barking and snarling.

Stoker continued leading the way, keeping Florence at his side. He took them east along the northern border of the property. They were all breathing hard, tiring as much from the fear as from the exertion.

Doyle drew up beside Irving and began reloading the Webley. Not a simple task at a full run. "They won't stay in there long," Doyle yelled, taking deep breaths. "They'll either break through or go out the way they got in."

He reached into his pocket for more cartridges. "Damn bloody hell!"

"You've no more shells?" Irving asked, alarmed.

"I've got four shots, but that's it."

"How could you bring so little ammunition?" Irving asked.

"Well, I suppose I didn't count on having to shoot at a pack of wolves. Especially the variety that keeps getting up after you shoot them."

"We can't just keep running. What do we do now? Where do we go?" Irving asked.

"There's a superintendent on the grounds," Doyle said.

"Yes!" Stoker shouted over his shoulder.

"He'll have keys. He'll know the routes out."

"But where is he?" Florence asked.

Doyle snapped the cylinder shut and pointed with the gun barrel. "This way!"

They cut through a flower garden surrounding the Pavilion Pond and emerged onto a walkway. It sloped down to the tunnel passing under Outer Circle, leading to the north section of the Zoological Gardens.

Another frenzy of howling followed them into the tunnel. It reverberated off the walls, seeming to last forever. They ran faster, their footsteps slapping against the bricks and echoing through the passageway.

The Stokers exited the tunnel, with Doyle and Irving close behind them. Already tired, everyone's pace slowed as they made their way up the incline leading to the north section of the zoo. Reaching the top, they found themselves at an intersection in the walkway between a large monkey cage and a kangaroo pen. A howl pierced the night and then another.

They broke into a fast run. There was no reason to look behind them. The baying and snarling that echoed through the tunnel told them the pack was giving chase.

They saw the elephant pen ahead of them, across a wide, open area. The superintendent's office and cottage were on the far side of the pen. Stoker looked back. The wolves appeared at the top of the incline.

"The elephants," Stoker shouted. "Head for the elephants."

They reached the elephant pit and scrambled under the outer guardrail. In only a few steps, they reached the inner rail at the edge of the pit wall.

Stoker and Florence ducked under the guardrail. She held fast to the rail as he jumped down to the ground seven feet below. He then wasted no time, reaching up as she lowered herself into his arms. He placed her on solid ground as Doyle and Irving leaped down after them.

Four adult elephants and a large calf inhabited the pen. Two of the adults and the calf were lying down sleeping. The other two adults stood near the others, their trunks swinging back and forth in a shallow, lazy arc.

"We'll cut across," Doyle said.

"Past those, those elephants?" Florence asked.

"I'll wager they'll object more to the wolves than us," her husband assured her.

They started across the pen, doing their best to keep as much distance as possible between themselves and the elephants. The two elephants lying on the ground climbed to their feet.

"They're getting up," Irving shouted.

The calf climbed clumsily to its feet. Its mother snorted, raised her trunk and draped it over the baby's neck.

"Follow the wall, and make sure you stay away from that baby," Doyle instructed them.

The elephant nearest the calf trumpeted a short warning and took one or two steps toward the human intruders. It kept its eyes on them, but made no further aggressive moves.

The humans stayed close together, running along the base of the wall. One elephant stepped into their path and trumpeted. They veered out toward the center of the pen to avoid the animal. Hearing a piercing howl, they all looked back to see the wolves jumping over the wall, hurdling down into the pit.

Their survival instincts triggered by the wolves' intrusion, two of the adult elephants moved up beside the calf. The elephants trumpeted and stomped at the approaching pack.

The wolves scattered, intimidated by the enormous animals. They ran in tight circles, growling, looking for the safest route across the pen.

Approaching the opposite end of the pen, the Stokers, Doyle, and Irving raced to a stable-like structure housing a large supply of hay bales. Beside the structure was a narrow access ladder bolted into the wall.

The wolves darted across the pen, doing their best to stay clear of the elephants. The elephants, protecting the calf, charged at the wolves.

One wolf passed too close to an elephant. The elephant blocked its path with a single step. Cornered, the wolf snarled and jumped at the angry elephant. The elephant swung its huge head, knocking the wolf out of the air. It reared and brought its front feet down on the wolf. The animal emitted a hideous yelp as it was crushed to death.

The humans reached the access ladder and Stoker helped Florence up.

Irving looked back at the pen. "I count eight now," he shouted.

Doyle turned into the pen and provided cover, aiming the Webley and opening fire. The first shot missed. "Three shots left," he announced.

Florence swung her legs over the wall and Stoker hurried up behind her. Irving was right behind him.

The wolves spread out as they ran toward Doyle. The revolver jumped in his hand. A hit, and the wolf tumbled into the dirt.

Doyle retreated to the ladder. He fired again. Another wolf yelped and fell. Doyle began climbing. As he pulled himself over the wall, the two animals he had shot climbed to their feet.

One wolf, larger than the others, launched itself through the air, attempting to clear the wall. Doyle turned and fired at it. A miss. The gun was empty.

CHAPTER 100

T he pack leaped at the top of the wall. They fell to the ground, circled around, and tried again. Their barks and howls grew in ferociousness with every attempt. The big wolf ran for the hay bales stacked against the retaining wall. It scrambled up the bales, bounded onto the roof of the shelter, ran across it and jumped over the top of the wall. The rest of the pack soon followed.

They passed the superintendent's office at a full run, heading for the cottage set against the back wall of the property. All the windows were dark.

Stoker hammered his fist against the door of the cottage. "Open up! Hello!" he shouted.

Florence looked back and saw the wolves run into view around the side of the deer pen. "Hurry," she screamed.

"Open up. Please open up," Stoker yelled, slamming his fist into the wood.

Light appeared in the front windows and a few moments later, they heard the bolt being drawn back. The door opened, revealing a sleep-hazed and bewildered superintendent. The man was in his early forties, barefoot and wearing a long, white nightdress.

"Escaped wolves," Irving yelled.

They shoved past him and pushed into the cottage.

"Here, now," the man complained. "Who do you think—?" the barking and snarling drew his attention. He looked through the open door and saw the wolf pack bearing down on the cottage. His jaw dropped open.

Irving pulled the superintendent inside, slammed the door shut, and slid the bolt into place.

The cottage was small. They were standing in a main room lit by wall lamps. An open kitchen area adjoined the room. Next to the kitchen was a small storeroom, its door ajar. A slept-in bed was visible through the open bedroom door.

The superintendent started when the first wolf pummeled its body against the front door. Snarls and growls seeped through the walls and door of the cottage.

"What in 'ell is goin' on?" the baffled man asked. "An' what're you people doin' in here after hours?"

"The wolves escaped," Doyle gasped, still trying to catch his breath.

"Well, I can see that. What'd you do to make 'em so mad?"

"We did nothing. They're trying to kill us," Irving answered.

The clamor from the wolves grew louder as the superintendent scratched his head, trying to make sense of it all. Then he walked across the room and pulled down a shotgun from its wall rack. He broke the gun open, checked for shells and then snapped it shut. Leaning against the rack was a long pole with a noose attached to the end. The man picked it up with his free hand.

"Is there a back way out of here?" Stoker asked. "Out of the zoo?"

"Got a gate right behind the place. But don't you worry. I'll take care of the beasties for ya', straight away."

"You're not going out there?" Irving asked, horrified.

The superintendent shrugged. "Now I told you not to worry. I been handling these animals for going on twenty—"

The window exploded in a shower of glass and wood. Florence screamed as a wolf hurdled into the room. The enraged beast smashed into the super-intendent, locking its powerful jaws over the man's throat. The shotgun dropped to the floor as the animal's weight propelled the man across the room. Blood spurted into the air as the wolf ripped open its victim's throat.

Irving grabbed Florence and pushed her into the storeroom.

Stoker ran forward to help the poor man, but a second snarling wolf leaped through the window, knocking him to the floor.

Doyle dived for the shotgun and got it in his hands.

Stoker wrestled with the wolf, gripping the animal by the flesh beside each ear to keep its teeth at bay. The animal broke free and lunged at Stoker's throat. Stoker twisted away and felt the fangs sink into his shoulder. He screamed at the tearing pain.

Doyle reversed his grip on the gun and clubbed the wolf over the head. The wolf yelped and rolled aside, stunned. Stoker scrambled to his feet. The wolf was already beginning to recover from the blow, blood matting the fur above its ears.

Doyle raised the shotgun to fire, but the rest of the wolves began pouring into the cottage through the shattered window. He squeezed off one wild shot. The pellets did no damage, but the exploding cartridge rattled the wolves long enough for Doyle and Stoker to make it into the storeroom. The pack rushed after them.

As Doyle moved to slam the door shut, a wolf wedged his snout into the doorway. The rest of the pack, barking and snarling, threw themselves at the door behind their comrade. Stoker joined Doyle on the door, desperately pushing to close it. The animal cried and barked, but did not back down. It just pushed back harder, snapping and growling.

Irving reached over to a wooden storage shelf and grabbed the first tin he saw. He pulled the lid from the tin, leaped to the doorway, and threw its contents in the wolf's face.

The animal yelped, twisted its head and pulled back out of the doorway. Doyle and Stoker shoved the door shut and threw the bolt.

The pack continued assaulting the door, throwing their bodies against it with a rabid ferocity. For several moments, the humans could only stare at the wooden barrier, gauging the movement of the bolt and the hinges against the constant battering.

The storeroom was small, with just enough room for all of them to fit comfortably. A single gas lamp provided light from a low flame. Irving had stood Florence against the rear wall, next to a small window, and placed himself between her and the door. Maintenance tools leaned against the walls and littered the floor. The wooden shelf housed a variety of cleaning and painting materials.

Blood had soaked through the shoulder of Stoker's coat and the dark stain was spreading. Florence went to him as he ripped open his collar and pulled a handkerchief from his inside coat pocket. He placed the handkerchief inside his shirt and pressed it to the bleeding wound.

"The superintendent!" Florence cried, embracing her husband.

"He's beyond our help," Stoker replied.

"The poor chap was dead the moment the damn beast struck him,"

Irving said. "Good heavens, man!" he added, alarmed, seeing the blood on Stoker's handkerchief.

"I'm all right."

A sudden, violent volley of thuds against the door drew their attention. The screws holding the bolt plate vibrated loosely. The hinges weren't faring much better.

"They're coming right through the bloody door," Doyle said.

Stoker glanced at the window at the rear of the storeroom. "We've a window, but they'll just be after us again if we use it."

"And we'll be out in the open again," Irving added.

The door shuddered again. Everyone stepped back from it. Something caught Doyle's attention. He sniffed the air.

"What's that odor?" he asked.

Irving looked closer at the tin still in his hand. He held it up to his nose and sniffed. "Kerosene, I think," he reported.

"There's more?"

Irving shook the tin. "Almost full."

Stoker grasped Doyle's train of thought. "Capital idea. It might even work," he said.

CHAPTER 101

D oyle examined the contents on the storage shelf. He found a stained preserves jar containing an assorted collection of screws and nails. Taking it from the shelf, he removed the lid and dumped the contents on the floor.

"What are you doing?" Irving inquired.

Doyle ignored the question as Stoker took the tin of kerosene from Irving. Doyle held the jar while Stoker poured in the kerosene until it was about three-quarters full.

Turning back to the storage shelf, Doyle found a filthy rag wadded up next to a box of rat traps. He took the rag and shook the dust out of it.

"Turn down the gas," Doyle instructed Irving.

Irving lowered the flame.

"No, no," Doyle said. "All the way."

Irving extinguished the flame. Now, the only light in the room came from the window, and from the thin strip creeping under the door along with the moving shadows of the wolves.

The pounding at the door grew heavier and the snarls more rapacious. The wood around the bolt began to splinter.

"Over to the window. Quickly!" Doyle ordered.

Stoker tripped the window latch and swung the sash outward.

Doyle reached for the gas jet and twisted the valve wide open. The gas hissed into the room.

"Everyone out, but be quiet about it," Stoker instructed.

Irving crawled through the window first. The early morning fog was thick behind the cottage and soon chilled him. As soon as his feet touched the ground, he turned back to help Florence.

The pounding against the door grew in intensity and the snarling was so loud it seemed to pierce their skulls. The door vibrated, the bolt and hinges dangerously loose.

"After you," Doyle nodded to Stoker.

Stoker climbed through the window. He leaned back into the cottage and took the jar of kerosene from Doyle.

About to pull himself through the window, Doyle spied a tool consisting of a wooden shaft about five feet long, tipped with a metal, barbed point. He retrieved the tool and passed it out the window to Irving.

There was a loud crash against the door. Doyle whirled around to see the wood splinter around the latch screws. More thuds and the door shook in its frame.

The smell of gas had grown heavy in the small room. Doyle scrambled through the window and closed the sash behind him.

"We've got to wait 'till the last second. Get as much gas in there as possible," Doyle said, handing the dirty rag to Stoker.

Stoker twisted the rag and pushed its end into the jar of kerosene, saturating it.

"Sir Henry, the gate," Stoker said, nodding toward the heavy gate set in the wall behind the cottage.

Irving took Florence by the arm and escorted her to the gate. It was bolted shut but not padlocked. Irving slid the thick bolt back and pushed the gate open.

"Ready here," Irving reported.

Doyle scavenged around in his pockets and produced a small box of matches. "I suggest you both get to the other side of the wall," he said to Irving and Florence.

"But you two," Florence began, anxiety in her tone.

"We'll be right behind you," Stoker assured her with a nervous smile.

CHAPTER 102

The waiting was unbearable. It had only been a minute since they climbed out the rear window of the cottage, but it seemed infinitely longer. Stoker stood with the kerosene-filled preserves jar ready to throw. Doyle stood beside him, ready to strike a match. Both kept their focus on the storeroom window.

Stoker and Doyle saw it, a dull flash of light from within the storeroom as the lower corner of the door caved inward. Doyle struck a match, and sheltering it in the palm of his hand, held it ready near the kerosene-soaked rag.

The door sprang open, hanging loosely on its battered hinges. Stoker and Doyle had been staring through the darkened window long enough that the light was almost blinding.

Irving dropped the tool Doyle had handed him and shoved Florence behind the wall.

Doyle moved the match toward the rag. The flame flickered out before it made contact. Frantically, Doyle struck a second match. The flame sprang to life and Doyle touched it to the rag. Feeding off the kerosene, the flame spread.

Stoker waited just long enough to make certain the rag was burning. As Doyle ran for the gate, Stoker hurled the jar at the storeroom window.

Like a flickering comet, the jar soared toward the window, a jet of flame trailing behind. Stoker watched long enough to make certain the crude bomb would indeed strike the windowpane, and then he turned and ran.

Stoker never heard the glass break. The explosion was deafening and the unexpected force of it knocked him to the ground. He felt hot air pushing against his body and rushing over him.

Doyle did not have time to reach the gate and threw himself to the ground when the gas exploded. Glass and other debris began raining down on them, some of it burning.

Stoker sat up and then got to his feet. He looked toward the gate and was relieved to see Irving and Florence staring back at him. He gave them a reassuring wave of his hand. They stepped back in through the gate, but remained near the wall.

Nearby, Doyle was climbing to his feet and dusting himself off. Stoker turned again to look at the cottage. Doyle joined him and together they surveyed the carnage.

Most of the rear section of the cottage was on fire and the flames were spreading to the front of the building. The rear portion of the roof and most of the rear wall was gone. They could see several wolf carcasses, some dismembered, lying charred and smoldering among the rubble. The smell of burning flesh assaulted their nostrils.

The heavy mist combined with the smoke made it difficult to see. Stoker couldn't be sure, but he thought he detected something out of place just outside the burning cottage wall. A slight movement.

As if drawn by an unseen force, Stoker stepped closer to the burning ruins.

"What is it?" Doyle asked.

Stoker didn't answer, peering hard through the smoke and the fog. Then he saw it.

Illuminated by the flickering firelight, the body of an enormous wolf stirred. The beast growled and slowly raised its head.

As Stoker watched, his face drawn in horror, the wolf climbed to its feet, rising out of the smoking rubble. Its matted fur was charred and stained with blood. Wisps of smoke drifted up from its blackened coat. The creature fixed its glowing, dull red eyes on Stoker.

Behind him, Doyle uttered, "My God."

Stoker knew he should run. God knew he wanted to get away from this place, but something was keeping him from moving. It was not an unfamiliar feeling.

The wolf snarled as a large billow of smoke surrounded it, shrouding it from view.

They strained to see through the thick, purling cloud. There was a movement and Florence gasped.

Tepes emerged from the heavy smoke. He stood straight and still, his black coat wrapped around him, the bottom of the long garment appearing to dissolve into the smoke. His face was streaked with soot, or perhaps the skin was burned. Tepes stared balefully at Stoker, his hard mouth set in a frightful, hateful grimace.

Just when Stoker thought he could witness nothing more horrible, an agonizing howl emerged from the smoldering cottage. The burning body of a wolf tumbled from the window, disappearing into the smoke and fog hovering near the ground. The glow from the flames on the animal's body broke through the swirling haze.

As they all watched, the flames rose higher and the tormented howls grew louder. The flames, smoke and mist appeared to take shape, converging into human form. As the howls became anguished screams, the apparition solidified into Lucinda Westen. The flames burned her burial gown and engulfed her body. Her face was contorted in hate and rage. With a last chilling scream, the flames consumed her and her body fell to the ground, dead. The thick haze mercifully hid her from view.

CHAPTER 103

Tepes, having dispassionately watched Lucinda's gruesome cleansing, turned his baleful eyes back to Stoker. He snarled in rage and lunged, locking his hands around Stoker's throat.

The man was still strong. Tepes stared, unblinking, into Stoker's eyes as his grip tightened. Stoker realized Tepes wanted him to die slowly. The creature could have snapped his neck and been done with it. But his eyes were searching Stoker's face for pain. He wanted to see it and he wanted it to last.

Stoker could hear Florence screaming as Tepes lifted him off the ground. The sound was hollow and distant, competing against the pounding inside his head.

How ironic that he at last saw it, now, as he was about to die. Tepes was all about pain, all about selfish gain, all about death, all about destroying souls. He did not differ from any other demon found in the world, using half-truths and blatant lies to lure victims away from all that is good and right. He was no different from any evil that preys on human weakness with the goal of depriving the living of life.

Doyle and Irving slammed into Tepes with all the force they could muster. Tepes staggered but stayed on his feet, and held his grip on Stoker.

Doyle locked his arms around Tepes' forearm and fought to pull his hands from Stoker's throat. Irving was holding Tepes' coat lapel in his left hand and was thrusting the cross, gripped in his right hand, into his face.

Tepes swung his body, using Stoker as a club to strike at his assailants.

He dragged the men, their feet hardly touching the ground, but Doyle and Irving hung on. Irving kept the cross in Tepes' face, pushing it closer.

A low, ugly scream began deep in Tepes' throat. It grew in volume and intensity as he tried to draw his face away from the cross. The scream became an angry roar and Tepes jumped backwards. He released his grip on Stoker, his arms springing outwards, catapulting all three men away from him.

They tumbled across the ground. Stoker came to rest on his stomach and felt the air rush back into his lungs. His head cleared. He was alive. Miraculously, he was alive, and he had to stay alive. Florence was only yards away, and he had to keep this fiend away from her.

Lying in front of Stoker, only a few feet away, was the pointed tool Irving had dropped before the explosion. Stoker drew his legs under him and pushed off, leaping for the makeshift weapon.

Tepes was already moving toward Stoker with long, swift strides. Doyle and Irving intercepted him, again throwing all their weight against the man. This time, Irving was too slow with the cross. Tepes took hold of them both, stopping only long enough to toss them out of his way. Doyle and Irving arched through the air and landed hard, stunned.

Stoker reached for the tool and picked it up. He jumped to his feet and whirled around. Tepes was only a few feet away. He became wary when he saw the shaft in Stoker's hands. Stoker saw it in his eyes. There was some small hope, after all. Stoker prayed a silent prayer, asking God to forgive his foolishness, his weakness, and to grant him the strength to overcome this evil.

The two adversaries circled each other, each looking for an opening to attack. Stoker thrust his weapon at Tepes' chest and lunged forward. Tepes parried the thrust, stepped aside, and drew back his arm. Stoker felt the blow connect at the base of his neck. The force of it hurled him to the ground.

Stoker rolled with the momentum and brought the shaft up in time to fend off Tepes. He got back on his feet, found another opening, and leaped forward. The barbed tip of the shaft missed Tepes' heart, but the point found his shoulder. Tepes grunted as Stoker pulled back the shaft. His hand went up to the wound. Blood covered his fingers when he drew it back.

Tepes' face contorted in renewed rage. He charged Stoker with a blinding swiftness. Stoker brought up the shaft, but Tepes blocked it, grabbed hold and yanked it from his hands. Stoker watched the wooden shaft tumble through the air and land in the burning rubble of the cottage.

Tepes advanced, his red eyes burning through the shadows and smoke. Stoker stumbled backwards. He thought he could hear Florence screaming again, calling his name and crying, but her voice sounded far away.

Tepes was almost on him now, his clawing hands reaching out. But the monster stopped in his tracks. Tepes hissed a short, vicious phrase in his native tongue. There was no understanding the words, but there was a no question they were a vile and angry curse.

Stoker realized he was sitting on the ground with his back against the wall. He felt himself breathing again, and his head began to clear.

Florence, Doyle, and Irving were kneeling next to him. Florence was crying.

Tepes was still within view, but his image was a dark blur. He was backing away, his silhouette framed by the flames consuming the cottage behind him.

The mist swept in toward Tepes, swirling around him, growing denser. Tepes' dark form appeared to fade away into the eddying cloud. The mist thinned and he was gone.

CHAPTER 104

S toker's eyes focused on the flames devouring the superintendent's cottage. Awareness returned to him and he bolted upright. A throbbing pain shot through his skull and he moaned.

"I suggest you take it easier from this point on," Doyle advised.

"Where is he?" Stoker demanded.

"He's gone," Florence replied, stroking his cheek with the back of her hand. "Please be careful," she continued as Stoker struggled to get to his feet.

Doyle and Irving helped him. Aside from his throbbing head, he felt better.

"But where is he? What happened?" Stoker asked again.

"We don't know," Doyle replied. "He just stopped his attack and then escaped in the fog."

"I thought you were a dead man," said Irving. "Thank God he stopped, but I don't understand why."

"I'm rather prepared to believe *that* is the reason," Doyle said, looking to the east.

They followed Doyle's gaze.

A paper-thin line of purple ran across the horizon. The dark, red-orange pigment just visible below it hinted at the sunrise to come.

"He has to return to Chicksand Street," Stoker said. "There are still two more boxes. They have to be there. That's where he'd have to go. We'll find him when he's powerless."

Irving arched an eyebrow toward Doyle. "I notice this time you aren't rolling your eyes."

"Let's get on with it," Doyle answered.

Daybreak was cutting through the morning fog by the time they pulled up in front of 197 Chicksand Street. Irving, Stoker and Florence had waited at the gate while Doyle walked around Outer Circle and then made his way along the Zoological Gardens' west wall to retrieve their four-wheeler.

The ride back to Whitechapel provided them with a welcome rest. Even Doyle, though he was driving, was glad for the opportunity to just sit and hold the reins. Although tired and hungry, they all felt somewhat revived by the time they reached their destination.

They found the outer cellar doors. Tepes had not concealed them, and this time they had the added advantage of daylight. The padlock lay in the dirt beside the opening.

Stoker led the way down the steep stairs. Florence insisted on going. Irving followed her and Doyle brought up the rear.

The light streaming from the open doorway revealed the Carter Paterson & Company box resting in a damp corner of the damp room.

"Only one," Stoker said in dismay.

"There's still the fifth," Doyle added, annoyed.

"But what's he done with it?" Irving asked.

Stoker walked over to the box. "The crowbar, and the ax, they'll still be upstairs."

"I'll fetch them," Irving offered. He started for the stairway he had just descended and then noticed the second, steeper set of stairs. "We'll just try this one, then."

Irving climbed the ladder-like stairs and pushed open the trapdoor at the top. He pulled himself up. A moment later, his face appeared in the opening. "The kitchen," he reported.

Doyle and the Stokers listened to Irving's footsteps above them. In less than a minute, he leaned down through the trapdoor, dropping the crowbar and ax to the floor below.

Stoker picked up the tools and approached the box. He leaned the ax against the wall and then positioned the flat edge of the crowbar under the box's lid. The lid slid to the side.

"It's open," Stoker informed them.

While Florence watched from the foot of the stairs, Doyle and Irving helped Stoker push the lid aside. Like all the others, a simple, coffin-like box lay within the crate.

Stoker lifted the lid. The box was empty except for the odorous, moldy soil.

Stoker grabbed the ax. Doyle and Irving backed out of the way. With a vengeful energy none of them had witnessed before, Stoker chopped the boxes into pieces.

"What about the fifth one?" Irving asked.

Doyle shook his head, perplexed. "Let's look upstairs again," he suggested.

The parlor was still in shambles from their earlier skirmish. But now, paper and coined money were scattered across the floor, and several documents lay near the ruined table.

Irving and Stoker pulled open the old draperies. Doyle knelt down beside the scattered papers and began leafing through them.

"Travel papers," he told them. "In different names. And the fifth box, a bill of lading, but not from Carter Paterson." Doyle stood up, the mess of papers in his hand. "He used another cartage house for that one."

"But how?" Stoker asked. "Carter Paterson confirmed they delivered all five boxes."

Doyle shuffled through the papers. "Here it is. A transfer order. Carter Paterson delivered two boxes here, and then turned one of them over to," Doyle hesitated while he located the name. "To Smyth and Pierson, Carriers."

"So, where did they take it?" Irving inquired.

Doyle squinted at the paper. "A storehouse on the docks."

"The docks," Stoker repeated.

"What does it mean?" Florence asked.

Doyle looked through the documents, finding the answer in one of them. "He insured himself a way out," he answered. "Doolittle's Wharf. The Czarina Catherine. Sailing this morning."

"This morning," Stoker repeated. "When?"

Doyle consulted his watch. "We'll have to hurry."

"He's leaving the country!" Irving observed.

Stoker nodded. "We left him nowhere to hide. There still may be time!"

CHAPTER 105

The morning mist was heavier than usual at Doolittle's Wharf. It was still quite early and the little light provided by the rising sun was subdued even more by the haze. The Czarina Catherine, a side wheel steamer, swayed in the river's current beside the wharf.

Two dockworkers rigged ropes around a large wooden box. They worked quickly and efficiently, going about their business with no unnecessary words passing between them. The name of the shipping company was stenciled on the sides of the box: SMYTH & PIERSON, CARRIERS.

One man raised an arm to signal the men manning the hoist. "Go ahead, then," he shouted.

Stationed on opposite sides of the windlass drum, the two men turned the hand cranks. The rope drew taut and the box jerked into the air. The rigging men walked on either side of the box, pushing it, guiding it toward the ship, and the boom arm pivoted with the load.

When the box was high enough and close enough to the rail, two crewmen leaned out and pulled it on board. The winch men lowered the cargo until it was only a few feet above deck.

The crewmen pulled the box along until they had it positioned over the open hold. After a few more minutes of work and sweat, the cargo rested in the blackness below decks.

Several minutes later, smoke puffed in black clouds from the Czarina

Catherine's chimney stacks. Dockworkers cast off the lines and a second crew pushed the steamer away from the wharf with long poles. Orders were shouted and the ship's signal bell sounded. A low rumble came from deep within the vessel. The big wheels began turning, their paddles churning up the water. The ship steamed away from the wharf and headed into the river.

CHAPTER 106

D oyle drove the four-wheeler like a madman, east toward the Left
Bank. This time, Irving sat beside him on the driver's seat, his hand
on his hat, anchoring it against the wind. Doyle didn't understand the
actor's desire to leave the comfort of the coach. Irving explained he required
the fresh air to keep him alert.

They raced toward the Long Shore, a district that extended along the
bank of the Thames. It comprised quays, wharves, storehouses, and engine
factories.

"You know where you're going?" Irving asked, holding on to the rocking
coach.

"I do. The river's just ahead."

They drove on in silence for some time and then Irving glanced at
Doyle. "Nothing like it, heh, Arthur? The thrill of the chase."

"Nothing like it," Doyle replied. "Although I've found that the business
of helping a friend has its benefits as well."

Irving nodded. "I want to offer my apologies, for uh, doubting your
abilities of detection."

"And my apologies as well, Sir Henry," Doyle replied. "For underesti-
mating your grit."

Doyle kept the horse galloping along the bank of the river. Ahead of
them they could see a sign reading DOOLITTLE'S WHARF. There was no
sign of a ship at the wharf, just a few dockhands going about their work.

Doyle reined in the horse, stopping the four-wheeler at the wharf. The Stokers leaned out the coach window as a dockhand passed by.

"The Czarina Catherine. Can you tell us where to find her?" Stoker asked the man.

"If you look right hard, you can see her downriver," the man replied, pointing.

Stoker opened the coach door and stood up in the doorway. Doyle and Irving looked from the perch at the top of the four-wheeler. The steamer was heading away from them, about a mile down the river. Beyond the steamer, they could see one of the several bridges spanning the Thames.

"Headin' for Varna an' up river to Transylvania," the dockhand offered.

"Get in," Doyle ordered Stoker.

The four-wheeler was moving before Stoker got the door closed.

Doyle snapped the reins, urging more speed from the horse. The four-wheeler rocked along the river road, heading for the bridge ahead.

Stoker leaned out the coach window. "What do you hope to do?" he shouted up at Doyle.

"The bridge," Doyle shouted back. "The ship'll have to pass under the bridge. A challenging height to the deck, I'd think, but if we get there first, perhaps we can board her."

The four-wheeler was closing the distance to the steamer. Soon they were parallel to it. Doyle drove the horse hard and they pulled ahead of it. The bridge was just ahead.

Doyle cut across the road, but the turn onto the bridge was still sharp. The coach made the turn on two wheels. It was with great effort that Doyle and Irving stayed aboard. The bow of the steamer was already passing under the bridge as the four-wheeler stopped.

Doyle and Irving jumped down from the driver's seat. Stoker climbed out of the coach with Florence following him. The steamer's whistle sounded.

Stoker broke into a run, heading for the middle of the bridge. He was already pulling off his hat and coat when Doyle and Irving caught up to him.

Doyle looked down at the ship deck, passing some twenty feet below them. "No, Stoker. It's a greater drop than I realized," he cried.

Stoker didn't seem to hear, driven forward by the obsession to finish what he had started, driven forward by a need for revenge. Before Doyle or Irving could act, he swung his legs over the rail and lowered himself onto the outside ledge.

"Bram!" Irving shouted. "You hit that deck, you'll kill yourself."

Smoke from the steamer's chimneys floated up from below.

Bram gauged the height, hesitated at the distance to the steamer's deck, uncertainty growing in him. No, he had to try.

Doyle and Irving grabbed hold of him just as he let go of the rail.

"Bram!" Florence screamed.

Suddenly realizing his foolishness, Bram grabbed hold of Irving's hand. Doyle had hold of the back of his shirt and one of his suspender straps.

The steamer's stern passed under them. Deck hands stared up at the bridge, some of them pointing.

Irving lost his grip on Stoker's hand just as the ship cleared the bridge. He lunged and reclaimed Stoker's shirtsleeve. The sound of ripping cloth blended with Doyle and Irving's shouts. Stoker's shirt ripped away in Doyle's hands. The cloth pulled away from Irving's grip and Stoker dropped into the river below.

"Bram," Florence shouted.

They leaned over the railing, searching the water below. At first, there was no sign of him and then Stoker broke the surface. He caught his breath and began swimming for shore.

They rushed back across the bridge the way they had come. Florence stopped at the four-wheeler and retrieved a lap blanket from the passenger seat while Doyle and Irving hurried on to the riverbank.

Stoker, gasping, reached the shore. Doyle and Irving helped him from the water and sat him down on a small boulder. Florence joined them, wrapping the blanket around her shivering husband.

"I'm unsure which of you is the bigger lunatic," Florence scolded, her relief obvious.

They were silent for some time, watching the steamer fade from view into the morning mist. Stoker wore a mask of defeat.

"That's it, then," Doyle growled. "We can at least notify the authorities in Budapest."

"And tell them what?" Irving asked. "Are you going to tell them what you've seen? You think they'll believe it?"

"They won't believe it, but it's one cable I need to send. I won't be able to live with it if I don't at least try to warn them," Doyle mumbled.

"So, he won after all," Stoker muttered.

"No. We sent the devil back home," Irving said.

"But he got away. It's not over." Florence said.

"Isn't that the way it goes?" Irving answered.

"How do you mean?" asked Doyle.

"Good and evil, a staple in the theater, you know. There's always been evil in the world. There always will be. It continues on and on. All we can do is fight it where we find it. With God's help, we won this battle." Irving rested an encouraging hand on Stoker's shoulder. "Can't you see that?"

"Faith in an invisible God," Doyle sighed. "Somewhat overrated, if you ask me."

"The only faith worth having if you ask me," Irving retorted.

"I was such a fool," Stoker said.

"But you did everything within your power to put it right," Doyle answered. "And you're not responsible for what he is."

"What's to be done now?" Stoker wondered aloud, the pain obvious in his question.

"You're already well on your way to doing it," Doyle replied. "Your book."

Stoker looked at Doyle, his face darkening.

"Your book, of course," Irving agreed. "The power of the pen."

"My book? No," Stoker exclaimed. "Look what it's caused us. I'll burn every page and have nothing more to do with any of it."

"But you must finish it. Give warning by it," Doyle reasoned.

"All I want to do is put this behind me, behind us. No, I can't bear any more of it," Stoker shook his head.

Doyle sighed in surrender. "Well, it's your decision. But don't destroy the manuscript. I urge you not to do that. If you do, there'll come a time you regret it."

Stoker digested Doyle's words. "I'll consider it," he muttered. "But I promise nothing."

EPILOGUE

hey were all exhausted long before Doyle reined the coach up in front
of 27 Cheyne Walk. With hasty "goodnights," Doyle and Irving drove
off to their own beds as Bram helped Florence inside.

Florence began preparations for bed, but despite the fatigue he felt,
Bram could not embrace the idea of sleep. Images of their near calamitous
night rushed through his head like a surging stream.

He went to his study and built a small fire in the hearth. Once it was
burning, he went to his desk and unlocked the side drawer. Pulling it open,
he reached in and removed his notebook and the manuscript.

He stared at the mass of paper in his hands. He'd loved creating these
words inked into paper; he had loved the wonderful dreams of how they
would change his life. But now, all he felt was loathing.

Stepping over to the hearth he felt his grasp tighten on the papers. He
felt the heat of the flames as he struggled in anguish with what he should
do. Stoker didn't know how long he stood there. He felt beaten into defeat
and retreated to the desk. He returned the notebook and manuscript to the
drawer and slammed it shut.

Aside from the haunting memories, the days following Tepes' departure
from England returned to normal. Doyle and Irving returned to their

routines, and to their negotiations to bring the Sherlock Holmes play to the Lyceum. There was still only minimal progress, but Stoker took note that at least the two men were friendlier in their parleys.

Florence had slept soundly in the first nights following her ordeal, but then began having nightmares. They were mild in the beginning, but grew in intensity. As she described them to him, he understood the bad dreams were forcing her to relive the traumatic events she had experienced. Bram felt intense waves of guilt as he listened to her trembling voice.

He had never been that much of a praying man, but now he prayed often. He prayed for Florence, that the nightmares would end, and that her emotional wounds would heal.

Work proved to be a healthy distraction from the bad memories and Stoker threw himself into it with admirable energy. There was never a lack of tasks demanding his time at the Lyceum, and now he welcomed them.

Returning home from the theater each evening, he made it a point to spend time with Florence. After coming so close to losing her, he vowed to never take her for granted again. They would chat over an apéritif and then continue their conversations through dinner.

Only after they had finished dinner, and when Florence had retired to read, would Stoker venture off to his study. Before a fire crackling in the hearth, he would sit with a good book. Sometimes, alone with the flames, he would set his mind to thinking of new stories that might make another book worth his writing. But his thoughts always returned to the horrors that he, his wife, and friends had survived by the grace of God.

He stared at his desk, knowing the unfinished manuscript, inspired by Tepes, was locked within. It was as if it contained some power of its own. But night after night he resisted the oddly magnetic pull.

More than three weeks after they had driven Tepes from the country, Stoker again sat in his study reading before the fire. But he could not keep his mind on the Thackeray novel in his lap. His eyes kept wandering to the desk.

He believed the potential in the manuscript was still strong. But who would believe him if he wrote the truth? He might be labeled a liar or even crazy and the warning in the book would be ignored. Possibilities took shape in his mind. Perhaps the key was to treat it as a fiction. It might work. There might be a way, he thought.

He rose from his chair, leaving the Thackeray, and made his way around the desk. He gazed at the drawer for several moments. "I'll write my version of the truth," he muttered.

Drawing the drawer key from his pocket, he placed it in the lock and turned the bolt.

DID YOU LIKE THIS BOOK?

You Can Make A Big Difference!

Reviews are the most powerful tool I have when it comes to drawing attention to my books. I can't emphasize enough how valuable they are.

Honest reviews help bring my books to the attention of other readers.

If you enjoyed this book, I'd appreciate it if you could spend just a few minutes leaving an honest review (it can be as short as you like).

Simply visit the *Black Shadow Moon* book page where you made your purchase (Amazon, iBooks, Barnes & Noble, or Kobo) and look for the "leave a customer review" link.

Sincere thanks in advance, P.G. Kassel

THE STORY CONTINUES...

Don't wait to discover what happens next.
Read **Black Hunters' Moon** now!

Available at your favorite book seller.

BOOKS BY P.G. KASSEL

Siphon

A Cayden March Thriller

Black Shadow Moon

Stoker's Dark Secret Book One

A Supernatural Vampire Thriller

Black Hunters' Moon

Stoker's Dark Secret Book Two

A Supernatural Vampire Thriller

Dark Ride: A Novella

Get your FREE digital copy at www.pgkassel.com

(paperback for sale only)

ABOUT THE AUTHOR

P.G. Kassel (Phil to his readers) is a former film and television writer-director turned novelist. With over 30 years working in the entertainment industry, his teleplays have been produced for television, and his feature length screenplays optioned by major studios and production companies.

Phil is married to an amazing and beautiful woman who puts up with all his artistic moodiness. They make their home in Los Angeles, California.

If you have any questions or comments for Phil connect with him online:

phil@pgkassel.com
www.pgkassel.com
https://www.facebook.com/pgkassel

Made in the USA
Columbia, SC
05 May 2025